# APPOINTMENT IN PARIS

Also by Jane Thynne

*Midnight in Vienna*

AS C. J. CAREY

*Widowland*

*Queen High*

# APPOINTMENT IN PARIS

## JANE THYNNE

QUERCUS

First published in Great Britain in 2025 by Quercus
Part of John Murray Group

1

Copyright © 2025 Thynker Ltd.

The moral right of Jane Thynne to be
identified as the author of this work has been
asserted in accordance with the Copyright,
Designs and Patents Act, 1988.

All rights reserved. No part of this publication
may be reproduced or transmitted in any form
or by any means, electronic or mechanical,
including photocopy, recording, or any
information storage and retrieval system,
without permission in writing from the publisher.

This book is a work of fiction. Names, characters,
businesses, organizations, places and events are
either the product of the author's imagination
or used fictitiously. Any resemblance to
actual persons, living or dead, events or
locales is entirely coincidental.

A CIP catalogue record for this book is available
from the British Library

HB ISBN 978 1 52943 071 4
TPB ISBN 978 1 52943 072 1
EBOOK ISBN 978 1 52943 073 8

Typeset in Bembo Book by CC Book Production

Printed and bound in Great Britain by Clays Ltd, Elcograf S.p.A.

Papers used by Quercus are from well-managed forests and other responsible sources.

Quercus
Carmelite House
50 Victoria Embankment
London EC4Y 0DZ

John Murray Group
Part of Hodder & Stoughton Limited
An Hachette UK company

The authorised representative in the EEA is Hachette Ireland,
8 Castlecourt Centre, Dublin 15, D15 XTP3, Ireland (email: info@hbgi.ie)

*For Adam*

He who fights with monsters should be careful lest he thereby become a monster. And if thou gaze long into an abyss, the abyss will also gaze into thee.

> Friedrich Nietzsche

They took the upward path, through the still silence, steep and dark, shadowy with dense fog, drawing near to the threshold of the upper world. Afraid she was no longer there, and eager to see her, the lover turned his eyes. In an instant she dropped back, and he, unhappy man, stretching out his arms to hold her and be held, clutched at nothing but the receding air.

> Ovid, *Metamorphoses,* Book X

# PROLOGUE

Midnight in April. A hard moon in a chill sky. Even this late in spring there was a touch of frost in the air, crisping the grass and causing the two men in army uniform to shiver as they leaned against a grey classical urn, smoking cigarettes and surveying the horizon.

'Charlie Chaplin was here.'

'What you talking about?'

'If there was graffiti, that's what it would say. He was here. And Winston and the Prime Minister and Noël Coward and whatever. Stanley Baldwin. George Bernard Shaw. All friends of Lord Aberfeldy. The Duke of Kent. Celebrities. Hollywood people. They all came to this place.'

'You're kidding me.'

'It's true. They'd come up for the weekend. All kinds of larks.'

'The things you know.'

'I'd give something to earwig those conversations.'

'Beats the guests we get now.'

Private Fred Jenkins and Lance Corporal Sid Nolan always chose this spot for a smoke during their night patrol. It was effectively out of sight of their superiors and a brief pause there, even in moonlight, afforded a panoramic view of the surrounding countryside. It was a vista that had been specifically designed for contemplation. To one side, a shadowy tangle of birch and oak formed the fringe of what had once been Enfield Chase, a vast and ancient royal hunting ground, four hundred acres of it, visited by both Henry VIII and Elizabeth I. Straight ahead, beyond the wide sweep of lawn, lay the dark mass of an ornamental lake reflecting a sky scattered with stars. Further on, the eye was drawn up an avenue of lime trees, planted by Humphry Repton, to an obelisk on the crest of the hill.

And directly behind, the beneficiary of this splendid panorama, was the house, a grand and imposing neo-Georgian mansion of flat-faced red brick and mullioned windows.

The life of leisured gentility and unsullied ease that was once enjoyed by the house's inhabitants, however, was over now. In the space of a few months, endless lines of trucks had trundled up and down the long drive bringing concrete and bricks, throwing up Nissen huts and unravelling rolls of barbed wire, fencing off the glass-roofed greenhouses and the nursery garden and erecting watchtowers in the grounds. The previous winter had brought diggers, hacking into the frozen earth to create an exercise yard and an administration block before the first inmates arrived. Now the courtyard was bordered by a double barbed-wire fence and shelter trenches.

Fred took a languid drag of his Woodbine and relaxed, for all the world as if he was one of those high-society visitors of former days, breaking away from dinner to savour the night air. With his dark good looks and demeanour of louche ease he might even have passed for an upmarket weekend guest, unlike Sid, with his thin ginger moustache, spots and shivering, bony body.

'Better get on, Fred, hadn't we?'

Night patrol was always the same. Their route led around the perimeter of the grounds, past the cells and interrogation blocks, alongside the exercise yard's high fence and watchtowers, through to the more charming terrain of a fruit and vegetable garden. The contrast between the brutal fortifications and the mannered ornamentation of the eighteenth-century garden could not be more stark. Past a small, rectangular pond, its surroundings planted with bedding flowers and shrubs, came the wisteria walk, a long pergola that would soon be entwined with sweet-smelling purple blossom, before the path took them round the stable block and back to base.

Fred thrust his stub away.

'If you say so.'

There was a sudden movement. A barn owl, swooping in a white flash of silence out of the dark blur of the woods.

The glimmer of its moonlit wings caught Fred's attention, and he followed its flight until something made him start.

'What's that?'

He was staring at an oak tree: a magnificent specimen, said to be three hundred years old, which bore a tree house in its sturdy boughs because its graceful limbs were easy for children to climb. Fred was fixed on the point where its roots writhed out of the ground.

'I don't see nothing,' said Sid, peering into the gloaming.

'There. Bottom of the tree.'

Fred pointed to a place beside the trunk where shadows gathered and pooled. At first, he had thought it was a knot of roots, but it seemed to him more like a huddled shape.

'Something's there.'

He moved closer, then dipped down into the darkness and prodded the shape with his boot. It didn't budge.

'Christ! It's a Jerry. A bloody Jerry.'

His voice was high with shock.

'What is it? Is he drunk?'

Fred took out his torch. Its narrow beam illuminated a man in uniform, propped against the tree, legs akimbo as if he had just fallen asleep, one arm flung outwards, the other touching his chest.

Fred crouched down and turned the head. In the narrow blade of light, the face was marble, its features finely chiselled and the eyes open and sightless, as though one of the park's own Greek statues had been toppled from its plinth. It gazed up blankly at a sky it would never see again.

The beam of the torch danced as he took a quick survey of the surrounding area before coming back to the bleached face.

'I don't think he's drunk. Look at that.'

In the place where the fine, white temple receded into the hairline, the bone was shattered, and a mass of blood marred the strands of blond hair. It had dripped down one cheek and trickled below the neck into the tight collar.

'He's only gone and shot himself.'

Sid sank to his heels and gripped the man's shoulders, as if to shake him into life.

'No. Don't move him!' said Fred. 'You could disturb things.'

'Who d'you think he is?'

Fred stared sombrely at the supine form.

'I recognize him. I've seen him in the exercise yard. He arrived months ago.'

Once the men had hastened back to the house and reported the find, proceedings moved swiftly. The door to cell number 9 was found to be unlocked. Colonel Thomas Kendrick, head of Camp 11, was roused from his bed, dressed quickly and came down to his blue-walled office, where he spent the rest of the night in hushed conversation with his deputy.

When Mrs Leak the housekeeper went to light the fire in the Blue Room early the next morning, she was startled to see Colonel Kendrick already at his desk. He greeted her with a terse nod and confirmed that he did not require a fire or toast or a pot of tea or anything except not to be disturbed. Mrs Leak was a local lady from Cockfosters who had previously been housekeeper at a nearby manor house and had acquired a reputation for discretion. She was well aware of the secret nature of her workplace – *Work of National Interest*, was how it had been described at her interview. That could mean any number of things, but it required that she did not go blabbing around town, and she had kept her mouth shut, even though there were plenty of events she could have blabbed about.

Yet although Mrs Leak knew how to keep quiet, except in the company of her married daughter, that didn't mean she could not observe details and make her own deductions. In this case, all she was able to observe was that Colonel Kendrick, while always impeccably polite, was not his usual genial self. He had smoked at least ten cigarettes – she did a quick count of the stubs in the cut-glass ashtray – and his clothes looked crumpled, the tie askew. The diplomat's charming smile was only fleeting, and his face settled into an uncharacteristic frown.

Once Mrs Leak had left, she decided to brush down the parquet in the adjacent corridor. This was a job that always needed doing and it required an unspecified amount of time. Yet it was not until six thirty that the clatter of the telephone receiver from behind Colonel Kendrick's door suggested that he had placed an outside call.

# CHAPTER 1

*London, May 1st, 1940*

There is a myth that losing your sight means that all your other senses – hearing, touch and smell – become enhanced and extra sensitive to compensate. The truth, Stella Fry reflected, as she walked home that afternoon, was that the blackout which had been in place for the last six months only made you more clumsy and accident-prone.

That was why everyone was hurrying back in the last vestiges of daylight before the encroaching gloom descended. A blacked-out pavement, with its potential to make you stumble and trip, was a minefield, which explained why a couple of pedestrians she passed sported plasters or bandages after taking a fall. Paperboys were calling out the evening headlines, but the pedestrians were not listening. Most were thinking only of supper and getting back before the blackout made their journey even more arduous.

Stella Fry was no different to anyone else hurrying home that Friday. She got off the number 52 tram and walked along Queenstown Road, skirted Battersea Park and turned right into Prince of Wales Drive. She was a slight, tidy figure, with dark auburn hair rolled off her face, level brows and lips outlined in her favourite new plum lipstick by Maybelline. She was thinking of the evening ahead with mixed emotions. She had accepted an invitation to see Ivor Novello's *The Dancing Years* from a man in the office, Toby Enderby, but while she knew that he was keen on her, she did not reciprocate his feelings. She was not relishing the moment – almost certainly that evening – when she would have to rebuff his advances. Traffic might slow down in wartime, but courtships, she'd discovered, accelerated, and no man who could be called up at any moment saw the point in extended courtesies.

What made it worse was the fact that the two of them sat side by side where they worked at the GPO Film Unit in Soho Square. Both were involved in editing scripts for documentaries and short information films. Though it was a workplace filled with eager young film-makers, prepared to work for pennies for the chance to make art, the job was far from glamorous. When she had applied, Stella imagined that she might be meeting film stars but instead the director, Humphrey Jennings, a tall man with a short temper and an intense, artistic manner, preferred to portray ordinary people. Their latest documentary focused on working men's hobbies and the only cast members Stella had got to meet were two wrestlers, a football team and a man who bred lurchers in his back yard.

The thought of Toby Enderby and the need to let him down gently engendered a familiar sinking feeling. At thirty-one, Stella found most of her female friends were either married or defiantly single, whereas she was neither. She wondered why she was not attracted to Toby, who despite his old flannel trousers and sagging corduroy jacket was not bad-looking. But there it was. At least, as he had no money, he would not be suggesting they go on to dinner afterwards, or even have an interval drink. She only prayed that he didn't plan on bringing fish paste sandwiches, the way he did at work.

Despite these misgivings, she was looking forward to the play. She loved the theatre, and she liked dressing up. Half of London might be wearing khaki, brown and grey, but Stella could not exist without colour. Perhaps because she had lived so long on the Continent, she was passionate about pattern and style. That day she was wearing a lightweight fawn coat with padded shoulders cinched with a red belt, and a small green pillbox hat. For the evening she planned to change into a dress she had made herself from blue-checked Liberty print, together with her diamanté necklace and best shoes. *I will make it clear to Toby*, she told herself, *that I enjoy his friendship, but nothing more.* Just saying this to herself dissipated some of her anxiety and raised her spirits.

It was a surprise, therefore, when she reached her address, to break out of her thoughts to find a crowd gathered, craning up to gaze at a window on the second floor. The building, Primrose Mansions, was a handsome mansion block with a privet hedge on the street front and a white arched door to the hall. It overlooked Battersea Park, an urban idyll of elms and oaks and a bandstand, from where Stella would hear faint strains of brass bands floating up on weekend afternoons. Yet now a police car was parked outside, and an officer was standing on the pavement, urging people to pass along, which they were conspicuously declining to do. As she approached, the policeman's heavyset colleague trudged out of the apartment block, helmet in one hand, notebook in the other, and joined him to talk in a low voice. Both men shook their heads.

Even then, Stella was not immediately alarmed. She slowed down and lingered behind the onlookers who exuded a low hum of anticipation like the agitated buzz of a bees' nest. Most had abandoned their natural British reticence and were gawping openly while the police officers conferred. Stella could see barely anything and eventually curiosity drove her to question a woman in a floral housecoat with a headscarf over her bleached hair.

'What's happened? Do you know?'

'There's been an accident.' Behind her heavy spectacles, the woman's eyes gleamed with excitement. 'A young woman. Not expected to live.'

'Oh, how awful!' Stella paused for a shocked moment. 'From this actual block?'

Another woman leaned in. 'Primrose Mansions.'

Her own. Burning to know which of her neighbours it might be, Stella persisted.

'Have they said who it is?'

'They're not telling. It's procedure.'

The bespectacled woman was visibly relishing the incident. Death, or potential death, had become the acceptable stuff of drama, now that the prospect of it was everywhere.

'Fell in front of a bus.'

'A train, I heard.'

'Broke every bone in her body. Wonder if it was deliberate?'

'I'd say.'

The neighbour crossed her arms and craned forwards again, determined not to miss any of the theatre that had unfolded so unexpectedly and thrillingly on her doorstep.

'Unlikely to survive, poor soul.'

A third housewife leaned over, unable to resist yielding her own small nugget of knowledge.

'Actually, I heard the policeman, just now. Talking to his friend. He did let slip a name.'

'Go on, then,' said the yellow-haired woman.

'He said the poor lady was called Fry. Miss Stella Fry.'

The words hit Stella like a physical blow. She ducked and knelt for a moment, as if fastening a buckle that had come loose on her shoe, and bent her face down, breathing hard. She stared fixedly at the paving beneath her for several moments until it stopped moving. Why she didn't stand up and announce herself – protest that it was all a mistake, that she was perfectly fine and present, and prepared to prove her identity to any doubters – she could not at that moment understand.

Instead, after a minute, she rose, turned on her heel and walked swiftly away.

# CHAPTER 2

*Earlier That Day*

The harsh cry of wolves rose and mingled with the scent of lion dung in the soft morning air. The strangeness of it, so far from the Serengeti, could not match the weirdness of this new world they were in.

Harry Fox was staring into a pane of glass, gazing at nothingness.

The aquarium had always been his favourite spot at London Zoo. There was nothing like the sight of drifting fish to calm him down and ease his habitual edginess. Now, however, the aquarium had been drained and the fish were gone. They had probably been fed to the seals, while the poisonous snakes and spiders had been chloroformed and the manatees shot. A few surviving reptiles were still in evidence, slinking around a glass enclosure crisscrossed with gummed paper, but the pandas, elephants and chimps had all been evacuated to Whipsnade, leaving only lions and wolves as well as the odd goat and horse to represent the mammal kingdom.

And they were proving a devil to keep, according to signs around the zoo appealing for 'countryside visitors' to bring acorns with them for feeding. Thinking about it, Harry immediately pictured his nephew Jack, who was never far from his mind since he had been evacuated to a village near Stow-on-the-Wold the previous year. Maybe next time he visited Jack they could gather some acorns, if acorns even existed in May, and bring them here for a day out. And what would happen if bombs did fall? Would the wolves and lions here escape? He had heard the keepers had been provided with guns for that.

Running a fingertip along the pane of glass, Harry shifted from foot to foot. Whatever the fate of the aquarium's residents, it was not so different from his. Life had clouded over, and no one had any idea if it would clear again.

Zoning out from the empty tank, he focused on his own reflection. It was a physique that looked like it would be handy in a fight. Tall and broad-shouldered, his saturnine looks, the wide face with a square chin, were interrupted by a six-inch scar on his left cheek extending downwards from the side of his eye. He had dark-circled eyes, no matter how well he'd slept, and despite a sharp morning shave his jaw was already bristling, as if laughing at him for the price of razor blades.

He was a mess, he knew that, and above all a mess of

contradictions. He was an MI5 operative who did not formally work for MI5. An avoider of physical confrontation who nonetheless bore the legacy of a vicious brawl. A negligent dresser who managed to look good in a rumpled mac and battered trilby, at least that was what women told him. A romantic who worked on adultery cases.

And most of all, a patriot who couldn't fight.

Since the outbreak of hostilities the previous September, Harry had been desperate to join the war effort, but at forty-one, he was a few cruel months over the conscription age. Now that spring was here, seeing the green space of Regent's Park dotted with khaki was almost unbearable. People ran judgemental eyes over a man in civvies, before concluding that he was too old to be called up. Nothing made you feel your age like war and here he was, stuck with the halt and the lame. He felt utterly useless. As his sister Joan said, it was a toss-up whether he would die of cirrhosis of the liver or a German bomb. Though truth to tell, the sight of a whisky now felt not so much convivial as purely medicinal.

He had spent the weekend installing an Anderson shelter in Joan's garden – two curved sections of corrugated steel bolted together and sunk into the earth. The components were provided free by the government, but Joan wasn't in the least grateful. If bombs did come, she said, she would rather die in the warmth of her house than in some freezing shelter with rain pooling around her ankles.

Harry had no shelter of his own, but that morning a leaflet had dropped through the door of his basement flat in

Battersea: 'Beating the Invader'. *Where the enemy lands there will be most violent fighting. When the attack begins it will be too late to go . . . STAND FIRM.* There was more about disabling your bicycle and destroying all maps and removing the carburettor from your car. Harry owned neither a bicycle nor a car and all the maps he needed were in his head. Even though everyone was laying in sand for sandbags and blacking out windows, and mass graves were being prepared in the local cemetery, to Harry the whole thing still had a play-acting quality. The previous evening a 'bombing truck' had come down his street. In the back, a young air-raid warden with a theatrical air was throwing out different-coloured tennis balls to signify which attack was incoming: red for high explosive, yellow and green for gas. Harry had watched the lad impassively. Even if he could remember which was which, he knew he would forget how to react accordingly.

A flicker of movement in the glass's reflection caused him to turn. A man was lingering at the entrance to the air-raid shelter beneath the rodent house. He was middle-aged, and wearing a tweed suit, a checked shirt and a trilby. Beneath the hat's brim were a bulbous nose, large ears and beetle brows, yet these singular features were transformed by the warmth of his debonair smile.

Maxwell Knight, agent runner, head of MI5's M section and occasional employer of Harry off the books.

'Harry Fox! It's been a while.'

'Mr Knight. Good to see you.'

'Major Knight now, as it happens. But you can call me mister. How are you, Harry? Busy?'

'Crime waits for no man.'

Knight removed his hat and used it to fan his face for a moment.

'And your sister?'

'She's fine, thanks. Misses her boy, of course. I never hear the end of it.'

'Where is he?'

'Evacuated to a farm near Stow-on-the-Wold. Milking cows, probably. Shouldn't think he's ever met so many animals.'

'Good for him! We can learn a lot from animals. We should all spend more time looking at them. Useful tradecraft.'

Knight replaced his hat and cast a quick glance behind him.

'Thank you for coming out. I do like to chat here, as you know.'

The zoo was the place they had first met. Knight had taken him on a short tour of the cages and enclosures, and at the end of it enquired, mildly, if Harry had noticed anyone queuing at the ticket office and if he could describe them. That, it turned out, was Knight's method of assessing potential recruits and judging their observational prowess. Harry, whose work as a surveillance operative meant these routines were as natural as breathing, was instantly able to describe the powdery old lady with the twinset and pearl necklace and the man in the bowler hat with the silver cane, neither of whom seemed likely customers for a day at the donkey enclosure.

Knight had listened approvingly.

'They told me you're not the conventional type of animal. You don't like running with the herd. As it happens, that's exactly the kind of animal I like.'

Though Knight was employed by MI5, and indeed was its leading agent runner, he had always been a maverick. At the start of the war, MI5 had thirty-six officers and around a hundred other staff, run under the aegis of Major-General Sir Vernon Kell, known as 'K'. In the midst of this Knight had fashioned for himself an autonomous department, B5 (b), concerned with infiltrating potentially subversive groups, with agents hand-picked for their tenacity and loyalty. Knight ran his agents like a doting lover. He made it his business to know about their families, their hobbies and their insecurities. He chose individuals who craved excitement in their lives, coupled with a feeling that they would never properly belong. Harry wondered if, when Knight had first approached him, he had recognized a kindred spirit.

A bird alighted on the ground close to them and Knight stared fixedly at it.

'What do you make of that?'

'It's a pigeon.'

'Obviously it's a pigeon. I mean, what do you make of its gait, its origin?'

Harry shook his head. Wildlife was not his speciality. Lowlife was.

Sensing their interest, the bird stopped its strutting, tilted its head to regard them with a bright, beady eye, then ruffled its feathers and resumed pecking.

'We're getting reports of pigeons flying in a suspicious manner. People think they're German carrier pigeons, bringing messages for spies with notes wrapped around their legs.'

Harry shrugged.

'I wouldn't know what a German pigeon looks like.'

'Very much like a British one. It's the quality of the bird that differs. Apparently, the Nazis have seized all the pigeon lofts in the country and are using the very best of the racing birds. We've established a falconry unit stationed on the south coast to counteract them. Pick them off as they arrive. But it's an ongoing battle. D'you know, a good carrier pigeon can fly six hundred miles in a day? The Nazis use a technique called Widowhood where they remove its mate and take the bird away from its nest, so it has all the incentive to fly back to its young as fast as possible. I tell all my people to spend their time observing birds. In our business, we can learn a lot.'

The pigeon took wing into a nearby tree, and Knight followed its flight with a kind of rapture. Then the reverie ended, and his focus snapped back to Harry.

'I have to admit, I'm combining business with pleasure today. I'm hoping to secure a three-toed sloth. You know my enthusiasms, Harry. I've not forgotten your help in sourcing me the bushbaby from that man – Jessop, wasn't it?'

Harry nodded. Knight was famed for his devotion to animals. It was said that he always carried something alive in his pocket. He had an entire menagerie in his Sloane Street flat. Kenny Jessop, now a garage proprietor, had once worked in the circus and was able to magic up any number of exotic pets.

'How is our Mr Jessop?'

'Still in Clapham Junction mending cars.' Harry paused. 'So, you're looking for another bushbaby?'

'Ha! No.' Knight laughed. 'Not this time. I'm looking for a person. That, in fact, is the chief reason I asked to see you.'

He had been carrying a commodious, stained canvas bag, which he had placed on the ground. Now he crouched, delved into it, and bought out a manila file. Fastened to the top of the file with a paperclip, Harry saw a photograph of a brunette woman with regular features and brown eyes. She had an air of defiance in the pout of her full lips and the frank, unreadable gaze. Knight took out a sheet of paper and read.

'Stella Fry. Born London, August 19th, 1907. Father, William Fry, deceased 1916, mother, Nancy Fry née Cook. Read Modern Languages, Somerville College Oxford. Worked for publishing house, Hodges and Pettigrew, 1927–1928. Employed as a tutor to Austrian family, resident in Vienna until 1938. Fluent German, French, some Italian. Currently employed at GPO Film Unit. One brother, Alan Fry, still living. Unmarried.'

'What of her?'

'You've worked with this lady?'

Harry tore his eyes from the photograph and dug his fists deeper into the pockets of his mac.

'I have.'

'Very successfully, too, I understand. The Service is still digesting the after-effects of your discoveries, and it will be for some time to come. That novelist Hubert Newman. Extraordinary how he managed to escape our attention. To be honest, I was quite an admirer myself.'

Harry knew that Knight, like himself, was an aficionado of pulp fiction. A devotee of detective novels. Indeed, he had even written a few thrillers himself. Once he had told Harry that all true detective novelists were forged in childhood. *When Humpty Dumpty fell from the wall, the enquiring child will ask, did he fall or was he pushed?* That was the kind of kid who would go far, Knight said. He had long been a fan of Hubert Newman, so the revelations after his death were all the more grievous to him.

'What do you make of our Miss Fry? Solid, is she?'

'Rock solid.'

'Are you in contact?'

'I've not seen her for more than a year, Mr Knight. I'm not even sure where she's living now.'

'No matter. I know. I have all her details. She recently moved flats. The current address is . . . let me see, here.'

Knight detached a scrap of paper from the file and handed it to Harry, who stared at it, bemused.

'You want me to send her a postcard?'

'Not exactly, dear boy.'

Knight was stowing the file back in the jumble of his canvas bag. At the bottom of the bag, though it should not have been a surprise, Harry glimpsed something shifting and glittering like loose change. It was the metallic gold and yellow of a snake. 'Then what, may I ask?'

'I want you to approach her. It's nothing complicated. But first, I need her to disappear.'

## CHAPTER 3

It was hardly even a challenge. Shortly after leaving the zoo, Harry caught a number 88 bus to his office in Soho, where he opened what he called his 'prop cupboard' and collected a large case stencilled with the legend *Ealing Electricians* in red ink on the side. Then he caught two more buses to the address Knight had given him and by midday he was standing outside a large red-brick apartment block, resting his electrician's case on the pavement. There he waited until an elderly lady emerged, attempting to manhandle a wheeled tartan shopping trolley out of the mansion-block door without it slamming on her. Springing forward, Harry held the door gallantly open and then, accepting her thanks, slipped into the building, lugging his case behind him.

That part had been easy. Standing in the unlit stairwell, he prepared himself for the next.

*Just a quick visit. Let the neighbours know an accident has occurred.*

Those were Knight's instructions. He need not even enter the flat, but he couldn't help himself.

Had he not followed the path of pure virtue, Harry would have made a magnificent criminal. Because there were times when, for him, burglary was sheer joy. Indeed, it was an art, like ballet, with every step synchronized into a perfect and apparently effortless pattern. Breaking into Stella's flat was one of those times.

Knight had assured him that she was out during the day – doing something in films – and that she would not be home before five at the earliest. From Harry's career in the security services – employment from which he had been abruptly and disgracefully suspended – he had kept a skeleton key. After a swift glance up the stairwell and having established that Stella left her Chubb unlocked (bad practice, because you never knew who was around), he proceeded to work the Yale. A second later, he was in.

Standing in the narrow hall, he took a beat to enjoy it. He didn't like to admit it, even to himself, but he had missed Stella badly over the last year. After their joint success in uncovering a ring of Soviet spies they had gone their separate ways with no particular reason to continue an acquaintance. They had no mutual friends and not even the flimsiest of pretexts for ongoing encounters. These obstacles would not normally have deterred Harry, who was assiduous when it came to women, but Stella was a different proposition entirely. Therefore, as the glory of their espionage triumph faded, he had buried himself in freelance work – frauds, adulteries, missing persons – and tried to forget his dream that they might ever be partners.

He began to look around, yet each step, and each glance, felt like an almost physical intrusion. Every space and item spoke of Stella, as though the flat and its contents were part of a single nervous system that resonated with her energy. The desk, the chairs, the clothes in the wardrobe, the pots of Nivea and Johnson's talcum powder ranged beneath the bathroom mirror, even the toothbrush and the tube of Colgate, seemed not merely random objects but intimately connected to her. He could barely bring himself to touch a thing. Added to which, it was all so – *tidy*. The bookshelves, bowed with books, and the breakfast things washed and stacked beside the sink. Her coat hung neatly on a peg by the door. His sense of intrusion came to a head as he peered into her bedroom, where he tried not to snoop but did, in fact, manage to check for the sight of a man's shoes beneath the bed, or a tie slung on the back of the chair, or a razor on the chest of drawers, or any other telltale trace of masculinity that might suggest that Stella was not living alone. All he saw, however, was a blue dress on a hanger and a pair of her shoes ranged neatly beneath.

These he bundled into an adjacent suitcase, along with a pair of blouses and a couple of skirts from the wardrobe and a jumper of soft green wool. Then he took a final look around.

A copy of yesterday's *Evening News* lay folded on the table. He read a little.

*Experience in other lands has brought home to the Britisher that stricter measures must be taken against espionage, sabotage and 'fifth column' activities. The Germans' easy success in occupying the Norwegian ports is known to have been largely due to the activities of traitors like Quisling and German agents . . .*

The Enemy Within. Going by what he knew, Maxwell Knight's unit in MI5 was still concerned largely with his favourite subject, communist spies, yet since the outbreak of war, the focus had shifted to the right. In particular, towards any potential fifth columnist. That term included actual Nazis, fresh from the Continent, as well as Nazi sympathizers, sleeper spies, resident aliens and anyone involved in promoting German propaganda. Amid the British establishment the hunt for fifth columnists was close to an obsession. The belief that Germany was preparing for an invasion of Western Europe had inspired deep anxiety about every kind of domestic subversion.

And not without reason.

Visiting his sister Joan the other day, Harry had been greeted by the sound of fruity upper-class voices floating from the wireless and although Joan had jumped up with alacrity and switched it off, Harry recognized the NBBS – the New British Broadcasting Service – a station that sounded like the BBC but in fact emanated from a studio in Berlin, and employed a cast of expatriate fascists in an effort to sap British resolve. When not lampooning the upper class, the programmes featured an array of British cockneys complaining that Jewish bosses were planning to bomb their own factories. The general theme was that the war was all the fault of the upper classes and the workers needed to wake up.

Harry said, 'You know who runs that station? Joseph Goebbels.'

'I don't care,' said Joan mulishly. 'It's funny.'

In the past he had come across her listening to Lord Haw-Haw, 'for a laugh'. Whatever Harry thought about his sister's taste, he knew she was not alone in that.

How hard it was to persuade people of what they were up against. To get them to see the reality of the situation. *The Times* was still referring to *Herr* Hitler and *Signor* Mussolini and refusing to call savages savages. That was the problem with everything, Harry thought. A refusal to see savagery for what it was.

Then again, he didn't blame Joan. There wasn't much pleasure to be had from listening to the radio these days. Laughter was thin on the ground and all the news was bad.

Pulling himself together, he left the flat as quietly as he had come and proceeded to his main task, which was to press on the bell of the neighbouring apartment and inform the owner that Miss Fry had been involved in an accident.

'Who are you?'

It was an elderly lady. Her whiskery face twitched with suspicion.

'Electrician, madam. Your neighbour, Miss Fry, called me out, Mrs . . .'

'Mrs Delacroix. I'm very busy at the moment. How does this concern me?'

'Miss Fry had some problem with her electrics. We agreed that I would come in her lunch break. But when I got here, she wasn't answering the bell.'

'Well, I can't help you. She was probably held up. Or busy at the office. I don't have a key and I can't go imparting details of my neighbours' whereabouts. I can't be expected to tell you where she works. Not in these times. It's confidential.'

'Respectfully, Mrs Delacroix, you don't understand.' Harry was humble. He was decent. He was the salt of the earth. 'When Miss Fry didn't answer, I went down the street and telephoned the office. It was bad news. They'd been sent a message that Miss Fry was in an accident.'

'What kind of accident?'

'Couldn't tell you. But a bad one. Very bad. May have involved a train line.'

'You mean she threw herself on the traqks?'

'I couldn't say, missus.'

'Was it deliberate?' The watery eyes gleamed with intrigue.

'All I know is, the young lady's in the hospital. It's touch and go, apparently. Police will be arriving to check out the flat.'

'So why are you here?'

'Goodness of my heart, Mrs Delacroix. I thought a decent person such as yourself would want to know. Maybe you could let the neighbours know too. Respectfully, of course. Wouldn't want people to worry unduly.'

Job done, Harry departed the premises with a spring in his step. He had no idea why Mr Knight might want Stella Fry to disappear, nor why he might want to see her, but as he headed back to St Martin's Lane, he felt a quickening anticipation that something good was coming and it quite cancelled out his earlier gloom.

CHAPTER 4

Moving swiftly away from the scene outside her flat, Stella walked across Chelsea Bridge towards the underground station at Sloane Square. She felt watched, like an actress, and drew her jacket more closely around her, as if to shield herself from any curious gaze. It was uncomfortable to be at the centre of attention for all the wrong reasons and the feeling persisted until she made it to the station, where she caught the first train and sat in the semi-darkness, trying to fathom what had just happened.

After a few minutes, in which she reached no conclusion, she looked around her.

It was a strange sensation, knowing that something was coming – and indeed in Eastern Europe it had already come – but not having any real idea how it might erupt. As she sat on the crowded Tube train, breathing in the smell of oil and smoke and unwashed clothes, her fellow passengers looked sallow and unemotional, locked in their own inviolable worlds. They were the perfect embodiment of the famous British stiff upper lip and yet she wondered how they would react if actual, raw courage was required of them. War would mean cities levelled, people exiled, dreadful deaths. If the sea routes were cut off, Britain might starve.

If these same thoughts were playing on their minds, however, most commuters gave no sign of it. They jolted stoically with the train's starts and stops. The wooden floor beneath their feet was dirty, and the plush upholstery of the seats was worn and shabby, but they merely buried themselves in their newspapers, holding them up close to their eyes because the Tube lighting was dimmed and the windows crosshatched with tape.

The newspapers themselves had changed too. Since the German invasion of Denmark and Norway on the 9th of April, Scandinavian pulp supplies had been cut off, with the result that newspapers had shrunk to six pages. In terms of their content, however, they were fuller than ever. The classified advertisements were sprinkled with 'Help Wanted' messages but most of them stipulated that 'No Germans' were welcome. Elsewhere, Continental Jews were trying to advertise their way out of danger in terms both pleading and agonizingly genteel. *Would a generous English family consider hosting my daughter, 12, a fine musician, intelligent. My two sons, fifteen and nine, are willing, strong and ready to help in your household.* Recalling her time in Vienna, Stella remembered all too well the terror that caused families to send their children away.

★

Dusk had fallen when she emerged from the underground. The streets were busy with trams and taxis, moving slowly, the huff and throb of their engines sounding through the dusk. Cars crawled along with one headlight taped up and the other hooded, following white lines laid out in the road to guide them.

Along the dilapidated Georgian terraces of Mecklenburgh Square, the picturesque Victorian gas lamps had been decommissioned, so Stella groped her way armed with her blackout torch, trying to avoid the disintegrating sandbags that made the pavement an obstacle course for unwary pedestrians. It crossed her mind that moving in the blackout was not very different from how she had always progressed – sounding out the margins of her familiar environment and feeling for another world at the edge of her senses. It was that impulse which had taken her to the Continent in her twenties, finding a new home in Vienna as tutor to three intelligent Austrian children, with frequent forays to Italy and France. Two years ago, she had returned briefly to Vienna, but since war had been declared, she had no idea when, or if, she would travel to Europe again.

She had no plan for if Evelyn was out. The idea of begging a bed from her brother, Alan, and Vanessa, his formidable wife, was off-putting, especially at this time in the evening. Her funds barely stretched to a hotel, and she didn't relish the idea of hunting for one. But to her relief, her friend answered the door.

'Stella! It's you! You just caught me.'

'Can I come in?'

Evelyn stood aside.

'Of course.'

'Were you expecting someone?'

Evelyn was dressed as if for a party in a tight red dress and black seamed stockings and surrounded by a cloud of French perfume which Stella guessed had been bought by an admirer. Her mouth was a scarlet bow, and she was running a finger of Vaseline over it to give her lips an extra shine. She looked fabulous.

'I was, as a matter of fact. He'll be here any minute.'

'The thing is,' said Stella, dumping her handbag on the hall table, 'I've got a favour to ask. I might need to stay a night or two.'

'Here?'

'If that's OK.'

Stella was not going to tell Evelyn that she could barely afford a hotel. Evelyn's friends might call themselves bohemian, but being bohemian was expensive. It involved parties and clubs and weekends away, and neither Evelyn nor her set were ever really short of funds.

'Of course it's OK, but why? What on earth's happened?'

'Nothing serious. The flat flooded. A pipe burst, apparently, in the place upstairs and they'll need to go in and mop up. The floor's awash. My Turkish rug is ruined.'

'Poor you.' Evelyn seemed preoccupied. She was fiddling

with a pearl earring that she was in the process of fastening. 'You know I only have one bed.'

'I'll take the sofa. It's only for a short while. You won't know I was here.'

'I don't have any food. I mean, I'm living on powdered egg. Though I do have some smoked salmon.'

'Smoked salmon!'

Even in Stella's mental turmoil, this astonishment was enough to distract her.

'A Polish officer gave it to me. Witold. I met him at the Milroy. I'd never have guessed London could be such fun, Stella. I've been out dancing every night this week. In fact, it's Witold I'm expecting now. He's taking me to the Bon Viveur in Shepherd Market. Then we're going on to the Players' Theatre to see Peter Ustinov.'

The idea of knitting socks for soldiers, or spinning dogs' hair into yarn, which were currently recommended as spare time endeavours for women, had plainly not occurred to Evelyn.

'So many people are away already. They're either in the BEF or they're being posted. You have to make the most of it while you can.'

Wriggling her feet into a pair of high heels, she continued, 'Who's to say it'll happen anyway? It's just the Bore War. Apparently, the Italian ambassador said, I've seen several wars waged without being declared, but this is the first time I've seen it declared without being waged. That's quite amusing, isn't it?'

Outfit complete, she posed hand on hip.

'Will I do?'

Stella smiled. It was Evelyn's characteristic pose, the same one she had assumed at the age of thirteen, in a Panama hat and school tie.

'Very glamorous. And you're taking your gas mask!'

Evelyn opened the cardboard case to reveal not a mask but a packet of cigarettes and a hairbrush.

'It's terribly useful. You can get such a lot in it.'

'How's your play? *Private Lives*?'

'Wonderful, actually. I adore Noël Coward. We open in a week, unless Hitler thinks otherwise.'

'Who are you playing?'

'Not Amanda, unfortunately. Sybil, Elyot's young wife.'

'Can't wait to see it.'

'It's set in Paris. I suppose it's the nearest any of us are going to get to Paris for quite a while.' Drifting over to the mirror, she patted her hair and began to hum 'Someday I'll Find You'.

Though she was glad to see Evelyn again, Stella was finding it hard to focus. The shock of the past few hours, coupled with the uncertainty of her next move, had rendered her unusually quiet. She wanted to puzzle it out, yet now was not the time to unload her worries onto her friend.

'It's quite a coup to get that part, even so, Eve.'

'I know. And we're all awfully lucky to be working, to be honest. There are no staff. Jasper, the producer, is having to double as front of house manager. But what choice do we have? Jasper says it's all very well making sure people don't die of gas, but if they keep closing theatres and cinemas, people are going to die of boredom instead.'

Back in September, when war broke out, the theatres had gone dark, and even though many had reopened, work was thin on the ground.

Evelyn checked her watch.

'Witold should be here by now. As I say, there's not much to eat.'

'That's OK. And I have my ration book.'

Stella flourished the small brown book that everyone had been issued with, back in January. Sixteen coupons a month to spend on rice, sardines, milk, biscuits, oats, or anything else they were able to find in the shops.

'Oh good,' said Evelyn vaguely. 'Leave it on the table. And I do have alcohol, though they say even that's going to run out soon. Let me get you a drink. I can't find gin for love nor money so I'm making all my cocktails with rum. I'll do you my version of a martini. Vermouth, a squeeze of orange and rum.'

She crossed to a burr walnut cocktail cabinet that opened at the push of a catch to reveal a range of cut-glass decanters, bottles of spirits, a lemon squeezer and ice tongs.

'After dinner there's a party for Peter. He's joined the RAF so there'll be plenty of Brylcreem boys. And there's an American broadcaster called Ed Murrow who's invited. Do you want to come?'

'I can't. I'm done in.'

'That's a shame. Apparently, Peter wants me to look after his pets. Three ferrets he bought from Harrods. So don't be alarmed if I come back with a cage. Chin-chin.'

Proffering a glass of what looked like pure rum, Evelyn opened a packet of Kent cigarettes and sat on the sofa, folding her legs beneath her.

'You're not in any trouble, are you?'

'No. I told you. I'm just flooded out.'

'That's a relief. After what happened before. You do seem to get involved in some extraordinary ventures.'

'Hardly. My biggest excitement tonight would have been going to the theatre with Toby Enderby.'

'The one with the ginger hair?'

Stella smiled, astonished at Evelyn's near-photographic memory concerning aspects of her romantic life. She felt another pang of guilt. She had called Toby from the telephone box at the end of her street, but he was out – probably on his way already – so she had left a message with the landlady making her excuses.

'Toby Enderby's still on the scene, is he?'

'Not really. It's never going to work. He's not a listener. I sometimes test him by inserting something extraordinary in a sentence to see if he notices, but he doesn't turn a hair. I told him I'd tracked down a circle of Soviet spies in London and he thought I was telling a shaggy dog story.'

'You can't blame him. That's exactly what it sounds like. You can hardly expect him to have believed you.'

'Anyway, I've resolved to tell him to look elsewhere.'

Evelyn smiled sympathetically. Like all the Lamonts, she had the kind of face whose features went well together, well-proportioned and harmonious, and Stella could not look at her without recalling her brother, with whom she had shared a brief summer before university, and who she had met again before the war.

'How's Tom?'

'He's moved. He's been assigned to Churchill and he's working at Admiralty House now. You haven't seen him in a while, have you?' Evelyn paused, frowning slightly. 'And you ought to know, I suppose. I should have told you.'

She exhaled a jet of smoke, with a graceful tilt of her head. 'Tom's engaged. To an American, of all things. He met her at a party for Kick Kennedy, the daughter of the American ambassador. It was a debs' ball, after Kick was presented at court. Not really Tom's scene, but there you are. He's a spy.'

'A spy!'

'Not a real spy. Only in a manner of speaking. Between you and me, Churchill asked Tom to stick close to the Kennedys and their circle and to report back anything important that he learned. The thought is, they're friends of President Roosevelt and they could be influential in getting America into the war. I think that was the logic. Anyway, in the course of doing that the two of them met, and now they're getting married. She's called Meredith Meadows and my mother loves her. She's become quite boring on the subject. She's always listing Meredith's good points.'

'Oh . . .' Stella paused so infinitesimally that only the most attentive would have noticed. 'And what are Meredith's good points?'

'Her family owns a stable of racehorses and a thousand acres.' Evelyn cast a sideways glance. 'The acres are in Kentucky, though.'

'Nice for Tom.'

'Even nicer for our mother.'

Sidonie Lamont was a woman of beauty, frosted elegance and intense social ambition who was determined that her only son should marry a woman of both means and breeding.

'She wants them to marry quickly. Everyone's getting married now, just in case.'

'In case . . . ?'

'Anything happens. Besides, she's desperate for some grandchildren, and it's no good looking in my direction.'

All Sidonie Lamont's hopes rested on Tom's shoulders. It was not that she disapproved of her daughter's rambunctious party lifestyle, nor the acting profession – Sidonie was far too cultivated for that – but Tom was her golden child. As far as Sidonie was concerned, Tom had the talent, the ability, and the family responsibility to rise to the top.

'Meredith's holding a dinner for friends on the 13th. I'm sure they'd both love you to come.' A wry smile. 'You know, it's funny, I would have thought getting engaged would cheer Tom up, but he's looking awfully dour.'

'You can hardly blame him for that. Considering the circumstances.'

'I suppose.'

'I should send congratulations.'

'Oh, I think I can hear Witold on the stairs.'

Evelyn leapt up, pulled on a pair of scarlet kid leather gloves and gathered up her gas-mask bag.

'Tom's coming over tomorrow. If you're still here, you can congratulate him yourself.'

Once Witold had taken Evelyn off, Stella looked around her. No matter that this was a different flat, Evelyn had managed to recreate her precise environment, as though it was some kind of psychic aura that followed her around: a turbulent, untidy aura full of art deco items and junk shop finds. She browsed around, glancing at an opened copy of *Vogue*: *Siren suits, one-piece and cosily cowled, respond to a profound need of mind and body to be warmly, safely enclosed against fear and danger.* A programme for Evelyn's most prestigious performance, *The Importance of Being Earnest* at the Golders Green Hippodrome, with John Gielgud, Edith Evans and Peggy Ashcroft, was tucked into the corner of a mirror. Another for a recent revue, Noël Coward's *All Clear*, opposite it. Stella plucked it out and scrutinized it. Evelyn was photographed in soft-edged monochrome, caressed by a fur wrap, her chin cupped stagily on her palm, emitting a smile of rigid gaiety.

Replacing this flattering vision in the corner of the mirror, Stella stared at herself, as if through other eyes. Brown hair with glints of russet, complexion a little flushed from the rum, round-necked sweater and single-strand pearl necklace. Her eyes were ringed with tiredness from the day's unsettling events, and she could not help thinking that a little artificial light and a fur wrap would improve things greatly.

So Tom had a fiancée. She was not sure how she felt about that.

Apart from the help he had given her a year and a half ago, she had not had any connection with Tom Lamont. She kept her memories of him, like her time on the Continent, strictly compartmentalized, and only allowed herself to see them with a deliberately vague, sepia tint. She had known his stolid frame and his wise, kindly face since the age of thirteen, when he was nothing more than Evelyn's older brother. Then, shortly before she left for Oxford, she had spent a summer at the Lamonts' country home, a Palladian edifice of tawny stone in Berkshire, and a romance had flowered between them. It had faded like a spring bloom when she went off to university and Tom to his job, and it was not until a year and a half ago, when she had been involved in a dramatic investigation into the death of a crime writer, that he came back into her life. Now her feelings about Tom occupied a deep, unexplored layer far below the business of her ordinary existence.

The last time she had seen him, he had walked her back to her flat after a supper, paused at the door and put his hand on her arm.

'You know, Stella, you continually surprise me.'

'Thank you, I suppose.'

'You're not planning any more adventures?'

'I think war will put paid to any adventures.'

'I wouldn't be so sure. It's more likely to be the beginning of them.' He hesitated. 'You will be all right, won't you?'

For a second, the scent of him and the feel of his hand was so familiar that she felt an almost irresistible urge to fold herself into his arms, but instead she had turned away.

'Of course I will! Thanks for supper. Goodnight!'

She shook herself. Why was she bothered about Tom Lamont? She didn't want him. She was happy for him, delighted at his engagement, and she would tell him so just as soon as she got the chance. Meredith Meadows, whoever she was, was a lucky girl. Though God forbid Stella herself should have to attend the engagement dinner. She would need to dream up an excuse.

Besides, she had far more pressing concerns. Someone had told her neighbours that she had been seriously injured. It was clear that she should stay away from her flat. Her life had been uprooted, and nobody was explaining why.

Taking the tea cosy off the pot, she poured herself a cup, thanking her time on the Continent for the fact that she was able to contemplate tea without milk. She looked in the cupboard for food and was disappointed to see that Evelyn's comments about powdered egg were completely accurate. The only other nourishment was a few slices of bread, a packet of Jacob's Cream Crackers, a couple of Oxo cubes and a jar of Bournvita. She ate a couple of the crackers and followed that with a cup of black tea.

Then she ventured into Evelyn's bedroom in search of a blanket. The dressing table was crowded with bottles: Worth's Je Reviens, Chanel No5, Lanvin's Arpège, Leichner make-up, Cyclax Stockingless Cream. She ran her fingers over Evelyn's enamelled hairbrush and comb, her hand mirror, and the small cut-glass dish of hairpins.

Rifling in the wardrobe, past the umbrella with a broken rib and the crocodile-skin suitcase, the ratty fur coat and the satin dresses hanging like glistening ghosts of Evelyn herself, she found a rolled-up tartan rug. She considered switching on the wireless to hear the latest bulletin but instead she lay shifting restlessly on the sofa, turning over the events that had unfolded outside her flat. She thought again of the women's excited faces, swapping their nuggets of news: *There's been an accident. A young woman, not expected to live.* This incident was not, she felt sure, a case of mistaken identity. Someone had gone to considerable lengths to upset the predictable pattern of her life. They had staged a thrilling little drama, prompting a chorus of neighbours, crafted for her sole benefit. *Unlikely to survive, poor soul. Fell in front of a bus.* What kind of person would arrange such a brazen stunt, and why? Yet even as she asked herself these questions, she knew the answer. As she settled into the knobbly discomfort of the sofa and pulled the blanket over her, the face of Harry Fox, with his downward-turned smile, loomed in her mind, arousing a surprising mixture of outrage, apprehension and above all, excitement.

# CHAPTER 5

## May 2nd

'I suppose this is all your doing.'

Harry Fox's office was up an inconspicuous alley called Goodwin's Court just off St Martin's Lane, flanked with bow-fronted, iron-barred windows that dated from the seventeenth century. At its narrowest point the passage was no more than six feet wide and the soot-blackened buildings on each side leaned towards each other, as if conspiring to shut out the light. Heavy gas lanterns, at least a hundred years old, helped the customers of the Seven Bells on their unsteady way home, but since the blackout they had remained unlit and pubgoers were obliged to stumble precariously over the cobbles in the dark.

The bell to number 6 was graced by a faded placard that announced *Simpson International Investigations and Enquiries*.

It was ten thirty in the morning and Harry had come

down the stairs himself to open the outside door. This was the first time Stella had seen him for almost two years and in the swift transit of the moment, which can only have been two seconds, she registered the bandage on his hand, and a face which had barely aged except for a few lines around his eyes, and the scar, which was now not much more than a faintly puckered silver line. He leaned against the doorjamb with a lazy grace, a smile dancing on his lips.

'Good morning to you too.'

He gave her an appraising look. She was wearing the same clothes as the previous day: the fawn coat cinched with a red belt, the small green felt hat, and underneath it a grey flannel skirt and lambswool cardigan with a row of glass buttons.

Harry's smile, and the fact that he did not seem surprised to see her, was absolute proof for Stella that he had been behind the previous day's events. Yet at the sight of him, the indignation that had broiled through her during her journey deserted her. The pleasure of being reunited with Harry, even in these circumstances, instantly outweighed the inconvenience and annoyance of the previous day. The drama of their earlier liaison came back to her as she followed him up the stairs, through the frosted-glass door, into his office.

It was a cramped space. On one wall, a set of bowed shelves was stacked with wire baskets overflowing with yellowing papers. More papers were stashed in a couple of metal filing cabinets buried under a pile of manila files. To one side was a chess set with a game in progress, that she guessed he had been playing against himself. At the far end was a sink, with a kettle beside it, a bottle of milk and several unwashed cups. A mahogany bank manager's desk stood in the middle, its scuffed leather top coming unstuck at the edges, and in an apparent stab at interior decor, a portrait of the Thames at Hammersmith Bridge hung above a worn purple chaise longue. The window looked directly into the upper rooms of the pub opposite.

'How are you, Harry?' Stella nodded at the fraying gauze tied round his hand. 'Was that attack or defence?'

'Self-defence. I was putting up my sister's Anderson shelter.'

'You should get it looked at.'

'Don't worry. It's not like I'm going to be playing the piano anytime soon.'

'I thought you might have joined up.'

'They thought I was too old and wise.'

'Oh, I see. Are you still shadowing, then?'

'A little. There's plenty of other business too. Rackets, missing persons. I can't keep track of all the missing persons. War's a perfect time for people to disappear. Not to mention the fifth columnists.'

The outbreak of war had led to a flood of reports from observant members of the public which were delivered by the sackload to MI5's counter-espionage department. Strange marks on telephone poles, flowerpots placed strategically on windowsills, circles of stones in fields. Nothing was too minor to escape the attention of the patriotic and the paranoid. Hotel owners called to report guests who had left without paying their bills, abandoning suitcases of Nazi literature behind them. Fishermen reported anglers on the coast who remained for long stretches with no apparent catch. In the absence of general internment, it fell to MI5's counter-espionage unit to investigate every report and Harry had been engaged on a freelance basis to tail, track and vet them. He had spent a whole day following a nun who was supposed to have hairy arms and a Hitler tattoo under her habit. All the way to Walthamstow on the top deck of the bus until she reached the convent. Another afternoon was taken up with a pensioner in Sutton who had, his neighbours insisted, planted white flowers in his front bed to guide invading planes. Most of Harry's enquiries turned up nothing suspicious, but the British imagination was a lively one, and easily convinced that every postman, milkman or bachelor in next-door's semi-detached must have a malign and secret life.

'How's your nephew? Jack?'

'He was evacuated. He's learning to milk cows.'

Stella felt curiously reassured to find the office almost exactly the same as when she had last seen it. Same spider plant, still dying; same dust, still thick; same files, still disordered; same photograph of Jack with a deep and dimpled smile; same tattered paperbacks. A copy of Hubert Newman's *Appointment In Paris* lay on the desk, alongside a leaflet advertising Beethoven's Appassionata and Bach with Myra Hess and the London Philharmonic Chamber Ensemble.

'Ever been to one of those?' said Harry, picking it up. 'Lovely, they are.'

Myra Hess was a pianist who had started giving lunchtime concerts at the National Gallery. The Old Masters had been removed and sent for safe storage to a mine in Wales, leaving only their blank frames on the walls, but in the place of art, music had blossomed. The concerts were hugely popular and drew audiences quite different from the usual type of concertgoer: from office boys to soldiers, nurses and typists. The music seemed to provide pattern and soothing order in a turbulent world.

'No.'

'You should. They're terrific. I go every day if I can. Especially as it's just around the corner. More elevating than spending lunchtime in the Seven Bells. Don't stand there like that, it's unsettling. Why don't you sit down?'

She did.

'When I got back to my flat yesterday, I found policemen there. People were saying that I'd been involved in a serious accident. I'm guessing you might have had something to do with it.'

'I may have spread a little rumour.'

'A rumour that I had been run over by a train! Why did you need to do that, Harry? People are going away all the time. There's a war on. If I vanish, nobody's going to ask questions. I could have joined the Wrens, or the WAAF or . . .'

Harry held up a hand.

'It wasn't my idea. He's going to explain everything.'

'Who's he?'

'The person who wants to see you. A friend of mine. An employer. An old colleague.'

'Does this colleague of yours have a name?'

'I'll let him tell you that.'

'For Heaven's sake, Harry! What does this mysterious person want?'

'He wants to meet you at Brown's Hotel this lunchtime.' He checked his watch. 'In two hours' time.'

'How could he possibly know I would come here? That I'd guess you were responsible for this whole . . . charade?'

'He's a good judge of character.'

'Well, he . . . whoever *he* is . . . is going to have to wait. Apart from anything else, I don't have anything to wear.' She gestured at her clothes. 'I need a fresh blouse. What about my things?'

'I took the precaution . . .'

Harry gestured to the corner and Stella glimpsed her old valise, patched with tattered labels from Monte Carlo and Vienna and Prague. The one from Paris was peeling off, as though all those days sitting in cafés and bars and visiting the opera were now definitively over and no longer had any relevance to her life.

'I'm sorry. It's official business,' he added, passing her a cup of tea. 'A formal summons, really. He works for the government. And even I don't know what he wants to discuss. I'm just the messenger here.'

'If I do go, how will I know who to look out for? And please don't tell me he'll have a carnation in his buttonhole.'

'He'll find you.'

'So, the idea is, I miss a day's work to meet a complete stranger in Brown's Hotel wearing yesterday's clothes.'

'You look all right from here.'

He watched her face, curiosity warring with indignation, and understood how she felt. Curiosity would come out on top, he felt sure of it.

'I should be in the office,' she said.

'You can call in,' he said, knowing that she would already have done that. Women like Stella Fry didn't disappear into thin air, not unless they actually wanted to.

'I've told them I had a family emergency. I hate doing that.'

'Being run over *is* an emergency.'

'But I *haven't* been run over, have I? I'm sitting in your office, drinking tea.'

As she looked at him, time seemed to blur and she saw herself the last time she was here in the autumn of 1938, buried in the couch opposite being fed whisky in a mug.

She got up, took a deep breath as though internally bracing herself, and said, 'Anyhow, I'm here now.'

'Good. It's been quiet without you.'

'I might as well go. Just to see what he wants.'

'Great idea.'

She gave a tiny, defiant shrug of the slim shoulders.

'See you later then, I suppose.'

'You bet.'

After she had gone, Harry shut the door and leant against it, closing his eyes.

When she left the office, Stella went to the bank on the Strand and cashed a cheque for two pounds, then walked across Trafalgar Square. A small throng of people were queuing along the north side of the square and threading into the National Gallery, presumably going to one of the Myra Hess concerts. For a moment Stella yearned to be among them, forgetting everything around her in a transport of beauty. She loved the piano. She had learned as a child, but after her father died and they had moved to the small house in Chiswick, there was no room for the old upright and she missed it badly. Part of the joy of staying at Evelyn's country house as a girl had been the freedom to play Bach on their glorious Bösendorfer, with no one to protest or disturb her. Later, when she was living with the Gatz family in Vienna, as a children's tutor, she had constant access to the piano in their baroque drawing room, where she would secretly imagine herself back in the days of Mozart, Haydn and Beethoven.

She went into Hatchards and browsed, picking up one novel after another, scarcely able to focus on the titles. *How Green Was My Valley*, *Farewell, My Lovely*, *Fame Is the Spur*. Love affairs, country-house murders, underworld criminals;

how bizarre it seemed that people should still want to read about such subjects when the world was going to war. Surely, when everything changed, tastes should change too? And yet, she knew it wasn't like that. Thus far, the arrival of war had been more like a magician's tablecloth trick, where the cloth was suddenly whipped away by sleight of hand, but the cups remained untouched.

She dawdled along Piccadilly – Swan & Edgar were showcasing all-in-one suits with contrast stitching and a detachable belt, for hurried dressing in night-time air raids. A pair of mannequins were modelling gas protective outfits that looked like something a deep-sea diver might wear. Under the slogan *As Smart as a Soldier*, a slacks suit in narrow chalk-pinstripe flannel was displayed. Jacket shoulders were broader now, and hats were smaller, as if even those not in uniform might prefer to look as if they were.

At two minutes to one, she reached Brown's Hotel and passed through the revolving brass doors.

The lobby was filled with people meeting for lunch. Women in twinsets and hats, young men in khaki, being treated by their parents before they were mobilized, couples, either married or lovers, reuniting with the intensity of imminent parting. Stella peered around her. The smell of roast meat and vegetables hung in the air, and from the dining room came the clatter of cutlery and the hum of conversation. Yet she had no appetite at all. Her stomach was tight with nerves at the prospect of Harry's mysterious colleague, and whatever 'official business' he might have to convey.

At that moment, a shadow moved on the far side of the lobby, and a man came striding across, holding out his hand.

'Miss Fry. What a pleasure to see you again.'

For a second she blinked, then he came into focus, and she recognized him at once.

# CHAPTER 6

They had met before. It was the summer of 1939 and the invitation to visit Trent Park for the weekend had come courtesy of Roger Anson, a theatrical producer with whom Evelyn was conducting a fling.

Roger was driving up, but his Aston was occupied by his wife, so Stella and Evelyn arrived by underground and took a taxi from Cockfosters station. Their cases were taken by a uniformed maid and transported up a grand central staircase. Their room was a chintzy and floral space, with two narrow beds, but it also had an adjacent bathroom with a deep claw-footed bath which Evelyn swiftly filled with a froth of luxurious bubbles.

'What about this then? Beats the Ritz!'

'I'm still not sure what I'm doing here.'

'Oh, stop fretting, Stella. It's just a weekend. Enjoy yourself.'

Stella knelt on the window seat and looked down at the

acres of parkland. This was, without doubt, the most elegant and luxurious place she had ever stayed in. The lawn was, apparently, planted with a hundred thousand daffodils and the wide herbaceous borders foamed with purple sage and blue delphiniums, undercut by pastel roses and soft lavenders waving in the foreground. Beyond lay a lake dotted with wild ducks, and further on, the parkland merged into a charcoal strip of ancient woodland. To the back of the house was an airstrip and a golf course, and directly beneath their window a procession of gleaming Rolls-Royces and taxis were crunching on the immaculate gravel before disgorging a cargo of dinner-jacketed men and women in vivid evening dress. The house's owner, Sir Philip Sassoon, was a spectacularly wealthy Member of Parliament whose social circle ranged from royalty to Hollywood stars. Evelyn had flicked through the visitors' book as they arrived and pointed out the signature of Edward VIII, as well as Wallis Simpson, Charlie Chaplin, and Winston Churchill, before scrawling her autograph with a flourish, and urging Stella to contribute. Yet even as Stella inscribed her name in her own neat, anonymous hand, she wondered why she had agreed to come. She would know no one, and probably wouldn't want to, either.

By seven, guests were beginning to leave their rooms for drinks and the ordeal could be delayed no longer. Evelyn had disappeared to discuss 'casting' with Roger while his wife rested, so Stella made her way downstairs alone. Her flatmate had lent her a dress: a flimsy confection of fluted silk and slender straps, with a bodice far lower than Stella would have chosen, and in a shade of bold turquoise. The colour brought out the Titian tints in her hair, the bias cut emphasized every curve of her figure and somehow the dress had the effect of making her feel like another person entirely.

She wandered through the rooms, looking out for any face she might recognize. Everything about the place was sumptuous, from the silvery dazzle of candlelight on the pendant prisms of the chandeliers to the pearls of caviar on the blinis. Footmen in white coats with red cummerbunds weaved through the throng to the backdrop of a band crooning 'Pennies From Heaven'. On every surface, vases were filled with lilies brought up that morning from Covent Garden, and roses cut from the garden. The floors were laid with silk Persian rugs and the Chinese lacquerwork cabinets bristled with photographs. Pride of place was given to a picture of Queen Mary in battleship grey with wedding-cake coiffure, cruising at stately pace through the hall, a flotilla of flunkeys trailing in her wake.

In the ballroom, Stella spotted paintings by Gainsborough, Zoffany and John Singer Sargent. They looked down on a cast of actors, writers and socialites drinking gin, their buzz of conversation periodically pierced by sharp shrieks of laughter. The women shone with jewels and the men gleamed with brilliantine. At the centre stood the host himself, Sir Philip Sassoon MP, in a blue silk smoking jacket and zebra-hide slippers. The whole scene reminded her of one of Evelyn's society magazines come to life, with a carousel of vaguely familiar faces reflected back by giant gilt mirrors perfect for the twin functions of admiring themselves and spying on others.

Stella escaped onto the terrace and collided with a flamingo.

For some reason, there were birds everywhere. Exotic birds: pelicans and penguins, flamingos and peacocks, black and white, pink and glinting turquoise, pecking their way between the gossiping guests.

'Frightfully amusing, aren't they?' commented a young woman, with the basalt bob and steely stare of a young Cleopatra. 'And have you seen the black swans on the lake? He has everything except pigeons. Pigeons have to be shot.'

'Really? Why is that?'

'Philip doesn't want to encourage inbreeding.' It was her companion who spoke, a young woman with tight bubbles of blonde hair like cauliflower. 'They're pollutants. A single pigeon can turn the entire dove flock grey.'

'God knows what will happen to these birds if war comes,' said Cleopatra.

'They'll probably be eaten,' said the blonde with a weary sigh. 'Such a shame. Why go to war for the Poles and the Jews? Ooh, hold on. I'll have one of those.'

She flagged down a passing tray of oysters bathed in Tabasco and tipped one expertly down her throat.

'If we're going to starve to death in a war, we might as well eat up.'

'Hello, Iris, Vera.'

It was Roger Anson, Evelyn's friend. He was flabby and five foot six, with small bearlike eyes buried in folds of flesh.

'And is it . . . it is! Stella Fry!' he exclaimed. 'How goes it with you? I hear you've a job in the movies.'

At this, Iris and Vera looked around with interest.

'It's not the movies. It's the GPO Film Unit.'

'Still, frightfully interesting,' said Roger. 'What sort of films do you make?'

'Oh, mostly politics. Current affairs. We've just finished a documentary on working-class entertainments. Wrestling and dog racing.'

Roger gave a theatrical shudder and stroked his cravat. 'Don't talk to me about current affairs. I've given up on them. Too depressing.'

As soon as politely possible, Stella smiled and made her way out into the shadowy garden beyond the terrace.

She wandered past the swimming pool and orangery, then through a walled garden thick with the scent of stocks to where a pergola stood, covered in twining honeysuckle and clematis. The aroma of damp earth rose up from the flowerbeds and distant, mingled laughter carried on the breeze. Stella ducked under the trailing stems and leaned back in the shadow of the marble pillar, wondering if she could reasonably disappear to the room for an early bath.

'Mind if I join you?'

The voice came from the semi-darkness behind her. She started and turned to find a man who had emerged soundlessly, his tread so soft on the manicured grass that she had not even heard his approach. Her first impression was of a tall figure with a powerful build, who had eschewed the dinner jackets of the other guests for an ensemble of thick herringbone tweed.

Should she know him? He seemed to know her. Scrutinizing his face, illuminated by a Chinese lantern in the boughs of the tree above, Stella recalled what Evelyn did when approached by someone she didn't recognize. Unleash a brilliant smile, while simultaneously turning the shoulder and edging slightly away.

'Of course not. I came out for a little air,' she said, neutrally.

Then it came to her. He must have overheard her telling Roger about the GPO. No doubt this man was a writer, wanting a slot or to script a film, and imagining she had some influence. She hadn't the slightest bit, but he seemed the persistent type and might not take no for an answer.

'Forgive me, have we met before?'

'No, but I've heard a lot about you.'

Feeling in his jacket pocket, he withdrew a gold cigarette case, tilted it in her direction, and when she declined, extracted one for himself. The cigarette was long and unbranded and the tobacco smelt Turkish.

'Really? From whom?'

She was still trying to place him. While not at all good-looking, his wide mouth and muscular build were attractive. He had huge ears and a large beaky nose. His skin was lightly tanned, suggesting an outdoor life, and his manner was confident and purposeful.

'I'm a friend of Cecil.'

'Oh!'

She almost laughed with relief. Cecil Fairfax was her beloved German professor at Oxford. Beloved, because he treated his students like fully fledged adults, introduced them to a roster of eclectic dinner guests, held famous Sunday lunches at his cottage in the Oxfordshire countryside and gave them free range of his personal library. She had not seen him for far too long.

Relief was succeeded by a jag of alarm.

'Is Cecil all right?'

'Perfectly. One might think that a professor of German would have fallen out of favour in the current circumstances, but instead he finds himself with more work than he can manage. Nonetheless he was on particularly good form yesterday evening when I dined with him.'

'Oh good, Mr . . .'

'Knight. The name's Knight.'

He cast a glance up at the darkening sky.

'Looks like it's going to rain on Philip's parade. Perhaps we should find somewhere warmer. If you've not seen the library here, you have a treat in store.'

Without waiting for an answer, he led the way back through the garden to a side door into the house, across a gleaming chessboard hall and down a corridor to the most sumptuous library Stella had ever seen. Great cliffs of books covered the walls floor to ceiling, and the light from the fireplace glimmered off the gilt letters on their spines.

A fire in midsummer seemed incongruous, but then everything about this evening had turned out to be odd. The floor was laid with a ruby-red Bokhara, and green-shaded lamps threw a comforting glow over a selection of volumes displayed with their pages open on mahogany tables. Plump pillars supported an elaborately corniced ceiling and twin masks of comedy and tragedy were carved into the fireplace. A pair of deep leather armchairs stood before the marble fireplace and an aroma of polish and sandalwood mingled with the woodsmoke from the grate.

Somewhere inside Stella, a note of caution sounded. She did not, as yet, know what to make of this man. He said he was a friend of Cecil's, yet he didn't seem like any of Cecil's fellow academics, nor did he resemble Evelyn's theatrical pals, with their boastful, self-regarding anecdotes and roving gazes. He had neither the diffidence, nor the overt pomposity of the writers she'd encountered, and his courtly manners seemed to conceal something far less comfortable: a sense of cunning and an edge of danger.

She wondered if Knight was even his real name.

'Drink?'

He was standing before a table, surfaced with tooled Morocco leather, and crowded with a selection of decanters and cut-glass tumblers.

'Thank you.'

He handed her a glass of brandy and glanced down at an array of newspapers fanned out on the library table, full of rumours of war.

'*Alea iacta est.* The die is cast. It won't be long now,' he said.

He removed another long handmade cigarette from his gold case, and Stella noticed that the case bore what looked like a coat of arms and an inscription, Maxwell Knight 1931. So that *was* his name. He gave her an inquiring look but she declined again so he tapped the end of the cigarette against the case, lit it and shook out the match.

'Shall we sit?'

She braced her shoulders, clasped her hands on her knees and assumed an air of polite distance.

'You're close to Cecil, I understand. Your father died in, what . . .1916?'

She nodded, startled at how upsetting it still was to be reminded of it. Despite everyone's assumptions, which she never bothered to correct, her father had died not on the field of battle but struck by a bolt of lightning while crossing Clapham Common in a rainstorm. She wondered if Knight assumed that Cecil Fairfax was some kind of father figure to her. She had wondered that herself.

'Mr Knight, you said you wanted to talk to me. I think I know what it is, and before we talk I should explain, without wanting to be rude, that I have absolutely no authority at the Film Unit as far as contributors go. I mean, I could always mention a name, but . . .'

'God help me, it's nothing like that.' He steepled his fingers, then angled them towards her like a gun. 'It's about *you*.'

'Me?'

'Cecil's told me all about you. He says you're resourceful and independent. Have a good mind. And he thinks you're exceptionally observant.'

Stella shifted in the deep leather armchair. Generally, she prided herself on being able to read people; their expressions and behaviour gave far more away than they would ever articulate. A psychologist had once told her that you could know a person was telling the truth from the direction of their gaze, and whether they tugged their ears or touched their nose. Yet this man gave no such indications. In all respects he was utterly elusive.

Perplexed, she said, 'That's kind of him.'

'It's a quality I admire. I'm the same.'

He paused and she noticed his toes tapping to the distant rhythm of jazz music issuing from the ballroom. Catching her glance he said, 'Sorry. Gets in the blood. I used to play the drums in a band at the Hammersmith Palais.'

'Are you a musician?'

A wide smile.

'Among other occupations. I've also been a Latin teacher, a hotel keeper, an author and a naturalist.'

'A zookeeper, you mean?'

'A student of animals. Though I do have something of a private zoo in my flat – just a bushbaby, and a few snakes right now – so you could be forgiven for calling me that. I've always been interested in animals, since I was a boy. I must have spent thousands of hours looking after small creatures, learning how they communicate; how they show if they're sick. There's nothing more rewarding than hand-rearing a wild fox, or a bird that one has rescued from a predator. Damaged creatures respond so well, if one only understands their ways.'

His voice was soft and mesmeric; hypnotic, almost. She could see how an animal might find it soothing. It was easy to imagine those leathery hands, currently cradling the brandy balloon, holding a fledgling thrush, or a robin with a broken wing. Yet at the same time she sensed that those hands were capable of less gentle skills.

'When you're studying wildlife, you need to notice things other chaps might miss. Being observant is essential in that line of work. And, indeed, in my other occupation. My *chief* occupation.'

'Which is?'

'I work for the government.'

'Like a civil servant?'

'In a manner of speaking. Something between the War Office and Scotland Yard. I safeguard the interests of our country from foreign powers. Collecting assets who can keep an eye on developments in potentially hostile nations.'

Stella stared into the amber glow of her brandy. First wildlife, then foreign powers. What on earth was all this about? It was like some kind of scrambled code. Making a little show of consulting her watch, she said, 'You mentioned you'd seen Cecil . . . ?'

'At the Royal Geographical Society. He was giving a talk on labyrinths.'

That sounded like Cecil. His love of German culture had led Cecil Fairfax to a passion for the nineteenth-century archaeological excavations of Ludwig Borchardt and Heinrich Schliemann, who had unearthed the mound of Troy. Cecil had also devoted much of his life to Sir Arthur Evans' excavations at Knossos to find the Minotaur's lair.

'Labyrinths are Cecil's obsession,' said Knight. The thin lips lifted into a smile. 'Mine too.'

That made sense. This entire conversation was a maze of meaning, with abrupt turns and unexpected dead ends, frustratingly hard to follow.

'Cecil mentioned you spent several years in Europe.'

'Mostly in Vienna, but I also visited France, Germany, and Italy.'

'So your German and French are up to scratch?'

'German, pretty fluent. And as you know, I read Modern Languages, so I get by in French too.'

'I envy you. What did Charlemagne say? To speak another language is to possess another soul. Is that how it feels?'

'A little, sometimes.'

The fact was, following Maxwell Knight's drift was like translating from another language – trying to grasp the rhythms, working out the grammar and the circumlocutions.

Then, in a flash, it occurred to her. This must be one of those party games that people in grand English houses played: a type of charades, or sardines, or hide-and-seek, with Stella as the unsuspecting victim. No doubt a group of guests — perhaps Iris and Vera — were hidden behind a secret door, hands over their mouths and ready to burst out laughing when she agreed to the wild goose chase.

'Look, forgive me, Mr Knight, but I don't really . . .'

The blunt features were illuminated by another brilliant smile. He untangled his long legs and chuckled.

'Of course. You want to get back to the party, and I don't wonder. A young lady doesn't want to get landed with an old stick. Please don't let me keep you. It's been a pleasure.'

She had escaped, as swiftly as possible within the bounds of polite behaviour, and although she kept an eye out during the rest of the weekend, Maxwell Knight seemed to have disappeared entirely.

She had not given him another thought until that moment.

In the seconds that it took him to cross the hotel lobby, that late-night encounter at Trent Park flashed through her mind. This lunchtime Knight was wearing what looked like the identical jacket of hairy tweed, and under it a checked shirt and tie. He might have been a farmer up from the country for a day out in the Smoke.

He took her hand in his rough palm and shook it briefly, then turned abruptly, not into the dining room but up the stairs, into a barely furnished first-floor room. A narrow bed stood in the corner, and two ugly chairs faced each other under a badly executed copy of Constable's *The Hay Wain*. Once he had closed the door behind them, Knight crossed to a side table holding a single bottle of gin, and measured out two glasses, topped up with tonic. Stella was not used to drinking spirits at lunchtime on an empty stomach, but then she was not used to being summoned anonymously to hotels by virtual strangers, so she took one.

Knight sank into one of the ugly armchairs.

'You're working at the GPO Film Unit, I remember, Miss Fry. How d'you find the place?'

'Everyone seems to be holding their breath.'

'Understandable, I suppose, with what's going on.'

He was studying her with a keenness that in another setting might have been flattering, yet in effect was disconcerting. His head was to one side and his eyes bright, as though he was some intelligent, inquisitive animal.

'Forgive me. I owe you an explanation. You're probably wondering why you're here. When we met last summer, we were in a different situation. We were not at war, though it was plain to me that we soon would be. My meeting with Cecil Fairfax was not entirely social. I was making a point of running through German speakers who might come in useful to us, and I had contacted Cecil to that end. He singled you out as exactly the sort of person we could work with.'

'I don't quite follow . . .'

'Cecil believed that, aside from your linguistic proficiency, you possess the appropriate qualities. So, I made sure to meet you.'

It was quiet in the hotel room. From below came the sounds of conversation and in the distance a door banged. Maxwell Knight had not taken his eyes from her face.

'And when I did meet you, I liked you. I could see at once what Cecil meant. As I place great trust in Cecil's opinion, I would like you to undertake some work for me.'

'You mean a job?'

'I mean a task under my direction.'

'That's very flattering, but as I said, Mr Knight, I'm afraid I already have a job.'

She braced her shoulders.

'And I should add that I'm not at all happy about what happened at my flat. Harry Fox told me that you were behind the events yesterday afternoon. The policemen and so on.'

'I'm sorry.' Knight swirled the gin in his glass. 'I would have preferred to approach you in a more gentlemanly fashion – a letter or some such, followed by dinner at my club – but time is pressing and the matter in question won't wait.'

'Why was it necessary to spread rumours among my neighbours that I'd been in an accident? Injured, or even dead? How will my family feel if they hear? I'm going to have to go and explain.'

He raised a hand.

'No need. Your family won't hear a thing. We will keep the information completely secret. Your name will never appear, and you'll be yourself again before you know it. Lady Lazarus. Back from the dead, so to speak.'

'Then what was the point of staging my disappearance?'

'The precaution was essential. After the events of last

year – your tackling of Mr Hubert Newman and his Soviet friends – we had an inkling that you might be watched, and your flat might be monitored.'

She stiffened in shock.

'An inkling? What do you mean, an inkling? Am I being watched?'

'We think so. At least at some point you may have been. We can't be certain, but what we are about to ask of you is important and it's essential that you're not observed.'

The thought that she might have been surveilled and that agents of a hostile power would have bothered to track and monitor her movements was terrifying. Could it be true, and if so, who might be doing the watching? She straightened in the chair.

'Exactly what are you asking of me?'

'You remember Trent Park?'

'How could I forget?'

'I would like you to go there again.'

'To a stately home?'

'It's not that any more. Trent Park has been requisitioned. Officially we tend not to mention its former name. It's now the Combined Services Detailed Interrogation Centre. Also known as Camp 11. Or Cockfosters. It's a holding centre for captured enemy troops.'

'What would I do there?'

'You will be enlisted into the ATS.'

The Auxiliary Territorial Service – drivers, cooks, clerks, dispatch riders – came complete with a frumpy khaki uniform and a brown cap. It was the last service Stella would have chosen.

'Your duties will be outlined by the chap who's running the place. A man called Colonel Thomas Kendrick.'

'And what would those duties be?'

Knight put down his glass.

'First you need to know that everything I'm telling you is highly secret. You will be required to sign the Official Secrets Act, you understand?'

She blinked and nodded.

'As I said, Trent Park is no longer a private home. Last year, as you may know, shortly after we met, Sir Philip Sassoon, the owner, sadly died. It was a tragedy, very premature. But Philip had no heirs, and he wanted the estate to go to the nation, so the nation has taken him up on it. Trent Park is now a holding camp for captured prisoners of war. We had been keeping these men in the Tower of London, but if there's a German invasion and London is bombed, that may not be secure. So operations were moved to Trent Park.'

He paused, then leaned closer.

'Trent Park is not only a prison – it is also the site of the biggest bugging operation ever mounted against a British enemy. Every conversation there is recorded, every chance remark, every quiet confidence. There's not a spot in the house that is not wired. The inmates have no idea that their every word is recorded, transcribed and analyzed. The people listening to those conversations are wholly concealed, mostly below stairs. They are equipped with state-of-the-art microphones and they both translate and transcribe everything they hear. All of our listeners studied languages at Oxford or Cambridge or are German refugees, so they are entirely fluent.'

'And you want me to join them?'

'Precisely. You will become part of the listening team.'

'But Mr Knight, I've never done anything like this. I may understand German, but I could never transcribe very fast without making a lot of mistakes. I don't have shorthand. If, as you say, you have listeners there already . . .'

He shot her a quick, penetrating glance. 'It doesn't stop there. You will also be engaged in a second act of subterfuge.'

He cast a glance around, as if even in this quiet room they might be overheard.

'I want you to be my invisible ink. I want you to make friendly acquaintance, chat, seek confidences among the listeners. Report back everything that you learn. Make a record of everything you find until we settle the matter in question. This job won't take long.'

'How long?'

'No more than a couple of weeks.'

'Weeks?'

'Yes. And who knows where we'll be in a few weeks' time.'

'Sorry . . . you mentioned the matter in question. What is the matter in question?'

Maxwell Knight lowered his voice.

'The matter in question is murder.'

For a second, surprise sucked the air out of her lungs.

'Is this a joke?'

'I only wish it was. A few days ago, there was an incident at Trent Park. A murder. We can't get the police involved – the entire set-up is highly secret, and we can't risk any leaks. But we are convinced that the staff there know more than they are saying.'

'Who was murdered?'

'The dead man was called Oberstleutnant Gabriel Fassbinder. A Luftwaffe officer whose aircraft was downed a few months ago.'

'Where was he found?'

'In the grounds, not far from the main house.'

'And how was he murdered?'

'He was shot. At first it was thought to be suicide, but there was no weapon. The key point is that on the same night as his murder, one of the listeners disappeared. Then it was discovered that a gun had gone missing at the same time. This man has, by all accounts, entirely vanished.'

'And you think . . .'

'I want to know exactly what happened.'

'But Mr Knight, I really don't see why you would ask me to do something like this.'

Knight pointed his cigarette at her.

'Ordinarily, it's true. You might not have been the first

person to spring to mind. But the fact is, Miss Fry – Stella, if I may – the reason I ask you is because this man is known to you.'

'You mean the man who disappeared?'

'Indeed. His name is Robert Handel.'

Robert Handel. She saw his face at once. It appeared in her mind like a postcard one might use as a bookmark and forget about, then find years later, when least expecting it.

He had been a contemporary for a year at Oxford, having come over to study philosophy after finishing a degree at Munich University. It was appropriate that his name evoked a composer because there was a harmony in Handel's features. The high brow, wide mouth and grey eyes seemed to fit together with finely tuned precision. He might have been a Protestant nobleman in a Dürer sketch, Stella thought, with his pale skin and level gaze, yet in character there was nothing Protestant about Robert Handel. He exuded an undercurrent of glamour and passion. She remembered the rumours that swirled about him. His family owned a castle in Prussia, his parents were refugees from the Russian Revolution, he was the most brilliant chess player of his era. Whatever the truth, it had seemed odd to her that such a figure should be engaged in anything so sedate as a year in Oxford studying philosophy.

Stella recalled the day she had first met him, as they wrestled their bicycles out of the rack after a lecture at the Taylorian, and he had asked her to his college rooms.

A group of them were discussing the early German Romantics. Would she like to join? After an hour, as she was leaving, she dropped a book from her bag and Handel had retrieved it, then as she reached out for it he held on to her hand, pulling her towards him and giving her a kiss on the cheek that lasted a fraction of a second longer than expected. She had wondered at the time what that fraction of a second contained.

Yet she had given him barely a thought for a decade.

'You think Robert Handel was involved in this?'

'That's what I would like to discover. You ought to know – Handel was another of Cecil's recommendations. He was sent to Trent Park two months ago at my suggestion. As he's vanished from sight, the only way anyone is going to find out what happened and where he is – let alone his intentions – is to analyze his last movements. As you knew the man once, you seemed like the perfect choice, which is why I enlisted Mr Fox to approach you. I understand you work together.'

She recoiled slightly.

'Well, we *did*. More than a year ago. It was just an encounter. A brief encounter.'

'Nonetheless, your efforts made their mark. Your discoveries about Hubert Newman's circle were quite extraordinary. It was a major coup for British intelligence. You impressed at the highest levels. I heard you like to work as a team. What brought you two together, may I ask?'

'As I said, we're not together.'

It emerged a little more vehemently than she intended and later she would ask herself why. 'It was just . . . we both had different reasons for wanting to find the truth about Hubert Newman's death.'

'Either way, it was a great success. If you will forgive me for saying, I'm interested in women like you, Miss Fry. Our world is very much a male world and often women are used, forgive my directness, to seduce. But I look for those who are not obviously oversexed. I tend to think of women like porridge.'

'I've heard a lot of things, Mr Knight, but that's a new one on me.'

'What I mean is, they need to get it just right. Neither too sweet or too salty. Too hot or too cold. We don't want to frighten anyone. I think you have that talent, Miss Fry. You are the perfect . . .'

'The perfect porridge?'

'If you like.'

'Well, I should say right now that I have no intention of seducing anyone.'

'Quite so. Perhaps we should stay on the metaphorical plane. But the fact is, I see more than your charms, Miss Fry. I see your brains. That's why I'm sending you to Trent Park. And I would add that nobody, not even Harry Fox, must know anything more than your destination.'

Knight's gaze was still fixed on her.

'This is highly confidential, you understand? It's imperative that nobody hears about this case. And that nobody at Trent Park itself knows exactly why you are there. Take the Piccadilly line to Enfield West station tomorrow morning and a military car will meet you at 10 a.m.'

For a second Stella hesitated. She felt giddy, as though she had been lifted by some fairground big wheel and the whole panorama of her life lay exposed before her. And there was every chance, once the wheel had turned, that she would be landed in a place she had never envisaged.

Fiddling with the edge of her cuff, she looked up at him.

'I'm flattered that you ask me, really I am, but as I say, I have a job with the Film Unit, which I enjoy, and Mr Jennings – he's the director – is quite a hard taskmaster. Even if I said I was taking a few weeks' holiday, I really don't see that at such short notice . . .'

There was a knock at the door, and it opened to reveal the face of Harry Fox, full of trepidation and excitement.

'Ah, Harry, do come in. I think we're finished here. And thank you for briefing Miss Fry earlier. It's been a terrifically fruitful exchange. Just terrific. I know you like working as a team . . .'

Stella stared from one man to the other with bewilderment.

'And it's on that basis I would like you to operate. Initially, you have different tasks, but the overall aim remains the same. To track down the missing Robert Handel, or whatever he may be calling himself now, and to discover just how far our operations have been compromised. It's essential that both of you report to me the moment you find anything of note.'

'What will Harry be doing?'

'I've tasked Mr Fox with a different line of enquiry.'

'Which is, exactly . . . ?'

'He will be observing the émigré communities throughout London. I'm sure he can share a certain amount of detail in due course.'

'But I still haven't said . . .'

Quietly, Knight interrupted.

'Miss Fry, you do, of course, have the prerogative of refusing. But if I may observe. There are a handful of moments in every person's life when they have to make a choice between acting and simply coasting along. This, I suspect, is the time for you. This afternoon the Prime Minister will be obliged to inform the House of Commons that the navy is evacuating eleven thousand troops from central Norway. The whole Norwegian episode has been a disaster. German invasion of Britain seems almost inevitable. God knows what's coming, but of one thing I'm certain. If Robert Handel is not what we think, and he is taking our secrets to the enemy, we may have just days to find him.'

His eyes lost their focus, as if they were fixed on something else entirely. As though he was contemplating vast armies moving across distant battlefields.

Then he stood up and extended a hand.

'So all that remains right now is to say jolly good luck.'

# CHAPTER 7

'Was it you who told him we liked to work as a team?' she said, as they walked back along Piccadilly in the afternoon sunshine.

'I might have said something.'

'So you're a mind-reader now?'

'Comes with the job.'

She rolled her eyes. 'What do you make of him?'

'He's been good to me. After my suspension, he was one of the few who still bothered to employ me. Frankly, that kept the wolf from the door. It meant a lot. I guessed he would like the sound of you.'

'I wonder why?'

'He admires women. Most of the Service is angled against them, but Knight's had great success using women in his work. He has some impressive cases under his belt.'

'What exactly is his work?'

'Complicated.'

'And what is it he asked you to do?'

'He wants me to keep a watch on the cafés and pubs for this man Handel. Apparently you knew him?'

'A long time ago.'

'What did you make of him?'

'He didn't look like a murderer.'

'That's always the problem. If murderers looked like murderers it would make life so much easier. Did he say what happened to the victim?'

'He was shot at close range.'

He grinned. 'I suppose we're lucky,' he went on. 'Normally, Knight doesn't like his people knowing about each other. It's quite unusual that he's recruited us together. What about you? What are you to do?'

'I can't tell you.'

He stopped in his tracks.

'That's ridiculous. How the hell are we supposed to work as a team if we can't communicate?'

'He's sending me to a government facility called Trent Park. I can't say anything about it, Harry, because it's classified. It's just for a few weeks, he says. I'll keep in contact. And I'll let you know anything I discover.'

'Keep in contact? Where on earth are you going?'

She looked up at him.

'Right now, I'm going to your office. It looks like I'll need my suitcase.'

As she lugged her case back to Evelyn's flat, Stella's mind was full of the encounter with Maxwell Knight. The idea that she might be under surveillance, due to her accidental discovery of a ring of Soviet spies, was terrifying. Automatically she scanned every person she passed, analyzing them, looking out for repeated figures or faces.

Yet at the same time, she was pondering Maxwell Knight's other revelation: that her long-ago acquaintance, Robert Handel, was wanted for murder at Trent Park. That he had gone on the run, potentially with the aim of taking intelligence secrets to the enemy. And that she and Harry Fox might make a difference to the outcome.

She walked swiftly northwards, through the backstreets of Bloomsbury. She had lost all sense of time. She had eaten almost nothing that day, and drinking a tumbler of gin on an empty stomach had only increased her hunger, excitement and fear.

The fact was, it was impossible to square Maxwell Knight's story with the Robert Handel she remembered from all those years ago. He seemed the most unlikely murderer. She recalled his commanding presence and extravagant gestures in the small room overlooking the quad in Merton crammed with eager students reading Goethe and Schilling and Heine, or walking beside her along the High, quoting Rilke's *Sonnets to Orpheus*. Charisma seeped from his every pore. Sometimes, when he had drunk too much beer, he strayed onto the subject of politics, and then his conversation was tinged with a sharp bitterness. He deplored the Treaty of Versailles and thought it was foolishly punitive towards his countrymen. When drunk, his German accent hardened, his eyes narrowed and she glimpsed a darker layer beneath the charming surface.

Yet despite this passionate nature, she simply could not connect these memories with the idea of Robert Handel as a criminal. Let alone a murderer.

She reached the corner of Mecklenburgh Square, unlocked the outside door and climbed the stairs to Evelyn's flat. Her mind was so full that it was a shock, just as she had her key in the latch, to find the door opened, not by her friend, but another figure she had known for half her life.

Tall, solid, with thick dark hair that was just showing its first threads of grey, Tom Lamont was dressed in shirtsleeves and braces, and his familiar ruddy face looked as startled as her own. He was holding a brown china teapot.

Flustered, Stella said, 'Oh, Tom! Hello. I just . . . I'm just staying with Evelyn for a few nights. My flat's flooded out.'

He blinked at her momentarily, then found his manners and said, 'Come in, come in. Evelyn didn't mention you were here. The fact is, I arranged to drop in to see her, and she entirely forgot I was coming. She's had to go out. Some chap in Polish uniform turned up and carried her off.'

'Witold?'

'Yes, I think that was his name.'

Stella put her bag on the table and stood hesitantly. Tom seemed equally nonplussed.

'I thought I'd make tea anyhow, while I was here.'

'Oh, let me.'

As she busied herself with the kettle and teapot, he stood with his back to her, looking at Evelyn's bookshelves, inspecting one volume after another. *Brave New World*, *The Rainbow*, *Decline and Fall*, *Persuasion*, as though he was genuinely contemplating reading them. She could not help but think that he welcomed the opportunity to talk with his back turned.

'How are your parents?' she said.

He turned towards her and replaced *Persuasion* on the shelf.

'They've left London. Mother's packed away all the art and gone to the country. She's tacked a map of Scandinavia on the wall and is following Hitler's progress with dressmaking pins. She's also refusing to drink German wine so my father has left all the hock and Riesling in Chelsea where either the bombers or the thieves will get them. I must admit, I have thought about moving my books, too. It would be sad to see all those go up in flames.'

'Herodotus and Gibbon and Carlyle and the rest?'

'You remembered.'

She brought over two cups and settled on the lumpy divan.

'Rather surprised to find that Evelyn has sugar,' he continued, stirring a teaspoon into his tea.

Stella realized that Evelyn had made quick use of the ration book she had left on the table.

'You look pale, Stella. Have you eaten? Have some chocolate.'

He brought out a bar of Cadbury's Dairy Milk. 'If there's anything to eat in this flat, my sister's hiding it well.'

'Thank you.' She took a square. 'I hear you're working in the Admiralty.'

'Yes. It's rather extraordinary. And tremendously grand. The doorman wears a frock coat. I'm working directly to Churchill. I'm in the room beneath him and I can hear his feet pacing around all day above me.'

'How are things? Am I allowed to ask?'

'Between us? Manic. We're in the midst of a political crisis. Winston's drinking too much. But he won't listen to anyone. He makes light of it. He says he won't drink tea on medical grounds. That his doctor has ordered him to take nothing non-alcoholic between breakfast and dinner.'

'That's funny.'

'Yes, he's irrepressible. He never loses his sense of humour. And in most ways, he's having the time of his life. I think a crisis brings out the best in him. Norway was a rout – we sent an expeditionary force and it ended badly. Winston knows that they're going to try to pin the blame on him. He thought the Norwegians would fight like Vikings, he said. But we were caught napping by the Germans, and it mustn't happen again. It looks as though Chamberlain will go. MPs are saying he's not fit to run the war, and if Chamberlain goes, Winston wants to be prime minister.'

'Will he be?'

'Not sure. There's a crowd of candidates, and the King prefers Lord Halifax. Halifax is the establishment choice. He's more predictable. He said it would be an entirely different world if Hitler and Goering had been to Oxford.'

'Lord Halifax said that? Really?'

'Quite. But the tide's flowing in Winston's direction. The thing about Winston is, he would bring such energy to the office. He works tremendously long hours, whereas Chamberlain needs his rest. Apparently, they're saying Chamberlain's seriously ill, while Winston's full of the most tremendous brio. He says he knows that Germany may soon rain down steel and fire on us and bring death and destruction, but they *can* be beaten. If only we can find a way of dragging the United States in.'

'Which doesn't sound likely.'

'I'd agree. The Americans seem set square against involvement in another European war. Ambassador Kennedy's favourite phrase is *Include America out*. There's a new Gallup poll out today that says ninety-three per cent of Americans are against it. But Winston doesn't let the bad news deter him.'

'Do *you* think the Germans will attack Britain?'

'Pretty certain. There's every chance a blitzkrieg will start within weeks.'

*Within weeks.* Stella imagined the throb of planes overhead and the dreadful, screaming moment when they loosed their cargo onto the city beneath. Explosions blossoming in the sky and scarring the earth beneath, firestorms of heat and familiar buildings blazing, glass melting into drops of light, and flames leaping out of windows. Then afterwards the city with all the life sucked out of it, a terrain of ash and ghosts, and the bones of buildings shrouded with dust.

Almost absently she said, 'Do you remember when we visited King Henry's Mound?'

It was a spot in Richmond Park where they had walked many years ago. They had gone there to see the deer, and Tom had led the way up a small hill to a place where the line of sight to St Paul's Cathedral was protected by ancient rights. The tiny, bone-white cathedral dome could be glimpsed through a keyhole of trees, as though it was floating in a cloud of leaves.

'Of course I do.'

'That's what I picture whenever I think about London being bombed. I just can't bear the idea that St Paul's might be demolished.'

'There's no saying that will happen. We have air defences. And civil volunteers. Even Evelyn has decided to volunteer as an auxiliary fire warden. At least she will once she's finished her current run.'

He frowned and drained his tea.

'What will you do, Stella? How long do you think you'll stay at the GPO? There might be a job for you at the Ministry of Information, with all your languages.'

'I'm not sure.'

She could not possibly tell him that a most extraordinary job had been suggested to her that very lunchtime, and she had resolved to leave the next day.

Instead, to change the subject, and because the subject

could no longer be avoided, she said, 'Evelyn mentioned that you're engaged.'

'Oh. Yes.' He looked quickly away. 'Meredith. Meredith Meadows. She's a good woman.'

'I'm glad.' She paused. 'Where did you meet?'

'Oh, Meredith's a friend of Ambassador Kennedy's daughter. Kathleen. Who everyone calls Kick.'

Stella felt a small heave in her chest.

'What's Meredith like?'

'Oh, she's a smart cookie.'

A smart cookie? When had Tom started talking like that?

'Have you known each other long?'

He shrugged.

'Six months, maybe. There was a party for Kick being presented at court. Rather ludicrous, these events. Ridiculously old-fashioned. I can't believe they haven't died out, but anyway . . .'

'Congratulations.'

'Thank you.'

'I hope I'll meet her soon. When's the wedding?'

'Oh, plenty of time for that.' He rubbed his hands as if keen to cut the conversation short, and jumped up. 'Now I'm afraid I must leave.'

He put on his raincoat, and she watched his turned back, noting the familiar, slightly sloping shoulders, and the freshly shaved nape of his neck. She recalled seeing the softly lit portraits of his grandfather and great-grandfather in their family home and being startled at the likeness – the same features, the same taut mouth — as if she had never encountered biology before.

She wondered what memories of herself existed in his head.

In the midst of tying his scarf, Tom said, 'Stella . . .'

'What?'

He shook his head.

'Oh, nothing. It doesn't matter.'

But when he reached the door, he turned back.

'Actually . . . I'm free tonight, if you'd like dinner.'

She found herself torn between wanting to go and knowing that she would only ask more questions about the smart cookie Meredith Meadows. The less she knew about Meredith, the better.

Swiftly, she doused the prospect.

'I can't, I'm afraid. I have a very early start.'

'Soon, then?'

'The thing is, Tom, I'm not sure where I'll be.'

He looked at her, perplexed, but the code of silence, so deeply entrenched in him, prevented him from enquiring. Quietly, he said, 'I see. Well, if you find yourself free, give me a call. Admiralty 251.'

'Yes. Soon, maybe. I'd like that.'

# CHAPTER 8

The statue of Charles I in Whitehall was surrounded by a wooden dome. Kings and statesmen and earls on horseback had been sandbagged. William III had vanished from St James's Square and Viscount Wolseley from Horse Guards Parade. On his way up Regent Street, Harry Fox thought of the Elgin Marbles, stashed away in the tunnels of Aldwych underground station, safe from the threat of bombs. How would it be, descending to those murky depths, to find oneself surrounded by the stone goddesses of antiquity, Aphrodite, Gaia and Thalassa?

It wasn't only goddesses. When he reached Piccadilly Circus, he noted that Eros, too, had disappeared from his plinth, just as completely as he had from Harry's life.

High above, two barrage balloons, like great silver elephants sixty feet long, floated improbably in the sky. People were constantly looking up at them, or at least they were constantly looking up, as if the sky might be darkened at any minute by circling planes. On every scarlet pillar box squares of yellow detector tape had been stuck, designed to glow luminously if poison gas was released. London was in a liminal state, waiting to be transformed.

An invasion could begin at any moment. Anticipation rang like tinnitus in the air.

Harry Fox, however, was contemplating his reunion with Stella Fry.

He could not deny a stab of annoyance at being excluded from the precise details of Stella's task. Maxwell Knight was employing them as a team. He had been led to understand that this job was a joint effort – indeed, that the whole point of their involvement was their skill in working together – and yet Knight had instructed him to arrive at Brown's Hotel at one thirty, only after Knight had had a chance to speak to Stella privately. This annoyance, however, was mingled with a nobler emotion. Harry felt protective of his friend and hoped that whatever Knight had asked of her was not dangerous. He still remembered the agony of guilt he had suffered during Stella's journey to Vienna two years ago at his behest. This time it was Maxwell Knight issuing the orders and Knight was known to be a tough taskmaster, especially where young women were concerned. In the past, it was said, from his semi-autonomous desk at MI5, Knight had used well-bred young women to penetrate the closeted circles of the far right. Knight's girls, with their sweet, guileless manners, had charmed their way into the confidence of the hoariest fascists. Harry guessed that whatever was being asked of Stella Fry would be risky if not downright perilous.

As to the precise circumstances of the crime, all Knight had told Harry was that a German officer called Gabriel Fassbinder had wound up dead, another German called Robert Handel had gone missing, and he wasn't going to trouble the police with the details.

'So we're looking for one German who's killed another German. That's good, isn't it? Two less Germans. Win win?'

Knight had responded with a cutting look.

'This is no time for frivolity. It concerns top-secret information. It's essential that we solve this murder, and that will start with finding this man. He may very well have secreted himself among the émigré community. As you know, we do have people in position, keeping an eye out, but since you frequent these circles, it makes sense that I ask you to look.'

Harry thought he might as well start with Luigi's.

The idea that an agent of German military intelligence might be concealed among the shabby ranks of customers at Luigi's café in Greek Street seemed fanciful. The place, with its fine green tiles, walls ambered with cigarette smoke and its gouts of steam issuing perpetually from the Gaggia machine, was at least half a home to him. Its fug of nicotine and coffee was his own version of Proust's madeleine. Luigi's was the only place in London that served proper Italian coffee. The British, as a nation of tea drinkers, never saw the point of the bitter, highly caffeinated liquid that issued in tiny dribbles from the machine on the counter, but Luigi's clientele did. That was why they congregated there, the disgruntled, the intellectuals, the distressed. Foreigners with alien faces and pain behind their eyes, keeping up a low murmur of Czech and German and Yiddish. Most had accents as thick as Harry's forearm and would make a poor show of passing themselves off as skilled members of the espionage community. The thought that this diaspora of the dispossessed might form a network or a cell was for the birds, but all the same he needed to start somewhere.

Entering, he glanced around at the usual denizens and noted that his regular seat was occupied by a surly Eastern European giant scowling over a chessboard. He was a well-muscled man, the kind you saw on stucco housefronts holding up porticoes like Atlas, and he looked up belligerently when Harry approached. The last thing Harry wanted was a staring contest with a Baltic hulk, and besides, the man was playing Igor. Igor was a former Russian sailor with a tattoo of a woman on his bicep that jiggled her rear when he flexed it. Despite this frivolity, on the chessboard Igor was deadly. Harry had played against him many times and always had to retreat, begging for mercy.

Instead, he went to lean against the bar where Luigi greeted him, his face creased in apology.

'I am so sorry, Mr Fox, we have no space. What can I do? They keep coming. Perhaps they find no coffee in London. Is all tea in this country. Tea! What do they want with tea?'

'No problem. I was just looking in.'

Luigi spread expressive Italian hands. He might have been born in Deptford, but his gestures went generations back to the distant streets of Naples.

'Tell the truth, I'm glad of the custom. There's a lot of people out there who aren't too friendly to Italians right now.'

Since Italy had signed its Pact of Steel with Germany, several of Luigi's waiters had been classed as enemy aliens and banned from owning bicycles or cameras or maps.

Luigi busied himself at the sparkling coffee machine, then produced an inky cup of espresso, which Harry downed in one.

'I can't stop, but I wanted to ask. Have you ever come across a man here name of Robert Handel?'

Luigi frowned then shrugged.

'Is this gentleman a friend of yours?'

'More of a business interest.'

'And you think he will come in soon?'

'Maybe.'

'You want me to tell him you're looking for him?'

'Better not. In fact, don't say a thing. But if you do hear of anything, please let me know sharpish.'

He handed over a card, which Luigi scrutinized.

'Sure, Mr Fox. And I meant to say, I have a message. Someone was asking for you. Karl. Bavarian Karl.'

Everyone called him Bavarian Karl, probably because they could not remember his actual surname, which read like a bad hand at Scrabble. Karl was one of Luigi's most loyal patrons and an artist. A shambling figure in an ancient brown cord jacket, with skin the colour of nicotine, a bony jaw and an oversized nose. It was a face made on a Friday, as Harry's sister Joan would have said. Badly put together. Nose too big, eyes too small, not enough chin. Yet this unvarnished exterior concealed a refined and sensitive nature.

'Karl says, would you come to his studio. He has a job for you.'

'Bavarian Karl has a job for *me*?'

'He give me the address. Here.'

Luigi fumbled in his capacious striped apron and thrust an old receipt towards him, on the back of which was inscribed an address in a spidery, Continental hand.

'Is not far.'

Karl's studio was at the back end of Camden, close to Mornington Crescent. It was halfway down a terrace of sooty stucco whose black railings looked like gapped teeth because half of them had been removed for melting down.

No sooner had Harry rapped on the door than the man himself was standing before him, dressed in a filthy smock the colour of mould, and holding a paintbrush. He had the dry skin and tiny eyes of a reptile in its lair and he extended a scaly hand.

'Mr Fox. Welcome to my studio.'

The room was the filthiest place Harry had ever seen, and he had walked among the lowest of the low. The bare floor was randomly littered with newspaper and the walls' scabrous masonry was covered with paintings, some on canvas, some framed, all vividly coloured and abstract: squares and rectangles bisected by great slashes of scarlet, splinters of grey and yellow, dense concentric circles of blue and green. Canvases smeared with clods of dark paint that might have been mud. Charcoal sketches were pinned randomly to the wall and gobbets of pigment seemed to burst out of their frames. The only furniture in evidence was two paint-encrusted wooden chairs.

'Afternoon, Karl.'

'Good afternoon to you too, though I'm not sure it will be good for much longer.'

He motioned towards one of the chairs and accepted a Woodbine with doleful courtesy.

'You mean in general?'

Karl was the kind of person who attracted bad news like a magnet. Doom hung above him like a portable thundercloud.

'I mean for us exiles. I hear a Conservative MP has asked in Parliament that there should be mass internment. He has said that the authorities should 'intern the lot'. Imprison us without trial. I expect very soon to be classified as an enemy alien. They even talk of deporting people to Australia or Canada.'

This was unjust, Harry knew. Karl was not an enemy of anywhere except his own Bavarian homeland, the place where he had grown up, and which had now decided he was not welcome. He shifted cautiously on the paint-smeared chair.

'Sorry about that. Sounds wrong to me.'

'They say the British will become paranoid and we will be safer locked up. I remember back in 1933 Heinrich Himmler making a similar argument. He said he could not guarantee the safety of the Jews.' Karl sighed. 'I am no stranger to being locked up for my own good. I was in prison in 1937. The Nazis put me in Dachau. It's near Munich. I did eight months there.'

'What exactly were you jailed for?'

'For the crime of being a degenerate artist. The Nazis, they don't like certain kinds of painting. Hitler says the sky should always be blue and the trees should always be green. To paint anything that doesn't look the way he thinks it should, he doesn't like that. He wants people to see the world the way he sees it.'

'Could you not just paint in private?'

'They are very thorough. The Gestapo used to come around to check my paintbrushes to see if they were wet. They would get the owners of the paint shops to report any sales of oil paint to people they suspected.'

Harry shook his head.

'You English are fond of irony, and I have to say it is an irony for those of us who have fled from the Nazis to be interned for our own benefit. When the Nazis arrest you, they call it *Schutzhaft*, protective custody. I expect soon to find myself protected all over again.'

'It may never happen,' said Harry. These days he said this constantly in different situations and every time he knew for sure that it would. He decided to get to the point.

'You sent me a message, Karl. How can I help?'

'If you can think of any way I can be useful, instead of rotting behind bars, I would be grateful, Mr Fox. I am an esteemed artist. There must be some kind of work for a man like me.'

'I'll ask around,' said Harry, half-heartedly.

'Whatever prevails – ' Karl gestured around the room. The sight of the paint-encrusted walls, and the spatulas and brushes on every surface, the heap of rags piled in the corner, appeared to revive him – 'I will never stop painting. Nothing will stop me.'

'I can see that.'

Karl cast a nod towards the variety of slashes and scrawls in their frames.

'Do you know, there used to be a time when I was happy. I was completely content. And I worried, with this happiness, that my art might dry up. I might have nothing to say, and I would settle down to painting watercolours of landscapes and wildflowers and still lives. Instead of which . . .'

He shambled across the floor towards a canvas daubed with indecipherable swirls. 'We have this. *Woman in Green*. The most authentic work I have ever produced.'

Harry stared at the painting. It was green – or rather lots of greens – but mostly a vibrant, almost lurid shade that he had never seen in nature. Not emerald or leaf or mint or sage but a violent green – the kind you might encounter in nightmares. The brushstrokes seemed applied at random, congregating towards the centre of the canvas in an aggressive collision of thickened circles and arrows. Harry thought he could make out a woman, the way you could see images in clouds if you screwed your eyes up, but it might equally have been an elephant or a butterfly or nothing at all.

'Very exciting.'

It might well be. Harry recognized that art criticism was not his strong suit. Sometimes he felt abashed at this, but other times he thought if knowing what you liked worked with food and clothes and women, why not with art?

'Anyone I know?'

Karl gave a dismissive shrug.

'Art is a feeling, not a likeness.'

Harry nodded. He was not a complete barbarian. He had heard of cubism and was tentatively familiar with the concept of looking at several perspectives at once. It struck him that the process wasn't too far from his own detective work, which required a simultaneous study of all angles and facets of a problem until they resolved into one essential truth. However, he was on uncertain ground here and decided that now was not the time to go into it.

'By the way, did you ever hear the name Handel? Robert Handel?'

Karl scrunched his nicotine face.

'I don't think so. I'm sorry.'

'OK. Doesn't matter.'

In that case Harry need waste no more of his time. Yet courtesy obliged him to linger.

'So is this why you wanted to see me, Karl? You thought I could find you a job?'

'No. It's a different problem. I have a young lady for you.'

Harry raised his eyebrows.

'At least, in the professional sense.'

'You captured my interest there.'

'Well, she is very beautiful. I say young, she is perhaps in her late twenties. She has a face like Adele Bloch-Bauer.'

'Not sure I'm acquainted with her.'

'She was a beautiful aristocrat painted by Gustav Klimt in a dress of gold.'

'And that's good, is it?'

'Klimt was a master. A genius. And Adele Bloch-Bauer was irresistible. She was known as the Viennese Mona Lisa. But Jewish, so the Nazis stole the painting, needless to say.'

'So this young woman . . . does she want something?'

'She would like your help. She's willing to pay whatever you charge.'

'A lady with a face like an oil painting wants my help and is happy to pay whatever I charge. What's the catch?'

'It's a hopeless mission. She's looking for someone but I fear she has little chance of success. Her name is Lieselotte Edelman. Obviously, you may need time to consider the commission, but can I tell her you will see her?'

For a fraction of a second, Harry pretended to consider it, then he said,

'Sure. Why not? Perhaps you could give her my number.'

# CHAPTER 9

*May 3rd*

The army jeep drew up before a pair of gates and Stella jerked awake from a semi-doze. She was bone-tired; the combination of Evelyn's lumpy sofa and the anxiety of the assignation meant that she had barely slept at all.

'Just a jiffy.'

The sergeant stopped the jeep and walked over to the barrier, which was guarded by an armed sentry. A sign on the gate said *War Office Camp 11*. Stella climbed down and surveyed the view.

In front of her lay an expanse of parkland, the morning silence broken only by birdsong and the distant sound of a train. The fields were hazed over with mist and the tracks of military jeeps had run ruts through the ground. The grass was dotted with bluebells, stitchwort and wild garlic and the air was tinged with the smell of hawthorn in flower.

At the end of an avenue of elms, in the far distance, stood the house. You could never have called it beautiful; handsome, maybe, but the memory of its previous glory was overlaid now with an impression that was far dingier. The long, graceful windows were shuttered, the rose-red brick dulled, and the neo-classical facade, with its stone balustrades and urns, was obscured by coils of barbed wire. The yew borders were still neatly clipped and the statues of Romans and ancient Greeks still gestured emptily on their plinths, but Neptune was listing slightly, sunken into the soft earth. To one side she glimpsed the fruit and vegetable garden and the greenhouses, and another scribble of barbed wire that punctuated the boundaries. In the distance was a watchtower, and where the stables and dairy had been, Nissen huts and accommodation buildings had been constructed.

'Nice gaff, ain't it?' said the sergeant, who had returned from the guard hut and was fishing out a packet of Craven "A" Virginia cigarettes. He leaned against the bonnet of the jeep to light up. 'Four hundred acres. Before the war it was proper grand. Weekend parties and the like.'

She had a sense of time blurring at the edges.

'I know this place.'

He did not appear to hear.

'I came here once. Before the war.'

'Righto. Best get going,' he said, climbing back behind the wheel.

As they progressed up the drive, they encountered an

extraordinary sight. A couple of men both wearing the blue-grey uniform of the German Luftwaffe were strolling beneath the oak trees. They looked up briefly as the jeep passed, and to her astonishment, the sergeant saluted. The officers responded.

'Did you just . . . ?'

'Protocol, Miss. Don't ask me why.'

The jeep pulled up at the side of the house, rather than the grand frontage that she recalled, and the sergeant hauled out her case and pointed her towards the door. The herringbone parquet and chessboard-tiled hall was busy with people coming and going. The clack of women's heels, the distant ring of telephones, the muffled sound of voices. A man in army uniform with a neat toothbrush moustache was leaning against a pillar chatting up a woman in the lumpen, belted khaki of the ATS. When he caught sight of Stella, he straightened up and hurried over.

'Miss Fry? Delighted to meet you. I'm Clem Beckwith. Hope the journey was OK, yes? I've instructions to take you straight to head office.'

'Oh. Thank you.'

'Pop that case over there in the corner. I'll deal with it.'

He had friendly brown eyes and an air of suppressed jollity, as if they were engaged in some kind of game.

'I take it it's your first time here. Just come up from London, have you? Ignore that if you can't say.'

'No, I can. I've been in London. Bloomsbury.'

'Very nice. Good for the British Museum, not that any of us have had time for antiquities recently.' He gave a little wave to the room they were passing. 'Though we have plenty of them here to be going on with.'

They were passing the grand salon, and Stella saw again the murals of frolicking dolphins, the elaborate coving, the marble fireplace and the French doors that opened onto the terrace with its lake views. The pattering ghosts of the people who had partied there were long gone.

'Here we go.'

Beckwith halted at a desk, behind which a beautiful girl with ash-blonde hair was bent over a list.

'To see Colonel Kendrick, Margy.'

Margy gave him a finishing-school smile and knocked at a door.

Stella remembered the Blue Room. It was one of the prettiest rooms in the house. Apart from the Rex Whistler mural above the fireplace, all the walls were painted a greyish green. It was more like a sitting room than an office, decorated with comfortable chintz armchairs and fine porcelain along the mantelpiece.

'Miss Fry.'

Colonel Kendrick was a tall, genial-looking man with intense, deep-set hazel eyes, large protruding ears and a jovial smile. He was sitting at a desk on which stood two telephones, one black and one red, but when she entered, he rose, came across and extended a hand with the easy charm of the diplomat he had so recently been. He closed the door behind her.

'Thank you for coming. You've seen this place before, as I understand it?'

'Last year, yes. Before the war.'

She got the impression he already knew every answer to the questions he was asking.

'I chose this room for my office because it's my favourite. Charming, don't you think? Churchill did a painting of it, when he was last here. Little did he know.'

Without warning he suddenly switched language, addressing her in German.

'I understand you lived in Vienna.'

'I was a tutor there for five years,' Stella replied, in German too. 'The family I worked for left before the *Anschluss* . . .' After a slight hesitation she added, 'I went back in September 1938. During the Munich crisis.'

'I heard. I had just left. Difficult time.'

'Yes. They told me about your arrest when I went to the British legation.'

'It was pretty hairy. And I can't recommend a stay in the Hotel Metropol. I spent a week in that place, courtesy of the Gestapo. One prays that Vienna will be restored to herself one day. How did you find it?'

'I can't think of a more wonderful city.'

'Get much time for the opera? Or the concerts?'

'Oh yes! I even attended a New Year's waltz. With my . . . then fiancé.'

She hesitated to mention Franz Lehner. The last thing she wanted to discuss was the Austrian lawyer who had joined the National Socialist Bar Association as a career move.

Kendrick had not asked her to sit down. He was perching casually on the edge of his desk. She wondered how long they were going to swap pleasantries about European travel.

'Well, we're a long way from Vienna now. And God save that beautiful place. But because you've lived there, Miss Fry, I feel sure you comprehend a little of the Austrian, and more particularly, the German mindset. It is that which we utilize here to our advantage. Compared to what the average German or Italian soldier might expect – and indeed in contrast to the work camps you will have heard of in your time there – this place offers an extraordinary degree of luxury. Our prisoners have free range of the outside lawn on the south side and the lawns on the west and north side. They are provided with billiards, table tennis, painting equipment, and musical instruments. Many of them are very musical, as it happens. We also have a vast library of German books, which we liberated from the German embassy. A tailor visits twice a week for their sartorial needs. They receive special rations of whisky, and their food is often brought up from London hotels. Sometimes, if a man proves especially promising, we might give him a nice trip to a West End theatre, or the cinema, or lunch up in London with one of the team.'

She must have been looking at him with astonishment, because he smiled, and steepled his fingers thoughtfully.

'I note your surprise. And yet, here at Cockfosters our

detainees themselves are not the least bit surprised by our largesse. They enjoy these comparatively luxurious conditions because they believe, and pray God they are wrong, that an invasion is imminent, and that Hitler will win the war. When that happens, they will be masters of all they survey. Therefore, they regard our behaviour towards them as purely rational. The British are known to be the most pragmatic of people and they assume we calculate that if we treat them well now, perhaps soon they will repay the compliment. The trick cyclists agree.'

'Trick cyclists?'

'Psychologists. They engineer the interrogations. Work out the best way to approach these men. I have a friend in the Admiralty, a man called Ian Fleming, who suggests we use women in the interrogation room. It throws the prisoners off guard, apparently. Makes them more cooperative. It could work. Stranger things have been tried.'

At that point he switched back to English once again.

'I'm sorry, I'm forgetting myself. Do please sit. From this time, you will not speak a word of German in this place. Should any of our inmates hear you – and that is an eventuality I will not countenance – our entire endeavour would be ruined. As far as any of our guests are concerned, not that they would ask, you are a new secretary, reporting to me, recruited to cope with an excess of prisoner reports.'

'Of course, sir.'

'It might be a good idea if I explained how things operate. Six of the bedrooms and five of the interrogation rooms have been bugged. Also, some of the rooms in the stable block. False ceilings are fitted, and walls soundproofed. The microphones are highly sensitive – we've overheard prisoners whispering as they look for them, but they won't find them. Every ceiling, every lamp, every piece of furniture, every plant pot has been miked. There are devices behind mirrors, and in the fireplaces. You might remember that rather attractive portrait of an eighteenth-century lady in the grand salon whose eyes seem to follow you around the room?'

'I think so.'

'Well, it's not just her eyes now – her ears follow you too. And it doesn't stop in the house. The trees in the garden are wired, as are the tennis courts.'

'Do none of the prisoners suspect?'

'Oh, for sure. Some of them are intensely suspicious. Germans know all about hidden microphones – the Nazis have been using them for years, in all the best restaurants, I understand. There are a couple of officers here who will only converse when leaning out of the window.' He chuckled. 'Suffice to say we have installed a microphone on their window ledge.'

'Who are the prisoners?'

'Most of them are German and Italian naval officers from U-boats, but we also have a handful of Luftwaffe men whose aircraft were downed. They're not obliged to give out information – the Geneva Convention requires them only to give name, rank and serial number and we don't go in for torture here, as I'm sure you're aware. But in the interrogations, we do question them on German strategy, Hitler's intentions, anything they might have garnered about invasion plans, troop movements, codes etc. Aircraft, new technology or the development of any secret weapons. If they're talkative, we tend to keep them here longer. There's a U-boat petty officer whose boat was scuttled at the end of December, and he's been tremendously useful on German naval codes. As far as the Kriegsmarine prisoners go, we're looking for information on the strength and movement of U-boats, the losses sustained, the progress of Germany's new battleship programme, anything that gives us an idea of German naval strength. From the Luftwaffe personnel we want information on enemy positions, movement of fighter squadrons and, in particular, engineering advances. We've been picking up mention of a new technology used by the Luftwaffe called *X-Gerät* and *Knickebein* – it helps the planes bomb us more precisely. But we're also very keen to hear what they have to say about time on leave – what friends and family are saying, and domestic morale and so on. Most importantly, we want any information about a possible invasion of the British Isles.'

'Have you learned anything about that, may I ask, sir?'

'Everyone we monitor is certain that invasion is imminent. This is a crucial moment. We need as much intelligence on the Luftwaffe – their technology, their tactics – as we can get. It will be vital if we're going to avert an invasion.'

As if conscious, suddenly, of the pessimism of his remarks,

he added, 'Though I say so myself, this venture has been remarkably successful. Since last September we have gained extensive knowledge of Germany's military capabilities. It will all be an enormous help.'

He walked across to the long window and gazed out. A gardener was clipping the box hedges and from a distance came the buzz of a lawnmower. A nuthatch issued a long trill from the nearby trees. It struck Stella that these sounds seemed too innocent for a place of such elaborate deception.

'We do interrogate; however, our interrogations are not enough. Most won't give anything away in the interrogation room. It's only afterwards that they begin to talk.'

'When they're unobserved.'

'Precisely. When they're back in their cells. Everything a man says in war is filtered. He can never tell his wife, or ordinary civilians, what is happening. The only people who understand are his fellow soldiers and to them he speaks without filter. They discuss everything – landscapes and art and women as much as bombs and war.'

He pointed to his desk, with its different telephones and a number of bells.

'That's where these come in. Directly below our feet is a room that we call the M Room. It is staffed by sets of listeners who work in shifts, recording and transcribing prisoners' conversations. When they first arrive the prisoners are housed two to a room – always of equal rank but from different units or services. The idea is that they will talk to each other about their experiences and that every word will be picked up. This equipment on my desk means that I can connect at any time with the conversations being recorded. The compiled transcripts are called Special Reports and are disseminated to the War Office or the Air Ministry or the Admiralty.'

Stella was still trying to take it all in.

'And Robert Handel was one of those listeners?'

'Until last week he was. I understand that Captain Knight has briefed you on what took place.'

'The murder, you mean.'

Kendrick ran a hand through thinning hair.

'A Luftwaffe man, Oberstleutnant Gabriel Fassbinder, was discovered shot dead in the grounds. A few hundred yards above the lake. Handel, a chap of some talent and resource, in whom I would have placed the greatest trust, disappeared the same night. Subsequently we found that a revolver is missing from our range – an Enfield No. 2 service revolver – and we believe it's the one which killed Fassbinder. It's impossible not to conclude that the same man is responsible for the killing. As to why, I have no idea.'

He ran a hand across his eyes and massaged his brow, and for a moment she glimpsed the fatigue that must consume him daily.

'The fact is, Miss Fry – and please don't take offence – you might not have been my first choice as a listener. Though your German seems pretty good, native speakers are far better with technological terms and dialects and so on. But we don't want to involve anyone internally in this affair until we have a clearer idea of what took place, and Knight himself, because he recommended Handel, is determined to get to the bottom of the matter. He feels responsible. As soon as he heard, he telephoned me, and said he had the perfect replacement. He organized your clearance and begged me to trust him this time. He's taking a chance on you, as am I, so here you are. We cannot involve the police. But it's essential that we get to the truth. My proposal is that you will join my listeners, but you will be seeking a very different kind of information.'

Stella nodded. 'I understand.'

'Anything you find, or uncover or overhear, you report to me immediately.'

He clasped his hands together decisively, and Stella understood the interview was over.

'We will pay you three pounds a week. Out of that you'll have to pay for your billet. I've arranged a room for you in town, not far from here. It's with a Mrs Pursglove, a very discreet lady. A widow. Not exactly a hotel, but it's clean and comfortable and there's a few of our female staff billeted there already. Sergeant Jenkins, who drove you here, will sort you out a bicycle and a uniform. Normally you would be kitted out at the central depot, but circumstances don't permit. I think your suitcase has been sent ahead of you. And to repeat, it goes without saying, you must not utter a single word of German while you're here. A mistake like that could cost us dearly.'

He slid a paper across the desk, and she saw the heading: *Official Secrets Act.*

'I should reiterate that nobody here – not the couriers or the typists or the cleaning staff or the cooks – has any idea of what actually happens in the rooms under our feet. This work is strictly secret. You will tell nobody of what you are doing, not even your closest family. You must utter no word of it. This unit's existence must be protected at all costs. Our kind of high-grade intelligence counts for as much as firepower: indeed, I like to think it's rather more important for the war than driving tanks or firing guns. If, as I fear, Robert Handel has gone, and intends to impart our secrets to the enemy, then our entire enterprise – every bit of intelligence that we have gained here – could be blown.'

# CHAPTER 10

Mrs Pursglove's home was a Victorian cottage, set in town around a mile from the gates of Trent Park. The front door was approached through a wooden gate up a narrow brick path fringed with a sentry line of orange tulips. The landlady herself had tight grey curls, tartan slippers and an unctuous manner belied by a flinty countenance which Stella felt sure noted every detail.

'We have plenty of young ladies coming and going from the big house. I'm sure you'll be comfortable here. I've put you in the top room.'

This phrase made it sound exclusive, but once Mrs Pursglove had panted her way up the stairs, Stella realized that she meant the attic – not much bigger than a cupboard – with a steeply sloping ceiling that would prevent sitting up in bed. It was chilly up in the eaves, and to forestall any comment, Mrs Pursglove said, 'Warm for spring, isn't it, miss? Only hope it doesn't turn cold before the apples have a chance to set.'

Stella unlatched the tiny dormer window. It looked out onto a large apple tree, its little buds of blossom opening into spring, and its boughs echoing with the screech of nesting crows. The rest of the garden had been dug up for vegetable beds, and in one corner stood a lean-to greenhouse in which she glimpsed early tomato plants. The blackout curtains were stiff and smelt of dust. Colonel Kendrick was right when he had described the billet as not exactly a hotel – the bare floorboards were decorated with a small rug, made of patched-together rags, and the only furniture was a large wardrobe, a long spotty mirror, a small basin in the corner, and a narrow bed with a threadbare yellow candlewick bedspread. The wind whistled through an empty grate, decorated with a couple of cigarette ends, which only made Stella think of its last occupant. Where was she now, the woman who had sat here smoking and tossed these stubs into the chilly grate?

Once Mrs Pursglove had left, Stella sank onto the bed and tried to collect her galloping thoughts. A khaki ATS uniform complete with cap and belt was folded over the back of the chair. Someone, Sergeant Jenkins she supposed, had parked her suitcase in the corner and she took out the few things and hung them up in the wardrobe. Maxwell Knight had suggested that the task would take 'no more than a couple of weeks'. She wondered what fictions they had told the people at work and found herself thinking irrelevantly of Toby Enderby. No matter that she was not attracted to him, she did not like to think of him believing that she'd had an accident and wasting his time fruitlessly searching London's hospitals to find her.

As to her own search, she had no hope that she would find anything at all. She would need to befriend, and probe, staff who were professionally trained in discretion. Indeed, public discussion of their activities was forbidden by law. How could she possibly go about it, given that, as Colonel Kendrick had said, even among themselves the listeners were not encouraged to discuss their work? And yet, her time at the Film Unit had helped her understand something about herself, which was that she possessed an unusually acute power of observation. She was often the one who noticed some quirk among the interviewees – a funny turn of phrase, or an idiosyncrasy, or a memorable face. A tugging of the earlobes or a nervousness concealed. She would watch people as they talked, knowing by the tilt of the head or the direction of their eyes how fluent their stories would be, and how fabricated. She only hoped this would help in what seemed like an impossible venture.

There was a knock at the door and a face peered around.

'Just wanted to say hello.'

It was a young woman in her early twenties who somehow managed to make the ATS uniform seem chic. She had a cheerful smile and abundant curly brown hair rolled off her face.

'I'm Mimi. Mimi Friedlander. Mind if I . . . ?'

She took out a carton of cigarettes and lounged against the doorjamb.

'No, please, do come in. I'm Stella Fry. I'm new and I don't know a soul.'

'You're a listener, right?'

Stella nodded.

'That's what I thought. I've just come off shift and I'm dead tired, but I thought I'd meet the latest recruit if only to warn her about the hot water. There isn't any — it's tepid at best — and if Mrs Pursglove finds you've had a bath above five inches, she files an official complaint.'

'Really?'

'No, not really, but she might. Then again, she'll probably forgive you because you're not foreign. I don't think she's ever got used to having real "Continentals" under her roof. There's three of us billeted here — me, Esme Muller and Gerda Sontag — we all work on a rota, so generally you'll only see us when you're queueing for the bathroom. Oh, and make sure you eat everything you can at breakfast — she's terrifically stingy with the margarine.'

'Oh. Right. Thanks.'

'And she only allows us in the parlour between five and nine, though why anyone would want to go in the parlour . . .'

Stella smiled. She had glimpsed the parlour on her way in: a mantelpiece crowded with china dogs, tasselled lamps, stiff, formal chairs and a carpet and curtains in violently competing patterns.

'I suspect she snoops in our rooms while we're out, so if you keep a diary, make sure you lock it up. And be glad you're on the top floor because she likes to have her wireless turned up full volume. I'm right above her and sometimes think if I ever hear Jack Wilson and His Versatile Five again, I'll scream. It's worse because I'm working nights at the moment so I need to sleep in the daytime. I'm sure she knows, but she takes no notice.'

'Did you work all last night?'

'We all do. On and off. I don't know if they've told you the drill, but you'll get your rota shortly. There are two shifts – breakfast till 4 p.m., and 4 p.m. until the prisoners go to sleep. And one unlucky person – me, this time – is on night-time duty, in case our guests wake up and start talking. Or maybe say something in their sleep.'

She grinned.

'Apart from that, Cockfosters is not a bad place to be. The rations are good and there's an officers' mess at the camp that I'll take you to, if you like. That can be an awful lot of fun. And we have use of the tennis courts. There's a gym and a rifle range and a badminton court – we play a lot of badminton – and there are always card games in the mess. And occasionally we go out to the Cock and Dragon in town.'

Although her English was fluent, the edge to her accent – a clipped hardening of the consonants – confirmed she was not native.

'Where are you from, Mimi? Originally?'

'Germany. I came over on a domestic visa. I got a position in service. I didn't know the first thing about housekeeping – we had a maid for that at home – and the only recipes I know are German ones, which I can assure you did not go down well. But eventually, thank God, this came up. Have you ever been to Germany?'

'I lived in Austria for five years, but we often made trips there.'

Stella was not going to say that three years ago she had broken off an engagement on the shores of Lake Starnberg. That episode, anyway, seemed like something from another life. A whole existence away.

'We used to go to Munich a lot, to the opera.'

Her employer, Herr Gatz, who was an opera fanatic, had taken the whole family to see *Don Giovanni* at the Opernhaus and it was so glorious he had vowed to make it an annual pilgrimage. The following year, however, the Nazis enacted the Nuremberg Laws, Jews were barred from German theatres and there had been no return trip.

'I miss music,' said Mimi. 'I can't bear it. At home I used to play the violin but now I never get the chance. It's like being separated from my own soul.'

'I have a friend in London who feels the same. He goes to the Myra Hess concerts at the National Gallery every day. He's not the sort you think would like classical music, but he adores it.'

'Ah! So this is your boyfriend?' asked Mimi, eyes sparkling.

'No, he's just a friend. His name's Harry Fox.'

'Handsome?'

'I suppose so, now I think about it. You could call him that. He's tall and dark-haired, though he'd be better-looking if he didn't have a scar down one side of his face.'

'Like a duelling scar?'

'He never said, though I find it hard to think of Harry in a duel. He's more the kind to go in with all fists flying.'

'Is he married?'

'No. I get the impression he takes women out like library books. A couple of weeks, then it's time for a new one.'

Mimi laughed. 'I know men like that. So what does your Harry Fox do?'

'He's a private investigator.'

'What does he investigate?'

'Crimes. Missing persons. People pay him to find things out.'

'How exciting.'

Mimi finished her cigarette and put the stub in her pocket. 'Do you miss it? Austria?'

'There's no point, is there? I can't see myself going abroad for a good long time. It must be much worse for you. Being away from your people. Your home.'

'My home is not a nice place to be right now. In fact, I don't even call it home any more. Perhaps I never will again.'

Stella wanted to ask about her family, but she sensed that Mimi herself was not ready to talk about it. She was turning away and showily stifling a yawn.

'Sorry, I'm dead tired. I'm going to bed. Hope your first

shift goes OK. I can't say enjoy it, because you won't. But see you later, I hope.'

Stella sat on the bed. The mention of her years with the Gatzes turned her thoughts to everything that had happened since she returned – meeting Harry Fox and their investigation into the death of the novelist Hubert Newman. Reuniting with Evelyn and her family. And now, this. The past two years had been full of unforeseen twists and turns. The combination of chance and connection that brought her to this narrow attic room seemed entirely random.

And yet, surely, that was how life was. Arbitrary. Coincidental. Entirely without order. When she had returned to England in March 1938 she had felt unmoored and without connection. Apart from Evelyn, all her previous social circles had fallen away and she had no idea how to reintroduce herself. Her university girlfriends were long married and most spent their time looking after their babies. The men were established in banking or law, or stockbroking, and their days were filled with work and their weekends with golf.

Yet how much more painful it must be for women like Mimi, hundreds of miles from her homeland, separated from her family and everything she loved. Despite the girl's insouciant '*I don't even call it home*', she sensed an anguish beneath the surface.

She tried on the uniform, which roughly fitted her, though the skirt was too roomy around the waist. The cut was appalling and guaranteed to flatter nobody. She tightened the belt, tidied her hair and secured it at the sides with clips. Then she washed her face, applied a touch of lipstick, and stared into the spotty mirror.

She shivered. It was either excitement or nerves, she wasn't sure which.

CHAPTER 11

The M Room was unlike any office she had ever seen.

There were three rooms in the basement, linked by bare arched cellars and walled in rough brick interspersed with patches of white tile. A smell of dust and damp pervaded the frigid air, and the underground gloom was lit in some places by dim ceiling lights and elsewhere by bare bulbs. A haze of tobacco smoke hung over several rough wooden tables piled with steel frames holding machines, each with a perplexing number of dials. Five or six people wearing headphones were seated in front of what looked like a telephone switchboard and every so often one or other would suddenly straighten, switch on a turntable and begin to record. An intense, balding young man in wire-rimmed glasses and an overcoat glanced up as she passed, issued a wintry smile, and said 'hello' before returning to the machine in front of him. Further along the basement, she could see several women typing. The only sounds to penetrate the hush were the rattle of typewriter keys and the click and whine of switches.

Stella had found a bicycle provided for her, as Colonel Kendrick had promised, and she had cycled back to Trent Park to be met at a side door by a stout man who introduced himself as Sergeant Hadley. He conducted her through a series of corridors before diverging suddenly, darting through a door, and descending a flight of unlit stone steps to the basement. They came to a steel door, and only once they were through it did he begin to talk.

'We have a number of recording engineers here, and at the far end, you'll see our stenographers, who type up the recordings.' He gestured to the women bent over typewriters, their fingers a blizzard of movement and wire baskets piled with paper at their sides. 'The transcripts are known as X reports and they are sent on to relevant departments for analysis. As you see, we have several female staff – some refugees from Austria and Germany, and I usually caution them . . .' here he turned to face her, 'that some of the conversations you will hear can be . . . distressing. Normally, Miss Fry, I would warn you about what you might hear concerning women, but in this case, there are even more shocking issues, especially about the SS and the treatment of Jews. You may hear men recount acts of brutality. Shooting, raping, robbing. They discuss atrocities committed against the Poles. Rest assured, there are some savage men among our guests.'

He gestured to a table, on which lay a pair of headphones and recording equipment.

'If you would sit here. Your shift runs from now until your prisoners go to bed. But be aware that often they go on talking for quite a while in their cells. We operate in teams of six. You will be next to Subaltern Susanne Frobisher.'

A fresh-faced, red-cheeked woman of around thirty looked up enquiringly. Her braided hair was clamped with a pair of headphones, and she gave a brisk smile that suggested she should not be interrupted.

'Subaltern Frobisher can answer any questions you have. You will be monitoring two prisoners – both Luftwaffe first lieutenants: Lieutenant Scholtz – he's a pilot, and Gruber, he's Bavarian, he's an observer. They arrived last week, and we thought it appropriate to pair them. Scholtz came after his Heinkel 111 crashed, and he's provided some very useful information about new enemy aircraft and their capabilities. It seems the Luftwaffe admire the Spitfire tremendously.'

'How will I know if they're saying something important?'

'If they start talking about anything other than their last meal, that's when you begin recording.'

He gestured to the equipment before them. 'This functions like a telephone exchange. You might be asked to monitor two or three cells at once. You insert the plug into a numbered socket here. It's important that you get to know your chaps' voices very well so you can follow them speaking easily. As soon as you hear anything that may be of interest to the authorities, you flick this switch to start up the turntable and pull this lever to lower the recording head. Each disc records seven minutes of conversation, after which you take what you have recorded to the playback room, transcribe it in longhand, have the transcript checked by the officer in charge. Then it will be typed up in German and translated into English. OK so far?'

She nodded.

'Always keep a log of what the prisoners are doing, what they're talking about and at what time they have each conversation. As I said, the prisoners are two to a cell. In fact, they're specially paired according to their voices. Each voice needs to be sufficiently different, so we know who's speaking. Fortunately, German comes in a number of dialects, as I assume you know.'

That was true. The soft and throaty Bavarian accent with its rolled 'rs' could not be more different from the hard edge of *Berlinerisch*, or the high-class *Hochdeutsch* you heard on German newscasts.

'Happy, Miss Fry?'

Quite the opposite.

'Yes.'

'If that's all, then, I'll leave you to it.'


Stella took the seat next to Susanne Frobisher and donned the headphones. Immediately, through the whisper of static, a voice emerged. It was a young, north German voice, Westphalian perhaps – she remembered similar inflections in the voice of Joseph Goebbels, which she had heard on Austrian radio during her time in Vienna. The prisoner was discussing the library.

Stella flicked the switch.

'Magnificent library they have here. Such a range. I never thought the British read so many German books. That's not what we're told, is it? We hear they're effete and insular. They have no interest in other cultures. But I found a complete collection of Karl May.'

Another voice interceded. This one was markedly different; it sounded southern, which would have been a difficult accent to follow had she not spent so many years in Austria.

'Winnetou! Ja?'

'Yes. I found *Son of the Bear Hunter*. I love them. I suppose now I'll have time to read them all over again.'

An inaudible comment followed from the man she took to be Gruber, then, 'How long do you reckon we'll be here, then?'

'Too long. Ask for another razor if you need one. I asked for a good razor and some cigarettes, and they delivered them straight away.'

'Should we try to escape?'

'Not me. I'm married. I don't want to be shot. Besides, it's not as bad as it could be.'

The conversation idled. She could hear the flap of a book's pages and assumed that Scholtz was reading.

She paused, pen in hand, trying to recall the name of the secret aircraft technology that Colonel Kendrick had mentioned. *X-Gerät? Knickebein?* It seemed unlikely that the two men might switch from popular literature to the fine detail of technical innovations.

Then Gruber said, 'They were asking me about Poland, in the interrogation. Naturally, I told them nothing.'

'Ah, Poland. It's beautiful flying there. The countryside, it's really something.' A pause. A sigh, as though he was stretching, then, 'When you're dropping bombs, it's interesting how quickly you get used to it. Do you know, I found I actively enjoyed it.'

'Hitler has lost a lot of blood in Poland,' Gruber commented.

Lazily, the conversation moved on. She could hear the sound of a match striking as the men lit cigarettes, and then the rustle of movement and the clink of an ashtray.

But Scholtz had not finished with his reminiscence.

'. . . operating the machine gun. I enjoy it when they run, hands up, and I give them the bullets in their back. I felt the urge to shoot every one of them.'

It was as though they were competing, like boys, in telling tales.

Her gaze was fixed on the recording equipment in front of her, soundlessly turning. It seemed less a set of neutral machines than a terrifying, interlinked confessional filled with the worst sins that could be committed and for which there was no atonement.

After seven minutes, the disc was full, and she put down the headphones. She was aware that the blood had drained from her face, and when she stood, she felt unsteady. Subaltern Frobisher glanced up.

'Go and transcribe that. Only two hours till tea.'

Stella inserted the disc into the machine and played it back. The tea break seemed infinitely far away. She knew she was supposed to be gathering intelligence on the recent death of Gabriel Fassbinder. At some point she should be asking leading questions and probing the rumours on the ground. But at that point the exchange she had heard, and the effort of transcribing it first in German, then into English, was so intense that she had no chance of thinking of anything else, even if she had wanted to.

It was ten thirty at night before Scholtz and Gruber finished chatting and the headphones transmitted nothing but the sound of snores. Stella was wrung out, her nerves taut. She cycled back to the billet, letting the cold air on her face blow every thought out of her head, except for the thought of getting into her room and falling into the oblivion of sleep. When she reached Mrs Pursglove's she parked her bicycle and went into the kitchen, desperately hoping that she would not encounter her landlady and her inquisitive eyes. Instead, she found only a tray covered in a tea towel under which was a lettuce leaf, two tomatoes, a wafer of ham, two thick slices of bread and a tiny scoop of margarine. She fell on it, famished.

After the solitary supper she curled into bed, staring out

at the apple tree's black boughs fracturing the sky, trying to obliterate the images of the day. Except, each time she shut her eyes, the pictures came back more vividly, so she tried to keep them open instead.

# CHAPTER 12

It would have made sense for Harry to meet Lieselotte Edelman at his office, but this was the finest spring anyone could remember, and she sounded like the kind of girl who would look good against a bed of roses, so he suggested a meeting in Hyde Park.

He liked a park. Nature was tidy there and well-mannered, even if, as it turned out, Dig for Victory had replaced the roses with cabbages, and a posse of Land Army girls with spades and khaki dungarees were on the lookout for anyone stealing the leeks.

When he reached the Italian Gardens with its white marble fountain, Lieselotte was already there sitting on a bench, a slight, upright figure in a tight-fitting pink cotton jacket, knitting her fingers in her lap. Her face was so pale it was almost translucent. Visible blue veins ran down the side of her cheek, her burnished brunette hair was piled above a slim neck, and she possessed the slender fragility of a whippet.

Basically, a goddess in a cotton jacket.

She proffered a small hand to be crushed in his enormous palm and looked up at him with large blue eyes that helped him decide, before he had heard a word about it, that he would take the job.

'Hello, Mr Fox. Thank you for coming.'

'Pleasure's all mine,' he said, settling himself next to her on the bench and taking off his hat.

'I am grateful to you for agreeing to meet me. Karl told me you're a detective.'

'Private,' he qualified, which sounded exclusive, rather than merely expedient.

'A private detective, yes. Of course. I don't expect any of the usual police would bother with my problem.'

His eyes crinkled with sympathy.

'And what is your problem, if I could ask?'

'I'm looking for someone. But I'm not even sure if he's here in Britain. He could be anywhere. Anywhere in the world.'

He offered her a cigarette, which she accepted, lit them both and stretched out his legs in front of the bench. Karl was right. This did not sound promising.

'Why don't you tell me what brings you here?'

Lieselotte leaned forward, crossed a pair of well-sculpted legs, and inhaled greedily on the cigarette.

'Mind if I start at the beginning?'

'Always a good place to start.'

'Do you have the time?'

'Sure.'

Usually, the life histories of his clients were concise. Their stories could generally be summed up in four words – started good, went bad. This story, he guessed, might be more complex.

'I was born in Berlin Mitte, and we lived in Rosenthalerstrasse. My father Bernhard was the manager of a textile factory, and my mother, Esther, was a Hausfrau. There were three of us, Mutti, Vati, and me. I'm their only child and I suppose they doted on me.'

Her voice was low and throaty, punctuated with soft sighs.

'But everything changed when Hitler came in. I'm sure you can imagine. Pretty soon, there were all kinds of new laws. You couldn't keep pets, you couldn't go to the theatre, you couldn't even smile at an Aryan in the street. Jews could not associate with Aryans in any way. I had to move to the Jewish Girls' School and I hated it. The lessons there were very basic. Heinrich Himmler said the *Untermenschen* need only to spell five hundred words. Why would they need any more than that?'

Did she want an answer to this question? Harry was dumbfounded.

'Luckily, I was in my last year at school, and besides, all I really cared about was art. My parents had such hopes for me – they encouraged everything I did – and when I said I wanted to be an artist, they paid for lessons. Of course, I was never going to be able to make portrait painting a career.

No artist is allowed to work in Germany now unless they are a member of the Reich Chamber of Culture, and you can't be that if you are Jewish, but I managed to get a job designing the sets for movies. Everything was getting harder every day, but somehow, while I was painting, I managed to escape it all. When I was making these glorious film backdrops I imagined myself melting into them – escaping through the painting into a mythical world; can you understand that, Mr Fox?'

He thought he could.

'Then something happened. I fell in love.'

Of course. That was a plot twist he could see from miles off.

'He worked for the government. His name was Paul Schilling. He had visited the film studios one day when I was painting and when I went out, I found him waiting for me. He had artistic ambitions too! He asked me to dinner. He took me to Ganymed, that's a restaurant on the Schiffbauerdamm, looking over the canal. It's a smart place, Mr Fox, though I was almost too excited to eat. Jews aren't allowed there, so I was nervous I would be found out. But we had so much to talk about. Right from the beginning, it was like we were twin souls, you know?'

Harry very much didn't, but he liked the idea.

'The only problem was, he was Aryan.'

'That's a problem?'

'You don't understand. As I said, Jews cannot associate with non-Jews, let alone marry them. It's against the law in Germany. I couldn't even tell my family about Paul. We started to meet in secret and began to talk about how we could be together. He said he could get hold of forged documents and I could change my identity so we would have a future. But how was that going to work? I would never see my parents. Eventually, Paul said he would help me leave Germany. I said we could go to France, but he said no. England was safer. He had contacts in England . . .'

'Contacts?'

'In the German embassy, I think. He had spent some time here, too. And I had a cousin in England so I would have somewhere to stay, at least to begin with. The idea was, I could work as a housekeeper or something. Paul was going to come too. He wanted to make a new start. But I had to keep it secret for everyone's sake. I hated doing that – I knew how much Mutti and Vati would worry. But also, I knew that if I did get to England, I could help them come too.'

'So that's what you did?'

'I tried. I arrived two years ago and as soon as I did, I sent my parents a letter, telling them what had happened and that I was now staying at our cousin's, and I would be trying to get them domestic service visas. They wrote back saying they were happy for me. I had caused them a lot of grief, but now they could rest easy. They forgave me. But Paul . . . he never showed up at my cousin's as we planned. I waited and waited. He had promised to contact me within a month, but the time went past and he never appeared. It was like he'd vanished.'

'Maybe he didn't make the journey?'

'That's what I thought. Only . . . I managed to get in contact with Herta, my best friend back in Berlin, and she told me that Paul's apartment was shut up. He had definitely left Germany.' Lieselotte took out her handkerchief and dabbed at her face. 'So, I need to know if he's here.'

'But surely, if your Paul had come over, after all that trouble, he would have got in touch with you?'

'He might not know where I am. My cousin moved away, and I was forced to find new lodgings.'

'Maybe you could approach his contacts. The ones who supposedly helped him.'

'They worked for the German embassy, Mr Fox, and as I'm sure you know, that's not there any more.'

Indeed. Harry remembered the day of departure. The embassy staff, among whom his friend Malone had had such a valuable contact, evacuating from number 9, Carlton House Terrace and loading their trunks into taxis while the press took excitable photographs.

Lieselotte sniffed. The cobalt eyes had glossed over with tears.

'I have to find Paul. I can't bear to think of him out there, searching for me. Besides, I need his help. It's hard being on your own in a foreign country.'

Harry hoped she was not going to start crying. Swiftly, he changed tack.

'So where did you meet Karl?'

'Oh, I'd heard of him, of course. Karl Zapf. Back in Germany he's well known. He's a friend of Otto Dix and he knows George Grosz and Max Beckmann. You know, the New Objectivist movement?'

Harry nodded sagely.

'They're a break from the Expressionists. Not at all sentimental. They see life with a kind of savage realism. Does that make sense to you?'

'Strikes a chord.'

'Anyhow, Karl approached me at a bus stop and asked if he could paint me. I recognized him at once. He said I had the kind of body he had dreamed of painting all his life.'

'You didn't let him, did you?'

'I didn't mind. I've done plenty of modelling in my time. And it was better than sitting on my own, going mad thinking about Paul. It was cold in his studio, though.'

'You mean you let him paint you . . . ?'

'Naked? Yes, of course. It's art.'

'Where's the painting now?'

'In the studio, I suppose. He was very proud of it, actually. He said it was the best work he'd ever done. He's called it *Woman in Green*.'

Harry recalled the swirls of meaningless paint.

'I think I saw it. Not sure it quite captures you.'

'Really?'

'Not got the hands right.'

'Oh.' She tossed her head lightly. 'Anyway, we became friends and when I told him about needing to find Paul

Schilling, Karl said he knew you. You were a top-flight detective, and you'd never had a case you couldn't solve.'

Where had Karl got that from? Despite himself, Harry glowed at such a testimonial. Then on second thoughts, he realized it sounded like something he might himself have said, on a late night in Luigi's after too much beer.

'I said if Karl could contact you, I would be willing to pay.'

The lovely eyes beseeched him once again.

'And I will. At least, I will just as soon as I manage to find a job.'

If Harry had a pound for every time a shortage of funds had been cited by the clients of his detective work, he would no longer be doing his detective work. He would be living at the seaside, reading novels and drinking by the fire.

'Do you think you could possibly find Paul for me, Mr Fox?'

'I'm going to try.'

'Does that mean you'll take the case?'

Take on an impossible task, which would be a total waste of time and energy, for no payment? What could possibly induce him?

'I think I can fit it in.'

The look on her face made it all worthwhile.

He passed her his card.

'Why not call me at my office in a few days and I'll tell you how it's going?'

## CHAPTER 13

For the next two days Stella sat among the filing cabinets and the recording devices alongside the other listeners, eavesdropping and transcribing discs. The atmosphere in the M Room was claustrophobic and intense and the smell of damp was intercut with the sharp metallic scent of the machines and the faint, sweaty odour of the listeners. Occasionally, someone would transcribe information and pass it urgently to a senior officer, and then a charged excitement would take over the room. Something significant had been found.

The man in wire-rimmed glasses, who had smiled at her when she first arrived, passed by and introduced himself as Helmut Monke.

'I'm from Düsseldorf. I'm sure your German is excellent, but should you come across any tricky translation questions, just let me know.'

'I'm Stella Fry. And thanks, I will.'

It was easy enough, however, to follow the language.

The difficulty lay in deciding which nuggets of intelligence might be useful to the war effort. Although Stella was alert for any discussion of technical details, it seemed the two prisoners had tired of discussing their aircraft and their conversation had dwindled to mundane chat. Yet even here, Stella realized that the most trivial exchange could contain insights pointing to the enemy's vulnerabilities. When Gruber remarked that his old mother must be missing him, Scholtz's rejoinder was downbeat.

'Germany is full of unhappy mothers right now.'

Then swiftly, as if keen to lift the mood, he could be heard crossing the room, opening the window, and leaning out.

'At least we're in a beautiful place!'

'I wonder if the rest of England is so charming,' said Gruber.

'We'll know soon enough, my friend.'

'You think?'

'I'm sure of it. It won't be long now.'

It was a strangely intimate experience, monitoring two men over several hours. Even though she could not see them, she became familiar with both Scholtz and Gruber – their personalities, their attitudes, the quirks of their humour. Scholtz was the dominant one, more confident and intelligent than his cellmate. Gruber was slower, less voluble, and rarely took the lead.

One subject Scholtz mentioned a lot was fun.

'Funny about the Jews,' he reflected, thoughtfully.

'Never found anything funny about them,' countered Gruber.

'No. I mean, I took part in all that business in 1936. Those poor Jews!' Laughter. 'We smashed the windowpanes and hauled the people out. They quickly put on some clothes and we drove them away. We made short work of them. I hit them on the head with an iron truncheon. It was great fun.'

At four o'clock on the second day, she was drinking a mahogany-brown mug of tea in the mess area. The listeners' mess was separate from that of the other staff, due to the secret nature of their work, and she was just finishing her tea when she felt a presence hovering at her shoulder and looked up to see Clem Beckwith.

'Don't mean to interrupt, but I have an awfully nice Chelsea bun to spare if you feel like it.'

He slid the plate in front of her. 'Mind if I join you?'

She smiled and gestured to the empty seat opposite.

'Call me Clem.'

'I'm Stella.'

'Hope you're settling in. I know some of the girls here find it hard going.'

'Do they? I'm not surprised.'

'I think so. I can't ask if you're enjoying the work because nobody could, but it helps to know we're doing something of great national interest.'

'It is, isn't it? Of national interest?'

'Very much so. You've no idea how valuable this information is. I haven't either, really – so much is above our pay grade – but we do hear about some successes.'

For a second she saw him hesitate, weighing the urge to disclose his knowledge against the duty of discretion. The urge won. Despite the background clash of serving trays, the chatter of the kitchen staff and the hum of conversation from officers in easy chairs, he lowered his voice.

'We had a U-boat petty officer whose boat had been scuttled and he started talking about the German code, Enigma. He confirmed that their navy spells out numerals in full, instead of just using the top row of the keyboard. May sound a small thing, but apparently it's of enormous help to the boffins who have to do the decrypting.'

He gulped down a mouthful of tea. 'You can't help but feel a bit of pride when something significant comes on your watch. I had a chap saying that Germany won't employ gas in an attack against Britain unless Britain uses it first. That sort of thing matters.'

Stella leaned forward; her fingers curled around her teacup. 'I still can't quite believe this whole set-up. It's just so ingenious. Are we sure the prisoners have no idea?'

'Absolutely none. I heard something awfully amusing the first week I was here. A prisoner spent twenty minutes examining the walls and the floor and the furniture in minute detail and finally he announced, "There are no microphones here!" I almost laughed out loud. The mikes are state-of-the art, though. All courtesy of the specialist chaps from the Dollis Hill Research Station. They've done us proud.'

He chewed his bun thoughtfully. 'The whole operation works so well. Sometimes the prisoners come back from an interrogation and boast about what they haven't given away, and that's usually where we get the most valuable information of all.'

Watching his cheerful, good-humoured face, Stella thought how recently he must have been at school. Clem Beckwith was much younger than she was. She sensed his eagerness for social life and female company. His desire to gossip even here, at one of the country's most secretive sites.

'How long have you been here, Clem?'

Now, at last, here was a chance to probe.

'Since the off. We were initially stationed at the Tower of London but the whole unit was transferred. Fears of bombing, I suppose, or invasion.'

'Why were you chosen?'

'I have German relatives. I used to spend summers near Munich, and I picked up the lingo then. The only thing I'm good at, languages, or so my schoolmasters told me.'

'How do you find it? Off duty, I mean. I imagine the social life's a bit dull. Does anything ever happen here?'

Beckwith hesitated and dabbed his moustache. She could see his eyes calculating. No one wanted to boast of a dull life. Not when they were trying to impress a new colleague. Or, more to the point, a woman.

'We had a little upset a couple of weeks ago. Can't talk about it, really, but it was pretty dramatic.'

'Dramatic? Really? What kind of upset?'

He glanced around the mess. Two women were doing the *Times* crossword together. An officer was applying himself to a plate of lamb's liver and reading a book propped against the water jug. In a place of professional eavesdropping, it paid to be cautious, but unless the mess tables themselves were miked, nobody was within earshot.

'A prisoner was assaulted. I can't say more than that. But it seemed to put the wind up the authorities. Now we have extra security checks and showing your pass all day and flipping night. It's a frightful bore. Apparently, some of the staff had their billets searched. Not me. Probably not important enough.'

He grinned and stood up.

'Maybe we could have a game of whist if you fancy it one night soon?'

'Oh yes. Rather. What fun.'

Hours later, cycling home, she glanced across the moonlit lawn at the front of the house, wondering where exactly the body of Gabriel Fassbinder had been found. Maxwell Knight had told her only that he was discovered in the grounds, not far from the house. As she looked, in the periphery of her vision a figure emerged from the deep shadow of an oak tree, walking alone across the silvery grass. She braked to a halt. Was it another prisoner, such as she had seen in the grounds when she arrived? Or a fellow officer, or one of the guards? He was facing away from her, but as the sound of her bicycle carried in the air he turned, and she thought she could make out the long overcoat and bony figure of Helmut Monke. Though it might just as well have been one of the administrative staff, or an interrogator, or another person entirely.

On the third day Stella was assigned to monitor a different cell containing a Luftwaffe pilot and an observer. When she first donned the headphones, they had just returned from lunch and were discussing the meal they had been served. The pilot, from Saxony, going by the voice, pronounced himself surprised by the quality of English food; they had been led to understand it was terrible, but really it was quite good, and this dish called Cottage Pie he would happily try again. His cellmate concurred. After a short lull, in which she could hear the two lighting up cigarettes, they started to reminisce, and at this point Stella began recording.

The pilot had been reflecting on his time flying over Poland at the beginning of the war.

'On the second day of the Polish war I had to drop bombs on a station at Posen. At first I didn't like it, but by the third day I didn't really care. On the fourth day I was enjoying it. It was our before-breakfast amusement to chase single soldiers over the fields with machine-gun fire and to leave them lying there with a few bullets in the back.'

'But always against soldiers?'

'People too. We attacked the columns in the street. You should have seen the horses stampede! In the end I cared more for the horses than the people.'

'Disgusting that, with the horses.'

'I was sorry for the horses but not at all for the people. I was sorry for the horses up to the last day.'

Stella frowned, checking the tape. The disc had six minutes to run.

'They all got bullets in the back and ran zigzags in all directions like mad,' the pilot recalled. His tone was frank, matter-of-fact.

'One becomes terribly brutal in such undertakings,' said the other voice.

'Yes, I've already said that on the first day it seemed terrible to me, but I told myself, "Hell, orders are orders." But as I said, the horses screamed. I hardly heard my own plane, they screamed so loudly.'

Stella clenched her fists beneath the desk. They enjoyed killing, there was no doubting it. It was like a hunt or a sport. Shooting defenceless women and children. Plundering private homes. Razing villages. Casual slaughter.

The only thing that had really annoyed them was getting shot down.

When the disc was full, she got up and took it over to be transcribed, but her legs felt as though they might give way beneath her. As she returned to her desk and clamped on the headphones again, she had a sudden mental image of an Old Master portrait she had seen in Brussels. Hieronymus Bosch, she thought. It was a picture of an earthly paradise – of gardens and hills and blossoming trees, all picked out in minute detail. Underneath these delights, however, lay the subterranean landscape of hell, convulsed with demons and torments. The inhabitants of the luscious gardens ate and drank and danced with no idea whatsoever of the terrors going on beneath them.

Such a painting might have been made for this place, where above ground existed the earthly delights of a stately home and below lurked an underworld, hushed and filled with horror.

At the end of the day, she returned to the billet to be greeted by a stomach-churning smell. It was heavy, greasy and slightly rotten, wafting from the kitchen.

Esme Muller put her head round Stella's door.

'Isn't Mrs Pursglove just the worst cook? She's boiling some creature's rib. She told me it's going to be stew and cabbage, with semolina for pudding. I'd rather go into town. Want to come? We're going to the Cock and Dragon with Gerda and Mimi and a couple of the other girls.'

Stella said she didn't want to. The truth was, she wanted to lie on her bed and wait for sleep to bring oblivion. She wanted to obliterate all the brutality she had heard and replace it with comforting thoughts of childhood holidays and old friends and favourite novels. But no sooner had she closed her door and lain down than she realized she would have to rouse herself. The whole point of her presence was not to listen to the prisoners but the staff. She needed to fraternize as much as possible with the others if she was ever going to find out more about the murder of Gabriel Fassbinder. She jumped up, changed out of her uniform into a skirt and blouse, and quickly inspected herself in the mirror. Her face was wan, with tired eyes, but she patted her cheeks to bring the blood up, ran a trace of lipstick round her mouth and hurried down the stairs, calling out to Mrs

Pursglove that she would have her dinner cold. Then she caught up with Esme in the lane.

Soon she found that the prospect of an evening out revived her. Esme was a clever, quick-witted girl, a little younger than Stella, with a cloud of dark hair, a sharp-featured, angular face and a ready smile. She must have heard precisely the same kind of talk that Stella had just recorded, yet she remained resolutely cheerful. She had grown up in Vienna before leaving with her family in the early 1930s to settle with relations in Kent.

'As a matter of fact, I lived in Vienna too,' said Stella. 'For five years.'

'You did? Where? Why? Tell me everything!'

The rest of the walk was filled with happy memories of more innocent times. Of palaces and parks, wine and cake, of the theatre and the opera and taking the tram to the Vienna Woods. For a while both women were utterly transported out of the gloaming of the English countryside and into another world entirely.

The Cock and Dragon was a solid red-brick place with an ivy-covered facade and a clock tower on which perched the eponymous gilded cockerel. The interior contained a broad fireplace fuelled by coke rather than coal, a snooker table with frayed baize and a pair of tables surrounded by old men playing dominoes. Mimi had changed into a white puffed-sleeve dress printed with cherries and found a corner table in the window. Three other women were gathered round it.

Stella ran through the few facts she had collected about

them. Gerda Sontag's family had resettled in Liverpool. The others, who were billeted with one of Mrs Pursglove's friends, were Daphne Longborne, a glamorous blonde and former debutante who leavened her refined manner with a salty laugh, and Helen Forsythe, who came from Dundee and, like Stella, had studied German at university. Daphne worked in the main building, censoring prisoners' letters for any snippets of information that might prove useful. Helen had been employed as a clerical officer in the WAAF when she came across a poster appealing for German speakers and submitted her name. She was sweetly pretty, with a peaches-and-cream complexion and a boyfriend serving with the British Expeditionary Force.

'Where's Tam now?' asked Gerda.

'Normandy. Or he was last week. They move around.'

'Go on. Show Stella the photograph,' laughed Daphne.

Helen brought out a picture of a man with strong, Celtic good looks, wearing the uniform of the Black Watch.

'Isn't he Errol Flynn to a T?'

All the girls laughed.

'Yes. I can definitely see it,' she said.

'Don't let Tam know it,' said Helen. 'It'll go to his head.'

'So what made you choose the ATS, Stella?'

'Well, certainly not the uniform.'

More laughter.

Stella smiled. 'It shouldn't matter, but it does. My friend can't decide between the WAAF and the Wrens. She's an actress, so costume's important.'

'Wrens every time,' said Daphne. Everyone agreed that the Wrens' outfit was the most stylish: a navy suit with a generously box-pleated skirt and brass buttons. An extra benefit was that it came with coupons for good-quality black stockings.

The conversation continued, light and teasing. Although it was surely the first time in their lives that these women had vaulted class boundaries to mingle side by side, an easy camaderie prevailed. When a group of men – fellow officers from the camp – entered and sat across the other side of the saloon bar eyeing them, the women responded with flicks of their hair and flirtatious looks. Everything about the scene was peaceful and ordinary: the soft thud of the snooker balls on baize, the murmur of conversation, the chink of glasses.

Yet Stella wondered what was really going through their minds.

Given that she had only just arrived, it was going to prove difficult to introduce the subject of Fassbinder's murder without revealing how she already knew about it. Yet the fact was, her thoughts were so full of the day's listening that it was almost impossible to think of anything else. She wondered what the others had heard today. Was it officers boasting of their exploits, or secret intelligence more useful to the war effort? Of course, they weren't allowed to say. Perhaps that was why they defaulted to a general discussion of Trent Park and their daily tribulations.

'What a place!' said Helen, in her soft Scottish burr. 'I've never seen anything like it.'

'Haven't you?' asked Daphne, languidly. Clearly, she had seen plenty of stately homes.

'Oh, Daphne! I'm surprised you haven't stayed here yourself, with all your *Tatler* friends.'

'As a matter of fact, Mummy and Daddy did come here for a house party before the war. It used to be glorious fun, apparently. I told them I was here, but obviously I couldn't tell them anything else. What they'd say if they knew, I can't imagine.'

'It scared me at first,' confessed Helen. 'When I first arrived, I kept expecting a body to fall out of a cupboard. All those panels and pillars. The place is like something out of a horror film.'

'Or a crime story,' said Esme.

At this comment, a tiny hiatus fell. It was the moment when Stella should have stepped in, probed with a question, but just as she was about to, Mimi changed the subject.

'Who needs a horror film when we already have a dragon? Mrs Pursglove! I swear she's swiping my sugar ration. Who's for another before we go home?'

On cue, the group of officers who had been eyeing them came over, and among them Stella recognised Helmut Monke, who proceeded to buy them all another round of drinks. After they had finished and were leaving the pub, Monke fell into step beside her.

'How are you finding it Miss Fry, may I ask?'

'Intense.'

'It certainly is. Sometimes, after a session, I need a long walk to cleanse my mind.'

In the darkness she could barely see his face, but she sensed the strain in his voice.

'To be honest though, when I arrived, I found it a relief.'

'A relief?'

Monke paused, then said, 'A relief in that the methods used here are preferable to the ones used elsewhere.'

'Where do you mean?'

He was speaking so quietly, she could barely hear and was forced to move closer.

'My previous deployment was at an establishment in London, in Kensington. At that place there was a different approach to getting prisoners to talk. It was rather more rigorous.'

'Surely not torture . . .?'

'Psychological. We had a cell in the basement. It was called Cell 14, and the prisoners were told they would be taken there if they did not talk. In fact, nobody was ever taken there. Merely the threat was enough.'

He fell silent and for a few moments, the only sound was the crunch of their footsteps on the road. Then he said, 'There were drugs too. Substances they injected to persuade prisoners to tell the truth.'

'And you saw this?'

'Yes. We never broke the Geneva Convention. But the reason I felt relief when I arrived here at Cockfosters was because I realised that ultimately nothing works as well as sitting a man down with a packet of cigarettes and a bottle of whiskey. Most of them are just longing to unburden themselves.'

Monke should not be talking like this, Stella knew, even if it was to a fellow listener. He knew it himself; she could tell. It constituted a direct breach of the Official Secrets Act. Yet she did not stop him. Asking people not to confide in her was the last thing to do if she wanted to glean any information about the death of Gabriel Fassbinder.

The fourth day was worse.

Stella worked constantly without a break. The other listeners barely registered each other. They were all, like her, immersed in the minds of their enemies.

She began the day monitoring a different cell, containing two U-boat crewmen who had been captured when their vessels were hit in the North Sea. She tried to picture the men as they talked, giving them seafarers' crewcut hair and tough, sea-wizened complexions. They were a taciturn pair, but they began to discuss, in a desultory way, the times when their submarines had targeted Norwegian and Swedish ships.

'What do you do with the ships you sink?' said one.

'We always allow the crew to drown. What else can you do?' replied his cellmate.

Stella was beginning to find a carapace hardening over her previous sensitivity. Perhaps this was what happened to everyone. There had to be some way that the men and women here, especially the refugees, were able to continue listening, day after day. She began to see herself as a ghostly third person in the cell, like some unfortunate psychotherapist, absorbing what she heard in silent confidence.

Intermittently she returned to the two Luftwaffe lieutenants, Scholtz and Gruber. They had resumed discussing the mechanical aspects of their planes. They were as fascinated by technical questions as they were by their attacks and kills. They relived each individual flight in detail: the weather, the performance, the missions they accomplished. Sometimes they sounded like tourists, reminiscing over the Polish countryside, and at other times the civilians themselves were the entertainment.

Gruber wanted to know what Scholtz had done when people on the ground surrendered.

'You surrender, you get hit all the same. We attacked from ten metres, and when the idiots ran, I had a good target. I had only just to hold my machine gun. I am sure some of them got a full twenty-two bullets in them. And then suddenly I scared fifty soldiers and said, "Fire, boys, fire!" and we just sprinkled them with the machine guns. In spite of that I felt the urge, before we were shot down, to shoot a man with my own hand.'

Eventually, at ten o'clock, Scholtz announced he was going to read his Karl May western, which he yet again recommended to Gruber, who replied that he was not a reader and was going to sleep.

Stella downed the headphones and collected her bicycle to go home. Wheeling it along the path past a sculpture of two Greek wrestlers, their lichened limbs frozen in an eternal grapple, she recalled Kendrick's remark.

*Everything here is miked. Even the statues in the garden.*

As she reached the lane that ran around the perimeter of the grounds, she caught a snatch of sweetness in the air and realized that it carried from the wisteria walk – the precise spot where she had first encountered Maxwell Knight eighteen months before. It smelt like the scent of a vanished world.

How impossible it was to connect these outer reaches of London, the unassuming stretches of meadow and park and woodland, with the scenes of brutality she had heard described. She dreaded to think that these rapacious men who had so efficiently conquered other countries might soon be here. She thought back to a film she had made with the GPO Film Unit; a documentary called *The First Days*, which was a compilation of scenes of ordinary British life at the start of the war: cheerful citizens filling sandbags and collecting tin helmets. Friendly dockers in neckerchiefs, miners and steelworkers holding singsongs in pubs. She wondered if war would unleash the same ferocious impulses in these people too. And what about the men she had known at work and university? Might Toby Enderby or Tom Lamont be capable of perpetrating acts of such unfettered aggression? It was too early to say. But dark forces lurked under every human psyche, that was what Harry Fox would tell her, and she forced the question from her mind.

Parking the bicycle up the narrow alley beside the house, she went into the back garden, where she found Mimi, smoking. The night air was mild, and a full moon was rising in the sky.

'I was moved shifts and I didn't want another evening in the officers' mess, so I thought I'd wait for you. Want a cup of tea? Though I have to reveal – cue fanfare – that Mrs P. has actually secured some Nescafé! So, which do you want?'

'Actually, I want a gin and tonic. But I suppose tea will do.'

In the kitchen, Mimi made a pot of tea, placed a cup in front of her, then settled herself down. Her eyes read Stella's face.

'I know how you feel. It's difficult to begin with. It haunts you. You can't stop thinking about what you've heard. But you need to, if you're going to get any sleep.'

'It's going to be hard to forget what I've heard today.'

'You mustn't forget. We need to understand what we're up against. I've been doing this for months now and every day I feel that more strongly.'

She sat, chin cupped in her hand, taking swift sips of tea, like a bird at a fountain.

'I had a pretty good idea already, of course. That's why I left. But the British need to know too. We don't want them thinking that these fine civilized Germans with their Beethoven and their literature and their philosophy aren't capable of turning into savages.'

*Savages.* This word was issued in a bitter hiss, quite at odds with her sweet countenance.

'I hate them all the more because I love my own country.'

Then she recovered herself and smiled.

'No point thinking about that now. Tell me about you, Stella. What brought you here?'

'I was . . . approached . . . by someone who knew I spoke German.'

'And where did you learn German?'

'I spent five years living in Austria. I was tutor to a family there – two boys and a girl. They were like a second family to me.'

'Oh yes, Esme told me that. How did you get that job?'

'I was recommended by my university professor. I'd read Modern Languages at Oxford.'

'Oxford! You went there!'

'Yes, I studied French and German. At Somerville College.'

'I wonder . . .'

Mimi was focusing on stirring her tea, then taking bites of a digestive biscuit.

'I mean, I imagine not, but did you ever come across a man there? His name was Robert. Robert Handel.'

Either it was the fatigue, or the emotional exhaustion of the past few days, but it was easy not to react. Stella didn't need a mirror to know that her face was inscrutable.

She frowned, as if searching her memory.

'Robert Handel? I don't think so.'

'That's a shame. He was a listener. We were friends, in a way. At least, we shared a desk. Or we did until last week.'

'Oh, really? Where is he now? Redeployed? Can you say?'

'Not exactly.'

Mimi shot a look at Stella, then glanced around, as if Mrs Pursglove might be hiding behind the kitchen door. Her fingers – violinist's fingers, with carefully rounded nails – twined nervously around the teacup.

'Something happened. Listen, I shouldn't talk about it, so this is just between us. Robert and I were working on a late-night shift. One of us would monitor and when we went off to transcribe, the other would take over. You know the form. We'd been assigned a pair of Luftwaffe men, and they were talking and talking. Rambling about everything. Life back home, their mothers' cooking, the films they liked, girls they'd had. It was late. I was longing for them to go to bed, but they just didn't seem tired. Every time the conversation seemed to be winding down, one of them would start talking again. I could hear them leaning on the windowsill of their cell, smoking cigarettes. They do that because they think it's less likely they'll be overheard, but we had a bug under the windowsill and you could hear them clear as day. Anyway, that's when they really began to talk.'

Stella sensed Mimi's knee, jiggling up and down under the table.

'The senior man was called Oberstleutnant Fassbinder. He'd been here a while, a month at least. He was tall and blond, like a north German. But the other man was new. He was younger, more junior. We had indications that this young guy would be a good talker – he'd already let out a bit of information about *X-Gerät* – that's an electronic system they've developed for their planes. It gives them direction guidance. But that night they weren't talking about technology. They were talking about Poland . . .'

Mimi paused and took a deep drag of her cigarette as if to sustain her.

'They had been in a group, flying over Poland. Fassbinder was talking mostly. It was almost like he was longing to talk about it – at night they relax a lot more and it gets more emotional between them. Fassbinder kept adding more and more detail. And the things he was saying were worse and worse. I remember him saying, *Throwing bombs has become a passion with me. One itches for it.*

'Then they began to talk about rape. Fassbinder said, *On the first day, we were being driven to the airfield and we passed a girl on the road. She was a lovely girl. When our truck went past, we all called out. I don't know what she said in return, but it wasn't friendly.* He laughed, and then he said, *Some men pulled her into the truck and you can guess what happened. She had to die the next day anyway.*

'Anyhow, at some point, the disc was full, so I passed the headphones to Robert and went to transcribe the conversation. But when I came back, Robert had become more and more tense. He didn't say anything, but his body was rigid, and his face was, you know, like thunder. At the end of our shift, when the prisoners had finally fallen asleep, he slammed down the headphones and marched out. A bit later I found him in a corner of the mess, drinking. I think he was pretty drunk already. I said something like, it was a bad day, and he said, "That Nazi bastard."'

'Fassbinder, you mean? Or the other man?'

'Definitely Fassbinder. Then he said something about Nietzsche. That Nietzsche had said something like, "He who fights with monsters should be careful in case he also becomes a monster. And if you gaze too long into an abyss, the abyss will also gaze into you."'

'What did he mean by that?'

'I have no clue. And I thought nothing more of it until the next day. That morning, Fassbinder had disappeared. And so had Robert.'

'Really? How did you know?'

'I didn't at first. I was simply told I needed to monitor a different cell. So I had no idea that anything had happened to Fassbinder until I heard a whisper among the other girls that something had occurred in the grounds. No one was quite sure what. And when I asked where Robert had gone, my officer said it was operational and I was to be assigned a new partner. It was all so confusing. And I'm still in two minds if I should say . . .'

'Say what?'

Stella drank some tea and waited patiently, knowing that when people said they couldn't tell, everything in them was longing to.

'I kept thinking about what Robert had said the evening before he vanished. How angry he was. Calling Fassbinder a bastard. Worrying about becoming a monster himself. Because after he said that, he said something else. He said an invasion was coming and he would be far more useful anywhere else but here – France, even. He didn't want to waste another minute.'

# CHAPTER 14

Harry walked through the indigo streets towards the Embankment. Behind him in the city twilight, unlit buses passed like dinosaurs, lumbering their way up the Strand. Ahead, the gunmetal-grey Thames flowed silently, massed with dark hulks of tugs and barges at its banks. He came to the balustrade beneath Westminster Bridge, from where, across the river, the fortress of County Hall loomed. To the right stood the Houses of Parliament, whose Gothic spires and turrets would once have been infused with the light of a hundred windows but were now shuttered and dark.

As the shadows of the city rose around him, a line ran through his head. *The night cometh, when no man can work.* It was a Bible quotation of which his father, Stanley Fox, was especially fond. He liked to chant it as he walked around the house. He said Samuel Johnson had had it carved on his watch.

It was also palpable nonsense. What was the Bible talking

about? In Harry's line of business, night produced endless work. Gloom, murk and confusion threw up all manner of crime. Theft, fraud and robbery grew like mushrooms in the dark.

The rush hour was long over and only a few pedestrians passed, oblivious to the figure in mackintosh and brown trilby with turned-down brim who was leaning against the wall and looking up at Big Ben. As Harry approached, the man said, 'You know that movie?'

'*The 39 Steps*?' Harry had seen it three times in a row. The first time with Jack, the second time with a woman called Violet, and the third time alone.

He followed Maxwell Knight's gaze.

'You're thinking of the part where Richard Hannay hangs on the hands of Big Ben to halt the clock.'

'That's what I like about you, Harry. A keen knowledge of popular culture.'

'Wouldn't have thought you had much time for spy stories, Mr Knight. Not when you get so much of the real thing.'

'There you'd be wrong. The fact is, spy stories are not always wide of the mark. And as far as Big Ben goes, the thought is we might have to do that ourselves, pretty soon.'

'What? Stop the clock?'

'The scientists say there's a chance that the Germans are able to determine British weather conditions from the sound of the chimes on the BBC news. It helps them work out the best weather to send their bombers.'

'You're joking.'

'It's physics, Harry. The toll of the bell sounds minutely different depending on fog and rain and so on. Something to do with acoustic energy and the atmosphere.'

Harry guessed this was the rationale behind their rendezvous. Their meetings were always arranged at different spots around London – for some reason, Knight never let him near the flat in Dolphin Square from which he conducted his agent running and where his case officers were established. Maxwell Knight, like so many in this game, liked to keep his life in compartments. The compartment with Harry's name on it involved a number of surveillance operations over the past few years – including, recently, a tail on Oswald Mosley, the fascist leader, and his beautiful aristocratic wife, Diana. Knight's intense suspicion of Mosley had been hampered by the refusal of several home secretaries to authorize a tap on his communications, with the result that Knight was obliged to deploy other methods, notably Harry Fox, in his pursuit.

'I assume you wanted to see me about this Robert Handel, Mr Knight, and I was going to say . . .'

The sentence petered out as Knight shook his head.

'No. In fact, Harry, I have a rather different reason. It's a delicate matter, but urgent all the same. You were the first operative to come to mind.'

'Pleased to hear it.'

'I don't mind saying, I have quite a regard for your work. Your memory, your persistence and so on. But most of all because certain elements within the Service warned me to tread carefully with regard to you. I always take that as better than a royal warrant.'

He paused, whipped out a handkerchief to blow his beaky nose, then pocketed the handkerchief with a snort.

'Anyhow, it's this. Intelligence has come our way in the past week from a source that we believe to be credible suggesting that the Abwehr has infiltrated three high-level spies into Britain. Two women and a man. Perhaps part of a larger German espionage network. We are, needless to say, very keen to track them down.'

Harry did not bother to ask about the source of the intelligence – that did not concern him.

'I do, of course, have a number of people reporting to me on the activities of German nationals in Britain. We have a hundred thousand registered foreigners already. But this is a matter of great importance, and the suggestion is that these characters have already spent some time in this country and know a bit about it. That way they will be able to pass credibly without attracting attention. My thought was, they may have inveigled themselves into the émigré community. Obviously, any location where refugees congregate is the perfect place for spies to hide. There's a classical story about a wooden horse . . .'

'The Trojan horse?'

'Indeed, very good.'

From the sniff of the bulbous nose, Harry got the impression that Knight was surprised at his knowledge of the Greek myths. People at MI5 were always trying to place him, but they were often mystified. He was a mackintosh-wearing freelance investigator who had read every detective novel published and could recite tracts of Shakespeare from memory. Generally, members of the security services liked their prejudices confirmed, and prejudice said that surveillance foot soldiers were rarely cultivated men of letters. But Harry's classical knowledge, not to mention his familiarity with the King James Bible and his worldly air, made him harder to categorize.

'The thing is, Harry, you already mix with these people. Foreigners. So I'd like you to take on the task of pursuing them.'

'What do we know about them? Names, ages?'

'We've no idea. And it would be foolish to ignore the possibility that this Robert Handel, or whatever he's calling himself now, could be involved. Even if he's not, we have to face the thought that the timing of these events is not necessarily coincidental. It may be that Handel is already in communication with them, and tracking down one agent may lead to the others. So I want you to step up your monitoring of the refugees you encounter.'

'You don't think the refugees themselves could tell who's a spy? Aren't these the same Nazis they're escaping from?'

'I agree, a genuine refugee might have an instinct about the people they're meeting and be naturally wary. We can deal with all that in good time. But in the meantime, I'd like you to watch out for anyone who seems in any way suspicious. Asking too many questions.'

'Sure, Mr Knight. And while we're here, I have a question myself.'

'Fire away.'

It was hard to explain. Locating needles in haystacks went with the job but Lieselotte Edelman's commission had proved more like one of those puzzles drawn by the artist Escher. On the question of finding Paul Schilling, he didn't even know where to start. However, her other problem – the lack of money – might be easier to solve, and it had occurred to him that Maxwell Knight could be the one to solve it.

'I don't want to waste your time, Mr Knight. But the fact is, I've come across a young lady who might be of value to you.'

He decided not to mention Liselotte's errant lover. The chap had plainly never made it to England and was no doubt right now being fitted for his Wehrmacht uniform.

'She's called Lieselotte Edelman. Jewish. From Berlin. She's an artist, and she needs a job.'

'How did you come across her?'

'In a professional capacity. She was looking for someone. I won't be able to help her with that, but I was wondering – what with her artistic skills – if you might be able to use her in some way.'

It was a gamble, but one of the many things that distinguished Maxwell Knight from his colleagues in the intelligence world was his penchant for employing young women in the belief that they made highly effective security operatives. A recent operation involving one of Knight's women, Olga Grey, who had infiltrated the Communist Party of Great Britain, had resulted in the trial of Percy Glading, one of the most important communist agents ever traced in Britain.

Also, Knight's eccentric curiosity made it hard for him to resist an unusual plan.

'An artist, you say?'

Exactly as Harry had hoped, interest kindled in his eyes.

'Very skilled, sir. She's a New Objectivist.'

Knight gave him a sharp look.

'And beautiful.'

Another steely glance.

'She needs a job.'

Big Ben began to sound the hour and instinctively they both glanced up at it, as though even now it was transmitting intelligence to the enemy through the vaporous air.

Then Knight said, 'Now you mention it, there might be something. In the artistic vein.'

He paused and fumbled for his pipe, then his tobacco pouch, and lit up, emitting an odour of cherry and charred wood, before continuing.

'As it happens, the problem of deterring Jerry bombers does not rest on silencing Big Ben. We have a new outfit called the Camouflage Directorate. They're gathering together artists, stage designers, cartoonists, technicians, all kinds of arty types, to engage in large-scale camouflage.'

'Painting out street names, you mean?'

'Far bigger than that. The plan is to camouflage key

bombing targets. Factories, installations, gas depots and so forth. They're fashioning nets over buildings, road signs on the rooftops. Everything that could confuse a Jerry in the air. They're building concrete cows so that from the air the rooftops look like fields. Painting scenes to make fields look full of Spitfires. You think your New Objectivist might be capable of that?'

'Certainly, sir.'

'I'll bear her in mind, then. But Harry, no matter how winsome she is, I'm not going to go employing a young German woman without the most rigorous of checks. I will make my own decisions, but you can make a start. She'll need checking inside, outside and upside down. I want you to know her better than she knows herself. I want her tailed and her flat dry-cleaned. Lovely young German ladies – and knowing you, she will undoubtedly be lovely – are not hired by British intelligence without the most intense scrutiny. She may be a little foreign bird blown off course, but she might just as well be a bird of an entirely different feather.'

CHAPTER 15

*May 7th*

Stella stood in a telephone box at Victoria station. All around her the babble of the station arose – the whistle of trains, the shouts of porters and the clatter of travellers hauling cases. A throng of troops with guns and knapsacks, heading for the British Expeditionary Force in France, were being sent off with a brass band. Families congregated amid the melee. Beneath a sign saying, *To Evacuation Trains Platform 12*, members of the Women's Voluntary Service in green tweed suits were shepherding crocodiles of evacuating children carrying small suitcases and wearing labels around their necks, alongside mothers visibly trying not to cry.

She knew that any moment now another person would appear, wanting to use the telephone, and she would have to relinquish it out of courtesy.

She had just called Harry Fox, the receiver still warm

from the previous caller and yeasty with exhaled breath. He sounded delighted to hear her voice.

'I was waiting for you to call. Mr Knight's getting nervous. He says it's an urgent case and we've turned up nothing. Unless you have something.'

'Not much.'

'We should meet anyway. Pool our thoughts.'

'I can't, Harry.'

'Why? Where are you?'

'At Victoria station, waiting for the boat train.'

'The boat train?' His voice emerged slightly choked. 'You mean the Continent?'

'Yes.'

'How long will you be there?'

'I don't know.'

'But . . .'

It was not like Harry Fox to be lost for words. At that moment, however, Stella was glad of it. Quickly, she jumped in.

'Listen, Harry, I have to go. The train's about to leave. I won't be long, and I promise I'll call you as soon as I can.'

Then she put her finger on the hook and cut the line.

Yet she did not go. Coins clenched tightly in her fist, she peered out at the concourse, reflecting on the conversation she had had at Trent Park only hours before.

★

She had woken at six and dressed swiftly. Mrs Pursglove was already in her housecoat, setting the breakfast table. Stella had refused either a bowl of porridge or a slice of toast, earning a suspicious look, and set off by bicycle before the other girls were up. As soon as she reached the big house, she had gone to Colonel Kendrick's office and told Margy that she needed to see him urgently. To her relief Kendrick was already in, sitting behind his desk bent over papers. He beckoned her in with surprise and took off his spectacles. She reported her conversation with Mimi Friedlander word for word.

Kendrick had received it all in silence. He had a way of listening that made it hard to read his thoughts – the essential diplomat's tool, that was doubly useful for a senior member of the intelligence service. He stayed intensely, formidably still, fingers steepled beneath his chin, and remained like that for a good few moments after she had finished. Eventually, he pushed back his chair and went across to the window, where he stood, hands on hips, staring out at the gracious vista.

'So, the same night Gabriel Fassbinder was murdered, Robert Handel was expressing his disgust. Calling him a bastard and swearing that something should be done. Worrying that he himself was becoming a monster. I admit, Miss Fry, it looks pretty cut and dried. You think it's true?'

'I think so. What Mimi said about him going to France; well, the fact is, it chimed with something Robert once told me. I would have mentioned it, if I'd remembered. Although he himself is German, I remember he said to me once that his sister had moved to France. She'd run an international bookshop in Berlin, and she dealt with a lot of foreign writers. Once the National Socialists arose, the pressure on her was tremendous. Her windows were broken by stormtroopers, and she was under constant suspicion of consorting with anti-Nazi elements. Eventually, she'd been forced to move. I think she married a Frenchman and went to Paris.'

'You think he might have followed her?'

'I couldn't say.'

Kendrick remained standing, back turned, studying the point at which the expansive lawn shaded into woodland.

Then he wheeled around decisively to face her.

'The only solution is to go there. To Paris. Catch the next train to London and proceed on the boat train. Sergeant Jenkins will provide money and a travel warrant. There's no time to lose. If Robert Handel has taken knowledge of this place with him, let alone any of the intelligence we have garnered, then all our endeavours are fruitless. If the enemy realizes that we have learned any of his secrets he will retaliate with false information, and we'll all be on a wild goose chase. If we have been nurturing a spy in our ranks, we can't possibly keep that information to ourselves. We might as well pack up and go home.'

The calamity of this prospect appeared physically to wind him. It had taken many long months, and the ingenuity of numerous specialists, to establish the operation at Trent Park. Now exhaustion seemed to press down on his shoulders like a lead weight as he strode across the room and sank onto the edge of the desk.

'I have faith in you, Miss Fry. Knight says you are quick-witted and resourceful. You speak French and, of course, you know Handel, so you'll have no trouble recognizing him.'

'I might have no trouble recognizing him, sir, but I'm not sure how I'd go about finding him.'

Kendrick was scribbling on a sheet of notepaper engraved with the address Hotel Victoria, Northumberland Avenue. He handed it to her.

'This might help. This chap seems to know absolutely everyone. I've never met anyone with so complete a list of contacts, and he never forgets a face. He's recently been appointed head of our Bureau of Propaganda in Paris. His job is supposedly liaising with the French Ministry of Information, but in practice he's sounding out the feeling on the ground, amassing information, recruiting informers. I'm sure you've heard of him. His name's Noël Coward.'

'The playwright?'

'That's the one. Amusing chap.'

She folded the note and stashed it in her pocket.

'A word of warning. Be careful, Miss Fry. Paris is already full of Gestapo spies. They're recruiting petty criminals and building their own network of informers. They'll be especially alert to an Englishwoman recently arrived with no apparent occupation. Stay alert, and if you are compromised, stay silent.'

He was regarding her solemnly. 'We have no time to lose. The German army is currently trampling Poland, but they have every intention of moving westwards. Every country in Western Europe is on edge. If – indeed, when – the German invasion goes ahead, Paris could be rapidly overrun.'

The whistle of trains and the calls of porters broke into her thoughts. Her train was due to depart from Platform 2 in ten minutes. A clergyman with clerical collar and bowler hat was marching in determined fashion towards the telephone box, with a look that said that this was wartime and feminine gossip should make way for important male communications. She turned her back on him and, ignoring the sticker demanding *Is Your Call Really Necessary?*, lifted the receiver once again and dialled Admiralty 251. It was picked up on the second ring.

'Hello, Tom.'

'Stella?' He sounded rushed.

'Yes. I'm sorry to call you at work. I just wanted to say . . .'

'Where are you?'

'Victoria station.'

'Oh. I see. Look, I'm sorry, but can this wait?'

'Yes. Of course.'

Clattering the receiver back into its cradle, she leaned her head for a moment against the cool glass of the cubicle, cursing herself.

# CHAPTER 16

For the last few days, Harry Fox had embarked on his own version of the Grand Tour, in this case a meandering journey through the dives and dens of the East End, the squalid pubs of Fitzrovia and Camden, and the plentiful cafés of Bloomsbury, Waterloo and Soho. Places where the conversation was not overly intellectual, and the alcohol was rough enough to dress a wound with.

He had sat. He had chatted. He had joined in singsongs, pledging along with Vera Lynn that 'We'll Meet Again', and chorusing with Elsie Carlisle:

> *Everybody says I'm old-fashioned*
> *To sit on the things that are rationed,*
> *So pinch all my ham and my plum and apple jam*
> *But please leave my butter alone.*

No amount of fraternizing, however, had turned up a trace of any recently arrived Germans.

Harry was frustrated. He was missing Stella. They had only just reunited and already she had disappeared. He was frantic with curiosity about her trip to the Continent and cursing himself for failing to discover where she had moved since the forced evacuation of her flat at his own hands. Now he had no way of getting hold of her and he was going to have to trust that she would come back to him as she had promised.

He had found in Stella Fry something that he never expected – a woman he could talk to without front or pretence. There was something about her that stimulated and resonated with him, as though his brain was a tuning fork and they were both in the same register. He might even call her a friend, until he came up with a better description. He was desperate to know what she might be doing abroad and deflected his annoyance onto the person of Maxwell Knight, who had set them on this two-pronged goose chase. How were they supposed to work as a team if they were unable to communicate? He was longing to interrogate Knight, but he could not plausibly get in contact again without something concrete to report. Consequently, he had no help to give Lieselotte Edelman.

This train of thought led, inevitably, to a familiar catechism of concerns. As he walked the streets of the city, his shadow-self loomed before him; the self that contained all his fears and doubts and dismays. Dismay at the relationship with his father, dismay at his relationship with himself, memories of the last war. Fears of what the next war would bring.

As he turned the corner into Fleet Street, however, his mood brightened. He had work. He had Jack. He had met Stella Fry. By every measure he was winning at life, or at least losing more slowly.

He headed for the Bell Tavern. The Bell was a popular haunt for employees of all the national newspapers, and Harry liked journalists. In another life he might well have been one. He admired their capacity to talk to anyone, high or low, their rapacious inquisitiveness and their cynicism about human nature, which tended to coincide with his own. They were fruitful sources of rumour and hearsay – whether about politics or show business – and they were always ready to share their intelligence for the price of a couple of pints. They understood that gossip was more than a social lubricant – it was an alternative intelligence network, and a route into the closed corridors of power. Detectives and journalists had a lot in common, except that journalists were social animals, hunting in packs, whereas his was a singular profession not known for its collegiate spirit.

The first thing he saw as he swung through the saloon doors was Sunny Hoss.

Sunny – whose parents surely could not have been responsible for this devastating misnomer – was a freelance journalist who had worked on most of the newspapers at one time or another. The *Daily Mirror*, the *Daily Mail*, and more august publications like the *Daily Telegraph*, had all called on his investigative skills. He was often to be found rooted in a pub corner, like some old gargoyle carved into a wooden bench, the sunken jaw and overhanging eyebrows suggesting a touch of the medieval. He had the deceptively rheumy eyes of a Rembrandt portrait, yet he was blessed with unusually acute powers of perception that were handy for a journalist but invaluable for his other profession, which was as a part-time MI5 operative.

They had met the previous autumn in the unlikely surroundings of Wormwood Scrubs prison. This grim edifice had been cleared of its inmates and, with no change of decor, other than the addition of a few metal filing cabinets, the odd bookshelf, wooden chairs and deal tables, reallocated to the staff of MI5. Behind a steel door, in a narrow cell, Harry's former employer, Mr Flint of MI5 B division, had effected a typically economical introduction.

'Hoss. Fox.'

The two men regarded each other with minimal interest.

Flint, grizzled and wiry, drew up his petite frame portentously.

'It won't come as news to either of you that my in-tray is overflowing. My card index now contains more than three thousand suspicious persons. I'm receiving a hundred new reports a day of the Enemy Within. I've got everything from mysterious figures who have been dropped by submarine off the coast to foreigners in Epsom holding maps. Collaborators, spies, saboteurs. And every one of them needs checking and eliminating.'

'I'm working through them, Mr Flint,' said Harry.

'I'm aware of that.' Flint smiled his cruel little smile. 'But I hope you won't mind my saying, Harry, you could learn a lot from Hoss here. He's half German, as it happens, and he's one of our most creative operatives. The other day he identified an enemy agent who was working as a taxi driver. Hailed the cab and started chatting to him in German. They got on like a house on fire. Then Hoss had him drive all the way here to Wormwood Scrubs, where we were able to arrest him on site. That's what I call imagination.'

Hoss received this compliment impassively.

'Anyhow,' Flint continued, 'this particular commission involves the both of you. We're getting reports that Nazi sympathizers may be infiltrating the Wembley engineering works. They need to be flushed out. I'd like you to work together on this.'

The plan was that Harry and Sunny should enter the workplace and approach potential traitors to assess whether they would be prepared to help the Fatherland in case of invasion. Harry would play the roguish spiv with flexible morals, calculating on a German victory, and Sunny the diehard Nazi agent. The people they approached were asked if they would be prepared to provide details of engines, machinery, or weapons manufacture. Perhaps the secrets of government ministries? To Harry's surprise, dozens volunteered. Some even offered accommodation for any Nazis who happened to arrive early. They provided their names for inclusion on a confidential list to be forwarded to the Gestapo, or in this case to the office of Mr Flint.

Now, months on, Sunny was huddled in a corner, his great Easter Island face scowling over a copy of the *Daily Worker*. At his feet, Max, a bull terrier, thumped his tail. Harry knelt down and ran his hands over the saggy skin of Max's thick neck, breathing in the musky dog smell and braving his ecstatic lick, before sliding into the seat opposite.

'Hello, Sunny.'

'Harry Fox.' He folded away the paper. 'This is a surprise.'

'Nice one, I hope.'

Sunny's expression did not confirm that.

'As it happens, Sunny, I'm wondering if you might be able to help me. It's a little piece of business.'

'Flint's business?'

'Very much not. Flint's not to know, actually. I'm after a German.'

'What kind of German?'

'Of great interest to the authorities.'

'You'll have to do better than that.'

Harry glanced around him.

'OK. This Jerry has killed another Jerry.'

The lizard eyelids rose a fraction.

'Own goal?'

'Yes, but complicated. Even I don't know half of it. The

man's name is Handel. Robert Handel. Or it was when they last looked.'

'Handel?'

'Like the composer.'

Sunny was giving nothing away. 'If your one Jerry is dead, and they know who killed him, why are they so keen to track the other one down?'

'Maybe they think he'll go after other Germans.'

'Like we do?'

'As I said, it's complicated.' Harry cleared his throat. 'The thing is, Sunny, you know I'm not allowed access, so I wonder if you might be able to help, off the books. Have a look at Flint's registry.'

Flint's registry was a card-index system containing the background and movements of any individuals considered subversive or hostile to the nation. Thousands of German, Italian and Austrian nationals were there, all graded according to their potential for subversion and the risk they posed to national security. Known agents were separated from those who were merely alien, and each was noted by age, address, aliases and profession.

'Have a chat with Janet. The brunette there,' Harry went on. 'Let you into a little secret, she's sweet on you. You never know where it might lead. See if my chap goes by any other names.'

'Do you know how many Germans they have on file? Must be five thousand.'

'Knowing Flint, he lists them alphabetically. It can't take long.'

'Sorry, Harry.'

'I'll owe you.'

'No can do.'

Then, perhaps because Harry was still looming across from him, cutting out the light, he said, 'Have you thought of asking Irene?'

*Irene.* The name caught Harry by surprise. But that was in another time. And besides, the woman was as good as dead to him.

Irene O'Malley was another of Maxwell Knight's employees, as well as a sometime lover of Harry himself. She had bright blue Irish eyes, skin like fresh milk and hair as red and gold as a sunset. She had worked as a croupier and a children's nanny, but when Harry first bumped into her in 1937, she was on an operation at the Hippodrome. She had been employed to stand stock-still in a cardboard shell, posing as Botticelli's Venus, wearing a nude body stocking and a flowery headdress. This act she had repeated at a series of London clubs and casinos, gathering handsome tips but more importantly, salacious gossip – what politician was sleeping with whose wife, which aristocrat was fraternizing with a hotel bellboy – all information that Knight could deploy in his arsenal of enticement and threats. As soon as they met, Harry had fallen hard for Irene, and they had enjoyed a happy summer in her spare afternoons, meeting up in her attic flat in Holborn, until she'd turned to him casually one day and said, 'This is only for fun, darling. You know that, right? Don't take it seriously. I have other fish to fry.'

For a while his heart was as broken as a beer bottle on a Saturday night, but time and Violet had helped mend it, at least well enough that it could be broken again.

'Irene O'Malley? How could she help?'

'She's working at the Danube Café.'

'Where's that?'

'The Danube Bar and Social Club. North London. It's full of Germans. Irene's keeping a watch there.'

It made sense that Knight would have put an agent into the epicentre of the émigré community. It was part of how he kept control, to have his people, especially his women, planted in those places where the safety of the nation might be undermined.

'If anyone can help you,' said Sunny, 'it's her.'

Buoyed by this lead, Harry hurried up Fleet Street towards the Strand and Trafalgar Square. It was almost lunchtime and he reckoned he might just be in time to catch Myra Hess at the National Gallery. He was there with two minutes to spare. He paid his shilling and filed into the hall just ahead of the pianist as she strode onto the stage — a Wagnerian heroine in a twinset, with a tight collar of pearls and hair in earphone braids. He found an empty seat next to a young woman and squeezed in, muttering apologies. She was sitting scar-side, and as the first notes rose she turned her head and smiled at him, before she caught sight of his scar and her smile faded.

It was often like that with women. Harry tried not to care. Until they had been exposed to the magnetism of his personality it was understandable. He recalled his last encounter with B4A, the clever woman who ran the Soviet desk in counter-espionage.

*You have a scar on your face, Harry, and don't worry, it's fading fast, even if you can't help being aware of it. But there are other scars, aren't there? And they haven't faded. I wanted to say, there are people — good people — who can help you.*

*Expensive people?*

*Maybe. But you may find it more helpful to consult them than the bottle.*

She had a point. It was certainly true that Harry had spent so long trailing other people, and rifling about in other lives, he barely knew himself any more. For a while, he had considered digging deeper into his psyche, and he could imagine paying good money to explore it further in the oak-panelled consulting rooms of Hampstead or Harley Street. For now, though, he preferred to consult the traditional amber wisdom, at least until it ran out, along with gin and chocolate.

He mulled over these thoughts throughout the concert, and when it was over and he reached Goodwin's Court, the telephone was ringing. He galloped up the stairs, heart pumping. It must Stella again, with more information.

But when he grabbed the receiver, it was quite a different proposition.

# CHAPTER 17

The boat train lurched past the London suburbs, then through the brilliant, luminous, spring-green fields of Kent until they reached Dover, where they were loaded onto a steamer. As Stella stood on the deck with the wind whipping her hair, she stared back at the receding cliffs of the English coast full of trepidation at the task ahead. Who was to say that Robert Handel's quotation of Nietzsche, *He who fights with monsters should be careful in case he also becomes a monster*, uttered to Mimi in a moment of high emotion, meant anything at all? Most likely this was a fruitless visit to a city living on its nerves. She did not have the faintest clue where to start her search. At least Colonel Kendrick had paid for the tickets.

Despite this, once the ferry reached Dunkirk and the sound of French voices rose up around her as the porters bustled with luggage and the passengers found their place in the connecting train, the familiar irresistible excitement of travel obliterated, for a moment, all these anxieties.

Stella knew nothing, really, about Paris. She had only ever seen it through a tourist's eyes. She had made a couple of trips there with the Gatzes, staying on the Left Bank in the 6th arrondissement, attending the opera, and drifting through the galleries. Staring up at the Eiffel Tower and at the splintered violet rose window of Notre Dame. Sitting in restaurants eating blanquette de veau, or white-fleshed fish with exquisite sauces, glistening chicken, caramelized potatoes, towering millefeuilles stacked with fresh berries and crêpes Suzette, swimming in butter.

Leaving the train at the Gare du Nord she decided to walk, even if it meant lugging her valise with her. Besides, it was not as if she could afford a taxi. Her plan was to make her way to the city centre, cross the Seine and find the cheapest hotel possible on the Left Bank.

Paris smelled exactly as she remembered. The little gusts of baking smells as she passed patisseries, the chastening, steel scent of incense issuing from a church door, the urinous stink of drains and the faint tang of something sweaty and animal. It conjured images of bars thick with the smoke of Gitanes and rats swarming up the riverside like a furry tide from the Seine.

Yet now the air was charged with something else. It was charged with fear.

As she progressed down the boulevard de Magenta, she passed knots of people standing on street corners in tense conversation. Posters announcing *Ordre de Mobilisation Générale* were pasted onto walls. At the place de la République a jostling queue had formed at a news-stand, as the afternoon editions were being unloaded from a van. No sooner were they on the stand than people fell on them, passing the papers to each other once they had scanned the headlines. Parisians sipping coffee at the pavement bars and cafés, who might normally be discussing the latest plays, or cinema, or love affairs, now had only one topic of conversation.

It might be springtime in Paris, but there was no joy about it, not this spring.

The streets were far dustier than she remembered, and the shop windows were crisscrossed with tape. The traffic was as choked as ever; the narrow streets were crowded with badly parked Renaults and Citroëns, and bicycles flung carelessly against walls. Towards the Marais, the cobbled maze of streets that made up the Jewish corner, a rash of graffiti appeared on the ancient walls: *Death to the Jews* and *Vive le Front Populaire*. On the door of one apartment a message had been posted: *Three Jews here killed themselves. Course of action recommended to others.*

She stopped at a small park in the 3rd arrondissement, the Square du Temple. The grass was lush and the pond in the centre was populated by ducks, paddling and quarrelling, oblivious to the human turmoil around them. To one side, in a sandy children's playground, small boys and girls were playing with yo-yos, reeling and unreeling them like prayer beads, as if dissipating nervous energy.

She sat on a bench in the dappled shade, next to an elderly woman in a black coat and hat who smiled at her broadly.

'What is everyone frightened of? We had this trouble a year ago and nothing happened.'

Although Stella had resolved to spend as little money as possible, she was hungry. Close by, on the corner of the rue des Archives, was a bar with a cheerful scarlet awning. She ducked inside and ordered a bowl of soup. The *soupe à l'oignon*, when it arrived, was richly aromatic, its surface glistening and crowned with a piece of toasted bread and melting cheese. A small basket of crusty baguette was placed on the table beside it. As she began to eat, the waiter stood by expectantly.

'You must pay before you eat.'

She looked up at him in surprise.

He nodded towards the unblemished sky and shrugged.

'We have sirens constantly, mademoiselle. We often find the meal is interrupted and our patrons forget to pay.'

As Stella ate, she tried to remember everything she could about Robert Handel. He liked poetry, she remembered, and enjoyed declaiming it. He knew his way around the paths and byways of European literature the way other men knew their way around their hometown. He carried a volume of Rilke everywhere. Once she'd asked for his help with a translation from Ovid's *Metamorphoses*. There had been no Latin at her school, and she had needed to cram in a hurry to pass the Oxford examination, but her ability was rudimentary at best and no match for the men from public schools who had studied Latin throughout their schooldays.

She had been working on the part where Orpheus the lyre player loses his bride Eurydice on his wedding day and descends to the underworld to claim her. Eurydice agrees to follow him up to the world of mortals, but only on the condition that Orpheus never looks back. If he did, she would be turned to stone. Orpheus did look back, and his wife was forced to return to the kingdom of Hades. At his own request, Orpheus was violently killed so that he could join her.

It went against Stella's independent nature – not to mention her pride – to solicit help from other undergraduates, but she was in a panic, close to an essay deadline, and Handel happened to be walking back from a tutorial alongside her. The episode had cemented their friendship. After that, the two of them had talked more often. Once he confided in Stella how he had first become interested in literature.

'My sister Ursula ran an international bookshop in Wilmersdorf, Berlin. She was older than me, and when I was a boy, she'd let me help behind the counter. I loved it. I used to stand in that bookshop and imagine that I could hear the whispered voices of all the poets and all the writers in history, speaking just to me.'

'How poetic!'

'I suppose it was. And it's probably why I ended up at Oxford.'

'What happened to Ursula?'

'She fell in love with a Frenchman and moved to Paris. She opened another bookshop there. It was a wise decision. Selling foreign editions in Berlin had become intolerable.'

Politics was never far from his thoughts and whenever they strayed onto the topic, Handel became bitter. The Treaty of Versailles was reckless and unfair, certain to stir up needless anger. The ending of the war had been badly handled. Germany had been dealt an injustice.

Stella racked her brains for any more memories, but nothing came. Other than the fact that even when Robert Handel was at his most argumentative and contrary, he was also at his most charming.

After finishing the soup, she headed down towards the Seine, and onto the Left Bank, towards the boulevard Saint-Germain. In the rue Jacob she passed a hotel with a grey shuttered facade, from whose window a plump black cat was watching. It blinked its golden eyes at her, and on this impulse alone she went inside.

It was a shabby place. The marble floor was pocked and cracked. The walls were decked with ancient monochrome photographs of Edwardian Paris – ladies in long dresses and high lace collars, gentlemen with elaborate waxed moustaches, promenading in the Tuileries. The reception was deserted, but when she rang the bell a middle-aged man with oiled hair and wearing a linen suit appeared.

'*Anglaise.*' His eyes narrowed distrustfully as he took her details. '*Quelle surprise. Vous êtes en vacance, mademoiselle?*'

'*Oui.*'

'*Il n'y a pas beaucoup de touristes ici en ce moment.*'

Up a flight of scuffed stairs, the *patron* showed her a room containing an iron bedstead on top of which was a thin, unpromising-looking mattress covered with an equally thin blanket, slightly stained. The window was lined by a green thread of mould and the air held a faint smell of sweat.

She took it.

# CHAPTER 18

*May 8th*

The next day the scent of jasmine drifting through the open window woke her up and for a moment she forgot where she was. The smell evoked a little fragment of her past, but she could not pin it down. All she knew was that it made her happy.

She lay in bed for a while as stripes of sun slid through the shutters, before jumping up and washing in the tiny basin. She hadn't brought many clothes, so she dressed as she had arrived, in a dark-navy skirt and jacket with a white blouse underneath. To brighten it up, from her suitcase she took a silk scarf printed with tiny blue birds, which she tied at the neck. Then she reached for a pair of sunglasses, grabbed her bag and hurried out.

It had rained overnight, but now the sun on the Seine was incandescent and beads of rain sparkled on windows and car bonnets. Along the river, the pale beige of the parapets was smudged with soot and patches of moss, and the lime trees, still clad in the bright green of spring, released bursts of fragrance to mingle with the smell of wet stone. Near-empty *bateaux-mouches* ploughed slow furrows through the water. Jackdaws with grey napes, slightly different to their British cousins, applied themselves to a discarded baguette in the gutter. Everything around her was humming with life: the cat whisking its tail on a windowsill, the fat little dog nosing the lamp posts, and the birds darting in the cloud-scattered sky.

A ripple of elation ran through her. Despite the urgency of her mission, it was May, after all, and this was Paris.

The vast facade of Notre Dame was piled with sandbags that reached the full height of the massive portals. Yet all around, the carts of the flower sellers still blazed with colour, as though to say that, despite such uncertainty, decoration was required. The streets and squares were dressed in a painterly beauty and waiters were setting out tables and red-and-white-chequered chairs outside their pavement cafés.

She stopped at the church of Saint-Gervais, walked along the rue des Barres, and found a café called Chez Julien, where she had breakfast, consisting of a large flaky croissant and a *café au lait*. As she ran her finger over the plate to collect every last crumb, she scanned *Le Matin*. RC Paris had defeated Olympique de Marseille 2-1 in the Coupe de France. John Steinbeck had won a Pulitzer Prize for

*The Grapes of Wrath.* The 1940 Olympic Games had been formally cancelled.

She brought out a postcard of the Eiffel Tower and paused for a moment, fingering her pearls reflexively, then took out a pen and wrote, *Dear Cecil, I hope all is well with you. I'm enjoying Paris and the weather is glorious. Hoping to see you soon, Stella.*

She had no idea what he would make of it. It was enigmatic at best, but then Cecil enjoyed enigmas. She hoped he would draw the conclusion that she had taken up Maxwell Knight's offer and was in pursuit of Fassbinder's killer. And it was true – she very much hoped to see Cecil again, before too long.

She addressed the postcard to Professor Cecil Fairfax, Elmwood Cottage, Elmwood, Oxfordshire, and dropped it back in her bag. She would post it later, but just the writing of it helped. It made her feel less lonely, and it reinforced the impression she was keen to convey: that she was simply a woman on holiday trying to escape the hotbed of international affairs with an improving trip to the Sainte-Chapelle or Versailles, taking a look at the Panthéon or Napoleon's tomb at Les Invalides.

Which could not be further from the truth.

Since the day, just a week ago, when Maxwell Knight had suggested to her that she might be surveilled, she had been intensely aware of her surroundings. The café was walled with mirrors, which helped her keep watch on the other customers and anyone who entered or left. She had attracted glances as she came in, but they were polite and, if curious, at least not suspicious. As the waiters delivered cups of chocolate and coffee, her ears strained for scraps of conversation, and she was startled to catch the sound of English alongside the French and Italian. Turning her head slightly, she saw two men who were discussing their 'company' and deduced that they must be officers, on leave from the British Expeditionary Force.

She had no idea where her gift for languages had come from. Her mother Nancy spoke nothing but English, yet Stella had found the rhythms of French and German easy to follow and had won a scholarship to Oxford on the strength of it. She guessed it was courtesy of her father, the charming Irishman who had loved language and revelled in the sound of words, whether it be Yeats or Joyce or merely the lyrics of 'Molly Malone', which he had sung to her as a child.

As she listened, she stared down at *Le Matin* without seeing it. How extraordinary to think that the murder of an unknown German officer should have brought her here. A person she had never met.

Who had been killed by a man she had not seen for a decade.

Yet she had no idea how to go about finding him. She walked north towards Les Halles, through the stalls with their mountains of vegetables and slabs crowded with fish, all rainbow scales and glazed opalescent eyes. She passed the Bourse, busy with dark-suited stockbrokers coming and going, and admired the flamboyant Gothic of Saint-Eustache. She lingered at the shopfronts. A confectioner on the Avenue de l'Opéra was selling chocolates in a box shaped like a gas mask. In the Champs-Élysées she stopped at the window of Guerlain and stared at the stoppered crystal bottles with their gilded lattice and velvet ribbons, knowing that in another world she would be trying on the perfumes and dabbing scent on her wrists. She drifted down the Galerie Vivienne in the rue des Petits Champs – an exquisite arcade walled with antique dealers and hat shops, yet even as she lingered among the racks of old prints, rifling blindly through pictures of Napoleon and Josephine, her mind was working hard. She was looking for a man, not a bargain.

At the Arc de Triomphe she turned left in the direction of the Trocadéro and heard, from an open window, the strains of Maurice Chevalier's 'Paris sera toujours Paris':

> *Plus on réduit son éclairage*
> *Plus on voit briller son courage*
> *Sa bonne humeur et son esprit.*

As a popular hit the song was hugely successful. Every waiter and shopgirl could hum it. Now, though, it sounded not sweet and jaunty, but fiercely defiant.

It took a while before the obvious solution dawned on her. Robert Handel's sister had owned a bookshop. Surely, if he had come to this city, he would have tried to make contact with her. Thus it followed, if Stella was going to stand any chance of finding him, bookshops were where she should look.

Paris was a city that loved books. From the damp cases of the bouquinistes, the outdoor bookstalls along the banks of the Seine with their mouldy leather volumes and uncut pages, all the way to the shops in the grand marble-floored nineteenth-century galleries that bisected the city. So it was impossible to know where to start.

She decided to begin with the only bookshop she had heard of in Paris: Shakespeare and Company at 12 rue de l'Odéon. She knew it was a legendary place, run by an American bookseller called Sylvia Beach and frequented by celebrated writers like Gertrude Stein, F. Scott Fitzgerald, T. S. Eliot and Ezra Pound. Samuel Beckett and Ernest Hemingway had used it as a lending library. Others crowded into its narrow confines for evening debates. She pushed open the door to find a warm, sunny space with bare floorboards, crowded with tables on which volumes were stacked, in no seeming order. On the walls, photographs of Walt Whitman, Edgar Allan Poe and Oscar Wilde stared down alongside a pair of watercolours by William Blake. Despite its celebrated popularity, the shop was completely empty apart from a silver-haired man with small round glasses and a goatee beard who was thumbing through the stacks on a table. Further inside, along a book-lined labyrinth, a passage led to an inner courtyard. There was no sign of Sylvia Beach herself, but when Stella went through, she found a girl with sleek brown hair, putting labels in books.

'Excuse me, mademoiselle. I'm looking for a German woman called Ursula Handel. She may not be called that any more, but I believe she used to have a bookshop here in Paris. And she has a brother, Robert. I wonder if you might have heard of either of them.'

The girl gave a Parisian shrug, the kind that mixed indifference with disdain in equal measure. A few minutes later Stella received a similar shrug in the bookstore opposite, on the rue de Condé, and later another at a shop on the corner of the rue des Écoles, where she noticed the goatee-beard man again, with his back to her, consulting a shelf of nineteenth-century novels She got the same response at another shop, beyond the Panthéon, in the rue Gay-Lussac.

Each place Stella visited she asked the same question, yet each time she encountered nothing but shaking heads and shuttered faces.

By late afternoon her feet were aching, and she had achieved nothing. She was beginning to realize just how crazy this hunt of hers was, and wondered why Colonel Kendrick had ever imagined she might succeed. Any confidence he had in her was surely misplaced, and she could only assume that Cecil, from old affection, had wildly overestimated her abilities. Well, Kendrick would soon find out the truth. She would return from the trip with nothing to show for it and would no doubt be back at the Film Unit within days. At least Toby Enderby would be pleased.

These reflections entirely crushed her earlier high spirits and she decided to return to the hotel and rest for a while, before finding a small café for supper.

The hall was deserted. The black cat was there again, curled on a chair, but there was no sign of the *patron*, nor any desk clerk lounging behind the reception table. She trudged up the stairs, shut the door behind her, and closed the shutters. Then she slipped off her shoes and massaged her feet before pulling off her skirt, jacket and blouse and lying flat out on the uncomfortable bed. To the sound of birds singing in the streets outside, she dozed off.

It must have been half an hour later when she awoke to an unfamiliar creaking noise. Without stirring, she could see across the room that the handle of the door was being slowly turned. The movement was gentle, yet purposeful. By sheer chance she had locked the door when she came in, but at the threshold, where the door met the floorboards, was a gap, and in the sliver of light she could just make out the shape of two dark boots. The handle moved up and down three times, and then, and after a small nudge and another attempt to shift the door, the unknown person retreated.

Stella lay motionless as the footsteps receded down the corridor. Her ears strained to analyze the sounds of the building: the clank and groan of the plumbing, the distant rattle of a window and the echoes of doors slamming down the stone staircase. She told herself there was no reason to be suspicious. This was a *pension*, after all, and it was entirely possible that the owner was performing some sort of check – an evening service – or maybe seeking to change the bed linen. Yet if that was the case, would he not have knocked? Or indeed have a key?

The words of Colonel Kendrick ran through her mind.

*Paris is full of Gestapo spies. They're recruiting petty criminals and building their own network of informers. They will be especially alert to an Englishwoman recently arrived with no apparent occupation. Stay alert, and if you are compromised, stay silent.*

Might it be possible that she had already aroused suspicion? Her mind was calculating rapidly. The impulse to flee was intense, yet she forced herself to remain still for several minutes more before getting up and putting on her clothes. Then she picked up her passport and the scrap of paper containing Noël Coward's address, stashed them in her bag, and left the room.

# CHAPTER 19

The location of Harry Fox's office in Goodwin's Court, just off St Martin's Lane, was superbly positioned for all the theatres and high-end restaurants he never went to. But it was also perfect for his favourite pub. As he walked through the West End that evening, the voice of his father, Stanley Fox, barged yet again into his thoughts, with one of his familiar Old Testament tags. *Eat, drink, and be merry, for tomorrow we die.* The British were certainly taking that to heart. Despite the blackout, the dance halls were bulging and the bars were full.

The French House in Dean Street had walls the colour of dried blood, which was convenient considering the brawls that erupted frequently amid its clientele at closing time. It was festooned with photographs of famous singers and Hollywood actors, giving the misleading impression that it was a favourite haunt of stars of the silver screen. The fact was, the tiny space and gloomy wood panelling was popular with artists, only they tended to be the penniless sort, along with street walkers and journalists, and a few actual French people, who could be found propping up the bar drinking Pernod and Ricard.

Harry thrust open the swing doors to a gust of beer and tobacco, caught his reflection in the mirror behind the bar and straightened his tie. The woman who had called him, Lieselotte Edelman, was sitting in a corner beneath a signed photograph of Maurice Chevalier, wearing a white blouse with a sweetheart neckline and puffed sleeves, a tight skirt and a little black beret on her glossy head. She was staring down at the sticky tabletop, immersed in her thoughts and nursing what looked like a port and lemon. In the smoke-filled air of the French House, she might have been a girl from a Renoir painting, symbolizing existential ennui.

When he approached, she looked up and her face fell.

'I'm afraid I'm going to disappoint you, Mr Fox.'

'I think that's very unlikely.'

A frown creased her clear brow.

'No. I am, really.'

'Is this about payment, because if it is . . . ?'

'No. Not exactly. It's more . . . it's more that I don't need you to do the job any more.'

'You don't want me to find your man?'

'He's not my man, but no.'

'You mean he turned up in the end without any help?'

Harry drew out a cigarette and patted his pockets for

a light. She unclasped her handbag and pushed a book of matches towards him.

'He didn't. But it doesn't matter any more. I can see there's no point looking for a person who could be anywhere. I don't want to waste your time. There's a war on and I know there are more serious jobs to be done, even for men who . . .'

She faltered to a halt.

'Men who aren't fighting,' he prompted.

She smiled. 'Detectives who have important cases to consider.'

On the one hand, that was true, but on the other hand, Harry badly wanted to keep doing an impossible commission for no money, so long as it meant seeing this goddess in a black beret.

'Is there nothing more I can do for you?'

'Well, I would still very much like to find a job.'

'As it happens, I made a start on that. I had a word with someone. I don't want to get your hopes up, but he might be able to find something for you in the artistic line.'

Lieselotte reached forward impulsively and grasped his hand.

'Do you really mean it? That's wonderful! What would I be doing?'

'I can't promise anything as yet.' He might have backtracked, but she was still holding his hand. 'My friend is working on it, and I'll let you know as soon as . . .'

As soon as he had performed an exhaustive battery of

background checks, visited her home and circulated her photograph among his more dubious acquaintance.

'I can hardly believe it. I was never expecting anything.'

The news seemed to overwhelm her. The pallid cheeks flushed, and her eyes brimmed with tears.

'I am so grateful to you. I don't know how I can express my gratitude. Art is my life. In fact,' she tucked an errant curl behind her ear and regarded him seriously, 'I would love to paint *you* one day, Mr Fox.'

'Call me Harry.'

'You have such an interesting face.'

He assumed this was an oblique reference to his scar, and while he didn't want to come across as Bill Sikes, if the scar were to raise his potential as an artistic subject, he was fine with it.

'And your eyes. They are so deep, and yet they're like the sea – it's as though I can see right through to the bottom.'

That was disturbing. What would it be like, if women could actually know what was in your head? What you really thought? He shuddered slightly and glanced around him. Already the pub was filling up with regulars who knew him and were likely to come over and question the identity of his attractive companion. The owner, Victor, who possessed an extravagant handlebar moustache, was beaming enquiringly in his direction.

'Listen. Let's not drink here. It's pretty crowded. Can't hear myself think. Why don't we go on somewhere quieter? Where are you staying?'

'I live with a friend. In Islington.' She fixed him straight in the eye. 'But it's best we don't go there.'

Half an hour later they had descended the dank steps to his basement flat and he was closing the blackout curtains and switching on the lights.

'You like books!'

Lieselotte was surveying the detritus of his apartment as though it was the lost library of Alexandria.

It had been so long since a woman had accompanied him into the bachelor underworld of his flat, Harry had almost forgotten that the sheer number of volumes he possessed might seem outlandish. Having run out of shelf space, he kept them in haphazard towers installed randomly around his living quarters. Lieselotte was running her fingers over the spines, picking up one novel after another and turning them over to look at the dust jackets.

'I've always loved reading. My favourite book is *Bambi*. It's a wonderful novel, all about the lives of little animals in the forest; a hare and a squirrel and an owl. I reread it all the time. But it's terribly sad. I can't read the part about Bambi's mother without crying. Have you heard of it?'

Harry nodded. Jack had read it when he was six.

'The Nazis burned it, you know. They said *Bambi* was un-German. How can a deer be un-German? I was horrified when they burned it. It made me think they were burning the little fawn himself.'

She picked up the top book from the tower and read the title.

'*The Murder of Roger Ackroyd.* What's this about?'

'It's a detective story. A classic. The first use of an unreliable narrator.'

'What's that?'

'It means the person who tells the story may not be telling the truth.'

'That's strange.'

'Not in my line of business.'

'I'd love to hear more about your business.'

She moved closer to him, looking up into his eyes. Secure as he was of his own appeal, Harry could not help a nagging sense that there were other motivations behind her seductive behaviour. All the same, she was close and getting closer. He could smell the sweet amber of her scent and the port on her breath. He could see the tendrils of hair at the edge of her brow and the pulse of the vein at the side of her neck. He was aware of the warmth of her body and the swell of her breast atop the sweetheart neckline. The effect was disconcerting and, unusually for Harry, he found himself prevaricating.

'Can I fix you anything . . . ?'

She took off the beret and loosened her jacket.

'Anything would be nice.'

He backed away into the kitchen and surveyed its unerotic contents with fresh eyes. A packet of biscuits, a hard heel of bread, sweaty cheese and a few cans of tomato soup. No milk, but fortunately, half a bottle of Scotch.

Hands shaking slightly, he returned with two glasses.

Lieselotte took one, drank a sip, then put the glass down on a first edition of *Gaudy Night* and kissed him.

Harry woke early and lay still, not wanting to wake her, feeling her ribs rise and fall. Her mouth was slightly open, and her eyelids fluttered with dreams. She was, quite simply, a visitation. Her body was curled to one side, away from him, and her pale skin was painted with light caramel freckles. She was like a fawn herself, one that had sought cover in the nest of his sheets and would take fright if startled. As delicate as a speckled thrush, trembling against your hand.

In the rush of the previous night's events, he had failed to close the bedroom curtains, and now the early sunlight was falling in squares across the carpet, motes of dust spiralling within it. He thought, as he always did, how strange it was that this same dust had once been other things entirely: trees, walls, books. Even people. People who had been loved and were now faded to nothing.

People persisted, though, just like dust persisted, and like dust, they were only sometimes visible.

Stanley Fox, for example, who barged into his mind on all occasions, no matter how private. Harry knew that in many ways he was an echo of his father – restless, quixotic, disputatious, mistrustful. A former employee of Britain's secret services. An undercover operative who changed identities the way other men changed their ties. Most fathers taught their sons fishing and football, but Stanley Fox had taught his son cynicism and sentimentality, which was a disastrous mix.

After a while Harry edged the sheet aside and crept out of bed. He did not want to rouse Lieselotte, who was still sleeping heavily, so he moved into the other room.

He didn't know what possessed him to look at the soft tan leather handbag that lay on the kitchen table. Habit, he supposed. A professional instinct as ingrained as breathing. Yet still it felt transgressive. Fumbling among a lady's things seemed more intimate than sex, even. When making love, a person revealed only what they wanted to reveal and the act of intimacy was often, equally, an act of concealment. But to rake through their belongings was a blatant violation.

He moved towards the bag, and the fingers that had, only hours before, undone a row of pearl buttons, now unclipped the clasp.

He pulled the bag open.

There was the book she had talked about. *Bambi*. A bunch of keys. A neat little toilet bag with a broderie frill, containing a powder compact and a lipstick. A comb. A lacy, embroidered handkerchief. A set of hair slides and a ten-shilling note. A tiny silver flagon of perfume that he couldn't help but sniff. Innocent female things that only endeared her to him more.

And at the bottom, under the sweet detritus of a woman's fripperies, was a gun.

# CHAPTER 20

The address on the scrap of notepaper that Thomas Kendrick had given Stella said 22, Place Vendôme. She knew that square – though to be precise it was not a square but an octagon: a colonnaded gem of eighteenth-century architecture in the 1st arrondissement, complete with a column of tarnished brass in the centre to celebrate the battle of Austerlitz. Directly opposite number 22 was the Ritz Hôtel, whose entrance was currently flanked by a row of gleaming sedans, from one of which a pair of elegantly dressed customers were emerging, accompanied by a dachshund in a quilted jacket.

Stella hesitated for a moment, prevaricating by staring into the window of the shopfront next door. It belonged to Maison Schiaparelli, the fashion designer's boutique, and a mannequin stood in the window wearing a chic satin 'siren suit' – a jumpsuit with large pockets, practical but still chic, to be donned hastily in the event of air raids. Stella was reminded of Evelyn's gas-mask holder full of cosmetics and cigarettes. It paid to be prepared, and Stella had always suspected that she herself would be far too impulsive to remember the essentials.

Eventually, she summoned the nerve to press the brass bell.

To her surprise, the door was opened by Coward himself, dressed in a red silk smoking jacket and black bow tie, smelling powerfully of pomade. She knew the playwright from posters and the cinema, of course, but up close, without the lacquered glamour of the screen, he appeared creased and careworn. His long horse face glistened with sweat and his hair was combed into tight Brylcreemed grooves. He seemed older than she had imagined, with enormous ears and a countenance that was lugubrious, until lit up by a brilliant professional smile. Even though she had been expecting to meet him, seeing such a well-known figure close up took her aback, and for a second she fumbled her pre-prepared lines.

'Mr Coward. My name is Stella Fry.'

'Is it? How charming.'

'I'm sorry to come here out of the blue. I should have put a letter through your door and made an appointment. Especially as you're going out.'

'What makes you think I'm going out?'

'Oh. My mistake.' She glanced again at the smoking jacket, its cuffs embroidered with oriental motifs, the stiff white shirt and patent-leather shoes.

'Anyway, I was given your address by Colonel Kendrick.'

The name worked like a spell. Coward opened the door wider and made a little gesture of welcome like a butler.

'As it happens, I was about to mark the cocktail hour. Perhaps you'd care to join me?'

She followed him through a marble-chequered hallway, up a set of grand stairs into a vast drawing room, with a dazzling chandelier hanging from the ceiling. On the floor, herringbone parquet was laid with Turkish rugs, and in the centre of the room stood a Steinway grand piano. He seemed to be alone.

'I do hope I'm not distracting you. I feel awful coming here without telephoning, but I didn't have your number.'

'Please don't worry. I could do with a little distraction, Miss Fry. Generally, at this hour I like to do the crossword to improve my French, but it seems they've discontinued it. Apparently, the fear is that the question setters might be using the answers to send a code. If they are, it would be lost on me. I wouldn't recognize a code if it was strung out in neon lights across the Champs-Élysées. Martini, or brandy and soda?'

He was presiding over a cocktail table arrayed with bottles and a silver shaker, his hands moving with proficient speed.

'Martini. Thank you.'

He brought over a martini garnished with an olive on a cocktail stick and threw himself theatrically into a white leather chair.

'So, Colonel Kendrick sent you. I don't know how much he told you about me.'

'He said you were running the Propaganda Bureau.'

'Yes. *Propaganda*.' Coward tasted the word in his mouth as if it was acid. 'It's hard to believe, in all honesty, that one has landed up here. They told me the job would suit someone creative. An artist, they said. But I'm afraid, although Joseph Goebbels might think Art is the same thing as propaganda, some of us have loftier ideas.'

He sighed, crossed elegant legs, and fixed a cigarette into a long ebony holder.

'If one must engage in propaganda, however, one should at least try to keep to the highest artistic standards, don't you think? I'm currently designing leaflets to be dropped from cotton balloons that will explode in mid-air above Germany. I did consider dropping miniature tricolours and Union Jacks too, so they would stick to German buildings like confetti. That would be amusing. And amusement is so important, don't you agree?'

'I do,' said Stella, thinking how much Evelyn would envy her, sitting here with Noël Coward.

'The authorities wanted us to drop long speeches by Chamberlain outlining the case that war was wicked, peace was good, and the enemy had better listen up. I said if the policy of His Majesty's government is to bore the Germans to death, I don't think we have enough time. The Jerries have been retaliating with lurid little leaflets showing British officers raping French ladies in looted chateaux. A touch heavy-handed, but then I never think of the Germans as particularly susceptible to humour.'

Stella sipped her martini and felt herself relax. Coward had not yet asked anything about why she was here, but that was the essence of charm, she guessed. This room was an oasis of calm English gentility in a frightened city.

'To my mind,' Coward went on, 'that's the great failing of Herr Hitler. He has no class, no charm, no wit, no warmth, no wisdom, no subtlety, no sensitivity, no self-awareness, but above all, no sense of humour. To lack humour is almost inhuman. Without it, there's no inner world, no soul. Fortunately for me, we British like to laugh.'

'Have you been here long?' she asked, almost reluctant to stem this flow.

'Since last year.' He finished his half-smoked cigarette, offered her one, which she declined, then immediately fitted another into the holder.

'Until the recent Norwegian escapade, it was frightfully listless. The French called it the *Drôle de Guerre* but there was nothing remotely droll about it, darling. It was very drab indeed. My opposite number is a tiny little cross colonel in the Commissariat à l'information and I fill my time doing dinners and lunches for big shots passing through. The food, of course, is the chief consolation, despite the meat-free days and the lack of hard liquor. It's marvellous, but to tell the honest truth, I do occasionally long for some steak and kidney pie and baked beans.'

Stella laughed. 'I hope you won't have to abandon your theatre career for long.'

'Oh, everything's acting, isn't it, darling? All one's world is a stage. I admit, I would never have cast myself in this particular role, but we all have our crosses to bear. And one does understand their reasoning. People will say all kinds of things to a man like me. A man who sings silly songs. They let down their guard – they regard me as the ultimate silly ass.'

'Actually, I have a friend who is rehearsing one of your plays right now. *Private Lives*, at the Queen's. Her name's Evelyn Lamont.'

'Yes, of course. Charming girl.' This was said with a vague smile. Then he brightened. 'Doesn't she have a delightful brother?'

'Tom.'

'A dear boy! How is Tom?'

'He's engaged to an American woman. A friend of Kick Kennedy's. She's called Meredith Meadows.'

Two raised eyebrows.

'Is he indeed? How curious. I've met Miss Meadows. She seemed a formidable character – "straight-talking" is I think how the Americans describe it. I encountered her at Holland House at the coming-out party for Rosalind Cubitt last year – my dear, that party was glorious. Rivers of champagne, butlers in knee-breeches and wigs. I can't imagine we'll see that again for a long time.'

Stella longed to ask more about the formidable Meredith Meadows and why the engagement should be curious, but Coward was unlocking his long legs and leaning forward. The charming facade sobered over.

'Enough about me. We should attend to more important matters. So what brings you to Paris, Miss Fry? And indeed to my door. You say Colonel Kendrick sent you.'

'I'm looking for a man. A German. He's called Robert Handel. We studied together at Oxford some years ago. Until very recently he was . . . helping the government . . . in Britain, but now he's gone AWOL.'

'Missing?'

'Yes, and there's good reason to think he may have come here to Paris. His sister ran a bookshop here, so I've been going into all the bookshops I can find, asking after him. But it's fruitless. No one's heard of him or his sister. It's obviously a dead end. I'm out of ideas, so I thought – or Colonel Kendrick thought – as you meet so many people, maybe you might have come across him? Or someone who knows him?'

'How long has this chap been missing?'

'About a week.'

'I imagine, from the short outline, that's there's a pretty dramatic story behind this tale.'

'There is. He has valuable information. And time's running out. The longer Robert Handel is missing, the more danger he could pose to British safety.'

Coward frowned. He steepled his fingers together and the clipped, patrician voice became more serious.

'What you need to understand, Miss Fry, is that Paris is a minefield. You may see a city full of pretty little bars and cafés and nightclubs, but what I see is a network of people fighting in the shadows. Communists, expatriates, anti-fascists, German refugees, Polish refugees, British, Hungarian, American. Many of the communists here, who were once Soviet agents, are appalled at the Nazi-Soviet pact, and I can tell you that little *entente cordiale* has been of great value to us British. They've turned to us; indeed, one pretty senior fellow who spent most of his life in tireless service of Stalin now gives regular lectures to my people in a Left Bank restaurant on the ways of Soviet spies. Then there are others still who are faithful to Stalin and who are spying on their former friends. On top of this, of course, the city is flooded with Gestapo agents, preparing the ground. So, there are numerous different groups of people, all with their own agendas.'

'Are you suggesting that Robert Handel might be in touch with one of these networks?'

'I don't know. But if he's fled to Paris, as opposed to, say, Bognor Regis, one would be sensible to suspect his interests are more than purely touristic. I do keep my ear to the ground, my dear – that is in fact my job – and if I come across your chap, if indeed he's still going by the same name, I will let you know instantly. You say he comes from a bookish family? As a matter of fact, I've taken to holding little lunches for bookish types – journalists, writers and so on. It comes as light relief from all those bureaucrats at the Ministère de'l'Information. I have all manner of interesting people. Vladimir Nabokov, the novelist. That Irish playwright chap, Samuel Beckett. Arthur Koestler. It may be that one of them has encountered him.'

'Does that mean you think you might be able to help?'

'I can only promise to look out for him. But I would remind you, relationships are what count in this business. That's what intelligence is. You say you yourself knew this Robert Handel. That matters. Thomas Kendrick will have recognized that. It may well be that whatever you knew about him will in fact be the key to finding him.'

'I don't see how.'

'If you would permit me a theatrical aside. When my darling actors are struggling to find what we must now call their "motivation", I tell them to look within their character. What's important to them? What happened to them to make them behave this way? Why are they lying to themselves?'

'Lying?'

He smiled.

'Would it be too frightfully immodest to refer again to that play of mine? *Private Lives*? Two divorced people, Elyot and Amanda, who simply can't admit they're in love with each other? Instead, they spend their time discussing trivialities.'

'I do love that play.'

'Kind of you to say. And thank you.'

'For what?'

'For not saying, *Very flat, Norfolk*.'

She laughed.

'You must get tired of people repeating that line.'

'It's true that I do occasionally wish I'd never written it.'

'But about lying . . .'

'What I mean to say, Miss Fry, is that we're all lying to ourselves, aren't we? Especially about what matters.'

He glanced out of the window. The light had drained from the sky and a twilit gloom had descended on the city. Shops were closing with a clattering of metal shutters. Grilles were clanging down. Stella wondered what lies Coward told about his own life, and what secrets he was obliged to hide behind his own private shutters.

'So your question should be, what is it that motivates Robert Handel and what has he lied about in the past?'

Coward gathered up his cigarettes into a crocodile-skin case, placed it in his jacket pocket and rose.

'You said there was not much time, and my dear, you were right. The French Prime Minister, Daladier, told me he's certain that France will be invaded and defeated and occupied very soon. By mid-June at the latest, he said. All the socialites have got the message. Everyone's leaving Paris, and Peggy Guggenheim's buying up their paintings. I'm not sure that the powers that be back home truly appreciate the situation.'

'Have you not briefed them?'

'It's hard to communicate with Britain. Even to place a telephone call. The authorities have given me a very complicated code made up of numbers that have to be added and subtracted and multiplied, and frankly, if I'm ever captured by the Gestapo, I'd never be able to betray it.'

He led the way towards the door.

'If you'll forgive me, I should be getting on. I'm expecting a guest soon and tomorrow I'm off to sing at the Maginot Line with Maurice Chevalier. I promise I'll do everything I can to look out for your man.'

'Thank you. And if you do find anything . . .' She took out another postcard of the Eiffel Tower and scribbled down the address of her hotel. 'I'm staying here.'

'It sounds delightful.'

He tucked the postcard in his pocket.

'I'm sorry this should have been such a brief encounter. I would love to talk more. Yet sometimes the briefest of encounters makes an impression, and you strike me as admirably determined, Miss Fry. If anyone is going to find this chap, it is probably you.'

At the door he paused, his hand on the handle.

'But I would warn you to be careful. There's a tremendous suspicion of strangers in Paris. It is not a safe place. You have been wandering the city, making enquiries in bookshops. That is very unwise. Remember what I said about the kinds of people who frequent the shadows. If you take my advice you will give up your search for the day. Go straight to your hotel and hole up with a good novel. Forget the world for a while.'

# CHAPTER 21

She sensed him before anything else, a sensation that made her body tingle and her skin creep with fear. It was not the normal fear of a solitary woman in an unlit city after dark, but a fear that made her chest constrict so it was hard to take a full breath.

She was being followed, there was no doubt about it.

Her eyes scanned the darkness, and instinctively she moved out of the deepest shadow towards the lighter edges of the pavement. Her ears strained for the sound of footsteps or the steady tread of boots on cobblestones. She could make out nothing either before or behind her in the strangely silent street.

She reasoned with herself that she was not about to be attacked. Though all her senses were on alert, maybe they had become extra sharp because her nerves were in overdrive. She had developed a hyper-acute sense of observation, as if her brain had lost its filter and every sensation presented itself to her at once.

*There is a tremendous suspicion of strangers in the city. It is not a safe place.*

Colonel Kendrick had warned her of the Gestapo's network in Paris. That they would be alert to an Englishwoman who had recently arrived with no apparent occupation. Might this be an amateur – a small-time crook paid to surveil her – maybe the man in the bookshop with the goatee beard or the person who had tried her bedroom door that afternoon? Or was it someone more official? And yet, if it was the authorities, why did they not make themselves known?

Above all, if she was being followed, what might her pursuer possibly want? She had nothing worth stealing, though she remembered that she had brought her passport with her and realized that if she was challenged, there was no chance of dissembling. She edged the piece of paper with Noël Coward's address out of her pocket, crumpled it, and let it fall down a drain.

Then she dropped her scarf and bent down, looking behind her to catch a flicker of movement from a figure she could not make out.

The sensible course of action, which would be to seek refuge in a house or a shop, was not available. The streets were unlit, and every window rigorously blacked out with thick curtains. Only the gleam of glass and chrome suggested shopfronts, and the buildings themselves were ghostly hulks, drowned in darkness. The painted street lamps emitted haloes of powdery blue. No matter how many Parisians chose to be bullish about the possibilities of invasion, at night they were taking no chances. Nobody wanted to be lighting the way for a Luftwaffe bomber.

She had reached the rue de Rivoli, with the shadows of the Tuileries stretching to one side. She walked along the colonnade, then diverted through the courtyard of the Louvre. Here at least she was in the open, and anyone following would be forced to show themself.

In that moment she remembered the first night she had met Harry Fox, when he followed her through the streets of London from the Café de Paris, and now she had a sudden craving for the muscular security of his presence. She wished she could have brought Harry with her – they were a team, after all – and besides, he was a better detective than she would ever be. But Harry was not here, and the only person who could help her was herself.

She glanced behind again and this time was certain that she saw the figure of a man a hundred yards distant, sensing his eyes fixed on her. She picked up speed and in doing so turned her ankle on a cobble, prompting a soft cry of pain. She snatched another glance over her shoulder, but the man, if he had been there, was no longer a presence. Turning left, she pressed on, hugging the river, dappled with oil and tar, a tide of foamy scum at its edges, until she came to the Pont Louis-Philippe and crossed onto the Île Saint-Louis. The streets here were narrow and shuttered. She needed to find a bar and secrete herself amid the warm press of its customers, and the safety of strangers.

Almost at random, she entered the first place she encountered, a facsimile of every Parisian bar there was, with green-painted shutters, wooden chairs and a zinc bar. The *patron*, rubbing glasses behind the bar, looked up and nodded. He was bald and missing most of his teeth, but at that moment his seemed like the nicest face she had ever seen. She took a seat at the back, beyond the bar, so that she could observe the door, and ordered pastis, which appeared in a small, smeared glass. A few men glanced at her but left her alone. She sipped the pastis, wincing at the bitter aniseed, and watched.

A few minutes later, a man came into the bar and took the seat next to hers.

He was swarthy, with a leather jacket and a scarf that obscured half his face. He drew out a packet of Gauloises Bleus, tapped it, lowered his scarf and lit up, the match glimmering in his hand. As he did so, hiding his mouth with his palm, he said, 'You walk fast, mademoiselle. I could barely keep up.'

'Who are you? What do you want?'

'I'm nobody. A messenger. And I have a message for you from a friend. He heard you were looking for him.'

'Is this . . . ?'

'No names here, mademoiselle. It's better that way. But yes, it is the man you are searching for. He is detained this evening, and he has to be careful where he goes. But he would like to see you. He says it has been a long time.'

'So where can I see him?'

'Go to the Denfert-Rochereau métro station in the 14th at nine in the morning.'

'How do I know this isn't some kind of trap?'

'My friend, he says, remember Orpheus.'

# CHAPTER 22

*May 9th*

The young man, who was wearing a flat cap and a serge workman's jacket, was leaning against the art deco entrance to the métro station with his hands in his pockets, a cigarette clenched between his lips. When Stella came up the steps at precisely nine the next morning he straightened, collected a bicycle and wheeled it off, his eyes telling her to follow.

She walked behind him a short distance to a bench beneath a horse chestnut tree, then he mounted his bicycle and rode off. On the bench a man was reading *L'Humanité*.

When he saw her approach, he put down the paper and stood up.

'Stella! What a pleasure to see you again. After all this time.'

It didn't seem like a long time. And yet she had not been able to recall his face in its entirety. Now the parts came together: the high brow, strong nose and intense virility. The cleft chin and hair receding at the temples, with a marked widow's peak. The clipped, German-accented English that lent his speech a certain formality and the eyes, grey as the North Sea, whose direct gaze sent a frisson through her.

Robert Handel. He held out his hand, which she shook, and inclined his head slightly towards her, as though making a bow. This Prussian courtesy, this fortress of manners around a passionate nature, brought back their encounters in a visceral rush: the debates in cramped rooms, teashops in the High Street, walks in Christ Church Meadow. Mahler and Beethoven on the gramophone in undergraduate rooms. Evensong, once, in Merton Chapel.

He was wearing a shabby blue jacket, shapeless khaki trousers, and a scarf looped the French way around his neck.

He gestured at the bench beside him and they both sat.

'Sorry for the elaborate directions. I'm having to be quite careful.'

'So I noticed. Why?'

He didn't answer directly. His eyes roved over her, and she sensed him taking in every aspect of her. Finally his glance took in her eyes, which she knew were circled after a night of restless sleep.

'You should be careful too. You were being watched.'

'By you? Or your friend? Whoever he is.'

'That's Achille. And no, not just us. My colleagues told me you'd been asking for me in bookshops and that a gentleman had followed you, questioning who you'd asked for.

He was armed with a wallet full of francs and probably more besides. Naturally my friends said nothing, but it behoves you to be observant.'

'I think one of them tried to get into my hotel room yesterday when I was taking a nap.'

'I hope you locked it.'

'I did.'

'They must have assumed you were out. They wouldn't normally make that kind of mistake.'

He rose to his feet.

'In light of which, perhaps we shouldn't wait around.'

He led the way across the square, and she followed him up the avenue Denfert-Rochereau, Handel scanning the wrought-iron balconies as they went and the young man with the bicycle weaving in and out of the traffic a few yards away. She was aware of him scouting out the passers-by, the flat-capped men, the office girls walking arm in arm, and the old women in black coats.

They halted as a policeman, with cape and white truncheon, directed the traffic, then crossed the road and entered the Jardin du Luxembourg. They continued walking along the wide sandy path to where the pond, like a dull metal coin, reflected the sky.

'I love this place.'

Handel surveyed the baroque geometry of the garden around them, with its colonnaded balustrades decorated with elaborate urns, and its manicured lawns. The paths, so hot and sandy in high summer, were still cool, and the beds were lush and damp.

'When this garden was made, it symbolized the apogee of human superiority. Reason had triumphed over barbarous nature. Nature must bend to man's will. What would they have thought now, if they could see the chaos and confusion that we've brought on ourselves?'

He glanced across the pond.

'I miss the little kids. For centuries, children have been sailing their model boats here, but now they're gone. It's like that fairy story. The city where all the children have disappeared, and we're left with the rats.'

'Who are the rats?'

'Oh, the rats are everywhere. Heydrich, the head of Reich security, sent in his spies months, even years ago. The people who were following you, no doubt. They're on the lookout for anyone unusual – Germans who have emigrated to France, communists, anti-fascists, Englishwomen on their own asking questions. Anyone who might be preparing for what is about to come. But Heydrich's recruits are locals; they're remarkably unskilled. Nothing like the real Gestapo. I can spot them a mile off. In this business you learn techniques – you stick to the same routes and routines day after day, then if you need to you can surprise them. It usually works. All the same, these thugs are not completely useless.'

'I met a man last night – someone who works for the British government – who says Daladier is expecting an invasion and the occupation of Paris by mid-June.'

Handel shrugged.

'I don't doubt it. I can see it already in my mind's eye, can't you? The swastika flags billowing over the Eiffel Tower, the soldiers in leather coats, the motorcyclists. All those decisions to be made. Which hotels will the bigwigs take? Who gets the Ritz? Which Nazis will enjoy the silk-lined rooms at the Crillon? How many distinguished murderers can they expect at the Continental?'

A cloud crossed the sun, and he shivered, as though the lines of German tanks were already at the gates, and his goosebumps were caused not by cold but fear. Then rain began to fall in heavy drops, sending up the smell of grit and sand.

'We're going to get wet. Let's find a drink.'

Out of the gate they walked, onto the Place de l'Odéon, where Handel diverged into a café. He selected a table where he could sit with his back to the wall and keep his eyes on the door. He pulled out a chair for her and she sat, taking off her hat. All the time they had been walking he hadn't looked at her at all, but now, having ordered coffee, his eyes did not leave her face. In a gentler tone he said, 'I remember the way you did that.'

'Did what?'

'Ran your fingers through your hair.'

Stella had no idea he had observed anything about her at all. Her hair was pearled with damp and beginning to frizz. She felt herself flush.

'You haven't changed, Stella.'

'Haven't I? You seem different.'

'I am. In every way that matters.'

'What happened to you? After Oxford, I mean?'

'You really want to hear my little history?'

She nodded.

'Then I'll tell you.'

He smiled. 'When I left, I followed the path that had been laid down for me. I went back to Berlin and began training as a lawyer. That's where I was living when Hitler came in. I remember that day like it was yesterday. It was bitterly cold, and I was working in a library and suddenly we heard feet on the street outside and the sound of a marching band. We rushed to the window. Stormtroopers in brown uniforms and policemen with searchlights scanning the buildings for troublemakers. Some of them muscled into the building where I was working, asking people if they were Aryan. One man, who admitted being Jewish, was beaten up on the spot.

'My own family was optimistic. Even if we were no Nazi lovers, at least we weren't Jews. Like a lot of people, my parents thought it wouldn't last, but I said, can people not read? Everyone's carrying *Mein Kampf* around, why do they not bother to see what it says? I guessed it wouldn't be long before I was arrested because I was already on their books. Not only had I spent time in England, but my sister Ursula had run an international bookshop in Wilmersdorf before she decamped here to Paris. My parents had been Social

Democrats. In every way, Hitler's enemies. Sure enough, in the summer of '36, they did come for me.'

'Were you arrested?'

'Yes. And I will never forget the Gestapo cellars in Prinz-Albrecht-Strasse. The shouts in the night. The screams from the beatings.'

He was staring into the middle distance, smoking now. 'Some of those screams were my own – I'm no hero.'

Softly she said, 'You are, though. You stayed.'

He shrugged.

'Yes. I stayed another year, talking to friends I trusted, trying to see what we could do. Those discussions were very dangerous, of course. One word astray, or one false friend and it would be the end of us.

'Then the day came when I was walking down Unter den Linden and I passed a man I'd trained with in law school. I knew this guy well. I'd been to his house; I'd met his wife and children. And yet he pretended not to recognize me. That's the thing about evil, you see, Stella. It goes in disguise. You think evil will come to your door in jackboots and uniforms, and sometimes it does, but more frequently it arrives in the form of a letter, or a summons, or a new law. Or a friend in the street who declines to say hello. Anyhow, that was all the signal I needed. I came here to Paris and stayed with Ursula for a while, helping in the bookshop. That's when I met the people I see now. Then I left for Britain in 1938.'

'What brought you back?'

'The truth is, I missed England. It was such a pleasure to return. Everything was just the way I remembered it – sad and damp and green. Beautiful England.'

His wistfulness reminded her of her own experience at Trent Park, thinking of the peacock lawns, the flowers and the fountains that were all, now, utterly vanished.

'And what did you do in England?'

'Oh, a little of everything. I didn't practise law, of course – we have a different system in Germany – but I found enough to occupy myself.'

She guessed he was not going to elaborate.

'And what brought you back to Paris?'

He laughed, briefly, and at last the wide grey eyes lit up.

'Do you remember that day when you asked me to translate a part of Ovid? Orpheus and the underworld? *Omnia mutantur, nihil interit.*'

'Everything changes, nothing dies.'

'I was thinking of that – of Orpheus – when I suggested the place to meet.'

'What on earth does the Place Denfert-Rochereau have to do with Orpheus?'

'It's the location of our modern-day underworld. The Catacombs. There are three hundred kilometres of tunnels down there. They built them when the churchyards could hold no more bodies – and they stashed the bones of the population of Paris there for two centuries. Today it has other uses.'

In all this time he had not asked Stella why she was in

Paris looking for him. Perhaps he didn't want to know. More likely, he already knew.

He tilted his Gitanes towards her, the packet with its smoky-blue flamenco dancer, the insouciant emblem of Parisian chic.

'Will you?'

She took one and he cupped a match in his palm and lit it.

'Thank you.'

This exchange was absurd. Like play-acting. How long could it go on? They were talking about everything except the fact that she had come to Paris specifically to find him. Yet still he failed to broach the subject.

She said, 'Where are you staying?'

'On the premises of a photo agency. They let me live above the shop. It suits me fine, for now.'

'Do you think it's certain that France will be overrun?'

He shrugged.

'There are dark days ahead, Stella. Commander-in-chief Gamelin may boast that the French army is better than at any time in its history and is prepared for a long war, but the truth is, the French have no idea what's coming. They're the most civilized creatures in the world. Whereas I'm a German, so I see it plainly. They say Hitler wanted to attack both France and Britain last year, but he was persuaded that the experience of the Wehrmacht in Poland suggested the army was not ready. But that's not the case now. Now, they're raring to go.'

He finished his coffee and clattered the cup back into its saucer.

'But you, Stella, you're in Paris! What a shame you won't have a chance to visit the museums while you're here.'

Suddenly he was as breezy and enthusiastic as though ten years had melted away and they were once again two students walking along St Giles' in Oxford, discussing art or poetry.

'Should I visit the Louvre?'

'It's almost too late. They've removed most of the pictures. There's nothing much left except the *Winged Victory of Samothrace* and that was apparently too heavy to shift. When I was living here before, I used to go all the time. All that beauty! It was like the room was on fire. I could hardly stay away. I loved feeling all those ghosts around me, watching me. Art's important at a time like this. It gives human life its value. It's what we're fighting for.'

'Who's we?'

'Ah, therein lies a story.'

He leapt up and held out a hand.

'And I promise to finish it. We have a lot to discuss, Stella, but this is not the place. Tell me, d'you like jazz?'

'Love it.'

'Have you ever heard of the Quintette du Hot Club de France?'

'No, sorry. What is it?'

'It's a band formed by Stéphane Grappelli and Django Reinhardt. They started out at the Hôtel Claridge but tonight what remains of them are playing at the Boeuf sur le Toit in the 16th. That's a nightclub, but it's really one of the great institutions of Paris. Like a gathering of all the best people you'd care to meet: Maurice Chevalier, Marlene Dietrich, Cole Porter, Kurt Weill, all the greats. Even your ex-king goes there. I'd like it very much if you could come tonight. I'll be there at eight.'

Before she could say anything else, he dropped some francs onto the table, strode out of the door and marched rapidly away, collar turned up against the rain.

CHAPTER 23

A gun in a bag. It was just Harry's luck.

Though he was hardly Cary Grant, he was generally successful with women. They liked his unfeigned, self-deprecating charm, his genuine interest in others and, before the scar, his looks. Yet recently, he had hit a dry patch. The months since Susie left had been a desert. And now, finally, when fate had delivered him a woman who was not only beautiful, but genuinely seemed to like him, this had to happen. Coming on top of the delight of Lieselotte's company, and to be frank, the sheer pleasure of her sharing his bed, this turn of events seemed especially cruel.

Once he had found the gun, he cautiously examined it, flipping it over in his palm and feeling the weight of it before instinctively covering it up again, as though it might go off right in front of him. An Enfield No. 2 Mk 1 .38 calibre revolver. Shock pulsated through him while his mind searched for possible innocent explanations involving rabbits and pigeons.

He made tea and clinked the spoon loudly against the china, prompting Lieselotte to wake. He carried two cups back to where she was sitting with the sheet bunched up to her shoulders in a kind of inviting modesty that had very much the desired effect on him. Indeed, he enjoyed the sight so much that he failed to challenge her. It was a tricky subject to bring up, especially when she was stroking his face with her thin hands and asking tender questions about how he had acquired his scar. The sunlight slanting through the curtain haloed her brunette hair and brought out the golden tints.

That was definitely the moment when he should have queried the need for weaponry amid her cosmetics, but to ask was to admit that he had rifled through her belongings, and it paid to be cautious when romancing a woman who was packing sidearms. So he decided to delay the question until he was better informed.

For another half-hour he submitted himself to her caresses and returned them in full. But all the time Maxwell Knight's warning rang in his head. *She may be a little foreign bird blown off course, but she might just as well be a bird of an entirely different feather.*

His heart sank within him. Not for the first time, he guessed Maxwell Knight was right.

She left a few hours later, with kisses and promises of a return visit. Sitting in an armchair, his mind and body full of her, he reached for a cigarette. As he patted his pocket for a light, he found the book of matches that Lieselotte had given him in the French House and drew it out.

He turned the matchbook over in his hands. It was a dark-blue square of cardboard featuring on one side a river running diagonally and on the other a white name written slantwise. As he looked at it, jagged pieces of information began to perform a slow dance in his head.

He remembered the name on the matchbook. Someone had mentioned it to him recently. It was Sunny Hoss. The matches said *The Danube Bar and Social Club.*

# CHAPTER 24

For one of Paris's great institutions, the Boeuf sur le Toit nightclub at 41 Avenue Pierre 1er de Serbie, had nothing on Les Invalides or the Louvre. It was located in the 16th arrondissement, the smartest in Paris, full of handsome apartment blocks and large mansions behind black metal gates, yet its frontage of mottled marble was no match for the glamour of the Panthéon or the Élysée Palace. It was not until you stepped through the curtained entrance, to encounter a blast of saxophone and chatter, that you felt the place pulsating with its own cultural importance.

Stella had been to very few nightclubs, let alone French ones. The modest evenings of her childhood were devoted to reading in front of the gas fire, attending concerts and playing Monopoly or Ludo with her brother, Alan. Later, living with Evelyn, she had been introduced to the more bohemian quarters of Chelsea, but a real French nightclub, with all its transgressive chic, was something else.

At least she was dressed for the occasion, no thanks to Harry Fox. When Harry said he had 'brought some things' from her flat, he meant workaday jumpers and blouses. He had not even provided a change of underwear, being either too squeamish or too gallant to rifle through her drawers, with the result that Stella had been forced to borrow some of Evelyn's clothes. Luckily they were almost the same size. Evelyn always dressed as if off to a cabaret, even in the daytime, so Stella was wearing a dress of dramatic cerulean-blue silk with a low neckline, which she had complemented with a single strand of pearls.

The dress helped, yet still she had no idea of her next step. Although she had located Robert Handel as Kendrick instructed, and he wanted to see her, he had not yet questioned what brought her to Paris, nor given any indication of what he himself was doing there.

That night those questions must swiftly be broached.

'Bonsoir, mademoiselle,' said a man in a dinner jacket, opening the brass door.

Inside, a vast Dadaesque painting overlooked an assembly of tables, crammed tightly together, at which men and women were making animated conversation against the backing of a ragtime band. The music was almost, but not quite, soft enough to allow conversation. Jewels glittered beneath the globe lights that shone on bare shoulders and gleaming hair, and cigar smoke plumed in the air.

Seeing her alone, a man with a clipped moustache and a glint in his eye began to move towards her, so she hurried to the bar and ordered a Cinzano. Next to her a girl with short, boyish hair overheard her accent and fluttered heavily kohl-lined eyelids.

*Well, hello. Can I trouble you for a smoke?*

Stella fumbled in her beaded evening bag, also Evelyn's, but no sooner had she brought out a cigarette than a hand offered a lighter, and she looked up to see Robert Handel, in dinner jacket and black bow tie.

'You came.'

He passed the cigarette to the girl and lit it, then, with one hand on her shoulder, steered Stella towards a booth at the back of the room, furthest away from the band, where they settled on deep banquettes, upholstered in crimson velvet.

'At least we can hear ourselves speak here. I'm surprised it's as busy as it is tonight. Until recently, this place was full of Americans in search of Ernest Hemingway and Scott Fitzgerald, but they've all gone home now, and the place has emptied out a little. Everyone misses the Americans. At least when they were here, the Parisians were able to be snobbish about the Yanks, and Parisians are never happier than when being snobs, but now they've gone everything's a bit duller. And it's about to get even less fun. What are you drinking? Not, God forbid, Cinzano. We need champagne.'

A waiter arrived, with a tray bearing a champagne bottle in a white napkin and two glasses. He filled the glasses and Handel raised his towards her.

'To Stella. Who's the only pleasant surprise I've had in a long time. You look gorgeous, by the way. You've grown even prettier. Tell me, are you married now? A wife with children? Or engaged to some handsome aristocrat or politician? I notice you're not wearing a ring.'

'That's because I don't have one. Or any of the above.'

'That amazes me. What happened?'

'I was engaged, when I lived in Vienna, but we were incompatible.'

'He liked Wagner, you liked Mozart?'

'He liked Nazis and I didn't.' She took a sip of champagne and savoured the bubbles pricking her mouth. 'I left for London just before the Anschluss.'

'Impeccable timing. That way you never had to see what happened.'

'I went back once, actually, so yes, I did see.'

Handel raised an eyebrow but probed no further. He sat, one arm flung over the back of the banquette, sipping his drink.

'Hungry?'

She said not, although she should be. She had eaten nothing since a piece of crusty baguette and ham earlier that day, but it was impossible to think about food just then.

'Never mind. We must eat anyway. The menu here is marvellous. The oysters are unparalleled.'

He ordered a dozen oysters, which came nestled in ice on a silver platter, and then a kind of chicken stew which was intensely aromatic, with tiny dumplings floating in the creamy sauce. No sooner had it arrived than Stella's appetite returned, and she began to eat eagerly, relishing the intensity of the flavours. If the English ate in black and white, then French food was Technicolor.

Yet she forced herself to pace her drinking. She must remember that the person so enthusiastically discussing oysters and filling her glass with Veuve Clicquot was no charming consort but a murderer.

As they dined, out of the corner of her eye she was aware of a man sitting on his own across the room, a small glass of cognac on the table before him, taking covert glances in their direction. He had broad shoulders, wavy hair and a high, intellectual brow. He was wearing a smart double-breasted blazer, silver tie and a navy-and-white checked silk scarf at the neck. Handel followed her gaze, then immediately leapt up, and brought the man over.

'You don't want to sit on your own, old chap! André, this is a friend of mine from university days, Stella Fry. She's here studying church architecture. Stella, this is André Simon.'

'*Enchanté.*' The man made a little bow. 'Would you prefer me to speak English?'

'André speaks seven languages,' smiled Robert.

'*Pas du tout. Parlons français.*'

'Church architecture?' The newcomer had a teasing air and penetrating, deep-set blue eyes that were analyzing her intently. 'That's a wholesome enthusiasm.'

'You sound like you disapprove.'

'Oh, I tend to think Christianity is rather an old-fashioned moral compass.'

'I suppose it is,' said Stella. 'But compasses are useful. Especially in these times.'

'You're right, of course.' A silky smile. 'French churches are the finest in Christendom, if you can see them behind the sandbags. And I suppose one might as well study them before the Nazis unleash their bombs. Enjoy the last of that sacred music. How about you, Handel? What's your enthusiasm?'

'Nothing so sacred, André. Jazz is my love.'

He gestured to the dance floor, which was a hot and airless press of rotating couples. 'Jazz starts in your head and travels along your limbs like a drug; it's intoxicating. And I love the clubs: the Foxtrot, the Grizzly Bear. That's where I find my relaxation. The Grosse Pomme . . .'

'The Caravan.'

'That too.'

'But most of them are gone now,' said Simon. '*Tant pis.* And very soon jazz will go too.'

'Really? Why is that?' asked Stella.

He frowned.

'Do you not know, Miss Stella Fry, that Hitler hates jazz? And swing. He's purged the cabarets in Germany and if he comes here, it's going to be closing time pretty soon. Curtain down.'

'I was just telling Stella that all the Americans have vanished, but you're the exception, André. You've been living in California, haven't you? What brings you back?'

'This and that.' He made a fluttering gesture with his hand.

'Where are you staying?'

'The Lutetia.'

Stella sensed that most of the conversation between them was not being expressed in words.

Then the band struck up Glenn Miller's 'Moonlight Serenade' and Handel leapt up, extending a hand. 'Shall we?'

Without waiting for a reply, he led Stella towards the tiny dance floor and took her in his arms. Her whole body leapt at his touch, and together they swayed to the music, and became part of it, and were closer than they had ever been before. Yet even as they danced, her mind refused to relax. Was this the reason that she had travelled all the way from London? Had she come to seek out a murderer, or an old friend for whom she had lingering feelings? Because she could not deny how attractive he was and how much she was relishing his company. Steeling herself to keep her distance, she moved slightly apart and said, 'Who was your friend?'

'He's no friend of mine. He goes by the name of André Simon while he's here, but his real name is Otto Katz. Or Rudolf Katz or Rudolph Breda. He knows everyone. Kafka, Brecht, Eisenstein, Fritz Lang. He's had numerous love affairs. His last lover was Marlene Dietrich.'

'He's not French, though.' Her ear had detected the accent in his speech.

'No. He's a Czech Jew. He has many different identities but in all of them he's an agent of the Communist International – the Comintern. I first met him in England years ago and it was clear then that he was being monitored by Special Branch. I remember how skilled he was at giving them the slip.'

'Are you saying he's on the run?'

'Not exactly. He's the hunter, not the hunted. For the past few years, he's roamed all over Europe hunting down communists who are disillusioned with Stalin. Paris is full of them. The Nazi-Soviet pact came as a bombshell to them. All these anti-fascists had been taken in for so long. Stalin was using them as a smokescreen for the fact that he had been making overtures to Hitler for years. André Simon, or whatever you want to call him, compiles lists of those people whom the Soviet Union regards as traitors. Presumably, they will be useful at some point in the future. If he's staying in the Hôtel Lutetia, he must be doing well. He's a very dangerous character.'

'Why talk to him, then?'

'I can't afford not to.'

As Stella absorbed this, Handel pressed his mouth to her ear and said, 'Actually, this was a mistake. I thought it would be a discreet place to talk but it's about as discreet as a Hollywood divorce. Shall we leave?'

The night was balmy and pungent with the scent of lime blossom. Handel took her arm, and she walked with him, not knowing or caring much where they were going.

'There's no chance of a taxi at this hour. We'll have to walk.' He was silent for a while as they carried on in the direction of the Seine but when they came to the Palais

Galliera they diverted left into a side street and he turned to face her.

'So now, Stella, we come to the main question. Why have you been searching for me?'

She stalled. The moment had come when she would have to explain herself.

'It's complicated.'

'No, it's not. It's very simple.'

Looking up at him, in his dinner jacket and silk scarf, she saw him again a decade ago, standing before her in St Giles', in a beige donkey jacket and claret university muffler, observing her with an air of jocular scrutiny.

'In fact, I scarcely need to ask. I can't have expected to disappear without them making valiant attempts to find me. My guess is, they chose you for the task because we have something – or someone – in common.'

'Who would that be?'

'Our beloved professor, of course. Cecil Fairfax.'

There was no point in denying it.

'It's true. They sent me because of Cecil. They knew I would know you and recognize you.'

'By "they" you mean . . . ?'

Stella was unsure how much she could say. How much he actually knew. Caution warned her to watch her words.

'People.'

'And what will you tell these people?'

'I'll tell them that I've found you.'

'Won't they want to know why I'm here?'

'Oh, I suspect they'll draw their own conclusions.'

Handel frowned. 'But they can't have any clue why I came to Paris.'

'Why don't you tell me, then?'

He hesitated, took her arm again and continued walking.

'If you know where I've been working, Stella, then you'll have a better idea than most of what's coming. But the citizens here, the very ones who will be first on the receiving end of it, well, they're completely oblivious. They have simply no notion what's about to arrive. They are obsessed with keeping up standards. Yesterday I saw Coco Chanel entering a shelter followed by a maid carrying her gas mask on a velvet cushion. Incredible. And do you know, the Académie Française is still meeting for Wednesday conferences to determine which words should be allowed into the *Dictionnaire Larousse*? Which definitions are the absolute correct ones? Is a chicken wing a wing, or a muscle?'

'So what do you think they should do?'

'They need to make ready. The French High Command is incompetent and refuses to grasp how the nature of war has changed. Politicians care more for their careers than about the nation. Many ordinary people are preoccupied with saving their own skins and are only thinking about who to bribe and who they might ingratiate themselves with. There's an insulting name for those people now. *Munichois* – it means cowards. Like those who supported the Munich Agreement.'

'Perhaps they're worried for their children's safety.'

'Of course. Not everyone's a hero. But it's deeper than that. The French don't understand the Germans. The anti-fascists here, the ones I work with, are rash, emotional, and bohemian – that's what makes them care. But they're going to need an entirely new set of attitudes. They're going to need detail, order and precision, because the Nazis are a formidable foe.'

Ahead of them, in the rue Goethe, a man emerged from a bar, staggering slightly. He halted, bent over with his hands on his knees, coughing. Once they had passed him, he followed in their wake.

'It was when the Nazis occupied the Rhineland that I understood. Neither the British nor the French lifted a finger to stop them. That's when I knew that France would be crushed by Germany when it came to war. It's only by sheer luck that an invasion hasn't come sooner.'

They had reached the Pont de L'Alma, and it was there, in the middle of the bridge, when he could be certain that they were being neither followed nor overheard, that Handel stopped. The wind was coming up from the river, whipping at their clothes, carrying away his words. He leaned his elbows on the stone parapet, forcing her to move closer to hear him.

'In Trent Park I sat and listened to my fellow Germans day after day. Can you imagine what that does to a man? To know that bomber planes may soon be circling that are sent by one's own compatriots? It's a kind of schizophrenia. One has to be grateful to Britain, because Britain is standing up to one's own homeland. But those planes are piloted by men whose blood and bones are the same as my own. Men who may well have been friends, schoolfriends, family, colleagues.'

'I do wonder if the ordinary Germans know what is being done in their name.'

'They do know. Maybe not on the surface of their lives, but in the deep undercurrent that knowledge is there. They don't want to look at it because it threatens to drag them down.'

He stared into the choppy pewter waters of the Seine as if he was staring into the abyss itself.

'One day, a little more than a week ago, I realized there was no time to lose. I needed to come here, to Paris, as a matter of urgency. I had to help the people who are planning resistance for when the Nazis arrive.'

'How could you do that?'

'There will be so many things to do. Transporting arms, printing leaflets, establishing underground printing presses. Cutting telephone lines. All kinds of sabotage. And building a network of people, too. The Gestapo have been organizing here for years; they have a formidable espionage network, so the French have plenty of catching up to do. We do have bartenders and prostitutes who will listen to talk, and a certain number of low-level informers. Many of those booksellers you visited, and the bouquinistes along the Seine. But it's not enough. The German army will go through this place like a firestorm.'

'Who says they will even get here? What about the Maginot Line?'

'There's a Maginot Line, yes, but it stops at the Belgian border. What's to stop them going round the edge?'

He pulled out a packet of Gitanes, lit two, one for himself and one for her, then he said, 'It's a cursed task, Stella, warning of what's to come. I feel like some ancient herald, like Pheidippides at Marathon, bringing news. Only this isn't news of victory – it's news that nobody wants to hear. They shut their ears to it.'

Suddenly, he fell silent. A policeman in a kepi was approaching, with a little torch muffled in blue, which he flicked in their direction.

'Bonsoir, monsieur. Madame.'

'Bonsoir.'

Handel tossed away his cigarette and it went flying, in a cascade of tiny sparks, into the river below. The wind was blowing her hair, and he lifted a hand to smooth it out of her eyes.

'Will you come to my apartment, Stella?'

How could she trust him, a man who had only recently committed a murder? Reason told her no, yet her every instinct urged otherwise.

'I want something of you,' he said. 'It's not what you think.'

## CHAPTER 25

Handel's apartment was in the rue des Saints-Pères, just off Saint-Germain, a street of well-appointed nineteenth-century buildings with sculpted pilasters and formal cornices. Stella recognized the name of a publishing company as they passed, alongside some academic printing houses and dusty, dark boutiques. They stopped at number 17, which had an elaborately carved wooden door with wrought-iron grilles and a shop window advertising *Henri de Leon, Photographic Agency, Commissions Taken*. Through the taped-up window, a montage of Parisian street scenes and a misty vision of Sacré-Coeur were just visible, along with a selection of formally posed families, husbands gripping the shoulders of their wives and cross-legged children in starched collars staring soberly at the camera.

The apartment was on the third floor. Once the shutters were closed, Handel switched on a lamp with an orange shade and the room leapt into view – a glimmer of books on the shelves, two armchairs, a crimson kelim rug. Against one wall stood a desk on which was a pile of paper and a typewriter. Alongside, a small gas stove with a coffee pot on it. Through a pair of double doors, an armoire and a bed were visible. She scanned his cramped sanctuary for what it might tell her about him.

'Let's have some music.'

He lifted the gramophone needle, and the sight of the record brought back with a jolt the claustrophobic hush of the M Room at Trent Park, the whirring of discs and the tapping of typewriters. As the jagged chords of jazz arose, he gestured to a chair, but Stella dallied. On the desk she noticed a small yellow origami stork. She picked it up.

'This is pretty.'

'Yes. I met the young woman who made it yesterday. She's a jazz violinist, but also an artist. She's going to be useful to us.'

Stella turned the little bird around in her hands.

'In what way useful?'

'Her name's Natalie. At least, that's the name she goes by. She makes these little figures for children. Tiny crocodiles and frogs and storks. All kinds of animals.'

He took the stork from her.

'They're so intricate. Kids love them. She'll make a little child whatever animal they choose, and they take them home. Then the parent unfolds the coloured paper, like so –' he splayed the stork's legs apart and the paper flattened back into a sheet – 'and they read the message.'

'How clever!'

'It's like jazz – you learn how to improvise. Like the agency downstairs.'

'How do you mean?'

'If the worst comes to pass, it will be useful to have access to cameras. We have accredited press photographers in our ranks. We can make photographs for false identity cards. I have mine already.'

He flourished a card from his inside pocket, and she looked at it.

État Français carte d'identité

Nom: Joubert

Prenoms: Patrice

Profession: journaliste

Nationalité: Fr

Beneath was a photograph with a round purple stamp. She studied the picture. The set mouth and narrowed eyes. A face as chiselled as a carving on a church front.

'Patrice Joubert. That's me. I'm an entirely different person. For the time being.'

He uncorked a half-finished bottle of Beaujolais that was standing on the table beside him.

'I need another drink. Do you want one?'

She nodded and he poured two glasses.

'How about you, Stella? Where are you living? When you're not in Paris?'

'Mecklenburgh Square, at the moment.'

'Mecklenburgh! Are you really? My family came from

there originally. I love finding traces of Germany in other places. Like little bits of living tissue scattered far and wide.' He laughed. A terse, dry little laugh. 'I rather like that notion, actually. It suits me. After all, I'm a man who's been completely torn apart.'

He passed her the glass.

'My family were Prussian by descent. My father moved to Berlin when he trained as a lawyer. He wanted me to follow in his footsteps, which is probably why I decided to escape to Oxford. Father indulged me. A year studying philosophy in a foreign country could not do too much harm. That was his reasoning.'

He turned to face her.

'When Cecil approached me, late last year, I thought of you immediately. D'you keep in touch with him?'

'We've not talked for a while, but yes.'

'Dear Cecil. All those stories he had! Working with Howard Carter in the Valley of the Kings. Meeting Heinrich Schliemann who excavated Troy. The Minotaur at Knossos. He was fascinated by labyrinths, wasn't he? Wasn't he writing a book about them?'

'*Method and Meaning in the Labyrinths of the Ancient World.*'

'That's the one. Strange that a skill for languages and labyrinths should go together. Do you remember those wonderful Sunday lunches he used to host?'

Cecil Fairfax had begun a tradition of inviting chosen students to his home, Elmwood Cottage, in a village a little way out of Oxford. Its low front door was approached by a brick path lined with lavender bushes and the latticed frontage was covered with Virginia creeper. Mullioned windows faced out across a wide lawn. Inside, exposed timber beams ran across the ceilings and lime-washed walls alternated with oak panelling. The drawing room was cluttered with ziggurats of books and manuscripts tied with garden twine, and every surface was decorated with souvenirs of his archaeological adventures. There, within this sanctuary, Cecil's undergraduates were treated to long, elaborate lunches that he had cooked himself.

'Cecil said his first thought was that I should work as a cryptanalyst. Bilinguists make good code breakers, apparently, because they're accustomed to looking for repetitions and patterns. But the need for German speakers at Trent Park was more pressing.'

Handel reached forward and touched her necklace, rubbing the pearls between his fingers, keeping his eyes locked on hers.

'Do you remember the first time you came to my college room? To discuss the German Romantics?'

'I think so.'

She had forgotten most of the German Romantics, but she had not forgotten the kiss that had lingered slightly too long on her cheek.

'You would sit there, your elbows on your knees, taking it in. Not interrupting. I used to wish everyone else would leave so that we could be alone. Since then, whenever I've thought of you, the background to you is always golden, like Oxford stone, never grey like Berlin or Paris.'

She was surprised he had thought of her at all. She'd hardly ever thought of him.

'That was a long time ago.'

He took her wrist in his hand, turned it over and stroked his thumb over the veins.

'I know. A lifetime. So much has happened since then.' He was very close. 'What would Cecil say now? Two of his students alone in an attic room in Paris.'

The air was full of energy. His words buffeted her cheeks, like little breaths, and the current of sexual attraction was too great to ignore. He leaned towards her, and they kissed. She put her hand to his chest and felt the slight dampness of the linen shirt. The scent of him must have lain deep in her memory, because it felt like déjà vu. An unexpected shiver ran through her as she looked at the map of lines on his face, wondering why this had not happened before. Time seemed to telescope so that it was both now, and a decade ago.

'I think Cecil would be surprised.'

He rubbed her lip with his thumb.

'I don't. I think he would have guessed all along.'

'Guessed what?'

He reached a hand around her waist and, so softly that she could barely hear, murmured, 'That we have unfinished business.'

Then he loosened her blue silk dress, and she shrugged it

off, letting it drop on the floor, and he pulled her towards him, as if he wanted to pull her into all the terrible things that he had seen.

Afterwards he walked across to the long windows, flung open the shutters and looked out over the jumble of lead roofs and chimney stacks. On the gramophone the record had finished long ago but the needle was still circling with a soft hiss. Stella pulled on his shirt and together they leaned out onto the balcony, their arms touching, gazing up at the pinpricks of stars in the night sky.

'Look at the stars. Aren't they astonishing? All those constellations. Galaxies. It reminds you that no matter how bright they are, darkness is the default setting. Light is the exception.'

'But light is more powerful.'

'Perhaps. Though you've not seen the kind of darkness I have. And you have no idea of the darkness inside me. I carry the things I've seen everywhere, like dreadful luggage. Often, at night, I can't shut my eyes for fear of what will be waiting for me.'

Gently, with a hand on his arm, she said, 'You were going to tell me what brought you here. To Paris.'

'I thought I'd made that clear.'

'But to take off like that. To leave so suddenly.'

'I've spent half my life leaving. It's ingrained in me now. As natural as breathing. But yes . . .'

He closed the shutters again, crossed the room and

switched on the lamp. He sat on the floor, in its orange glow, leaning back against the wall.

'I do need to tell you. I can't escape it forever, despite wanting to talk about anything else.'

He sighed and reached out for his cigarettes.

'I can talk about Trent Park, but only because you were there also. At least, I assume that's the case.'

She didn't answer, so he continued.

'I was first called for an interview at the Metropole building in Northumberland Avenue. When I arrived, I was interviewed by Colonel Kendrick, who pushed a pistol across the desk and said, *If you ever betray anything about this work, here is the gun with which I expect you to do the decent thing. If you don't, I will.* And I believed him.'

He sighed. 'But the fact is, there were times when I felt like using that gun on myself. It affected me, the listening. It shouldn't have come as a surprise, but it did. The extreme brutality, the lack of emotion and empathy. The way they talked about killing in such a matter-of-fact way.'

He paused to suck the smoke from his cigarette and blow it towards the ceiling.

'The first pair of men I was assigned to monitor had been rescued from a sunken U-boat. They talked of the drama – the terror of sinking, the damp bunks, the cold, the infernal noise of the engine, which never shut off and would have made it impossible to sleep, were it not for the fact that they were dead tired. But they didn't yield much of substance, and after a few weeks I was reassigned to a different pair of prisoners: a Luftwaffe officer around my own age called Oberstleutnant Gabriel Fassbinder, and his cellmate, a younger man called Georg Mandel. Mandel was much less interesting – he couldn't have been more than nineteen – but Fassbinder, well . . . I spent the best part of a month listening to him, day in and day out. Very often in the evening, when dinner and alcohol had loosened him, and he became more loquacious.'

Handel rubbed the line between his eyes with one thumb and she recognized the gesture with a jolt. It must have been buried in her brain, like information on a disc, waiting to be played back.

'As time went by, Fassbinder began to fascinate me. He might easily have been a friend of mine, I realized. We had so much in common. We obviously grew up close to each other – he talked about his family home in Schoenberg, which was very near mine. As a young man, he was mad about motor sports, just as I was. He would go out to watch the races on the autobahn and the Avus – that's the motor track out in the southwest of Berlin that goes through the Grunewald. They used to race the Grand Prix on there – Bugattis, Mercedes, Lamborghinis – half the boys in Berlin would go and watch. You see, Fassbinder could so easily have been my friend. We might have met, Stella. Do you see?'

'But you didn't meet.'

'No. Fassbinder trained as an architect, like my own uncle. And he must have been a promising one, because he told Mandel he had spent time in both Paris and London, studying there too. He had very modern views on style. And on his return, he won the biggest accolade a young architect could hope for – he became attached to the office of Albert Speer.'

'Speer?'

'The Nazis' chief architect. He ran the office of the General Building Inspector of Berlin. You can't imagine what a privileged environment that would be, Stella, for a young man like him. Those men who worked for Speer had limitless budgets and huge power. They called themselves Speer's Boys.'

'Like a gang.'

'More a brotherhood. They saw themselves as builders of a new world. They planned the clearance of the slum areas of Berlin. Fassbinder had helped Speer build a scale model of Paris for the sole pleasure of Adolf Hitler. Hitler, he said, would come into Speer's office in the evening just to look at the model and trace his finger up the boulevards and around the famous buildings. Every street in this city exists in Hitler's mind, even though he's never seen it.'

'Are you saying that Hitler's never visited Paris?'

'Not yet. But it's certainly on his agenda.'

He tipped more wine into his glass one-handed and waved the bottle at her. She shook her head. She was still naked, apart from the shirt and her pearl necklace, and she crossed her arms instinctively.

'There was something else about Fassbinder that made

him stand out to me. He had an undercurrent of humour that's rare among us Germans. His voice was warm, and *wry* — I think that's the word you would use in English. In fact, and this may sound strange to you, I *wanted* him to be my friend. It's a lonely life as a political exile. Fassbinder felt like a fellow spirit. Until he didn't.'

'You mean when he talked about the war.'

'Yes. That's when I really began to hate him.' He shuddered. 'When Fassbinder started boasting of the things he'd done, first in the Sudetenland, then Poland, I felt a pure, murderous rage. It's like what Nietzsche said, "If you gaze too long into the abyss, the abyss will look back into you."'

It was exactly what Mimi had told her. That Robert Handel had quoted Nietzsche.

*If you gaze too long into an abyss, the abyss will also gaze into you.*

'What does that mean? You can't say hearing about evil makes us evil ourselves.'

'Perhaps not. But it changes us, Stella. Evil can't be unseen or unheard. It's corrupting. Consuming. It can overwhelm you.'

She was leaning against the wall, the cool plaster at her back, knowing that she must not think of him as the man who had just made love to her. Though her body was still aching from his touch, she needed to remember that he had behaved with reckless anarchy. He had committed a terrible act. A murder, no less.

'If Fassbinder was an architect — and in Speer's office too, how did he end up fighting?'

'That's a good question. Georg Mandel asked that too. He definitely didn't need to. A man in Fassbinder's position could easily have remained on Speer's staff when war broke out. Instead, he joined the Luftwaffe. He said he felt a duty. He might have been expected to go into service at a higher level – the SS, maybe – but he chose to fly bombers. And that's how he was captured. Which was very much to our advantage. Because of his previous close relationship with Speer, he knew more than the average Luftwaffe officer. He knew about Hitler's plans for France. The Germans, he said, intended to subdue France entirely. He talked about *Fall Gelb*.'

'What's that?'

'Plan Yellow. The Wehrmacht plan to invade France. Last January, one of Goering's planes – a Messerschmitt Bf 108 – made a forced landing in Belgium and a top-secret dossier was lost. The passenger, one Major Reinberger, was on his way to a staff meeting in Cologne – he would have gone by train, but the plane carried more luggage and he wanted to take his laundry for his wife to wash. It is on these trivialities, dear Stella, that the fates of nations hang. The dossier exposed the intentions of the German High Command. It revealed that German paratroopers were to be landed behind the Belgian lines at Namur on January 17th.'

'But that never happened.'

'No. When Hitler learned that the dossier was lost, he immediately fired several senior members of staff and abandoned the plans. The King of Belgium sent a warning message to Churchill. But we'd be fooling ourselves if we thought the Nazis had abandoned their ambition to invade Western Europe.

'I realized that if what Fassbinder said was true, I needed to persuade my sister's family to leave Paris right away. But more than that – I knew it was essential that the French urgently improve their own networks of resistance. I had to get back in touch with people I had been in contact with when I lived here.'

He had been sitting head down and arms on his knees, but now he looked up at her.

'So that's how it was, Stella. I was appalled by Fassbinder. Appalled and, to be honest, disappointed too.'

'So appalled that you murdered him?'

He recoiled, startled.

'Murdered?'

'Murdered Gabriel Fassbinder.'

'What are you talking about?'

'That night. The night you left. His body was discovered in the grounds.'

'Are you saying . . . that Fassbinder's dead?'

'Yes. You killed him.'

'No. No. Not at all.'

'You said you hated him. You felt rage towards him. It's a bit of a coincidence that you should disappear the very night his body is found.'

'But how would I even know to find him? I'd never seen him. I only knew his voice.'

He got to his feet and paced the room for a few moments, then he said, 'Fassbinder's dead? I can't deny I fantasized about killing him. I felt pure anger, murderous rage. But then I thought, how would I even do it? Find out where he was and shoot him, perhaps? That would be pointless. A single bullet might be enough to end a man, but it would not end a war.'

He came over to her. 'You have to believe me, Stella. I never killed him. I had no idea he was dead.'

'Then why leave?'

'For all the reasons I've explained.'

'The authorities at Trent Park think you killed him. They think you're planning to take all the secrets you learned back to the Nazis.'

'No.' He was shaking his head vehemently. 'Not Cecil. Tell me Cecil doesn't believe that.'

'Cecil doesn't know what to believe.'

'And you, Stella?' He cupped her face in his hands. 'You know I'm not lying, don't you?'

She pulled away. 'I think you have to come back to England. You must explain to Kendrick and Maxwell Knight.'

'I can't.' He dropped his hands. 'Don't you see that what I'm doing here is more important? They need people like me in France. People with languages for once the Germans arrive. Once they get here, they'll bring with them reports on troop movements, ambitions, plans. We'll need people who can translate. And organize. There's no time to lose. Besides . . .' He flung himself into a chair. 'I have another motivation. Something a little more personal. I mentioned my sister Ursula.'

'The one who runs a bookshop.'

'Not any more. Because although her husband is still here, last year she went back to Germany to see our parents. It was a foolish move, born out of love, because they were getting older, and my father was ill. Neither of us knew how long he might live, and Ursula wanted to see him one last time. She wanted to persuade our parents to follow her here, to Paris. But she knew that her name was on a list of political exiles and that she was taking an enormous risk. Sure enough, she was very quickly arrested and transported to a camp called Ravensbrück north of Berlin. We don't know if she's alive or dead. My parents prefer to think the first, and I prefer – no, I fully believe – that she is herself dead.'

He reached out a hand to her, and she came and took it.

'We were talking about Orpheus. That story's been on my mind, Stella. We imagine it's about the desire of the living to revive the dead, but I think it's the opposite. I think it's about the way that the dead drag us down into their realm because we refuse to let them go. Ursula is always at my side, insisting that I follow her.'

'To death?'

'Who knows? Nobody can expect to survive. If the Nazis arrive, they'll arrest all the German nationals they can find.

I'll have to go underground very soon. What I'm doing now is more important than individual people. More important than families. More important, whatever we might feel, than love affairs. There will be other times for those.'

# CHAPTER 26

*May 10th*

Stella had spent a restless night. She was in bed with a man she had not seen in a decade. He had made intense love to her as though he had imagined it for years. For a while he had held her as if his life depended on it, then he fell away and dropped into a heavy sleep. Stella, however, lay awake. Feelings knotted in her, and through her churning mind images flashed. The secrets of the M Room, the sadism and the killings. Her everyday world, of the GPO Film Unit and Toby Enderby, which had never seemed so far away. The face of Harry Fox, leaning against the door of his office, smiling at her.

The normality she had known was in tatters. She had no idea what would happen next.

While Robert Handel slumbered deeply at her side, she turned over everything he had told her: about Gabriel

Fassbinder, about Ursula, his sister, and his denial of the murder at Trent Park. He would deny it. Of course he would.

And yet . . .

If Robert Handel was guilty, why not admit it, now that he was safely abroad and out of reach of the British authorities? He need fear no consequences. Who would blame him if he had killed a sadistic compatriot in a rush of blind rage? Many people would understand. Even applaud him.

Yet Handel was adamant. He didn't kill Gabriel Fassbinder.

And if he didn't, who did? Perhaps it didn't matter any more. That was the tempting conclusion. But if the secrets of Trent Park were at stake, it did.

She wondered what Harry was doing now. She was desperate to tell him everything but there was no way to communicate. If even Noël Coward, a British official attempting to contact the British government, had trouble placing an international call, what chance did a mere civilian stand, calling a detective of dubious repute? Besides, if she was being followed by Gestapo informers, telephoning Harry was out of the question. A telegram would be the better route. That was it. She would send a telegram first thing.

Eventually, towards dawn, she began to doze, thinking about the stars and the darkness. Tom Lamont, who had studied physics, had once told her that looking at starlight was literally looking at the past because the light had emerged millions of years ago and what you saw was no more than faint jolts of energy persisting into the present. The stars, he said, were proof that the past was always there, lingering and visible, even if it couldn't be captured.

This thought calmed her, and she dropped off to sleep.

She was woken by the scream of air-raid sirens. Handel was up, thrusting open the shutters. From all around came the clatter of windows being opened, and shouts echoed across the street.

'What's happening?'

'Come here.'

His face was still creased with sleep, but he was staring out across the rooftops. In the distance a billowing cloud of smoke was smouldering into the porcelain air.

'It's oil reserves burning along the Basse-Seine. They want to keep the fuel from falling into the hands of the enemy.'

'Why now?'

He was flinging on his shirt and underwear. She noticed he was shaking.

'Because it's happened.'

He crossed swiftly to the wireless. The voice of a BBC announcer emerged from the wavering static.

*. . . German forces have invaded Belgium, Luxembourg and the Netherlands by air and land. The invasion began at dawn with large numbers of aeroplanes attacking the main aerodromes and landing troops. Germany attacked through the Ardennes Forest in south-east Belgium and northern Luxembourg. The Dutch High Commission says more than a hundred German planes were shot down by its*

*forces. The British Foreign Secretary, Lord Halifax, received the Belgian ambassador and Dutch Prime Minister at 0630 when they formally petitioned for Allied help. Adolf Hitler has issued a proclamation to the German armies in the West, saying: 'The hour has come for the decisive battle for the future of the German nation.'*

Her heart began to race and she felt panic gathering in the pit of her stomach.

'We don't have much time left,' he said, buttoning his jacket. 'The Wehrmacht will reach Paris before we know it.'

'Surely not.'

'It's a blitzkrieg. Hitler wants a quick victory. Everyone here must get used to the idea that Paris may fall.'

Still, she stood, frozen.

Handel was rushing around the room, stashing belongings in a kitbag.

'You need to leave, Stella. You must leave now. I'll take you to the Gare du Nord and you must catch the first train you can for the coast. They'll start bombing the airports and the railway lines and we'll be caught like rats in a trap.'

She picked up the dress, which was lying in a puddle of creased silk on the floor.

'I need to go back to the hotel first. To collect my things.'

'Do you have your passport with you?'

'Yes, but . . .'

'Then there's no time. The trains will be full. Take this.'

He reached into a cupboard and brought out a pair of serge trousers and a rough white cotton shirt. She pulled them on and then he tied his own belt around her waist.

'Robert, about last night . . .'
He shook his head, sternly.
'Now's not the time.'

They stepped out of the apartment building into the bustle of the street outside. The sirens had stopped, but the chill morning air was still vibrating. She wondered what she must look like, in a man's trousers and shirt, and was grateful she had brought her woollen coat.

As they crossed the Seine, to their left more smoke drifted across the sky.

'The embassies must be making bonfires in the courtyards. They're burning sensitive files before evacuating.'

'Already? Who says the Germans will even get this far?'

'Adolf Hitler. And everyone here believes him.'

She stared around her. The testimony of her eyes told her that everything was normal. Men in broad-shouldered suits with white pocket handkerchiefs were heading for the office, elderly women were returning from the market with baguettes and baskets of vegetables, children were going to school. Workmen in overalls and corduroys were carrying tool bags. The pavement cafés were packed with customers taking their morning coffee and the tricolour waved bravely from government buildings. The idea that a few hundred miles away columns of German tanks were racing in their direction was not enough to disturb the Parisian sangfroid.

Yet as they crossed the Place de l'Hôtel-de-Ville, Stella noticed a group of people standing stock-still, staring up at the sky, as if they expected enemy parachutists to descend any minute.

The concourse of the Gare du Nord was already a seething mass of travellers, people laden not only with suitcases, but birdcages, typewriter cases, cat baskets, and rolled-up carpets. Men were shouting and children were shrieking. As she stood at the ticket office the young woman next to her had tears pouring down her face.

Once they had found the right platform, Stella halted in the melee and let the stream of people divert around her.

'Robert, I can't go without you.'

'This is no time for emotion.'

'No, it's not that. You don't understand. What I mean is, you have to come with me, because if you stay here you threaten everything those people at Trent Park have worked for.'

'But I thought I made it clear. How could you possibly imagine I would be a threat?'

'You may not mean to be. But what if the Germans do come and you're captured? What if, God forbid, you're tortured? You yourself said this city is full of Gestapo informers. One of them has most likely been following me. They'll get the information out of you, no matter how hard you try to conceal it. You'll compromise Trent Park and everything it's doing. It would be catastrophic. For the war and everyone back home. You can't want that.'

Soberly, he said, 'I can assure you, Stella, that I would

never give those secrets up. Besides, nobody in Paris would have the faintest idea that I was ever at Trent Park. Or what I was doing. The only people who know I was there are in England now.'

'And do you trust them?'

He recoiled, eyes widened.

'You mean, do I trust the other listeners? Do I think any of the listeners could be Nazi agents?'

'Who knows? At least one of them is a murderer.'

'Then that's a risk I'll have to take. France may not be my own country, but I would die for it. And Stella . . .'

He came closer and put his arms around her, murmuring in her ear.

'Everything I've told you . . . I wouldn't have said a word of it if I didn't think you were going back to England right now. You're just as much a security risk yourself, given what you know. I want you to go back and tell Kendrick everything I've told you. Give him this.' He slipped something into her pocket. 'It's my security pass – so he knows it's me. I need him to know that I'm in place. That I'm working here.'

He broke away and delved into his kitbag, bringing out a small box.

'I said I wanted something of you. It's this. I have something else to give you.'

He opened the box. Inside was a ring, blazing with diamonds.

'Wear it on your engagement finger.'

It was not the first time a man had presented her with

an engagement ring, but it was the most perplexing. Stella looked up at the cold eyes and the rigid jaw with its cleft chin.

'Go on. Let's see it on. What do you think?'

She slid the ring onto her finger. 'What does this mean?'

'It means five carats of diamonds, emerald-cut. Set in eighteen-carat gold. When you get to London, you must sell it. It's for the refugees. They'll need money when they come to Britain. They'll need plenty of things – people to vouch for them, find people willing to home them, assemble papers, rent apartments – but everything costs money and this can go a little way to help.' He shrugged. 'It suits you. We've tried other methods for transporting jewels – someone I know puts them in hollowed-out golf balls – but I think a ring is best.'

He heaved the bag back over his shoulder.

'And I suppose I should say, forgive me.' His tone was distant now, and businesslike. 'For last night.'

'For what?'

'For being sentimental. I was sentimental, and you indulged me.'

'Maybe I was sentimental too.'

His eyes were colder than ever and his accent more clipped and formal. The lips were a tight line. Already, their night together was speeding into the past. Already he was a thousand miles away from the handsome man at Le Boeuf sur le Toit who was intoxicated by jazz and by her.

'I know we'll see each other again, Stella. But in the meantime, I'm glad we agree.'

'What do we agree?'

'That war is no time for love affairs.'

# CHAPTER 27

'Finchleystrasse. Passports please.'

Going by the smirk on the face of the conductor of the number 13 bus, Harry guessed that this was not the first time he had made this joke. And going by the stolid, unsmiling countenances of his passengers, the joke did not get any funnier the more they heard it. Finchley Road in St John's Wood held the highest concentration of displaced Germans and Austrians in Britain. Chiefly this was because the area was full of large houses whose wealthy owners had fled to the security of the countryside, and in their absence the buildings were now subdivided into a warren of small bedsits and flats. The more refugees who settled there, the more others arrived to be with their compatriots.

He jumped off the bus and strolled a few yards down the road.

★

The premises of the Danube Bar and Social Club might have been situated in north London but to all purposes it was a perfectly formed segment of Continental Europe. It could as well have been the embassy of Austria, transported to English soil.

Harry pushed open the net-curtained door to find white linen tablecloths with folded napkins. Heavy, yellowing globe lamps and old wood-panelled walls with peeling varnish. Elegantly dressed women sporting elaborately styled hair sat at tables playing cards. Men in well-preserved suits were reading the papers, meticulously folding down each page as they went, presumably because each newspaper would be shared by several customers. On the tables stood tiny coffee cups and tall glasses of lemon tea with sugar cubes in the saucer. Nobody here was having any truck with Nescafé. Periodically, the doors to the kitchen swung open to emit wafts of Wiener schnitzel and apple strudel.

He found a booth that was partitioned from the main body of the café by a low wooden divider, sat down and withdrew a letter from his pocket. The letter was from his nephew, Jack. He had already read it three times.

*Dear Uncle Harry,*
*I hope you are well. I am having a great time. Mr Swiggs says I can ride the horses when they bring in the harvest in the autumn. School is fine – I have been moved up a class. They aren't half so strict as Hammersmith Boys and Mr Bannister says he might give me extra teaching two evenings a week.*

*I don't mind except I know Mr Swiggs would prefer me to help with the milking and Mrs Swiggs says he needs all the help he can get because Dick and Albert have joined up. I think I'd like to stay here after the war if they let me. Do you think they would let me? Perhaps Mum could move nearby.*

*Thank you for the modelling kit. I have finished the Ferguson tractor but I have not started the Lancaster bomber.*

*Hope to see you soon.*
*Your loving nephew,*
*Jack*

Frankly, he would rather have been stabbed with a knife. He was amazed what deadly wounds an eleven-year-old could inflict. In the old days, the Lancaster bomber would have been completed within days and the tractor left to one side. But it wasn't that which bothered him. It was the thought that Jack might become a country boy and Harry would see so much less of him. His nephew, who was as good as a son, might one day scarcely know him.

Instantly, he dismissed this thought. If that happened, Harry knew he would find some way of becoming a country dweller himself. A farmer, perhaps. How hard could it be? He worked his sister's allotment, after all. He knew about cabbages and beans. He understood that crops were like women: some, such as potatoes, would get on wherever they were, whereas others, like carrots, demanded constant attention and delicate treatment. Sandy soil, careful handling, soft words.

These thoughts were interrupted by a husky whisper and a gust of strong perfume.

'Harry Fox. What's my favourite detective doing here?'

Irene O'Malley had ditched the old nude body stocking she had worn as Botticelli's Venus at the Hippodrome, although the memory of it was unlikely to leave him anytime soon. Her new work wear, however, was just as liable to prompt lascivious thoughts, comprising as it did a black maid's outfit, with tight skirt, seamed stockings, white frilly apron and another little frill fixed in her hair. She looked how a waitress might look in an Edwardian gentlemen's cartoon.

Before he could reply she reached out and put a finger to his lips.

'On second thoughts, don't say. I probably don't want to know the answer. Let me get you coffee and you can tell me how much you're missing me.'

She disappeared for a moment, then returned and sat opposite him on the velvet-covered seat.

'Nice place,' said Harry.

'It is. They love it here, the customers. They live in tiny bedsits and some of them have no access to kitchens, so they come here for their meals. We make all their favourites from back home: breaded mushrooms, schnitzel, goulash, potato chips. The chef here makes a Viennese chocolate coffee eclair called a *Mohrenkopf* that's to die for. You must have some cake, Harry. What d'you fancy? We have all kinds: plum cake, cheesecake. My favourite is *Stachelbeerentorte*. It's made from gooseberries. The continentals have an awfully sweet tooth.'

'Very cosmopolitan,' said Harry.

'That's the idea. We have all sorts here. Austrians, Prussians, Hungarians, Spaniards. Even some Serbs. They don't like speaking foreign languages out in the street – they get funny looks – so they come in here and they go ten to the dozen. They're not all the same, you know. They're very particular. The Germans sit on one side, over there, and the Austrians sit on the other, right here. They hardly talk to each other. You wouldn't believe it.'

An elderly waiter shuffled towards them with two cups of thick black coffee and a large slice of chocolate cake.

'Thank you, Gustav. Go ahead, Harry. You'll never taste anything like that. It melts in the mouth. Sigmund Freud used to ask for it specially. He said it reminded him of Vienna. You heard of Freud?'

'The psychoanalyst.'

'He died, but half the gentlemen here are in the same game. They're so interesting to talk to. They can read your mind.'

Harry stiffened, as though even a stray glance from one of the clientele might discern his less respectable thoughts, then, plunging a fork into the cake, he said, 'Sunny Hoss told me you were working here.'

She nodded.

'I assume on the business of our mutual friend.'

A toothy smile.

'The fact is, our friend is after a particular individual. Handel. Robert Handel. German. Have you come across him?'

Irene frowned for a second, then shook her head. Her eyes were flickering around the room as they spoke, patrolling the customers, their interactions, their comings and goings. Knight had chosen well when he recruited her. Very little escaped her darting gaze.

'I'm afraid I haven't, Harry. And I'm being very . . . observant, if you know what I mean. These people love telling me their stories, so I do sit and listen. But that gentleman's name hasn't cropped up. I'd know if it had.'

Harry paused for a moment, as an explosion of chocolate ravished his tastebuds, then said, 'Never mind. That's not the only reason I'm here. It's something else. Or someone. I'm after a woman called Lieselotte. Lieselotte Edelman. Late twenties. Dark hair, blue eyes, very . . . very striking to look at.'

Irene grinned.

'This a girlfriend of yours?'

'I don't have a girlfriend.'

'An ex?'

He shook his head.

'A criminal then? Up to no good?'

'Not sure.'

He brought out the book of matches.

'She had these.'

Irene turned them over and gave them back to him.

'They're ours all right. Maybe she came in for a meal some time.'

'You're sure you don't recognize the name? Lieselotte Edelman?'

'Sorry, Harry. I'll keep a lookout though.'

'Thanks.'

She shuffled closer to him, and he felt a hand on his thigh. Her voice held a hint of treacly nostalgia.

'Shame you don't have a girlfriend, Harry. We were good together. Perhaps I shouldn't have let work get in the way. We're both rough diamonds, aren't we?'

Harry had never considered himself anything other than a cultivated man of talents, but if that's what Irene wanted to believe, he wasn't about to interfere, especially as she was reaching a perfumed face towards him to kiss. He almost let himself kiss her back, but this was a movie he had already seen, so he shrugged and said, 'I suppose.'

Irene took the hint.

'Oh, well. I'd best be going. Duty calls. Don't leave it so long next time, Harry.'

Then she was off, with a deliberate wiggle of her well-shaped hips to show him what he was missing.

It was only when Harry emerged from the underground at Waterloo that he realized something was up. The vast station concourse was always busy, but now it seemed to vibrate with nervous energy. Instead of milling beneath the departure boards, commuters were clustered around the newspaper stand that stood under the great clock. Civil servants with briefcases, clerks in flat caps, female typists making their way back to the Home Counties. Strangers exchanged anxious looks in a most un-English way. Harry strode across to take a look. The banner on the *Daily Express* news-stand read:

## CHAMBERLAIN TO RESIGN
### Churchill expected to be new Premier
Nazis invade Holland, Belgium and Luxembourg by land and air

So that was it, then. The interval was over, and the second half had begun. The refugees would no longer be the quiet sort, decorously eating chocolate cake in the Finchley Road. There would be legions of Dutch, Belgians and no doubt French, streaming in every which way, destitute, hungry, unsettled. The chances of finding a lone German were decreasing by the second.

He left the station, walked towards the river, and cast a weary glance at the scarlet poster tacked to the wall.

*Keep Calm and Carry On.*

It was good advice. Perhaps he should forget Lieselotte Edelman. She no longer had a commission for him and there was plainly more to her than met the eye. He could stop fretting about Jack, too. He would face the thing head-on; take the train out to visit his nephew next weekend and assess just what the chances were that this Swiggs family would steal him away long term. He would also try to cheer up Joan. Perhaps he could coax her out to the theatre, or the flicks. Instead of mooning after Lieselotte, he would focus on the more important things in life, which, right then, were absolutely everything.

# CHAPTER 28

*Saturday, May 11th*

She was neat as ever, in the same cloche hat and fawn belted coat, but it didn't take a detective to see that she was tired, and under the hat her normally smooth, gleaming bob was windblown. These details Harry could not help noting, even while he was overwhelmed with delight at the sight of Stella Fry, standing outside his office the following afternoon.

Almost immediately she lifted a finger to her lips.

'Not here. Let's walk.'

She led the way out of Goodwin's Court and towards Trafalgar Square. He walked beside her without speaking, hands in his pockets, through Admiralty Arch and into St James's Park. Beneath the canopy of birch and ash, they proceeded companionably towards the lake, and Harry felt he might not mind walking like this for a long time, now that Stella was back, and beside him.

They came to a place on the path where an old lady was scattering seed for the birds, and Stella halted. Harry leaned expectantly against a plane tree, looking at the play of shadows on her face as the light filtered through the leaves.

'Go on, then. Why the silence?'

'There was a man hanging around outside your office. I got the impression he didn't want to be seen. When I caught sight of him, he ducked into a doorway, but he didn't actually leave.'

'What did he look like?'

'Seedy.'

'That's no help. That describes most of my customers. Was he British? Foreign?'

'I've no idea. But Maxwell Knight thought I was being watched, didn't he? So I wonder if you might be too. And I don't want anyone hearing what I have to say.'

Harry rubbed his chin ruminatively, stowing away the information for later. Then he said, 'Where've you been?'

'Paris.'

'Paris?' he echoed, dumbly.

'I left there yesterday morning. It's been a terrible journey. I came straight to find you. And Harry, I tracked down Robert Handel.'

For a moment, astonishment rendered him speechless. He watched the old lady with the birds, delivering the seeds from her pocket mechanically, like a medieval peasant. The seed scattered high in a balletic arc before descending in a shower on the path where sparrows pecked at it with jerky clockwork movements and fat grey-liveried pigeons attempted to muscle in. Harry wondered irrelevantly if they were English or German birds. He was trying to marshal his disorderly emotions – jealousy, annoyance, relief – into some kind of pecking order. Annoyance won out.

'So, for the past three days, while I've been traipsing around the refugee circles, you already knew where he was? Could you not tell me?'

'I wasn't certain he was in Paris. And actually, I didn't find him – he found me. Besides, I had no way of getting hold of you, Harry. You can't telephone from France. I was going to send a telegram but as soon as I heard about the German attack, I left straight away.'

'You talked to Handel, though? You confronted him about the murder?'

'Yes.' She was twirling a large diamond ring on her finger. Her engagement finger, he noted with a shock. He would come back to that.

'The fact is, Harry, we discussed it, and he denied it absolutely.'

'That settles it, then.'

She frowned. 'Don't you ever get tired of being cynical?'

'On the contrary. I recommend it.'

'I know you don't believe me.'

'Oh, I like a criminal who tells the gospel truth. The only thing is, I've never met one.'

'I can understand why you think he's lying. But I knew Robert Handel before, ten years ago, at university. He's not a criminal, he's a remarkably intelligent man. With a deep integrity.'

'Sounds like it.'

'He told me he'd been engaged by British intelligence to monitor Fassbinder. That the more he came to know about him, the more he realized that this was a German man just like himself – probably the same age and from the same background. They even lived near each other in Berlin. He did feel a murderous rage towards Fassbinder, he actually said that, and he would never have risked admitting it if he was lying, would he?'

'Not unless he was a very remarkably intelligent man.'

Stella ignored the sarcasm. She was twisting the ring round and round, watching its chunky diamonds flash in the evening air.

'So Handel went off to Paris, what, on holiday?'

'He went AWOL the same night that Fassbinder was killed. He's urgently trying to help establish some kind of underground resistance network. He had no idea that Fassbinder was dead, and I promise you, Harry, I believe him.'

Harry pulled up the collar of his coat and looked gloomily around him.

'Right. Let's say, just for the moment, that this *remarkably intelligent* man is telling the truth. We still don't know who murdered Oberstleutnant Gabriel Fassbinder.'

Stella sighed. Exhaustion swept through her like a wave. The journey from France had been shattering. Once she had reached the French coast, she discovered that the regular boat train had been suspended and she had been obliged to talk herself onto a P&O ferry that was transporting other panicky Britons, as well as British troops, back across the Channel. From Dover, she found a third-class seat on the London train. The episode had cost the last of the money Colonel Kendrick had provided, and she could scarcely believe she had actually made it and was standing there, in front of Harry Fox, in the apparent tranquillity of St James's Park.

Emotional turbulence was exploding within her like a series of tiny bombs. First the traumas of Trent Park, then the nerve-racking experience of being followed in Paris, and ultimately her night with Robert Handel, and his curt behaviour afterwards. Reckless one-night stands were not her habit – indeed, she had never engaged in one before. Even if she had no interest in a love affair with him, she could not help but be stung by Handel's terse farewell, and the chilliness of his voice. She was angry with herself. It was humiliating, to be honest. Probing her feelings further she found, beneath it all, another dread lurking: the prospect of that evening's engagement dinner for Tom Lamont.

Not that she was going to tell Harry Fox any of this.

'What does it matter, Harry? In the end? A sadistic German officer got shot. He probably deserved it.'

'It matters.'

'Why?'

'Because I'm a detective who has been asked to investigate

a murder. With your help. Solving it is part of the job description. We're a team, Stella, remember.'

His face was uncomprehending. He was looking at her as though she was a puzzle to be decoded.

She shrugged, tiredly. 'I don't see what more we can do.'

'You're the tidy sort, aren't you? I've noticed that. You like everything neat around you. Surely you must want to tie up the loose ends.'

Something was stirring in Harry's mind – an evanescent, half-formed thought. An image, or some kind of connection. He tried to pin it down, but it slipped away, evading all examination.

'When Maxwell Knight told us about Fassbinder, he said he had been shot, didn't he? What was he shot with?'

'A gun.'

'Did they find it?'

'It went missing.'

'Hmm.'

He levered himself off the tree trunk and dug his hands into his pockets.

'Well, we'll need to relay all this to Maxwell Knight.'

Stella hesitated and, not for the first time, Harry felt there was a large part of this conversation that he wasn't hearing. Like those sounds so high that only a dog can pick them up.

'Harry, why don't *you* go? On your own. Tell him everything and I'll go back to Trent Park and inform Colonel Kendrick.'

'What are you talking about?'

'It's over. We've done what he asked. We found Handel. Mission accomplished.'

'Knight needs to hear that from you.'

'Does he? The Germans have invaded Western Europe. Frankly, I expect Maxwell Knight will have his hands full. As far as I'm concerned, I should go home and get back to my old job, at least until I'm drafted elsewhere.'

She pulled out a cigarette, and as she struck the match, he noticed that her hand was trembling. It was shaking so much that it threatened to blow out the flame. He felt a sudden, urgent desire to put his arm round her and protect her, but he reminded himself that Stella Fry didn't want protecting. If she was tough enough to travel around Europe unaccompanied, she was tough enough to manage a smoke on her own.

All the same, he reached out and steadied her hand with his.

More gently, he said, 'The fact is, Stella, we haven't completed the mission. If your chap's telling the truth, we still don't know who killed Gabriel Fassbinder. There may be a spy embedded at Trent Park. An enemy agent. At the very least, that person is still a major security risk.'

'I don't know what more I can do.'

'We can do what we were asked to do.'

'And I've done that. Why are you so keen to carry on?'

'Why? Because it's work, Stella, not a hobby. You don't do a crossword and leave it half completed. Something happens, we find the bad guys and turn them in. That's the job.'

Frustration was rising in him. Was it injured professional pride – that Stella had been the one to track down Robert Handel – or was it the idea that she would soon be returning to her film unit, and he would no longer have any reason to see her? Or was it something to do with the large diamond ring glinting on the third finger of her left hand?

'Nice ring, by the way. Are congratulations in order? Who's the lucky guy?'

She gave him a bewildered look, then said, 'Oh, that. As it happens, I'm planning to sell it as soon as possible.'

'Why are you being like this? This isn't like you. This isn't the Stella Fry I know.'

She gave him a fierce stare. Her eyes were shining, either with tears or tiredness.

'Really? Who is the Stella Fry you know?'

It was a good question. Harry knew her, and wanted to know her more, but he was gradually learning that Stella was made up of contradictions. She was both worldly and uncertain, tough yet vulnerable. Hot then cold. He had spent a decade in surveillance studying behaviour and motivation, but it occurred to him, not for the first time, that if the government really wanted to create an unbreakable cypher, they should take a look at women. Female minds were harder to crack than any code.

'What I mean is, you're just being . . . impossible.'

'Sure. Perhaps I am. I'm exhausted so I'd better get going. Sorry, Harry. Let's talk on Monday.'

She swung her bag up on her shoulder and turned.

Harry watched her go. The old lady flung a handful of seeds in his direction, but he barely registered. He remained there for at least a minute, staring ahead, as the sparrows squabbled and flustered about his feet.

To divert himself, he returned to the French House and ordered himself a weapons-grade Scotch, then another three, and sat at the same corner table that he and Lieselotte had occupied a few evenings before. After a while, however, his hungry gaze was beginning to attract the attention of a Continental lady in a leopardskin coat with a lascivious smile and skin as puckered as a peach stone, who was clearly angling for a free drink or maybe more, so he jammed his hat back on his head and left the place.

He walked a few blocks to Leicester Square. The Odeon was showing a matinee of *Busman's Honeymoon*. It was based on a detective novel by Dorothy L. Sayers that Harry had read and enjoyed, so he paid two and six and settled down in the flickering darkness, allowing a fictional murder to distract him from the real one. It was a decent film, featuring Robert Montgomery and one of his favourite actresses, Constance Cummings, but what Harry liked best about it was the fact that however much Lord Peter Wimsey and Harriet Vane quarrelled, they always ended up reconciled.

He was back in the office and had dozed off on the purple sofa when the phone woke him. Already the hangover was a gun to his head.

'Hey Sherlock.'

It was Irene.

'Want the good news or the bad news?'

'I've had plenty of bad news already. Don't want to be greedy.'

'The good news, then. That girl you mentioned. Lieselotte.'

'What about her?'

'I was thinking if Harry's chasing a woman, I bet it's a cute one. And I thought of one very cute girl who I've seen just recently. Gorgeous, really. Dark hair, legs up to here. Does that sound like the lady you had in mind?'

'Pretty much.'

'You're in luck, then. She was working here as a waitress. She called herself Lisa, not Lieselotte, but she's definitely German. She sat on that side of the room. And she had a lot of questions for the customers.'

'So what's the bad news?'

'Last week she's vanished. Left without collecting her wages. Disappeared without trace.'

His mind was turning over and over, fishing for the thought that had risen momentarily in his mind before submerging again. The gun.

Maxwell Knight had talked about three suspect Germans in the émigré community. Two of them women. Well, he'd found one of those all right. And she had a gun. The gun that killed Gabriel Fassbinder had gone missing. A gun, a German and a girl. Coincidence, as Harry knew from his devout study of detective fiction, was a rare thing, and this was the kind of join-the-dots exercise that featured on page one of the Private Detective's Handbook.

He waited until nightfall. It was drizzling slightly. The rain dampened his face like tears. Some way up the road a dog was having a nervous breakdown. As he approached the sooty terraces of Islington, he stumbled against a pile of saucepans, left on the pavement for the government to make Spitfires from, and set off an almighty clattering. He looked behind him, but the noise was too routine to prompt any surprise. A friend who knew had told him that the mounds of saucepans and frying pans left by the patriotic public had proved unsuitable for melting down. They were largely consigned to the rubbish, but it was the thought that counted, and people liked to think they were doing their bit, so the project continued.

He made his way towards the address Irene had provided. Most of the houses in the terrace were divided into flats. An arrow painted on the front door of number 18, Nottingham Street read, *Prendergast Flat A Basement Door* and above it was tacked a stained and faded piece of cardboard. It read *Arthurs Flat B, Price Flat C, Porter Flat D*. But the *Price* of Flat C had been scribbled out and the name *Edelman* inserted in pencil. So Irene had got this much right. On the first floor – Flat C's floor – blackout curtains were pulled, and no suggestion of light penetrated.

Opposite the building was a pub, which faux-medieval lettering proclaimed as the White Hart. The urge to toss down a quick one before work was powerful, but Harry managed to resist its magnetic pull. The dramatic political movements of the past few days had provoked even the most solitary barflies into lively discussion. In the Houses of Parliament, MP Leo Amery had directed a blistering speech at Chamberlain that evoked a historic moment from the reign of Oliver Cromwell. *You have sat too long here for any good you have been doing. Depart, I say, and let us have done with you. In the name of God, go!* Now Churchill was in. As a result, the deep peace of the saloon bar had transformed into the hurly-burly of the philosopher's salon – a place where people talked to each other, and worse, talked politics, which was the last thing Harry wanted.

Down one side of the pub he saw a slimy alley piled with old beer kegs and dustbins, and here he slipped in, leaning against the brickwork in the gloom, staring across the road. Half an hour went by. A man passed, walking a West Highland terrier that cast a beady eye down the grimy recess in which he lurked. Dogs may be man's best friend, but they were on cooler terms with private investigators. The animal tugged on its lead, wanting to come towards the alleyway and sniff at the contents, but the owner yanked its lead and the dog was pulled unceremoniously from sight. A few minutes later a tortoiseshell cat came prowling along the pavement, lifting delicate paws through a patch of weeds. Tortoiseshells were always female, Harry thought irrelevantly, and indeed there was something feminine about the insolent feline stare it directed at him.

He was pondering Lieselotte's comment in the French House. *I live in Islington, but it's best we don't go there.*

Why not? Was she married? Co-habiting? Lying? All of the above?

Suddenly, the cat lifted its head. Harry saw nothing, yet his senses quivered and in the next moment came the sound of a door opening and the patter of footsteps. They belonged to a woman who came out of number 18, clipped down the steps, and passed directly across his alleyway before crossing the road and disappearing in the direction of Upper Street. While it was hard to see in the gloom, he could tell from her shape and gait that it was certainly not the same woman who had left his flat only days before. There was nothing to say that she had come from Flat C — she might equally have been Prendergast Flat A or Arthurs Flat B or Porter Flat D — yet some aspect of this woman bothered him. She was familiar. Although he could see very little in the darkness, he knew that he had encountered that person before.

He waited for another half-hour, puzzling over this. Maybe it was a trick of the light. There was nothing so fallible as memory. No one else left or came, and his limbs were beginning to ache, so he decided to progress the situation.

Easing his way out of the alley, he rejected the idea of a frontal assault and instead walked along the street a little until he came to a side alley that led, as he suspected, to the back of the terrace.

Houses always show their best face to the world, but the back tells the truth about them. The narrow rat-run leading along the rear of the terrace was separated from the back yards by a five-foot wall. A cat, possibly the one he had seen earlier, was sitting on the wall observing him impassively. In the absence of a gate, Harry scrambled up the wall, vaulted over and dropped down on the terrain of weeds, rough turf and broken brick that passed for the garden of number 18. It was plain that the inhabitants were not meticulously house-proud. At the basement window, a dingy net curtain hung drunkenly above a pit of darkness. From the window of Flat B on the ground floor not a chink of light escaped, which meant that either the householder was out, or they were the kind of citizen that Home Secretary Sir John Anderson would be proud of.

He scanned the building for a means of entry. There was no drainpipe but, to his joy, an air-raid shelter had been constructed: an Anderson-approved roll of corrugated steel butting up against the side of the house, exactly like the one he had just installed for Joan.

Harry had always been interested in architecture, which came in useful when breaking into houses. His experience of nineteenth-century terraces had provided a connoisseur's knowledge of the sturdiness of brick walls, the thickness of doors, and the layout of the Victorian terraced house. This particular specimen, he reckoned, was early Victorian, going by its flat-fronted facade, long pedimented windows, three floors and basement. And that was good, because those

Victorian builders had standards, even when they were constructing homes for clerks and lowly office workers. They built them to last, with window ledges that would quite easily bear a man's weight.

Rolling himself up onto the curved roof of the Anderson shelter, trying hard not to put all his weight on one point, he reached up to the first-floor window ledge. For a few moments his feet scrabbled on empty air until he got a purchase on the brickwork. Gripping the ledge with his fingers he hauled himself up, balancing precariously on the narrow strip of masonry as he ran his fingers round the window. He was in luck again, for it was rotten and, even better, unlatched. Experimentally, he eased it open a few inches, waited a while, alert for any reaction, then opened it further and slid through.

Dropping down onto a ratty Persian carpet he inhaled, making a swift sensory inventory: a bouquet of damp, old masonry and cigarettes, the signature perfume of the transient lodger. He was in the back bedroom and, by his reckoning, the property would extend as far as a meagre sitting room at the front, with a kitchen and a bathroom off a narrow corridor on the way. The bed was empty and unmade, with clothes strewn across it. Women's clothes.

He got out his torch and cautiously took a few steps, testing the boards. While the exterior of these houses was invariably solid, he had yet to find a floorboard that did not creak. As his eyes adjusted, he found his way across the room towards the opened door and followed the narrow beam of light along the corridor to pass, as he had expected, first a bathroom, then a kitchen. He peered inside. On the small square table were two plates, a breadboard and half a loaf.

He moved into the front room. The parlour. His feet sank into a rug. The torch illuminated the shape of an armchair, and a small table on which a half-opened book was tented, with a standard lamp to the side, and a saucer full of cigarette stubs. He caught the glint of bottles and glasses on a small drinks trolley. He was about to examine the selection of postcards ranged along the mantelpiece when from somewhere in the house came a sharp noise, causing him to drop the torch.

He froze. Maxwell Knight had told him that some animals – alligators, he thought – could slow their heartbeat right down when they wanted to conserve energy. They could control their pulse at will. Harry's own pulse was dead slow. As slow as a dying clock.

Ten seconds passed before he heard a click behind him and the door slammed shut.

A figure was standing in the darkness, armed with a gun.

'What are you doing here?'

'Looking around.'

'Looking around? It's my flat, not Woolworths.'

In the dim light, only her outline was visible. She was as skinny as a Giacometti sculpture, and just as spiky.

'Harry? Is that you?'

'Put the gun down, Lieselotte. It doesn't feel very friendly.'

'It's not very friendly to break into a person's home.'

Her posture didn't change, but he could see her shoulders quivering like a tuning fork.

'What are you up to, Harry?'

'To be honest, Lieselotte, I'm more worried about what *you're* up to. And whatever it is, I don't like it.'

'How can you say that to me?'

'You mean after all the time we've known each other?'

Her voice hardened. 'I don't like your attitude.'

'I don't much like it myself. It doesn't change anything.'

'How did you track me down?'

'A friend of mine called Irene O'Malley. She said you'd been working at the Danube Café. I thought you said you didn't have a job.'

'I don't. I left that place. It didn't suit me.'

She was still facing him, arm rigidly in front of her, holding the pistol.

'Come on, Lieselotte. This is me, Harry. You don't need to wave that thing. It's making me nervous.'

'Why don't you tell me why you're here, then?'

'I was passing, and thought I'd drop in.'

'You might have called first.'

'Strangely, until I spoke to Irene, I had no idea where you lived. Nor could I find your telephone number. That gun you're playing with, on the other hand, I did find. I saw it in your bag the other night. The night you spent at my flat. What was it doing there?'

'It's none of your business.'

'It's exactly my business, in that my business is investigating murders.'

'Who said anything about murder?'

'So where did you get the gun?'

'Look, Harry. It's not what you think. I can explain.'

'Go ahead.'

At this, he sensed her limbs relax, and registered that the gun was no longer pointing at his face but at his stomach. Her voice softened. It was desolate, edged with tears.

'Let's not fight with each other, Harry. I don't have many friends here and you can't blame me for being scared when I come across a man creeping around my flat in the pitch darkness. I like you. You're a sweet guy. Actually, the nicest man I've met for a long time.'

'Really?'

'Probably the only one, truth be told. I've had a terrible time over the past couple of years. It's been so hard moving here, to a new country, so far away from everything I know. I know I should be grateful, and I am, but I've learned that there are very few people I can trust. Everyone's out for what they can get. Nobody cares. But when I met you, I knew straight away you were different. And the fact is, I wanted to go on seeing you. We had fun, didn't we?'

The wistful note in her voice chimed exactly with what he himself had been feeling. The other night *had* been fun, and he wanted more of it. And her. The memory of her soft white body curled in his bed evoked an aching tenderness.

She said, 'Why don't we sit down with a drink, and I'll put away this gun and tell you everything?'

'What do you have?'

'There's a bottle of whisky on the trolley there.'

'Now you're twisting my arm.'

'Pour me a glass too while you're at it.'

Harry turned, like the Pavlovian dog he was, and as he did so a shot rang out. It passed just below his outstretched arm and struck the bottle, which shattered in a shower of Scotch and then continued its trajectory to glance off the wall and ricochet towards the window, before finally embedding itself in the wood of the sill. Harry whipped round, but before he could stop her, Lieselotte had dropped the gun, run down the corridor towards the back window from where he had entered, slipped through, jumped down onto the air-raid shelter and disappeared into the night.

# CHAPTER 29

'Come in! Isn't this place glorious? There's even a movie room in the basement. It was so sweet of Ambassador Kennedy to lend it for our dinner.'

Stella and Evelyn were standing in an octagonal hall floored in black and white marble tiles beside a sweeping mahogany staircase.

Beaming at them was Meredith Meadows, a tall girl with wiry, brindled hair like a dog's, bundled tightly in a bun. Her face was a mass of freckles, her smile as bright as a Kentucky morning and her blue eyes as wide as a Midwest sky. She was wearing a long cream taffeta evening dress with a low neckline that emphasized her plump bosom, and a double-strand pearl choker set with rubies that had belonged to Tom's grandmother and which she fingered repeatedly.

'Oh, it is. Such a glamorous setting,' agreed Evelyn, scanning her surroundings with an expert eye.

For many years, the mansion in Prince's Gate just off Hyde

Park had been the official residence of the American ambassador, Joseph Kennedy, and several of his nine children. The pale-cream stucco facade and pedimented windows looking out onto Hyde Park were graciously Georgian, but inside, American money had bought new curtains and upholstery and tasteful, transatlantic chic. At the outbreak of war, however, the family had decamped to the United States leaving only Ambassador Kennedy himself, a thorn in the flesh of the British establishment, who he regularly infuriated with his predictions of a Nazi victory.

'Well, I'm glad you made it at last,' said Meredith. 'We were giving up hope!'

Evelyn had procrastinated endlessly that evening, spending far too long on her make-up – *better late than ugly!* – and running through all her outfits before selecting the most glamorous – a sheer column evening dress of dark-navy silk studded with tiny sequins. Stella had borrowed a black dress, a satin bolero and a fur wrap.

'I wouldn't miss it for the world, Meredith. This *is* your engagement.'

'Tom wanted to call it off.'

Evelyn gave her a sharp glance.

'This dinner, I mean. It couldn't have come at a worse time, he said. Churchill has been to the palace and the King has asked him to become prime minister, which means much more responsibility for Tom himself. He said considering the Germans have just invaded Western Europe, it's indecent to be partying. He point-blank refused to come to a dance at the Savoy last night. He was very fierce! It took everything I had to persuade him tonight. I said I will absolutely *not* let down our guests. Where I come from that is simply not done. That's what *I* call indecency. I said let's start as we mean to go on.'

'So where is he?'

'Even later than you, I'm afraid. He's been locked in rooms with Winston all day and he's only just coming from the Admiralty now.'

Meredith turned to Stella and thrust out a hand.

'So, you're Stella Fry! Evelyn says you're an old friend of Tom's. I don't think he's mentioned you, but then I do have so much catching-up to do. I said to Tom, I want to meet *all* your friends. If I'm going to marry you, I want to hear everything they have to say about you. The good, the bad and the ugly. Be prepared. Isn't that the Scout motto?'

'Tom hated the Scouts,' said Evelyn.

'How do you two know each other, Stella? Families?'

Stella nodded dumbly and accepted a glass from a waiter holding a silver tray. Her desire to avoid this occasion had arisen out of nowhere, and she had no time to analyze it. She had put on her evening dress and fixed her make-up with all the joy of a soldier preparing to face a firing squad.

'I'm so sorry Kick couldn't be here. I'd love you all to meet her but she's in Florida. Her parents absolutely insisted she return to America, even though she's head over heels in love with Billy Hartington. Do you know Billy? He's the heir to the Duke of Devonshire. Kick is pining for him, but her mother has put her foot down. I think because he's *not Catholic*.' This last in a theatrical whisper. 'Old Ma Kennedy is absolutely formidable. Nobody dare cross her. And the Devonshires are just as bad. They gave a dinner for Kick's twenty-first but spent the whole evening giving her dirty looks. Anyway, do go in.'

They mounted the sweeping staircase and entered the Long Room, a pillared drawing room walled with gilded mouldings, Old Master paintings and marble plaques. It was laid with Aubusson carpets, and crowded with Empire furniture, porcelain vases and chairs of burnished mahogany. Large palms stood in brass pots and orchids had been flown in from Paris. Rich tasselled drapes were drawn against the blackout and branching candelabras provided a soft, golden light.

The Kennedy family might have disappeared, but evidence of them remained on every surface. Silver-framed photographs of wholesome youths striding healthily across lawns, touting tennis rackets and sailing yachts. Children in ivory dresses and sailor suits, attending a tea party with their mother Rose. Ambassador Kennedy meeting the King. Teddy and Bobby petting an elephant at London Zoo.

'Tom's really landed on his feet,' murmured Evelyn in Stella's ear. 'He's going to be living like a lord when he gets married. That's where spying gets you.'

'He's not a spy.'

'As good as. You know Churchill asked all his people to get close to the Americans. His daughter-in-law Pamela is practically best friends with Kick Kennedy. It's the same for Tom. He went to mingle in Yankee circles and *voilà!* A betrothal.'

'I can't believe Tom would be that cynical.'

'No. Of course not. He's so honourable, my brother. Unlike the American ambassador.'

Evelyn nodded across the room, to where a craggy figure with horn-rimmed glasses and greying hair was holding court.

'That's our host. Joe Kennedy. Don't get too close to him. He likes to say goodbye to attractive females with a full kiss on the mouth. And don't, whatever you do, find yourself in an empty corridor with him.'

Despite the impending nuptials, the guests had only one topic of conversation.

'Churchill is capricious and rash. Who knows where this will lead us? It's a terrible risk.'

'People are saying Chamberlain will be back before long.'

'They say the King begged Halifax to take over.'

'He's full of more hot air than a barrage balloon.'

'Winston says that America must be dragged in.'

'What if we don't want to be dragged?'

Suddenly, the talk quietened, and a ripple of cries heralded the arrival of Tom.

'He's here at last!'

'The man of the hour!'

Tom hurried in, his face white and his hair rumpled. He passed within a foot of Stella but failed to catch her eye. His entire body seemed rigid with tension. She watched him approach a group of people and heard him say, 'Yes, very.'

She looked around her. Among the guests, she heard American accents and caught sight of a woman she guessed instantly to be Meredith's mother – an older, plumper version of Meredith herself, dressed in layers of fussy pink silk, like a blown peony. She was making towards Stella and Evelyn with steely determination.

Stella turned, and to the other side she saw Tom's mother approaching in a pincer movement. Sidonie Lamont had a way of drawing you aside, as if confiding some secret information, before pinning you to the spot like an invisible anchor with remarks of total banality. To Stella's relief she felt a tap on her shoulder.

'Hello, Stella!'

It was Tom's oldest friend, James Furneaux, a lanky aristocrat with a seraphic smile, who was now a major with the Coldstream Guards. He was towering over a pretty auburn-haired girl.

'How lovely to see you again. This is Camilla. I've been telling her all about guarding Buckingham Palace.'

Stella smiled brightly at Camilla, who said, 'Isn't this the most glorious party?'

'Yes, glorious.'

'Such happy news.'

'Isn't it? Glad you're here, James.'

'Oh, I wouldn't miss this for the world.'

'And where's Simon?'

Simon Montagu was the third in a trio of friends who had met each other at the age of eight. Stella could picture them, off to prep school wearing long socks and shorts and blazers that were too big for them. Over the course of the next twenty-five years, Tom, James and Simon had progressed in parallel through school and university, hiked across Greece and holidayed in the Alps. The three of them were always together. People often asked them about each other, and they never seemed to mind.

'Not invited, I'm afraid.'

James's face sobered, and through the well-mannered veneer she glimpsed a touch of distaste.

'Apparently, Meredith's mama is not over-fond of Jews.'

He fell silent as Meredith approached, arm in arm with Evelyn.

'I've been longing to see Evelyn's new play,' she announced. 'But I guess it's gonna be cancelled now.'

'Not at all. The dresser's on Monday. Why don't you come? I could get you in. Keep calm and carry on, after all. Jasper, our producer, is never going to be calm, but he's determined to carry on, even if it's by candlelight.'

'Oh, *shall* I come? I just love *Private Lives*. Do you know, I've met Coward. It was at a party last year. He's one funny guy. When I met him, I said, *Very flat, Norfolk*, and he laughed like a drain.'

Across the room, Stella noticed Tom helping himself to a cut-glass tumbler of Scotch, so she detached herself from the group and went over to him.

'Hello, Tom.'

'Stella. I'm sorry. I cut you off the other day, on the telephone.'

'It doesn't matter. I imagine you have a lot on your hands.'

'I do. You were in a call box. Were you . . . going somewhere?'

She hesitated.

'Don't worry if you can't say.'

She caught his familiar scent, of soap and skin and laundry starch, that she must have registered numberless times, and felt a pang of premature loss. How often again would she be this close to him? How strange that scents could lie in the brain for so long undisturbed, only to rise up in an unstoppable rush of emotion.

'What's it like there now? In the Admiralty?'

He shook his head.

'Yesterday was a day I'll never forget. Chamberlain held a meeting of the war cabinet at eight in the morning. By then we'd heard that Nazi Germany had invaded Holland and was bombing French airfields. The war cabinet met again. At teatime, Clement Attlee phoned Number Ten. Chamberlain had asked whether the Labour Party would be willing to form a coalition government with him or another PM. Attlee said the Labour Party would act as a full partner in a new government, but only under a new prime minister who could command the confidence of the nation. Not under Chamberlain. That was it, really. Chamberlain set off to Buckingham Palace to resign. Winston went to see the King. I keep reminding myself to call him Prime Minister.'

'And you, Tom? What will you do now?'

'Work harder, I suppose. One of Churchill's first aims is to root out fifth columnists. He's convinced that's what has sped the invasion of the Low Countries. He wants to intensify pressure on potential spies here. He's thinking about special measures.'

'What would they be?'

'Mass internment, I suspect. But the Americans are the priority. If America doesn't come to the rescue, there's little hope for anything else. The Prime Minister says . . .'

She was just taking a sip of champagne when he froze. It was hard to decode the look on his face, except that he seemed to have entirely lost his train of thought.

'Tom? What is it?'

But before he could reply, they were interrupted by Meredith, who advanced on them and plucked him by the arm.

'Come on, Tom, our guests want to know what Winston is going to do.'

'Stella, would you excuse me?'

He allowed himself to be led away.

Suddenly, the thought of staying any longer was unbearable. Stella was still trying to process the events of the last few days. Against all odds she had succeeded in tracking down Robert Handel, and ascertaining, as far as was possible, that he would not give up the secrets of Trent Park. She believed him when he protested that he had not been involved in the murder of Gabriel Fassbinder. In every way, events had been overtaken by the progress of the war, so why was Harry Fox refusing to let the matter drop?

*Something happens, we find the bad guys and turn them in. That's the job.*

Trust Harry and his ridiculous professional pride. How could it possibly matter who had killed Gabriel Fassbinder, or why? The Germans had bypassed the Maginot Line and were marching through the Low Countries. They would be at the gates of Paris in weeks. And then, no doubt, the coast of Britain. What would the death of one German prisoner matter then?

Yet even as she tried to obliterate Harry's frustrated face, telling her she was being impossible, she could not forget Colonel Kendrick or the tense urgency of Maxwell Knight, so desperate that Handel, the man he had recommended, should not have proved treacherous. And Cecil, too, who would feel the same. Maybe she owed it to Cecil, at least . . .

More important than any of that, though, was the fact that if a murderer remained in the ranks of Trent Park, one of the British government's most secret establishments, then it was crucial that they be found.

She trotted down the stairs to the hall. She was anxious to leave unobtrusively, but as she waited for the maid to fetch her wrap, she found James Furneaux looming behind her.

'Leaving already?'

'Afraid so.'

'Let me see you out.'

He drew back the heavy black velvet blackout curtain and they went out onto the porch. Across the road, the dark outline of Kensington Gardens stretched before them, its trees and the round pond lying in shadow and the ghostly shapes of barrage balloons shifting like giant moths in the moonlight. James leaned against the pillared portico and offered her a cigarette from a silver case.

'Can you not stay to dinner?'

'I'd love to, James, but I'm just back in London and I'm very tired, I'm afraid. I'm quite done in.'

'It might be the last good dinner we get for some time. Five courses, we're promised. I already took a look at the menu. Consommé, turbot, *côte d'agneau*, cheese, early-season strawberries and cream. All fresh from Harrods food hall. Ma Meadows does not cut corners.'

'I'm not sure I could stay awake for one course, let alone five.'

He smiled, took a drag of his cigarette and said, 'You two are as bad as each other.'

'I'm sorry?'

'You and Tom. You do know what he thinks, don't you?'

'Thinks about what?'

'About you.'

'I have no idea what Tom thinks about me.'

'How can you not know?'

'Please don't.'

The maid had returned with her wrap.

'I'm only saying . . .'

He held out her wrap for her and she slipped it round her shoulders.

'I'm sorry, James. It's not the time and I really do need to go.'

'Then forgive me if I spoke out of turn.'

'Not at all.' She laid a hand lightly on his arm. 'Thank you. And would you mind awfully telling Meredith that I've left?'

CHAPTER 30

*Sunday, May 12th*

In the middle of his dream, Harry came to a dark wood. Confusingly, his father was there. Stanley Fox. Always the one who walked ghostly beside him, like a latter-day emissary on the road to Emmaus. Stanley was looking up at the trees and remarking how subtly the shade of green changed throughout the year, from the pale, luminous lime green of early spring to the rich, dusty sage of summer. It was all about chlorophyll, Stanley said. Chlorophyll was something in the leaves and the more chlorophyll, the greener they would be. Those little nuggets of knowledge were just the kind of thing he knew, along with tranches of ancient literature, and fly-fishing and church history and how to abandon his family. Harry had spent most of his life assuming that his father was an unreliable fantasist and failed entrepreneur who was absent for most of his childhood. Only recently he had been informed that all those unexplained jaunts, the investment in South African diamond mines, the prospecting for gold in Ontario, and the gambling at Monte Carlo, were in fact missions for His Majesty's government, and he had still not come to terms with it.

Then, in Harry's dream, the wood darkened and closed in. Stanley departed, and Harry shuddered. It was 1916 again and this was Mametz Wood, the largest and thickest forest in the Somme, occupied by the Germans and subject to repeated attacks. During the day its huge mass appeared impenetrable, and by night it was lit up with shrapnel and heavy artillery. Eighteen-year-old Harry and his regiment were marching towards it, across open fields. They had been told to walk, rather than run, as they progressed uphill towards a wall of trees thick with the nests of enemy machine guns. And so they did walk, and as they did, hundreds of them were cut down instantly. Yet still they marched on. Once Harry and the others reached the margin of the wood, they began to fight hand to hand, but the undergrowth and summer foliage hampered every move and they stumbled on blindly through brambles and branches, while all the time British covering fire hit the treetops and their own shells rained down on top of them. It was a week before they took Mametz Wood; four thousand soldiers died for it and one of them was George. George Montgomery, who was always laughing and talking, known as Gorgeous George for his looks, and Harry's friend from the age of ten. George was talking when he fell, and the words died on his lips. Often,

Harry continued the conversation with George in his head. Sometimes he even had visions of returning to that place and hunting for George, then finding only his skull, chalk white, like a flint in the earth.

He stirred in his sleep. The green became more intense and vivid until it was no longer the colour of trees and leaves, but chartreuse or viridian, a shade of green not seen in nature. It belonged to a woman – the Woman in Green in Bavarian Karl's studio. The woman was Lieselotte. A modernist Mona Lisa with an enigmatic smile.

Swimming up to the surface with relief, Harry swung his legs out of bed, washed, dressed and left the flat.

Sunday gloom was a recognized condition among sinners, but the mood on May 12th 1940 was something different. The church bells had been silenced since the war began, but the faces of the people streaming out of the morning service reflected his own apprehension back at him. Londoners were not famous for being friendly and approachable but these days they seemed to have drawn yet further into themselves, as though they had taken refuge in their own internal bunkers and slammed the steel doors behind them.

He passed an ARP wagon organizing the evacuation of domestic pets. The van contained several baskets of cats with labels around their necks. A couple of little dogs were being loaded on too, and an old gentleman was sobbing as much as any parent, more, perhaps, as his Jack Russell's liquid eyes stared back at him out of its cage.

Harry looked away. Churchill might be insisting on fighting on, but nobody was taking any chances. The street names around Harry's flat in Battersea had not yet been painted out, but they soon would be. Many of them round his way were named after battles: Louvaine, Brussels, Cologne. But on the Continent, he'd heard, they preferred naming streets after bureaucrats. Presumably they could soon expect their roads to be named after some obscure German functionary nobody had heard of.

It wasn't only the street names. Time, too, might change. There was a rumour that when the Germans invaded, they intended to adjust the clock to their own time zone. Which meant everyone would be getting up earlier. And these cosmetic touches were the least of it.

Harry made a conscious effort to stop terrifying himself. Perhaps it wouldn't be so awful. He was used to ducking and diving, moving in an unofficial world, and whoever was in charge, there was always an underworld. That never changed. He himself was a denizen of that underworld, the great, uncharted nation of survivors, and he could be as bad as anyone if he tried. He had seen war right up close and knew that you did everything you could to stay alive.

He got off the bus and trudged along Whitehall. The air was still, and the quiet was magnified by the Sabbath hush, but as he passed Scotland Yard, the morning was suddenly shattered by a fleet of cars that roared out of the police headquarters and dispersed in both directions as heads turned sharply. In the heightened tension of the time, the sight provoked fresh alarm. What were the police doing? The images of Hitler's troops rampaging across the Low Countries played on every newsreel, and on every citizen's nerves.

Harry resolved to focus on the immediate problem, which was Lieselotte Edelman. He had no choice, because he couldn't get her out of his mind. Had she really intended to shoot him? Why had she run away? Where was she hiding, and was it fear or felony that prompted her to escape? If, as now seemed likely, she was one of the Abwehr agents Knight was hunting, perhaps his first action should be to report back and call for MI5 help in tracking her down.

To delay this eventuality, he decided to start with coffee.

Luigi's was deserted. Only one customer was seated, buried in the Sunday newspapers. The headlines were doing their usual trick of mixing false optimism with despair and serving it up with a cocktail of exclamation marks. *Nazi Advance Halted Near Frontier says High Command!* vied with *Nazis Warn We Will Bomb British Towns!*

Luigi was at the counter talking in Italian to a burly dark-suited man with the elaborate facial hair and theatrical gestures of an opera singer. He turned and poured Harry's coffee without asking.

'What's happened here? This place is like a funeral with no body.'

'I'm sorry, Mr Fox. This is my cousin. Giuseppe Franconi.'

Harry had heard of Giuseppe. He *was* an opera singer,

originally at least. Now he had fallen on hard times and was working as a sous-chef at the Dorchester.

'Did you not hear?' Giuseppi intervened. 'They've announced a mass internment. Churchill, he said, "Collar the lot." No half measures will do. Mass internment.'

So, it had happened. The thing that Karl had feared.

'What will happen to them?'

'They'll be handed over to the military authorities. Taken to camps.'

'Even refugees?'

'Everyone,' said Luigi. 'We had a visit at dawn, Mr Fox. All Italian places. Ice-cream parlours, cafés, they come for us. My waiters have been taken.'

'Marco? Antonio?'

'All of them. It's a round-up. The police they say, is in their best interests. They will be safe from the mob.'

So that was the reason for the fleet of police cars speeding out of Scotland Yard.

'They would have taken Giuseppe here, but he was not at home.'

'What about Bavarian Karl?'

'He's not been in. And Sunday, Karl is always in. They've arrested him for sure.'

'Thanks, Luigi.'

Harry dropped a handful of coins in the saucer and left the café.

Suddenly the scale of the task facing him seemed overwhelming. If Karl was in custody, Harry had no chance at all of tracing Lieselotte. He had no more chance of seeing her, let alone solving the task that Maxwell Knight had given him. Not to mention the small matter of the man Stella had seen lurking in Goodwin's Court.

He went back to his office, sat heavily at his desk and stared about him, as if seeing the place for the first time. He reached over and tilted towards him the framed photograph of Jack, the only picture he had ever been inclined to display, maybe because it was the only part of his life about which he felt unambiguously proud. The broad, gap-toothed grin and the oversized school blazer prompted a twist of the heart and then, because the boy's dark-lashed eyes so resembled his father's, a little shudder. He made a half-hearted attempt to sort his drawers, which were a riot of matches, cigarettes, staples, dead pencils and glasses he used as props. Then he turned to the shelves, which groaned under stacks of files bearing old cases: solved, unsolved, dead or merely sulking. He was just standing there, rearranging the dust, when the bell rang. He went down the stairs to open the door and was surprised to see Stella.

'Sorry. Am I disturbing?' she said.

'Very.'

'I know it's Sunday, but I took a wild guess that you wouldn't be in church.'

'Suppose you'd better come up.'

He led her into his office and shut the door.

'You haven't been drinking, have you, Harry?'

'When you drink as much as I do, you need to start early.' She sat down with a little sigh.

'Is that a more disappointed than angry sigh?'

'No. I just wanted to say I'm sorry.'

'It's OK.'

'No, it's not. We need to talk.'

'I agree.'

'Firstly, you're right, Harry. I was being impossible yesterday. Storming off like that.'

He was reminded of a remark Maxwell Knight had once made. *Secrets are things that are potentially knowable, but mysteries have no clear-cut answers.* By that logic, women were mysteries more than secrets, and Harry would never properly know them. He would not know if it was something he had said, or had not said, through ignorance, through weakness, or his own deliberate fault. He had made his peace with that.

'I wasn't expecting an apology.'

'Well, you're getting one. What you said yesterday about Gabriel Fassbinder. The murder. You were right. It's not over, and if it's true that Robert Handel didn't kill him, somebody else did. That person is just as much of a threat to classified secrets. I was thinking. There was a man there, a German called Helmut Monke. He seemed troubled by the way prisoners were treated. Then later, I saw him in the grounds after dark . . .'

'Wait.'

Harry was standing by the window, massaging his brow.

'There's something I haven't mentioned. I was going to say yesterday, but you didn't give me the chance.'

Although the door was shut and the building was empty, he lowered his voice. 'Maxwell Knight told me that the Abwehr has infiltrated three spies into Britain. Two women and a man. He's certain the report is genuine. He thought they might be hiding in the émigré community, and when Robert Handel went missing, it seemed too much of a coincidence.'

'That Handel was the man? But I already told you . . .'

'No. Stop talking. This is what I want to tell you. You see, in the course of my researches . . .'

He faltered to a halt. She was frowning at him, quizzically.

'In the course of your researches, what?'

'It's complicated. I met a woman. A beautiful woman, but that doesn't matter. She was Jewish. Or said she was. She asked for my help. She needed to find a man – a kind of good Samaritan – who had helped her leave Germany. During our . . . discussions . . . we went back to my place. I was checking her out.'

Stella smiled, wryly. 'You don't have to tell me this, you know, Harry.'

'I do. Because this woman had a gun in her bag.'

'Why would she carry a gun?'

'To shoot people with.'

She blinked. 'So where's this girl now?'

'She ran away.'

'And where's the gun?'

'I was hoping you'd ask me that.'

He reached into his inside jacket pocket and brought it out.

The weapon lay between them on Harry's desk, dull grey, glinting dangerously. They both stared at it.

'It's an Enfield No. 2 Mk 1 .38 calibre revolver. Light to use, not much recoil.'

Stella picked it up curiously, fingering the red plastic handgrip. Harry flinched.

'Careful with that.'

'And you think this might be the gun that killed Fassbinder?'

'It's possible.'

'So, who is this woman? Your friend?'

'I don't know. She called herself Lieselotte Edelman. If she is one of these three enemy agents, there's every chance she will have gone to meet the others. And because I know her face, either they will go to ground or . . .'

'Or?'

'They will try to find us. You said you'd seen a man lurking down there in the alley?'

'Yes. He vanished as soon as he saw me.'

'I've no idea what he wanted, but . . .'

He picked up the gun and stowed it away.

'All I know is, we should go to Trent Park straight away. See your chap there and discover if this is the same gun that killed Fassbinder. We need to leave, now.'

'The trains aren't regular on Sundays. Especially now.'

Harry's former gloom had lifted. Suddenly he was filled with energy. He had direction now. A path of sorts.

'It doesn't matter. I know a man with a car.'

# CHAPTER 31

The dark-green Riley Kestrel, with its gleaming flanks, leather upholstery, open sunroof and pre-selector gearbox, was a dream to drive. There was no need for double declutching and the engine sprang responsively to the slightest touch of the accelerator. It was hot for May, and in any other circumstances Harry would have luxuriated in the pleasure of purring along the road with a full tank of petrol, the wind in his face and Stella in a headscarf beside him.

Instead, he gripped the wheel and focused intently on the road ahead.

He had procured the car from Kenny Jessop, whose garage in Clapham Junction ran a sideline in supplying vehicles for the Service. Jessop had been an unofficial resource for a number of years: changing licence plates, respraying and ingeniously customizing cars, whatever was required, and because Harry liked cars he would sometimes drop in purely for the chance to admire Jessop's latest acquisitions. Perhaps that was why Jessop had proved impressively calm at being knocked up on Sunday afternoon and asked to provide a car and a full tank of petrol at extremely short notice.

The Riley hummed along, the fresh air in their faces. Petrol rationing and the Sabbath ensured there were few other cars on the road as they drove through the north-west London suburbs, past long, dull stretches of terraced housing and children riding out on their bicycles. Women chatted on their doorsteps, arms folded. A playing field went by, studded with cricketers in white flannels, and they heard the sharp crack of the ball and a little tide of cheers.

Eventually, the houses gave out and they were into fields and the countryside proper.

Being incurably urban, Harry rarely saw the countryside, and he might have enjoyed the view a little more were it not for the speed and the urgency of their trip. As a field of sheep flashed by, he recalled something amusing that Jack had written to him.

*Farmers can only kill their own animals if they're injured, but Mr Swiggs says a lot of sheep fall down holes around someone's birthday.*

Jack. Now was not the time to think about Jack.

'Where did you get the car?'

'I know a man.'

'And the petrol?'

'A full tank. He puts mothballs in it to make it last longer.'

The quality of wartime petrol was erratic. It contained

strange substances that made cars pink and judder, but Jessop had worked his magic and the Riley's engine ran smoothly with no problems.

They passed a road sign which said precisely nothing. Thank God Jessop had provided a map. Harry fished it out of the glovebox and passed it to Stella to study. Just as in the towns, all railings had been removed and the windows of pubs and garages they passed were crisscrossed with reinforcement tape. Even here, the heavy hand of Home Security had descended like a giant censor, redacting all the road signs and scribbling over everything with barbed wire.

'So, tell me about Trent Park.'

'I can't say much. I can't say what they do or what I was doing there, but you know Maxwell Knight sent me there, and I'll need to tell Colonel Kendrick, the officer in charge, everything I've found out.'

They fell silent again. After a while, he noticed that her head had fallen back in a doze. The headscarf came loose, and the wind blew her hair across her face. Travel and the lack of sleep must have exhausted her, he supposed, and he hoped that, despite the urgency of their endeavour, she might get a few moments of rest.

An hour went by before they passed a long stretch of parkland, fenced with barbed wire, and came into the outskirts of a small town. Stella asked him to pull over.

'I can walk from here. Remember, the whole place is classified, Harry. Even government ministers have to visit undercover. I'll have to go alone to speak to Colonel Kendrick.'

'Sure. And I will just . . . ?'

'Wait for me. If you head towards town there's a pub. The Cock and Dragon. Down Chalk Lane. I'll meet you as soon as I can.'

He parked by the side of the road, along from a row of shops, which were closed, and a line of neat terraced houses with miniature front gardens full of lupins and roses, and net curtains hanging primly at each window. Above the rooftops a plume of woodsmoke tangled in the air. Just ahead of him was the lane that Stella had told him led to the pub. It would only just be opening time. He lit a cigarette, rolled down the window, and leaned his elbow out to relax.

A few minutes later, from behind him came a babble of female voices. Glancing in his wing mirror, he saw a group of women approaching. The two at the front were dressed in the uniform of the ATS, and the other two were in civvies, wheeling bicycles. One was a dumpy, sandy-haired girl, wearing a short-sleeved jumper with pearl-buttoned collar and wire-framed glasses, and the other was prettier, in a white dress printed with cherries and a red bow in her hair. As custom dictated, Harry let his eyes linger on this girl as she passed, until she was drawn to look back at him.

Such was his magnetic pull that she did indeed glance backwards, and as she did so, her eyes widened. The next second she turned to address the group, then mounted her bicycle and rode off swiftly through a gap in the hedge, into an adjacent field.

Harry was startled. It was not often he had that effect, and it was a moment before he could analyze why. Then he realized something else. He had seen that slim build and erect posture before, silhouetted in a doorway in Islington in a glint of light. And before that, too. It was the young woman he had sat next to at the Myra Hess concert in Trafalgar Square. The one who had startled at the sight of his scar.

With a jolt of adrenaline, he opened the car door and prepared to follow her.

The girl had deviated from the road through a hedgerow to ride along the perimeter of the adjoining field, bumping along the lumpy terrain. Presumably she had calculated that the Riley would be unable to follow her here. The bicycle weaved from side to side, bouncing and juddering over the troughs, and Harry followed as best he could, stumbling on clods of earth, accumulating lumps of dirt on his shoes. Luckily, it had not rained properly for weeks, or he would have been up to his knees in mud. The gun, which he had thoughtfully placed in his inside jacket pocket, was slamming rhythmically against his chest like an impending heart attack. He staggered on through the furrows sweating, his mackintosh flapping behind him as his London shoes skidded on the rough ground. In Harry's line of business, running was sometimes required, but this was athletics of a different order — not so much a short sprint as the kind of long-distance effort that belonged to his schooldays, with the yells of a red-faced sportsmaster sounding in his ears. Immediately, he developed a stitch. He longed to stop but he stumbled on uncomprehendingly, unable to think about who he was following or why. All he knew was that the white blur of the dress was receding into the distance in the gathering dusk. And that he was most likely to lose her.

Then he tripped. He fell headlong, face down into a crust of mud and grass that smelt of cows. Getting to his knees, and checking that the gun was still in place, he dusted down the portions of field that had stuck to his front and staggered on.

Suddenly, a hundred yards ahead of him, the girl ditched the bicycle and darted swiftly through a space in the hedge and back across the unlit road, towards the underground station on the opposite side. Barely bothering to check for traffic, Harry tore after her, his breath ragged, his lungs heaving for air, and the stitch like a knife in his side, into the entrance to the station. Halting at the ticket office, he fumbled for coins, inwardly cursing the ponderous official who was issuing his ticket in slow motion as the girl crossed nimbly through the barrier and ran up the steps to the platform. Harry followed, into a vaulted hall lit by pendant globes painted blue, giving it the dismal air of an aquarium. There, with idling engine, a red Tube train was waiting.

He glanced from left to right, but there was no sign of the girl in the white dress, so he took a chance, darted into the nearest compartment and stared around. Red-and-blue-chequered plush seating, dusty wooden boards underfoot, red leather armrests. It being a Sunday evening, there was only a smattering of passengers as he made his way along the carriage: a couple of young men in army uniform, perhaps staff from Trent Park itself; a young man in a sports jacket, seemingly immersed in a library book, and an elderly woman, who raised her eyebrows pointedly at the sight of a middle-aged man, breathing heavily and beaded with sweat, floundering past.

As the train lurched off with a jolt and a screech of wheels, Harry pushed onwards, opening the connecting door to the next carriage. This one seemed to be empty. His eyes scanned the posters above the seats – *Keep Your Valuables in Milner's Safes*; *Wait! Count 15 slowly before moving in the Blackout!* A woman with rolled-up sleeves and large biceps announcing *We Can Do It!* – as if they could offer any indication as to the woman he was hunting.

To no avail.

Outside, dusk had gathered, and the vistas of fields bisected with hedges were visible only in outline. Harry pushed forward through the dingy light of the train, checking each compartment for the woman in the white dress. At one point, through the window of a connecting door, he saw a dark head but when he hastened through, an entirely different woman lowered her newspaper and raised her startled eyes.

A single sentence was running through his head.

*Three high-level spies Two women and a man.*

If he had found the two women, where was the man?

The train continued its reassuring rhythm, clanking along the track. At West Enfield, more people got in, and he waited for the slam of the doors and the guard's whistle before resuming his search, back through the length of the train, steadying himself on the overhead straps as it swayed.

Where was the girl in the white dress hiding? Or had she jumped? Perhaps she had never boarded the train at all, and he was here on a fool's errand while Kenny Jessop's Riley stood parked unlocked in a country lane.

At Southgate, the train stopped, and two more passengers entered his carriage. A man in a trilby, who immediately lit up, and his girlfriend, squeezing his arm and cuddling up to him. Harry peered out of the opened door and scanned the platform, but no young woman, in any kind of dress, was to be seen. The train pulled off, yet seconds after it had begun moving, it jolted to a sudden halt. Harry became aware of a commotion – a shout on the platform and the bang of a door, followed by footsteps. He barely had a moment to register, before a hefty young man had slammed through the connecting door and lunged towards him. Harry made to run, but it was too late. The man had him firmly by the arm and was speaking urgently into his ear.

'Don't make a fuss. Don't attract attention. You're coming with me.'

# CHAPTER 32

Southgate underground station was a strikingly stylish construction: a circular modernist building in reinforced concrete and glass, with a flat projecting roof, like a spaceship might look if it had landed unexpectedly amid the dreary suburban outskirts of north-west London. It had opened seven years earlier, and its streamlined shape, column lighting and bronze panelling had won widespread acclaim. Ordinarily, given his enthusiasm for architecture, Harry might have stopped and admired it. But that evening he was unable fully to appreciate this art deco marvel as he was marched, thoughts careering wildly, through the station and towards a waiting jeep.

They drove at speed along a country lane, beside a belt of woodland. In the darkness it was impossible to make out any more than the blur of trees to one side and stretches of agricultural land to the other. The last faint stain of light was fading from the distant horizon. After a few minutes, the jeep came to a red-brick neo-classical gateway topped with ornamental urns, and swerved through an opened barrier. Before them lay long, rolling acres of countryside, bisected by a drive, a cluster of cottages, and high wire fences, punctuated with watchtowers.

'Sorry for the confusion, sir, I'm Sergeant Clem Beckwith. I was asked to take you to Colonel Kendrick. I was just coming down the lane when I saw you get out of your car and take off through the fields. Once I realized you'd caught the train, I thought the best course of action was to follow in the jeep.'

'Impressive logic.'

'In a hurry, were you, sir?'

'Just stretching my legs.'

'I guessed you might be running for the train. They're not too regular on a Sunday. Quite a sprint you put on there, sir.'

Harry stared out of the window. Ahead, he could just discern the outline of a large country house before, with a crunch of tyres on cobbles, the jeep passed the main building and drew up at a side door. The man who had identified himself as Sergeant Beckwith jumped out and motioned him to follow.

'Maintain radio silence if you would, sir.'

They proceeded at a clip along wood-panelled corridors and across the parquet of a deserted hall, until they came to a door, at which point his escort left him and Harry entered to find Stella and an anxious-looking man in a dark-grey double-breasted suit.

They swivelled round when he entered, and to break the silence Harry reached into his jacket pocket and brought out the gun.

'What happened to you, Harry? You're . . . a bit dishevelled.'

'I'm afraid I fell at the first hurdle.'

The man in the grey suit advanced towards him, hand outstretched.

'Colonel Kendrick. I understand you're Harry Fox. Captain Knight did mention you. Miss Fry said you'd driven down together, so I had Beckwith come and fetch you.'

His eyes crossed from Harry's mac to the gun.

'What exactly is it you have there?'

'I'd say it's lost property.'

Kendrick took the Enfield and turned it over and over in his large hands. He stared at it as though he had never seen a gun before, which was crazy because a military man like him had undoubtedly seen a thousand guns and been at the wrong end of them, Harry thought.

'I can't be certain, but it certainly seems to be one of ours. We have a rifle range. Some of the staff here learn to shoot. This looks a lot like one of our guns.'

'And, presumably, the same gun that shot Gabriel Fassbinder,' said Harry.

'I wouldn't want to leap to conclusions.'

'Leaping to conclusions is my day job, Colonel Kendrick.'

'And the day job is, remind me . . . ?'

'Investigations specialist.'

'Very useful. Well, Miss Fry has told me about finding Robert Handel. She has brought his security pass back as proof and she believes he is not our man.'

His fingers played with the security pass that lay before him on the desk, swivelling it back and forth as though pondering a chess move.

Then, more decisively, he said, 'If that *is* the case – and I am not, as yet, suspending disbelief – then we're back to square one. It seems we may still have a murderer in our midst.'

'If you don't mind . . .' Harry hesitated. He was still trying to put things together in his head. Images came together and fell apart. Facts juxtaposed then drifted away like smoke. 'The reason why your Sergeant Beckwith took so long finding me is that I was chasing a young woman.'

Kendrick raised an eyebrow.

'I saw her outside the pub, the Cock and Dragon. I'd seen her before.'

'Where had you seen her?' said Stella.

'At Lieselotte Edelman's. That's the woman I mentioned.'

He caught Stella's sceptical glance.

'Are you saying Lieselotte Edelman was outside the Cock and Dragon?'

'No. Not her. This was a different woman. I recognized her, and at first I didn't know why. Then I realized I had seen her coming out of Lieselotte's flat in Islington. And before then, I remember her from somewhere else; it was a Myra Hess concert. One of those at the National Gallery. She was sitting next to me, and . . .'

'Please describe this woman,' said Kendrick.

'Pretty. Slim. Dark curly hair. Wearing a white dress . . .'

'Printed with cherries?' asked Stella.

Kendrick was staring from one to the other.

'Could you possibly explain . . .'

Stella said, 'That's Mimi. Mimi Friedlander. Sir –' she turned to Kendrick – 'she shares my billet. At Mrs Pursglove's.'

'I'm well aware of Miss Friedlander. She has been with us since last year. But the fact that you saw her in London is not in itself suspicious. All our staff are eligible for leave. She may well have been on a weekend pass and taken the opportunity to attend a concert. We can easily check that. However . . .' He paused. 'You did tell me, Miss Fry, that this is the same young woman who confided in you that Robert Handel had gone to France.'

Slowly, Stella said, 'I should have mentioned this earlier. Mimi said something that stuck in my mind. When she was talking about Fassbinder, she said, *He'd been here a while, a month at least. He was tall and blond, like a north German.*'

'Good God,' said Kendrick.

'What?' said Harry, looking from one to the other.

Stella said, 'When I confronted Robert Handel with the murder of Gabriel Fassbinder, he said, *But how would I even know to find him? I'd never seen him. I only knew his voice.*'

'Precisely,' said Kendrick. 'Our listeners do not see the prisoners they are recording. If the prisoners got sight of our people, it would compromise the entire operation.'

Harry said, 'So how could Mimi Friedlander know what Fassbinder looked like, unless . . .'

'Unless she had met him. Unless she shot him.'

The three of them stood motionless, lost for words, like guests at a terrible party. Then Kendrick said, 'Where is Mimi now?'

'She was heading towards the pub with a group of girls when she caught sight of me. As soon as she recognized me, she took off on her bike. She was moving fast. I followed her through some fields . . .'

Here he gestured towards the hems of his trousers.

'Then she jumped onto the underground. We got as far as Southgate before your man stopped the train.'

'Did you see Mimi on the train?'

'No sign of her.'

Kendrick said, 'Then it's possible she doubled back and decided to hitchhike. A lot of our girls do that when they're going into town.'

'Do you think that's where she's heading?'

'I can't say. I'll get Beckwith to double-check the billet first thing in the morning and see if the other women have any idea of her intentions.'

He put his head around the door and had a conversation with Clem Beckwith, who had stationed himself outside in the corridor, then returned to the room and went over to the window. Harry followed his gaze.

Outside, the grounds of Trent Park, the meadows, lakes and woodlands, slumbered on in the misty twilight just as they had since they were scoped out in the eighteenth century. Fleetingly, Harry wished he had the chance to observe the place better. He loved this kind of classical English country house garden, with landscape designed to evoke serenity, all rolling lawns, serpentine curves and whimsical tilts at the Gothic. It was an architecture that suggested the struggles of History were finished and had come down in favour of benign civilization. It seemed impossible that just a few hundred miles away, German forces were advancing across Europe and moving closer every hour to British shores.

Decisively, Kendrick turned.

'We may have to face the fact that we have been harbouring a cuckoo in the nest. We've wasted valuable time chasing the wrong man. I doubt we'll manage to apprehend her. God knows where she is now. Or what she plans to do with the information she has. Wreck our entire enterprise, I don't doubt. What do you suggest, Mr . . . Mr Fox?'

'First we should search the house in Islington where I found the gun.'

'The place where your young woman lives? Surely she will be long gone by now.'

Harry hesitated. He was aching for a cigarette and could not help glancing at the silver cigarette box and lighter on the desk. Kendrick recognized the signs and pushed the box towards him. He helped himself and lit up.

'I'm not sure you know, Colonel Kendrick,' he said, 'but Captain Knight told me that intelligence has picked up chatter of three German spies.'

Kendrick arched an eyebrow.

'Go on.'

'Reports said they had been infiltrated into the country some time back. Two women and a man. Captain Knight asked me to monitor the refugee communities. I can only assume . . .'

'Assume nothing, Mr Fox. Surely your time in MI5 taught you that.'

Colonel Kendrick seemed snappish. Worry had etched lines deep into his face. Then he managed a smile.

'Forgive me. You have both been exemplary in your work. Your trip to Paris, Miss Fry, was both courageous and invaluable. And you, Mr Fox, have been most helpful in tracking down this gun.'

Harry said, 'Seeing as the gun was found in the possession of Lieselotte Edelman, and Maxwell Knight is looking for two female spies, it would seem pretty important to find out what links these two women. If I may, I'd like to pursue some leads.'

'What leads?'

'I don't know yet.'

Kendrick gave Harry a look of deep scepticism.

'But I'm sure they'll come to me. That's the way it usually works.'

Kendrick seemed about to speak, but instead he merely nodded and said, 'Just at the moment, I don't see that we have any choice. But the matter is urgent. Now that Mimi Friedlander has absconded, we can't hope that our secrets are safe. It's Sunday night. I'll give you twenty-four hours, Mr Fox, but whatever you find you must report at once on pain of punishment. And there's another thing . . .'

On cue, a striking blonde entered the room and approached him.

'Margy wants your autograph.'

She slid a sheet of paper on a clipboard towards him and proffered a pen.

'Official Secrets Act, Mr Fox. Please sign.'

CHAPTER 33

Mrs Pursglove had just dropped off to sleep when she was woken by the noise. It was a sound which her finely tuned landlady brain would recognize anywhere; the soft click of a key in the lock, followed by the careful closure of the front door and the hushed, furtive tread of a lodger who did not want anyone to know of their late return. Her ears strained for the suggestion of a second visitor – a male visitor – which would be a grotesque and flagrant disregard of her rules and merit instant eviction. But it was just the one pair of footsteps that she registered, carefully proceeding along the corridor below and navigating the creaks in the stairs. She contemplated getting up to berate whichever of her lodgers had broken the rules, but the truth was, although the women were supposed to inform her of their shift patterns, they were often required to work late at short notice, and besides, she was warm and comfortable under her eiderdown, with the cat curled up asleep on what had once been Mr Pursglove's side. Her curlers were in, and her face lathered with Nivea. She would save the disciplinary chat until morning.

Stella unlatched the wooden gate as quietly as she could and trod softly up the narrow brick path, past the dustbins. Kendrick's men would be searching Mimi's room first thing in the morning, so it was essential that she see it before then. Luckily she had kept her key. Softly she pushed open the front door and stood for a second listening in the silent hall, dreading the sight of her landlady in dressing gown and slippers, ready to interrogate the stop-out.

But nothing.

Moving down the hall, she crept up the stairs, keeping to the central boards, which she knew instinctively were less likely to creak, to the first floor. Mrs Pursglove had the master bedroom at the back, overlooking the garden, and Mimi's room was on the second floor directly above it.

Rounding the landing, she crept through the sleeping house to the second floor and tried the handle of Mimi's room. As expected, it was empty.

Since they had left Trent Park, she had been haunted by something Mimi had said to her about Mrs Pursglove on the day, only just over a week ago, when they first met. *I suspect she snoops in our rooms while we're out, so if you keep a diary, make sure you lock it up.*

Stella knew she needed to treat this like an exercise, focusing on every inch of the room systematically. She tested the narrow iron-framed bed, which proved as hard as her own, but tidily made, with its lime-green candlewick bedspread smoothed down. There was nothing beneath the pillows but a neatly folded Viyella nightdress. She ran her eyes over the washstand, with its toothpaste, mug and toothbrush, and the low chair, across which an ATS skirt and jacket had been casually flung. Above the small fireplace, whose grate bore no trace of recent warmth, Mrs Pursglove had hung a reproduction of Holman Hunt's *The Light of the World*, showcasing Jesus in a long white robe and holding a lantern, as though to supplement her own frugal welcome. Stepping back in the gloom, Stella bumped her hip painfully against the corner of a table, and froze for a moment, trying to convince herself that Mrs Pursglove would be far too deeply asleep to investigate the late-night activities of one of her lodgers. She would surely save her disapproval for the morning.

The table doubled as both a desk and a dressing table, judging by the small wood-framed mirror to one side and the cut-glass perfume spritzer which contained – Stella checked – eau de cologne. An enamel tea mug stood empty, and in the drawers beneath she found pencils, a rubber, a lighter and a fold of Kirby hair grips. Mimi's dressing gown hung on a peg fixed to the door.

Other than these ordinary objects, it was plain that Mimi had made no attempt to personalize the room. This might be her long-standing billet, but in no way was it permitted to feel like a home from home. No photographs stood on the table and no trinkets or little objects decorated the mantelpiece. There was to be no softening of the stark, unwelcoming air of exile in this tiny corner of the diaspora.

It took another look round the room before it occurred to Stella to check under the bed. In the darkness she felt a rectangular object and slid out a suitcase. The metal edges scraped heavily on the floorboards as she drew it towards her and she stiffened, ears straining for any sign that her movements might be investigated, before clicking open the clasps. She pulled out heavy woollen sweaters, trousers, Mimi's winter clothing, and a make-up bag which she put to one side. Then she surveyed the contents underneath.

What was she expecting? A radio transmitter? Electronic equipment? Disguises? Instead, all she found was a notebook. A cheap A4 notebook with a cover of pale grainy card, the front of which was splashed with green ink and circled with the ring of a teacup. Exactly the kind of thing Mimi had suggested should be kept under lock and key.

Keeping this to one side, she refastened the suitcase and returned it to its place, quietly descended the stairs again, let herself out of the house and crossed to the other side of the road, where Harry Fox was waiting in his car.

'Find anything?'

Harry was regretting the false confidence that had caused him to tell Colonel Kendrick that a lead would come to him.

'Only this.'

Stella had her blackout torch out and was riffling through a book on her lap.

'What is it?'

'Mimi mentioned to me that I should lock up my diary if I kept one, because the landlady is so nosy. So it occurred to me that she might keep one herself. I found this in the suitcase under her bed. I was hoping it might give something away, but it's awfully banal. Just notes on her friends and meals she's had. A little bit about how much she misses her family in Berlin.'

'Show me.'

'I'll translate for you.'

Stella opened a page at random and read.

'*February 14th, 1940. Another early start and three inches of snow. I almost died bicycling in. My hands froze to the handlebars. Here they celebrate Valentine's Day, when sweethearts exchange presents and cards. All the girls were comparing what they'd got. Esme and Gerda, none, of course. Helen had a bar of chocolate from her boyfriend in the Black Watch. Daphne had most cards, naturally. Half the men in the county are in love with her. I had none, but Laurence Cottrell came up behind me in the mess and thrust a bunch of daffodils into my arms. All I could think was, why did it have to be Laurence? Home early, and Esme told everyone that dinner was to be Jambon Froid Haché en Gelée. It turned out that Mrs P. had made Spam hash with carrots and she didn't understand why we all shrieked with laughter when we saw it.*'

She flicked to another page.

*'March 18th. Mutti's birthday. What would she think if she knew I was here? I miss them so much. I can hardly bear to think about them. The last birthday I had with her was five years ago — Furtwängler conducting the Berlin Philharmonic — Beethoven. The* Eroica.'

Stella said, 'I was looking for the entries around the time of the murder, but she stops writing the diary midway through April. April 17th.'

They drove on towards London in silence. Through the streets, slumbering and hushed, the distant clatter of a train echoed in the emptiness. An entire skyline of offices, railway arches, houses and blocks hunkered in the darkness, with only a few chinks of light blinking like Morse from inadequate blackouts. The city had a brooding, apocalyptic air, as though it was waiting for something, and what it was waiting for wouldn't be good.

Suddenly, Harry said, 'Wait a minute.'

He drew the car to a halt by the side of the road and scrutinized the notebook with Stella's torch. Across the top, the words *Mimi Elisabetta Friedlander* were inscribed in graceful loops, but the rest of the jacket was dog-eared and scruffy.

He examined it a moment, then he reached forward, switched on the ignition, and resumed driving.

'Where are we going?'

'We're making a little detour.'

'To where?'

Harry had a sudden urge to be enigmatic. God knows he was entitled to it, having had no idea where Stella was for the past couple of weeks. It was his turn, and he relished the thought of Stella petitioning him for information. It would not take long to check out his theory, and besides, what else was there to go on?

'I said I'd follow a few leads, and I've just thought of one.'

It was almost midnight by the time they arrived on the outskirts of London. They came to a street full of tall, narrow rooming houses, divided into bedsits and squeezed together in a terrace like commuters on a rush-hour train. Harry drew up and cut the Riley's engine, then he got out and went up the steps of the nearest house, clattering into a pair of empty milk bottles on the way. Stella followed him, and when Harry knocked at the door they heard a bolt being drawn back.

A weaselly, apprehensive face peered out. It belonged to a man wearing a shapeless tweed jacket, bunched up around his shoulders like an old tortoiseshell. He had a brush in his hand, coated in purple paint.

'You're working late, Karl.'

'What can I do for you, Mr Fox?'

'You can let me in.'

'Are you part of the police, Mr Fox? Do you have a warrant?'

'What are you talking about?'

'I can't admit you without a warrant.'

From somewhere inside the house, a voice called, 'Oh, it's all right, Karl. Let them in.'

Mimi Friedlander was sitting in the model's chair – the one on which, Harry could never forget, Lieselotte had posed for posterity rendered in green paint. To his astonishment, he noticed a canvas on the easel and realized that Mimi too was being painted, though perhaps wisely she had kept her clothes on. She was perched upright and barely moved as Harry and Stella came in, as though she was expecting Karl to continue his work while they talked.

'Hope we're not interrupting.'

'It's fine. Karl has spent months on this portrait, so I deserve a break.'

Her face, with its scornful dark eyes and arched, finely drawn eyebrows, seemed entirely composed. 'I wondered when you'd get here.'

'I told Mimi,' Karl intervened. 'I said if it was Mr Fox following you, then Mr Fox would find you.'

Generally, Harry was open to any endorsements, no matter how dubious the origin, but in this case he was too distracted to properly appreciate it.

'The English, they always say, when you have a crisis, you must make tea,' Karl observed, as though this unexpected visit had awoken some dormant social graces.

'Why don't you, then?' suggested Mimi tersely.

She uncrossed her legs with languid grace and picked up

a cigarette which had been smouldering in a saucer. 'Stella told me your job was finding people, Mr Fox. But I didn't expect you to be so good at it.'

Harry glanced at the canvas. It was not finished, and the embryonic swirls of paint were purple this time, as well as green, but the subject was still recognizably unrecognizable.

'Why did you run away from me in the lane?'

'Because I knew you were coming for me.'

'How did you know?'

'My cousin told me.'

'Who's your cousin?'

'Lieselotte.'

Harry reeled a little.

'Lieselotte Edelman is your cousin?'

'On my mother's side, yes. She's a little younger than me, but people say we look alike.' Mimi arched a smile and tossed the rich brown hair. 'What d'you think?'

Harry ignored this. 'What else did she tell you?'

'She called me last night to warn me that she'd lost the gun. Then when I saw you in the street, in that car, well, I recognized you anyway . . .'

'You recognized my scar.'

'Not just that. Not at first. Stella told me you were good-looking and that you often went to the concerts. Then when I saw the scar, it wasn't hard to work out that the man I was sitting next to must be you.'

This distracting information caused Harry to glance at Stella, who smiled.

'So when I saw you earlier this evening, I reckoned you must have come to find me.'

'Was it you who gave the gun to Lieselotte?'

Mimi widened her eyes. 'Of course it was. I thought you'd worked that out. I came up here on a twenty-four-hour pass. Lieselotte always lets me stay with her. She wasn't happy about the gun, but I asked her to keep it until I worked out what to do with it. But then, when Stella arrived, I got a little worried.'

Stella said, 'Why should I worry you?'

'Oh, Stella. I'm not stupid. I knew you'd come to Trent Park to investigate the killing. You were asking questions. They were subtle, but they were questions all the same. We're all highly trained at Trent Park. We know you never get the information you want by interrogating someone head-on. You stay oblique. You use subterfuge. Once you told me you had learned your German at Oxford, I reckoned you must have known Robert Handel, yet you pretended you'd never heard of him. You didn't ask any more about him. So I decided, as Handel had already left, that I might as well point you towards him. There would be no harm in it. If he was going to France, he'd be far away by now. Far away and out of sight. They already suspected him because he'd gone AWOL, but if they thought he had gone to France, they would be convinced. They would stop bothering to accuse anyone else. I have to say, I hardly expected you to go after him.'

'How do you know I went after him?'

Mimi smiled at Stella and shrugged.

'Why else would you suddenly disappear? Even Mrs Pursglove had no idea that you were moving and she's normally briefed when a girl changes billets. She was most put out. She made an official complaint. She said she can't be expected to go tidying up after people when they vanish without warning.'

'Hey.' Harry held up his hands. 'Can we clarify here? You're saying it was you who shot Gabriel Fassbinder?'

'No. I didn't shoot Gabriel Fassbinder.'

'Then . . .'

'I shot Paul Schilling.'

The name spun in the air and dropped like a coin into the well of Harry's mind. It was a few beats before he connected.

'Paul Schilling was the chap your cousin was looking for. Until she wasn't.'

'Yes. She stopped looking because I told her he was dead.'

Mimi got up from the chair and drew her cardigan on.

'It's freezing in here, Karl. Can't you get more heat?'

She picked up a poker and prodded a couple of blackened sticks that were flickering ineffectually in the grate. The prod caused a shower of sparks, and the embers sank further into ash.

'I have no coal,' said Karl grumpily, as though Mimi had demanded caviar. 'Where would I get coal?'

'Can you make that tea, then? I'm frozen to the bone. Would you two like tea? Or something else, though Karl never has much in.'

'Sorry,' said Harry. 'Could we just get back to the subject? If that's not too much to ask. How did you even know Fassbinder? Schilling. Whatever you want to call him.'

For the first time since they had arrived, Stella detected a hint of emotion behind Mimi's defiant veneer. There was a glint in her eye, which looked like the edge of tears.

'You really want to know the whole sad story? There are plenty sadder stories to hear in this war.'

Harry took off his hat, sat on Karl's stool, and extended his legs.

'Why not? It's one in the morning. It's not as though we have anything better to do.'

Mimi jumped up and put her arms round Stella.

'Before I tell you about it, I'm sorry I ran away, dear Stella. Forgive me if I've caused you any trouble. I hope we can stay friends, whatever happens.'

Then she plumped herself back down in the model's chair and lit a fresh cigarette.

'We both knew Paul Schilling back in Berlin, but Lieselotte met him first. I mentioned, Stella, that I was a violinist. I was really quite a good one. All I wanted in my life was to play the violin and maybe, one day, to turn professional. It would have been my dream to play in the orchestra there – Berlin has such fine orchestras – even to play for the movies, or in the pit at the Winter Garden. Only once Hitler arrived it was impossible. Jews weren't allowed. I was reduced to playing in nightclubs and trying to make a living as a hat-check girl.

'I remember the evening I first saw Schilling. I'd gone to

visit my friend Etta. We used to play together at her house, just for fun, and on the way back I saw them. Lieselotte and this man. They were standing beneath the railway arches at Friedrichstrasse. I watched them kiss, quickly, as though they didn't want anyone to see. I waited until they parted, but on the way back Lieselotte caught me up and I told her what I'd seen. She was furious. She ordered me to keep the secret. She said he – the man – was going to help them. He wasn't Jewish but he was angry at how the Jews were being treated, and he had a plan to help the whole family. But if I told anyone then all his plans would be ruined.'

'Did you tell your parents?'

'No. Even after it happened, I never said a word.'

'After what happened?'

'A month later, I got a message to meet Paul Schilling in the Tiergarten. He had got me a visa to enter Britain as a domestic servant. He gave me money too. I said I didn't want to leave my home or my friends, but he said that was crazy. Someone had already painted a yellow Star of David on my parents' home. Things were going to get far, far worse for Jews. He knew that for a fact, because of the people he worked with. Soon the whole area where my parents lived would be razed for slum clearance. I had no choice. He was planning to do the same for Lieselotte and then he would follow us both here to Britain. But I was to go first. He said it was because I was older, but I think it was so that he had a little more time to spend with Lieselotte.'

Mimi swallowed, her eyes misty.

'So I came. And I worked in service for a couple in Godalming. That's in Surrey. The husband worked for the War Office. He used to grope me whenever he could, in my room, in the kitchen, in the corridor. Trying to kiss me when his wife was out. Until, finally, I got up the courage to complain to his wife, and then they couldn't get rid of me fast enough. I found new digs in London, and one day I got a telegram asking me for an interview in Northumberland Avenue. The husband had arranged it – out of guilt, I suppose. Anyway, I had two interviews and an assessment. I was desperate to get the job. I couldn't wait. Finally, they sent me to Trent Park.'

Softly, Stella said, 'If Paul Schilling helped you get to England, why would you kill him? Surely he was a hero?'

At this, Mimi gave a slightly hysterical laugh and Stella registered how exhausted she must be. Her eyes had deep shadows beneath them and she ran her hand through her tangled hair.

'A hero! Yes, I thought Paul Schilling was a hero too, until I got to Trent Park.'

She finished her cigarette and doused it in a brush pot.

'I was recruited as a listener for the M Room. They warned us, when we started, that we might hear things that would shock us. They must have said the same to you, Stella. But you yourself know that doesn't begin to describe it. Listening to those men, day after day, changes your soul. You start to realize that everything you believed about people is wrong. Then one night, shortly after I began, I was assigned a new cell and I heard a voice I recognized. I couldn't believe it at first. I told myself I must be mistaken. But I knew it was him. I knew it was Paul Schilling, only he was calling himself Gabriel Fassbinder.'

'Why would he do that?'

'I had no idea. But I couldn't stop listening. I was almost greedy to hear his voice. I was insatiable. I couldn't tear myself away. I made sure I had the responsibility for transcribing all his conversations. I knew, when he talked about the Jewish girls he had befriended, that he was talking about us. He was mocking us. Making salacious remarks. Telling terrible stories about what he had done to Jewish women in Poland. Then, that night I told you about, when Robert Handel was bursting with anger in the mess, I got my chance.

'It was very late. Both prisoners should have been asleep – I could hear the cellmate snoring away, he had a very distinctive snore – but then I heard footsteps and a man opening the door. Schilling was leaving the room! I was amazed. That should never happen, the cells were always locked, and I was about to report it, when I realized. This was my chance. It was a spur-of-the-moment thing. I had been learning to shoot on the rifle range – there was a very nice corporal guardsman there – and I knew where they kept the guns. I went out into the garden and there he was. Paul Schilling. Standing under a tree, looking up at the stars. I went up to him and he recognized me at once. I told him this was for Lieselotte – not only for her but for all the girls he had raped and the people he'd killed. He tried to talk to me, he was begging me to put the gun down, saying he could explain everything, and that's when I shot him. Because those things he had done, there was no explanation. They should never be explained. After I checked he was completely dead, I took my bicycle and went back to the billet. Everything else you know.'

'Except why he changed his name.'

Mimi shrugged.

'Men like that, they're capable of anything.'

She gave a little shake of her head. It was as though she was emerging from a trance. She braced her thin shoulders, tense as a bow, and resumed the bright, cocktail-party tone of before.

'By the way, you never said. How did you know I was here?'

'Teamwork,' said Harry.

'What does that mean?'

'We read your diary,' said Stella.

'You found my diary! But I don't see how anything in my diary would bring you here. I never mentioned Karl.'

Harry raised his eyes to the wall, where Mimi's cousin had been rendered in swirls of virulent green. Stella followed his gaze.

'It wasn't a splash of ink, was it, on Mimi's diary?' she said. 'It was paint.'

Harry smiled. 'That's a colour you never forget.'

★

It was as Karl was showing them out that Stella realized.

'I've seen you before.'

Karl affected a modest shrug. 'I must admit, I'm very well known in my home country. A little bit of a celebrity, I don't mind saying. I'm considered as one in the vanguard of a new artistic school. A forerunner of the emerging style.'

'No. I mean I've seen you in the street. You were hanging around outside Harry's office. You disappeared when you knew I'd caught sight of you.'

'Karl?' said Harry.

'*Ach*, that. Yes, it's true. I wanted to see if you could help me, Harry. I was worried about them coming to take me to an internment camp. I was thinking maybe you could make me disappear. Create some kind of official document.'

Harry opened his mouth to object, but Karl held up a hand.

'But then I realized, you're not that kind of man. I told myself, that's not how Harry Fox would do things. Nor should I ask him to.'

He turned up his palms with a deep, Mittel-European shrug.

'So don't concern yourself. I will take whatever Mr Churchill asks of me. I will make myself believe that if they arrest me, it is for my own good.'

# CHAPTER 34

*May 13th*

He had passed it occasionally in his travels and Harry had always admired the severe Bauhaus apartment building in Lawn Road. It towered over the semi-detached Victorian and Georgian villas like a small part of Germany transplanted to north London. When it was built, in 1934, its sleek white concrete decks and dazzling stone balconies had reminded him of an ocean liner – a likeness that was acknowledged when it was 'launched' with a bottle of beer broken symbolically over its side. As the first properly modernist construction in England, the Lawn Road flats had, in the past few years, attracted a bohemian mix of inhabitants: artists, intellectuals and free-thinkers. He had even fantasized about living there himself. The building had a communal restaurant, where a daily huddle of tenants would talk and dispute, and at times the place seemed more like a Viennese café than a residential block in an unassuming London street. Now, however, war had scattered the community, and the local council was in the midst of painting the gleaming white concrete sludge brown, presumably to avoid the attention of possible enemy bombs.

Stella and Harry had walked from Belsize Park Tube in the mild sunlight of late afternoon to find Maxwell Knight standing, hands in his pockets, staring up at the building.

'Extraordinary place, isn't it? They call it the Isokon building. They have all sorts in here.'

From 'all sorts', Harry knew that some of the residents must, at some time, have raised Knight's suspicions. Perhaps that was why he had chosen this block of flats as a meeting place. There seemed no other logical reason.

'There's one unit up for rent and I'm planning to recommend it to Mrs Mallowan – Agatha Christie to you. She's looking for a quiet flat in London to write her next novel. Apparently, she has an idea for a mystery about a hunt for German spies in Britain.'

Harry looked at him sharply, but Knight did not catch his eye. His tone was as breezy and jocular as ever.

'We've quite a bit to report, Captain Knight,' said Stella, quietly.

'So I hear.'

'I'm sure Colonel Kendrick passed on our findings to you. I met Robert Handel. He's attempting to assist with intelligence operations in France.'

'Is he, now? Good man.'

'He swears he didn't kill Gabriel Fassbinder – or Paul Schilling, as we should probably call him. He had no idea that he was even dead. And last night we found the person who did.'

'Mimi Friedlander,' said Knight.

'Yes. She bolted from Trent Park, but we followed her. It was Harry who realized where she must have gone. He recognized a splash of paint on her notebook.'

Knight arched an eyebrow, either in approval or surprise.

'She told us everything. How she'd known Paul Schilling back in Germany, and why she killed him. I don't think she would dream of betraying the secrets of Trent Park. She said she was planning to hand herself in first thing.'

'Yes. It appears she's returned this morning of her own accord and made a full confession. It will be up to the authorities to decide how to deal with her.'

Knight smiled. He seemed remarkably cheerful. Stella guessed it was relief.

'I don't mind admitting I'm pleased that both my recommendations, Mr Handel and yourself, have proved sound.'

'Thank you,' said Stella.

He paused for a while, perched on the low concrete wall of the property. He tapped out his pipe, refilled it, puffed it into life and soon a sweet-smelling smoke was drifting in the air.

'Considering everything that's happened, it's all the more tragic that Miss Friedlander's anger at Gabriel Fassbinder, or Paul Schilling as he really was, was entirely misplaced.'

'Misplaced?' Harry frowned.

Quietly, Stella said, 'I can't agree, Captain Knight. I think she was right to be angry. Murder was going too far, but I don't wonder at a person seeing red, listening to what that man had to say. Robert Handel was horrified too. And certainly, I heard things at Trent Park that I can never forget.'

She felt Harry's curious eyes on her, but Knight carried on.

'By "misplaced", what I mean is that Miss Friedlander's original assessment was correct. Paul Schilling *was* a good man. A remarkably good man. He helped several people out of Germany who would not otherwise have found their way. People who might indeed be sitting in one of Adolf's camps right now.'

'Yet he developed into a monster once he had been captured.'

'He was never captured.'

'But he was a Luftwaffe officer!' protested Stella. 'His plane was downed in the sea.'

'He wasn't.' It was Harry. He turned to Maxwell Knight. 'Schilling was never a prisoner, was he?'

'Quite right, Harry. In fact, he was one of us.'

Knight levered himself off the low wall.

'Let me tell you a story about a good man.'

He began to walk in the direction of Hampstead Heath and Harry and Stella fell into step on each side of him as he went.

'We first came into contact with Schilling in 1936, when he came over to England to take a look at that building behind us. That's why I brought you here. I thought it would be interesting for you to see it. Schilling was an architect, and he was very keen on Walter Gropius, who was the chap who inspired the place. Gropius was the founder of the Bauhaus school in Germany, but he had become *persona non grata* in his home country and turned up on these shores. Schilling had been working in the office of Albert Speer, Adolf's personal architect, and the fact is, or so the cognoscenti tell me, there are many similarities between Speer's own style and the Bauhaus, despite its unavoidably Jewish connotations.'

'Robert Handel told me that,' said Stella. 'He said Fassbinder was one of "Speer's Boys" but he had very modern views on style.'

Harry blinked, though whether he was surprised by this revelation about the origins of Third Reich architectural aesthetics, or was not following in any way, was unclear.

'Schilling's visit was not purely devoted to architectural sightseeing, however. As soon as he arrived, he took the opportunity to make contact with us, and he proved extraordinarily helpful. So much so, that in the summer before the war we managed to extricate him from Germany and bring him over to Britain. Then, when hostilities began, and we had to think about where to house captured Germans and Italians, Schilling came to the fore. Once Kendrick had assembled his team at Trent Park, he needed listeners, and as well as recommending Robert Handel, I also suggested Schilling.'

'Are you saying he was a listener?' asked Stella, incredulous.

'Not exactly. Colonel Kendrick decided to go one better. Installing microphones was inspired, but how much better would that intelligence be if one could install a human stool pigeon? A plant, whom the Germans took as another prisoner, and who would be able to provoke and prompt the release of even more information.'

'So, they disguised Paul Schilling as a German officer,' said Harry.

'They barely needed a disguise. SPs, as we call them, are outfitted in officer uniform and put in cells to encourage other officers to talk. They initiate conversations, speculate about the outcome of battles, enquire about technological developments and so on. Schilling was briefed to direct the conversation into areas that interest British intelligence. He fitted the bill perfectly. He was an educated, clever German who had worked closely with the Nazi High Command. He was able to move seamlessly among them. None of the other officers suspected him for a second. He was primed to discuss what we needed to know. In the course of that, however, he had to convince these men of his Nazi credentials, and hence the tales of horror that Handel and Mimi Friedlander were obliged to hear. Schilling would get other prisoners to let down their guard by confessing his own, invented crimes. Or even, as you must realize, boasting of them.'

'Why did you not tell me,' demanded Stella, 'who Gabriel Fassbinder really was?'

'What good would it have done, Miss Fry? You didn't need to know. We guard our secrets as jealously as we can.'

He paused, and pulled on his pipe before continuing. 'It's a great shame. Schilling used to tell me, if the war was won, he would stay in Britain and resume his work, trying in whatever way he could to undo the damage done. That will now not happen.'

'And Mimi Friedlander? What will happen to her?' Harry asked.

Crisply, Knight said, 'That's not for me to decide.'

After a few minutes the trio reached the edges of Hampstead Heath and crossed the road to progress through an avenue of plane trees onto the Heath itself. The temperature was perfectly poised between warmth and chill, and it was promising to be a nice day for everyone except the inhabitants of Western Europe.

Harry glanced round at the trees as though, even here, their vast, gnarled trunks might conceal eavesdroppers.

'There's something I have to admit, Mr Knight. I had a theory of my own.'

'You're going to say that you thought Mimi Friedlander, Robert Handel and quite possibly your other young woman were the three Abwehr spies I mentioned?'

Harry did not know whether to be insulted or impressed.

'Something like that.'

'Not a bad theory,' Knight conceded. 'Indeed, it would be perfectly plausible. But as a matter of fact, that job is done. All three have been picked up.'

'Picked up? When?' Harry failed to disguise his indignation.

'Yesterday. It has to be said, they were laughably bad spies. One of them tried to order a bottle of cider at nine o'clock in the morning in a Dorset pub. The landlord guessed he might not be a native and made a telephone call to the local police station. It took very little time for this chap to reveal the whereabouts of his fellow agents.'

'If that's what we're up against . . .'

Knight shot Harry a beady sideways look from beneath the brim of his trilby.

'That was, of course, one's first thought.'

'You mean, you think it was deliberate?'

'There's a theory that someone high up in the ranks of German espionage has intentionally sent poor-quality recruits.'

'How high up?' said Stella.

'It's no more than hearsay at the moment. And we are, all of us, bound by laws of strict confidence. But rumour suggests that it is possibly Canaris himself.'

'The head of the Abwehr,' murmured Harry.

'Indeed. Admiral Canaris is the chief of the Abwehr, the German foreign intelligence bureau. And a great animal lover, as it happens. Takes his dachshunds with him everywhere. I can't help feeling, in other circumstances, he and I might get along.'

A woman passed, pushing a pram from whose handles two small boys were hanging, and Stella waited until she was out of earshot before saying, 'Why would Canaris send incompetent spies?'

'We know that Canaris dislikes Hitler. We have a strong suspicion that he was party to an attempted coup against the Führer in '38. He was possibly even involved in sending advance plans of German intentions to other governments in Europe.'

'You're saying the head of Nazi foreign intelligence gives the enemy warning of their plans?' said Harry.

'Perhaps they're not his enemies. That remains to be seen. Either way, there is persuasive reason to believe that Canaris deliberately picked inadequate candidates – hapless agents who could be easily spotted. It may be that he actively wanted to send people who would fail. It may also be that he's behind deliberately poor intelligence-gathering designed to sabotage an invasion attempt.'

'So, all our hopes rest on Admiral Canaris?'

'All our hopes rest on Winston Churchill and the great people of Britain, Harry.' Knight smiled and shot a tweedy sleeve to look at his watch. 'Now, if you'll excuse me . . .'

He hailed a passing taxi and clambered inside.

Stella and Harry walked on for a while, back towards South End Road. The sun was slicing through the clouds in luminous blades, turning every surface golden. Ahead of them on the pavement a group of soldiers was milling, waiting to embark on a truck.

'What will you do now?' said Harry.

'Move back to my flat, I suppose. I'll need to catch a bus back to Evelyn's and collect my things. How about you?'

'I'll take the Tube to the office. Get on with work. Crimes won't solve themselves.'

'I'm not sure how long I'll stay at the Film Unit.'

'Really?'

'I should join up, don't you think?'

'I suppose.'

'I was going to say, Harry . . .'

'Yes?'

He stopped, dug his hands in his pockets and looked down at her. He noted how the faint peach down on her cheek caught in the light and the iris of her eyes was a braiding of brown and gold.

'What is it?'

Stella hesitated. She was thinking of what Noël Coward had said, just a few days earlier in his apartment in the Place Vendôme.

*What I mean to say, Miss Fry, is that we're all lying to ourselves, aren't we? Especially about what matters.*

'Oh, nothing.'

'Must be something,' Harry said softly.

'It's hard to explain.' She looked away, hurriedly. 'I'd better go.'

Harry remained motionless, as though he didn't want to move, then said, 'See you around, then.'

'Yes, fine. Goodbye.'

He crossed the street, and her eyes followed his footsteps, watching his back recede and the throng of soldiers enclose him in a cloak of khaki. At the entrance to the Tube she saw him hesitate, as if to look back, but instead he carried on into the underground and was lost from sight.

That evening, Harry went back to Bavarian Karl's. He couldn't help himself. He didn't know what he was expecting, but he wasn't expecting what he found.

Lieselotte was there. She opened the door and regarded him dully, as if he had come to read the gas meter, and returned to the table by the window, where she had been knitting. Karl was standing in the middle of the room, working on another masterpiece. The studio was filled with canvases, either half finished or possibly completed, some hung up and some propped against the wall. The colours throbbed with violent energy. They were alien, indecipherable images that seemed to say life would always be impossible to render or understand, but that Art was like a code or a pattern that would impart a great truth if only you could decipher it. When Harry came in, Karl stepped from behind the easel and stood motionless, paintbrush in hand. Then, with an unusual touch of sensitivity, he left them together. They listened to his tortoise steps shuffling up the stairs.

'I didn't think you'd want to talk to me again after what happened,' Lieselotte said.

'I didn't think I'd see you.'

'I'm sorry I didn't tell you about Mimi. It was just too complicated.'

He shrugged.

'Please don't get the wrong impression about me, Harry. I meant what I said. I like you.'

'You like me so much you tried to shoot me. I hate to think what you do when you really love a guy.'

'I didn't mean to shoot you. I'd taken off the safety catch and then the gun went off when I put too much pressure on the trigger. At least you weren't hurt.'

'Not that you stayed to find out.'

'All the same, I'm glad you're OK.'

'It's fine. I've been shot at by Germans before. Just not ones I've been to bed with.'

'I was in a state of shock, Harry. That's the only explanation. The fact is, I loved Paul. And I'd just learned that he'd died, and what was more, my own cousin had killed him.'

'Families are complicated.'

'I knew you'd understand. And on top of that, to hear what the man you loved was capable of.'

A tear trembled on her eyelid and threatened to roll down her cheek.

'He may not have been so bad,' Harry allowed.

A struggle was taking place inside him, between enlightening Lieselotte now as to the true nature of Paul Schilling or keeping the happy news for later. That would be the decent thing to do. Before he got the chance to decide, though, Lieselotte raised her chin defiantly and folded her arms.

'Whatever Paul did, the fact is, Harry, I'm not sure if it would ever work between you and me. Half of me is in another country. I could never really leave Germany. Not forever. And you're too good a man to mess around with. Besides, that woman you came with. I saw the way you looked at her.'

'Stella? She's just a friend.'

'If you say so.'

'What will you do now?'

'Keep looking for a job, I suppose.'

'I haven't forgotten about that. I'll see if I can help.'

'Do you mean that?'

She went up to him then, put her arms around him, and reached up her face towards his, but Harry didn't move.

He wanted to kiss her, really he did. He wanted to sit in Karl's chair and have her kiss him back and stroke his chest and unbutton his shirt and see where it led. But he was beginning to learn who was his own worst enemy, and just then it wasn't Adolf Hitler.

He left the house, closed the door behind him and went back down the street.

## CHAPTER 35

Stella walked along the river. In a tree-lined street behind the Tate Gallery she went up the steps to a block of mansion flats and rang the bell.

'Stella! I wasn't expecting you!'

'I brought something for you.'

She took out a bottle from her leather satchel and Tom held it up admiringly.

'Pol Roger. Churchill's favourite. This is kind of you.'

'It's to thank you for the other evening. It was a lovely party – I'm sorry I left early. And oh! You're in uniform!'

He was wearing a dark-blue outfit with a gold stripe on the shoulder.

'I'm a lieutenant now. Special Branch of the Royal Navy Volunteer Reserve.'

'I never thought of you as a seafarer.'

'I've sailed a little in the past and I can handle a small craft. But to be honest, I'd not expected it either.'

'What sort of thing will you be doing?'

'Mainly planning and liaison. And I suppose I can tell you this much: I'm about to be sent into France.'

'Oh, Tom.'

'How about you? Are you still staying with my sister?'

'No. The plumbing's fixed now. I'm back in my flat.'

'Are you thinking of war work?'

'Yes, but I'm not sure what. I'll stay at the Film Unit until I decide. Or until I'm drafted.'

'Evelyn's torn between joining the FANYs, who she says are her type, or the Wrens, who have the best uniform. So in the meantime, she's signed up for the Auxiliary Fire Service.'

'She told me. She hasn't stopped talking about it. For training she has to crawl through thick smoke, climb a ten-foot wall and drag a body down a flight of stairs. She loves it. She's going full-time as soon as her run ends. It's a long way from Noël Coward.'

'Oh, I don't know. Anything my sister is involved in has endless potential for farce.'

He ran a hand across his hair. It was freshly cut and made him look younger, but there were bluish circles under his eyes.

'Tell me what's happening, Tom. As much as you can.'

'The atmosphere's feverish. It seems the French are facing total collapse. This morning Churchill was woken by a call from the French Prime Minister, Paul Reynaud. He just said, "We've been beaten. There are tanks and armoured cars pouring into France." They expect Paris to be taken by

June 1st. Churchill is flying to France tomorrow to confer with the leadership.'

'Oh God! What does that mean for us?'

'There's no way to soften the blow. The Netherlands surrendered to Germany this morning. The Wehrmacht is advancing towards the Channel. Hitler's acting with lightning precision so we fully expect to be attacked both from the air and maybe airborne troops dropped in the near future. Obviously, we're increasingly desperate to bring the Americans in. Churchill wrote to Roosevelt to say the voice and force of the United States may count for nothing if they're withheld for too long. But if necessary we'll continue alone. And we're not afraid of that, Stella. Everyone at the Admiralty's pulling together.'

'It's just . . . so fast.'

'Yes. We're all shell-shocked at the speed of it. General Gamelin miscalculated and the German thrust came from the south, through the Ardennes Forest. Our forces in France are retreating.'

'No wonder you look tired.'

'It's one reason.'

'How are your parents?'

'My mother just telephoned. She's gone back down to the country. They had a photographer from *Country Life* come to shoot pictures of the garden and he was taking particular interest in the walls and gates. She asked me if she should tell him to leave. She was convinced he was a spy.'

Stella smiled, as she was supposed to.

'She's organizing all her friends to send in their opera glasses and hunting guns for the Local Defence Volunteers.'

'I should go. You have enough to do.'

'No. Please stay.'

He took up the Pol Roger.

'I know it's only late afternoon . . .'

'A naval man would say the sun is not over the yard arm.'

He laughed. 'You're right. But I say we drink some of this now.'

'If you like.'

He went into the kitchen to find glasses and Stella looked around her. She saw a vase of flowers on the mantelpiece, a cricket bat propped against the bookshelf, and an old chair with threadbare arms that she vaguely recognized from his family home. His gas mask was slung over a dining chair, and a writing desk was laid out with notepaper and envelopes and his pen, uncapped. She noted the gilt-framed portrait of his college first eleven, but there was no picture of Meredith Meadows.

She heard the voluptuous pop of the champagne cork and the soft hiss of gas, then Tom returned, handing her a foaming glass.

She held it aloft. 'Let's drink to your fiancée.'

'We could.'

The Pol Roger was crisp and flinty, with touches of vanilla and pear.

'We should.'

'Only I don't have a fiancée any more.'

Her eyes widened. 'What happened?'

'It wasn't going to work out. So we'll just have to drink to yours instead.'

'My fiancé?'

'The other evening I noticed you were wearing a very fine engagement ring. Though you don't seem to be wearing it now.'

Suddenly, she understood. It accounted for the astonished look he had given her at Prince's Gate and the abrupt way he had left her. He had seen the ring that Robert Handel had given her and made the wrong assumptions.

'That's not what you think. It's nothing to do with an engagement. I was given it so I could sell it and pass the money to refugees.'

He frowned at her for a minute, processing this, then shook his head.

'It appears that neither of us is engaged, then.'

'I suppose not. Tell me what happened with Meredith. Is it really all over?'

Turning away, he folded his arms and went over to the window.

'It's all a dreadful mess. We were up half the night discussing it. I can't tell you how appalling I feel. Meredith wants to leave Britain and return to America as soon as possible. The embassy has advised all Americans to leave. She wanted me to come too, but of course I said I wouldn't – *couldn't* – countenance it. She pointed out that Churchill might find it very useful to have one of his people stateside.

I never thought she had realized that . . . that was the original agenda for our meeting.'

'She's right. You might be far more use out there, arguing the case for American involvement.'

'I suspect that's so. But what would be the best way to serve my country?'

'Sounds like one of those philosophical conundrums you're so fond of.'

'It's not even a choice. We're at war and it's coming England's way. I simply couldn't leave. Not with my family and everything still here. So Merry said in that case, she would return to Kentucky by herself.'

'She didn't want to stay by your side?'

'It's more than that. I think — there's a saying. A cliché, really. The scales fall from your eyes.'

'Her eyes?'

'And mine. Have you ever felt that?'

Stella hesitated. His remark struck a chord deep within her. A thought darted into her mind and out again, too swiftly to analyze.

'I don't think so.'

'The strange thing is, when I finally told Meredith what I felt, she didn't seem too bothered.'

'Have you told your family yet?'

'I'm about to.'

He checked his watch, shook himself and went over to unhook his coat from the peg.

'I'm sorry. I'm late for a meeting. Then I leave tomorrow. I don't know how long I'll be away.'

'Let me walk with you.'

They headed back towards Whitehall. Outside the Admiralty, sentries were holding rifles with fixed bayonets and others were standing watch with Lewis light machine guns. Along the Mall, army convoys were parked, and Horse Guards was surrounded by barbed-wire entanglements. In front of the House of Commons, a stream of lorries rumbled past, transporting troops. The warm weather had brought out the crowds and uniforms were everywhere – the grey-blue RAF and the army khaki and the navy's dark blue, all interspersed with women in bright spring dresses, wearing their cheerful patterns and vivid colours as though to defy the gloom.

'Are you pessimistic about the war?'

'I refuse to be. I'm hopeful. I think that's our duty. Always to hope. We have to fight defeatism. Life's precarious but it's worth defending.'

'What will you do when it's over?'

'It's nowhere near the end. It's hardly begun.'

'Of course.'

Yet the idea of an end – any kind of end – was a consoling one.

As they reached Horse Guards he stopped, squared his shoulders, and almost off-handedly, as if it was the least important thing in the world, said, 'I wanted to ask you, Stella. May I write to you?'

## CHAPTER 36

*May 19th*

Harry came out of an avenue of trees, their branches interweaving into a tunnel of deep shade, and saw ahead of him a spire floating above a misty field. England seemed to him like a dream – an insubstantial dream of some great past, embodied in an expanse of billowing green.

Prelapsarian. That was a word Stanley Fox had liked using. It meant innocent, unspoilt, an Eden before anyone had ripped out the road signs and covered it with barbed wire.

It was still like that. The sun was lowering itself over the fringes of woodland and cows were moving slowly in a distant field, flicking their tails. England was at ease with itself, even when the threat had never been so high.

He had spent the day with Jack at Downland Farm, a mile up the road towards Stow-on-the-Wold. He had met the

Swiggs family, who showed no sign of wanting to steal his boy, and their Border Collie Daisy, who did. After a tour of the acreage, and admiration of the tractor, and discussion of chickens and a gift of eggs, he had taken his nephew off to the village pub. They had sat in the garden and ordered sandwiches made with fresh white bread and a pork pie and pickles. Harry had drunk a pint of the local ale and contemplated his boy Jack, who must have grown several inches since he left London. His face was ruddy with country air and losing its childish curves. He still had the same demeanour of eager excitement, even if the things that excited him now were herds and crops instead of football and his stamp collection. Yet he was undeniably pleased to see his uncle. He asked if he might have his own dog when he returned to London and Harry had suspended reality and agreed that he could. Then they turned to their books. The boy was reading a novel called *The Hobbit*, set in a place called Middle Earth. He told Harry that the author, Tolkien, had invented all kinds of strange languages, Elvish and Westron and Sindarin. Harry didn't know what to make of it, though he reckoned this Tolkien chap ought to be drafted sharpish to work in codes.

He'd brought his own book to look at – *The Observer's Book of Birds*. He turned to the page on pigeons. Next time he saw Maxwell Knight, he would be ready for him.

The previous day, Knight had called into his office. Harry was already focusing on a new case, involving a consignment of forged ration books. Knight's gaze roved around the room, taking in the piles of papers and the jumble of files spilling over every surface.

'One rather hopes the Nazis don't invade, because they certainly won't like your filing system.'

He glanced out of the window, and briefly examined the pigeons brooding on the sill opposite, before turning his attention back to Harry.

'In-trays, out-trays and ashtrays. Is that the general idea?'

'How can I help you, Mr Knight?'

'You've already been an immense help, Harry. This is by way of thanks. It's about that young woman of yours.'

'Not mine, I'm afraid, Mr Knight.'

'Either way, now that we know she's not been sent by the enemy to undermine us, I think I've found her a job.'

'As an artist?'

'That line of things. As I mentioned, there's space in the Camouflage Directorate. It's based up in Leamington Spa. They need people who can paint because there's a lot of it to be done. It's a little broad-brush, I fear. Making factories look like stables and aircraft hangars look like barns to confuse the Jerries. If she takes it, you won't be seeing a lot of her, I'm afraid.'

'I'm not seeing a lot of her already.'

'Think she'll be interested?'

Harry guessed she would. And he was grateful to Maxwell Knight, though not surprised. Knight was well known for his attention to animals and young women, and in a way,

Lieselotte was both: a stranded bird, blown off course by the currents of war and washed up far from home.

'More importantly,' said Knight, rocking back on his heels and digging his hands into his pockets, 'there's another woman I want to discuss. Stella Fry.'

'What about her?'

'I have a feeling that the pair of you could be very useful together.'

'In what way?'

'There'll be plenty of ways. I just wanted to let you know, I'll be in touch with you both very soon.'

After lunch, Harry had walked back to the farm with Jack and spent the afternoon inspecting the cows and sheep and drinking Mrs Swiggs's tea in the fug of the farmhouse kitchen. Then he tapped the whorl of hair on Jack's crown, scratched the dog's ears, said goodbye and left for the station.

The station was a minor stop on the Cotswold Line, consisting of a small brick building, two benches and some tubs of geraniums. Harry's train was not due for half an hour, so he sat on the bare platform and closed his eyes, feeling the warm kiss of sunlight on his face. A blackbird was singing – at least, it sounded like song, though he knew, because Maxwell Knight had told him, that most birdsong was generally not song, but a fight over territory.

He pondered again what Maxwell Knight had said about Stella Fry and how they might work together. He fervently hoped so. The thought of Stella evoked a feeling that was far too complicated for him to understand. It was unsettling and comforting at the same time. A sense of something unrealized, like the echo of music he had never heard.

A short way along the platform, the stationmaster was erecting a ladder beneath the station nameboard. The man seemed to make a great palaver out of the business. He opened the ladder, adjusted it, moved it, checked it, moved it again, and steadied it. Only then did he climb up and begin, with a pot of black paint, to erase the name. Harry watched the cream letters disappearing bit by bit, first *AD* then *LE*, followed by *STR* and the remaining *OP*. It was the same everywhere. Place names were vanishing across the country, but it didn't matter. Because this could be any place.

Someone in the ticket office had turned on the wireless, and from the opened window floated a familiar, slurred, magisterial bass . . . *After this battle in France abates its force, there will come the battle for our Island – for all that Britain is, and all that Britain means. That will be the struggle. In that supreme emergency we shall not hesitate to take every step, even the most drastic, to call forth from our people the last ounce and the last inch of effort of which they are capable . . .*

He reached into his inside pocket and brought out a paperback. The spine was cracked, and the cover scuffed. It was a Hubert Newman novel, *Last Night in Lisbon*, and he'd read it before.

But he reckoned that a novel, even the second time around, was a good way to spend his time. Whatever time there was.

# AUTHOR'S NOTE

The novel is based on real historical events. The Combined Services Detailed Interrogation Centre was established under the auspices of MI9, a division of British Intelligence which was formed at the outbreak of war to collate information from prisoners of war. The CSDIC was based in three locations, the first being Trent Park in north London (known as 'Cockfosters' or Camp 11), where initially U-boat personnel and downed Luftwaffe airmen, but later German generals and other senior ranks, were imprisoned. The dramatic part played by Trent Park in the Second World War is, even now, scarcely public knowledge. However, in November 2001, the German historian Sönke Neitzel, working at the British National Archives, discovered a cache of transcripts of German prisoners talking among themselves which had been secretly recorded by the Allies. In these apparently private conversations, the soldiers talked freely and openly about their hopes and fears, their concerns and their day-to-day lives, as well as their own brutality and sadism. Neitzel's book, *Soldaten*, became a number one bestseller in Germany, where it reignited the debate about the conduct of German officers and challenged the myth that high-ranking soldiers did not engage in brutal acts.

The hundred 'secret listeners', most of them German-speaking émigrés, worked in twelve-hour shifts, every day of the year. By the end of the war, they had amassed more than 74,000 transcripts of conversations from 10,000 prisoners, including Adolf Hitler's generals. Their work led to major intelligence breakthroughs, including details of Peenemünde, the German research base where the V-2 rockets were developed.

Trent Park also made use of 'stool pigeons', one of them being Brinley Newton-John, father of the actress Olivia Newton-John. Most of the quoted dialogue from German prisoners in this novel is taken directly from transcripts recorded at Trent Park.

The work of Trent Park has been superbly discussed in Helen Fry's book, *The Walls Have Ears* (Yale University Press, 2020).

Maxwell Knight, the maverick British spymaster and putative model for James Bond's M, liked to choose unattached young women as his agents because he believed they were better listeners. He recorded major counter-espionage successes with the help of two hand-picked young women, Olga Gray, who infiltrated the Communist Party, and Joan Miller, who penetrated Britain's anti-Semitic fascist network.

Paris fell to the Germans on June 14th 1940. On August 1st, Hitler signed the order for air strikes against Britain. What followed was the Blitz.

On May 16th, in a series of early-morning raids, 2,000 male German nationals in London were rounded up under Defence Regulation 18(b). Ten days later, 1,500 German women were woken at dawn by police and members of the Women's Voluntary Service and also taken to internment camps.

Agatha Christie moved into the Lawn Road flats in 1941 and wrote, unusually for her, a spy thriller, rather than a pure detective novel. It was called *N or M* and featured a hunt for undercover German agents in 1940s Britain. She cannot have known that the Lawn Road building itself was occupied by some of Britain's most notorious spies including Kim Philby, Arnold Deutsch and Edith Tudor-Hart – a talent-spotter for the NKVD (forerunner of the KGB).

JT, January 2025

ACKNOWLEDGEMENTS

It has been a pleasure to work with so many brilliant people in publishing this and my previous novels. Most especially Caradoc King, who is an engaged and inspiring agent and a dear friend. Alongside him, I'd like to thank Millie Hoskins, Becky Percival and all at United Agents. I owe huge gratitude to my editor, Jane Wood, who has been endlessly supportive and energetic, as well as Florence Hare. Many thanks, too, to Jon Butler, Emily Patience, and all the Quercus team.

In looking back at another period of geo-political turmoil, I should also thank all those friends who have patiently listened to me talk about this novel in progress. You know who you are! But especially Amanda Craig, Mark Stephens, Lizy Buchan, Joanna Coles, Mary Glanville, Sonja Churchill and Sonia Purnell. Lastly, but most of all, thanks to William, Charlie and Naomi.